THE CRIMSON MASK ARCHIVES

VOLUME 3

BY

FRANK JOHNSON

INTRODUCTION BY

TOM JOHNSON

THRILLING PUBLICATIONS

2022

TABLE OF

CONTENTS

Note: "Motto for Murder" is a Crimson
Mask story that was rewritten to remove
the character upon publication.

INTRODUCTION
BY TOM JOHNSON

THE CRIMSON MASK was another of those late creations from Ned Pines' Standard titles, appearing in *Detective Novels* beginning in August 1940. Bylined Frank Johnson, the stories were initially written by pulp scribe Norman Daniels before being handed off to Leo Margulies' stable of writers.

Pre-dating the Purple Scar by a year, Doc Clarke would be something of a chalkboard for plastic surgeon, Doc Murdock, whose police officer brother was murdered by gangsters. When Murdock's brother washed ashore, his face was bloated and discolored. The plastic surgeon made a hideous mask that resembled his dead brother's face, which he wore to frighten criminals. Doc Clarke's father, also a police officer, had also been murdered; shot in the back of the head. The result caused a strange crimson discoloration around his eyes. A pharmacist by trade, Robert Clarke dons a black suit and crimson mask to battle gangsters. Another similarity in the Purple Scar and Crimson Mask, both had offices in a poor neighborhood, where they helped the down-trodden and were well thought of by the community. Doc Murdock was active with his plastic surgery clinic, while Doc Clarke was a pharmacist at the corner drugstore on Carmody Street.

There's little doubt that both series were created by Leo Margulies through editorial committee.

The novelettes were typical formula, and so too were the characters. Sandra Gray, a nurse at the local hospital was Doc Clarke's love interest. He was also aided by David Small, a friend and former classmate. And the ever-present police official, in this case former Police Commissioner, Theodore Warrick. Naturally, the Crimson Mask would step in when a case surfaced that was too baffling for the police.

Oddly, for a pharmacist, Doc Clarke is a scientific criminologist as well as a ballistic expert and make-up artist. He can crack a safe, use ventriloquism, and has knowledge of the nerve centers in the human body. No science escaped his study in the pursuit of criminals. I might add that these traits were part of the make up of all of the masked crime fighters. And there's also little doubt that the same authors who were churning out the Phantom Detective and Dan Fowler also were involved in the Crimson Mask's adventures, as well as Standard's other lead stories.

That the series lasted for 16 stories is proof that it was successful. The Purple Scar only made it for four adventures, and the Masked Detective ended after thirteen stories. But this success might be attributed to the magazine title, *Detective Novels*, which was running numerous short story characters at the time, including a very popular Jerry Wade, the Candid Camera Kid.

Unfortunately, very few of the late pulp entries had a successful run beyond a few years. The war in Europe, coupled with the paper shortage in America, and many of Standard's stable of writers heading off to the war effort forced a shortage in the pulp industry. Not to mention the poor economy at the time. And with the price of the magazines jumping from a dime to fifteen cents by the mid 1940s, readers were undoubtedly being more selective with their change; Standard would end up dropping most of the late-comers, relying instead on the original titles that that had brought them this far. The Phantom Detective and Dan Fowler (from *G-Men Detective)* would continue until the end. Only one of the 1940s title would make it, and that was the Black Bat in *Black Book Detective*.

All in all, it was a shame, though. Characters like the Crimson Mask were a lot of fun, and added much color to otherwise formula detective stories. They deserved to have their day. Too bad, it was so short lived.

Happy Reading.
Tom Johnson

FOUR MEN OF MURDER

CHAPTER I

VOW OF TERROR

IT WAS quite a layout. Even in Nazi Germany it would have been considered really something, but here in the United States, in one of its greatest cities, the thing was bordering on the colossal.

First of all, it was a meeting room capable of holding two hundred people. However, only about fifty were present. The walls were hung with swastikas and pictures of a rug-chewer with a Charlie Chaplin mustache and a wayward lock of hair that was plastered against his forehead.

There were rifles, automatics and even a machine-gun. There were short-wave radio sets, blinker lights, photography equipment and maps in abundance. Maps which showed the locations of docks, gas plants, railroads, subways and defense plants.

There was a reason why only a quarter of the usual attendance was at hand. Lately, the F.B.I. had sadly depleted their ranks. The fifty present were nervous right now. They had seen men like themselves hauled out of their homes and dispatched to internment camps.

But on the platform, and facing the audience, were four men. Two were of average build but with criminal faces that smiled only when they watched someone die. The third was a gangling, raw-boned individual, and the fourth a man of slight, wiry build. He had cold, malevolent eyes and lips so thin as to be hardly more than a line to break his facial contour, making his mouth seem to be nothing more than an ugly gash in his face.

1

The two average-sized men were named Karl and Gottfried. The skinny one was known as Paul, while the wiry one called himself Werner. They had last names, but did not advertise them. None were citizens, although they had lived a long time on the bounty of a nation they hated.

Werner was the leader and the most dangerous. That was evident when he spoke.

"This may be one of our final meetings," Werner said. "The cursed F.B.I. are getting closer and closer. You can see how badly we have suffered already. But they shall suffer, too, and when the tidal wave of Nazi manhood sweeps across the Atlantic and crosses this nation to the Pacific, our friends will be freed and the F.B.I. shall be hanged from the nearest poles."

ONE OF the men in the front row raised his hand. Werner called him by name.

"Yes, Lommel, what is it?"

The man called Lommel arose.

"I do not wish to deny what you have said, *Herr* Werner," he said, "yet there is always the chance that we might not win. Or, if the war goes on for a long time, that we shall be interned, and that is not pleasant. I suggest that we disband immediately and lay low."

"Disband?" Werner shouted. "Are you a Nazi, Lommel, or a weakling like these Americans Has their decadence entered your blood-stream to turn it into water? Disband! Never! Never, do you all hear me? We have hardly begun our work—and it shall go forward!"

Lommel spoke again. He seemed less frightened of these four than any of the others.

"With continued respect, *Herr* Werner, I think we could do more good by not showing our hand. By simply getting information quietly, sending it over the regular channels and not bothering to hold any more of these meetings. Many of us are watched. One day, the F.B.I. will close in on all of us."

Werner scowled blackly.

"I am giving the orders here. Later, I shall see what is to be done about you, Lommel. We cannot tolerate such weakness among

He raised the knife and poised it above the man who apparently lay so helplessly at his mercy

us. No, we shall continue. Suppose some of us are caught? A few will be left."

"A pitifully few," Lommel broke in again. "Hunted like wild beasts. And the end is inevitable."

"So you think!" Werner shouted back. "Perhaps so, but before we are done, these Americans will know of our presence. Yes, we have broken up. There are too few for us to carry out great projects—but it takes only one man to fire a bullet into someone essential to this country. It requires but one man to place a bomb, to start a fire, to derail trains. That is what we shall do! All of us!"

"Still the end is just as inevitable." Lommel protested quietly.

"Then let it be so." Werner declared. "What matter? Perhaps—we shall die. But—listen to me now—we die for the glory of the New Order. We shall make history. Sometime in the future, our names will be written into the books of the New World, respected and honored.

"Very well then—we die. All good Nazis are prepared to die but, mind you this, we shall make those who kill us pay for our deaths. We shall do more damage than a Panzer division. Our actions will encourage our own people, give them backbone to continue the fight. What we shall do will become the most potent propaganda in existence. Have I made myself clear?"

"You have, *Herr* Werner," Lommel said, "but I still believe that throwing our lives away will be of no avail. These Americans are like the British. The more you punish them, the tougher they get. The more defense factories that are demolished, the more will be erected. I do not have to tell you that!"

Werner said nothing for a moment or two, then his voice rose to a screech of hatred.

"Lommel, you know we consider ourselves as soldiers of the Reich! We obey orders. We do not challenge them. We do not give advice to our superiors. Therefore, you are under arrest and you shall be tried immediately. We four who lead you shall decide your fate."

INSTANTLY THREE men, wearing swastika armbands, closed in on Lommel, who remained seated and just shrugged at the sight of the loaded clubs this trio brandished, he knew what the outcome of this so-called "trial" would be.

Werner announced it after a ten-seconds' consultation with his colleagues.

"*Herr* Lommel, you are sentenced to death. Effective immediately. We cannot tolerate traitors in our ranks. Karl will take command of a firing sound in the cellar. Now, Lommel, we shall see if you know how to die like a Nazi."

Lommel smiled slowly.

"Nazis die the same as anyone else, *Herr* Warner. It makes little difference to me, because I was ready to do the same thing for myself out of disgust. Disgust that I was once weak-brained enough to listen to your supercilious speech-making. That I once believed in the prophecies of a madman. That I did work for murderers, not soldiers.

"Where do you think this will all end? For the greater glory of the Reich? No! Because the Reich is not Germany. It does not represent the will of the German people, but the mad domination of someone who holds himself higher than any deity. I tell you the end is already in sight. A hideous, inglorious end."

Lommel didn't say anything more. One of those loaded clubs crashed down on his head. Werner, crimson with rage, snapped orders. Lommel's unconscious form was drugged into the aisle and along it toward the cellar doorway at the rear of the hall.

"Wake him up before you shoot him!" Werner screamed. "Make sure he knows what is happening. And as for the rest of you—"

Somebody gave a loud yell outside the hall. All heads turned. The double doors caved in. Police and G-men burst through it like a flood-tide. The men who were dragging Lommel away for execution tried to use their clubs, and went down under a barrage of police night-sticks. None of the others offered any resistance.

But on the stage, Werner spoke softly. Karl sidestepped to a small switch and snapped it home. There was a mild explosion and a curtain of thick smoke rose up from the edge of the stage.

G-men barged through it with drawn guns, but the stage was empty. All the back of the place was foggy with these fumes.

The G-men and police stumbled around for ten minutes and finally discovered what they feared. There was a secret door leading into an alley. Directly across from this door was another which offered ready passage for the quartette. They had evaded the guard thrown around the outside of the building and had vanished as completely as those yellow fumes were being fanned away by the drafts which blew through the big meeting hall.

Lommel was treated on the spot. G-men knew they had something on him. He was taken downtown to face the special agent in charge, and Lommel talked. His words made even tough cops turn pale and mutter savagely among themselves.

"YES, I was one of them. I am ashamed to say so, but I did believe in what those Nazis encourage. Destruction and death. Ruin and desolation. Lying and treachery. I was sent here years ago, to help prepare the ground for this war. I worked faithfully, but those years did things to me. I began to see what really free people were like. What kindness and faith brought forth. Then I returned to the Reich. The New Germany. My insides turned at what I saw there. I couldn't get back here fast enough."

"Why didn't you come to us with this information, then?" the special agent demanded.

"Why? Because it requires months to rid the human body of a poison such as Werner? They are fanatics. Even Hitler himself could not be more fanatical. They live for the day when they will rule this nation or destroy it. They are ready to die for the New Order. But first they intend to create as much mischief as possible. I warn you, it will be serious. They do not resort to half-way measures and they are clever."

The special agent whistled softly.

"You mean those four men intend sabotage and murder? That they'll keep doing it until their last breath?"

"Exactly," Lommel answered. "I said they were fanatics. Perhaps crazy is a better word, but do not underestimate them. They are hand-picked killers, that which Naziism instills. Very quietly, I tried to convince some of the others how wrong they were. It wasn't hard in a few instances, but that poison runs deep, and there is little in the way of an antidote."

"All right, Lommel," the special agent said. "We believe you. We've checked on you long ago. Now what about these four men who escaped?"

"Karl—Gottfried—Paul and that beast. Worse than any of your gangsters, because they are trained and smart."

"But why on earth would they sacrifice their lives for something that will never happen? I mean, a dozen nations of the New Order type couldn't conquer me. We Americans are dumb, Lommel. We don't know enough to quit. If things get tough, we throw back our shoulders and yell for more bullets."

The Crimson Mask

Lommel nodded. "I know. I have read American history. I have seen your soldiers and sailors and marines. I know the stuff they are made of, but you cannot think in the same terms with those four murderers. They will destroy everything in their path and die gladly if their actions benefit the New Order. They are more interested in creating a niche in history than in saving themselves. They are interested only in manufacturing propaganda to keep the German people soft, and to soften up their conquered lands."

"We'll stop them in their tracks," the special agent said.

He picked up the telephone and began issuing orders. All city, county and state police were warned. Waterfront guards were doubled. The F.B.I. threw out its entire local force to round up these four mad dogs.

Lommel just sighed deeply as he listened to these preparations. When the special agent hung up, Lommel spoke in a weary voice.

"You will get them eventually, yes. But mark my words—first they will destroy anything and everything in their paths. They may work together or they may separate. It makes little difference. Each one is mad—and their first objective will be me."

"Why you, Lommel?"

"Because I was sentenced to death by Werner. He and the other three will risk anything to carry out that order. When Nazidom issues a command that a man is to die—he dies."

"Nonsense," the special agent answered. "We'll guard you as if you were the United States Mint. Now suppose you visit one of our artists who will draw pictures of these four killers. Pictures from your description of them. That may help."

Lommel arose and drew himself erect.

"Whatever I can do to exterminate those men, I shall do willingly and gratefully. You see, I have a son who was born here and who goes to your schools. To him you may give all credit for my conversion. Even a small child has been able to offset the lying propaganda of the Nazis—because a child speaks the truth and sees the truth through young and innocent eyes. Take me to your artist."

CHAPTER II

THE CRIMSON MASK MOVES IN

THERE WAS a drug-store down in the slum areas. Not a flashy place selling ladies' hosiery, coffee pots, lunches, dinners and breakfasts. This store didn't even sport a soda fountain nor a showcase filled with candy. It sold nothing but medicines and drugs.

In gold lettering on the door was the name and license number of the owner. It read:

ROBERT CLARKE, PH. G.

Bob Clarke was behind the prescription counter preparing a dozen capsules according to the doctor's prescription before him. He was tall, good looking and had strong, slender hands. He whistled cheerfully and kept a weather eye out for customers who might come in.

Someone did enter, but it was not a customer. It was Dave Small who entered, and Small was Bob Clarke's assistant. Rather short, a little overweight, Small was usually the picture of happiness. It was a rare occasion when he was not smiling, but one of those occasions was at hand now. He carried a newspaper and was excited.

The first thing he did was to turn on the small radio and then he brushed aside the paraphernalia with which Bob Clarke was working. He spread the newspaper on the bench.

"Take a look at this. Four Nazi madmen are loose and sworn to inflict as much damage as possible before they are caught. Boy, if they get away with it, the Huns will throw out their chests and start bragging again!"

Bob Clarke read the item and frowned deeply.

"You're right, Dave. Dead right. The Nazis have always boasted about the kind of men they produce. These four must be some perfect examples."

"Sure they are. Well, aren't you going to do something about it?"

"Me?" Clark asked, and then he smiled a little. "I think the police may be able to handle them."

"Look," Small argued, "this is serious. Those four must not be allowed to get away with it. You could stop them. You—and me and Sandy."

Bob Clarke did not have time to answer. For his eyes was on a tiny red bulb that was hidden behind rows of reagent bottles. It winked a couple of limes, indicating that he was wanted on an unlisted phone. He turned the capsule job over to Dave Small and hurried toward the back of the store.

He opened a door which looked as though it was made of thin oak. In reality, the oak was thinner than it seemed, and between its two wooden surfaces was a panel of the strongest steel. This led into a laboratory that would have put many police criminal labs to shame. Here was everything with which to fight crime. Microscopes, spectroscopes, chemicals, books and apparatus.

Bob Clarke climbed a single flight of stairs and reached his living quarters above the store. He picked up a phone and a soft, pleasant voice reached him.

"Sandy!" he said. "Now wait a minute before you bawl me out. I know I have a date. I know I'm late, but Dave was out and I had to compound—"

Sandra Grey to whom he was speaking was as pleasant to look upon as her voice was to hear. Yet there was a strain of excitement in her tones right now.

"Never mind that, Bob. Have you read the papers? About those four Nazi gangsters?"

"You too," Clarke groaned. "Dave was just impressing me with his ideas on the subject. Yes, I read the story."

"And aren't you going to do anything about it, Bob? Anything at all?"

"Well, I don't know. The police and the F.B.I.—"

"Can't do what the Crimson Mask is able to accomplish," Sandy cut in. "Bob, we've fought criminals of all kinds, but this time four super-criminals are loose. Men whom a whole regime has trained to kill and destroy. I—"

"Hold it," Bob Clarke said. "I hear Dave coming up the stairs as if Hitler were at his coat tails."

DAVE SMALL burst into the room. "The radio!" he panted. "They just interrupted a regular broadcast to say that somebody had heaved two grenades into the booster plant of the electric light company on Malloy Avenue. Two men were killed and the plant pretty well smashed up. The cops think those four mugs did it."

Bob Clarke spoke into the phone again.

"Sandy, you'd better come over. Our mad dogs are already at it. I'm going to move in as soon as I have a plan."

He hung up, waited a moment and then called Theodore Warrick. At one time Warrick had been the ablest police commissioner that New York had ever enjoyed. He was retired now, but he was by no means inactive.

"Mr. Warrick," Clarke said grimly, "I want you to visit Headquarters or the F.B.I. Find out all you can about those four Nazi rats. I'm going to run them into a hole and cover it up. Better get down here as soon as you have enough dope to help us."

Lommel threw himself
directly at Werner

Bob Clarke hung up and sat back. Dave Small was down in the store again. Through Clarke's mind ran a stream of thoughts having to do with the creation of a crime fighter known as the Crimson Mask. The man who now wanted to bring four Nazi criminals to book. He was a man with a price on his head—placed there by wealthy crooks who were in constant terror of him.

Bob Clarke was the Crimson Mask, although only Dave Small, Sandy and ex-Commissioner Theodore Warrick knew this. Even before Clarke had finished college, his mind had been made up to fight the elements which had destroyed his father. He had seen his father dying of a gangster's bullet.

Just before his death, Police-Sergeant Clarke's face had become strangely suffused with blood. It had formed an odd shape around his eyes—the shape of a mask. From that phenomenon came Bob Clarke's symbol under which he battled enemies of a decent, law-abiding world.

Ted Warrick, who had been a friend of Police-Sergeant Clarke had helped young Clarke greatly. His experience was immense and he kept nothing from Clarke. Gradually the young man had mastered languages, the art of disguise, the science of criminology, ballistics, toxicology, and all the associated subjects having to do with detective work.

A crimson mask covered the upper part of his features when he worked, and nobody suspected that Bob Clarke, drug-store owner, was this scarlet-masked avenger.

Now Clarke was getting ready to fight one of his grimmest battles. Against four men who had already resolved to die rather than be captured. Men who could inflict a tremendous amount of damage if they got the breaks. They had already struck, in fact. That blasting of the booster plant had been their work without question.

Perhaps that plant supplied electricity for a number of defense factories which were now stopped. Every moment so lost was a gain for the Axis powers. Something to make Hitler and Tojo smile and rub their hands. Once a blow-hard called Mussolini had rubbed his hands, too, but lately he had been spending his time rubbing his head. Mussolini had discovered what Nazidom really was.

"Ted" Warrick, as his older intimates knew him, came shortly after nine o'clock that night. He was tall, as erect as a soldier, and still capable of a good fight. Warrick was the Crimson Mask's only contact with the rest of the world. Through him, came the start of many interesting cases.

Warrick sat down and looked grave.

"It's worse than I thought," Bob," he said. "Those four men are extremely dangerous—capable of any crime on the calendar. A fellow named Lommel, who was caught in the raid, gave enough evidence of that. Lommel had been sentenced to execution just before the F.B.I. broke in because he dared to challenge the leader of this quartette—a slightly built man known only as Werner."

BOB CLARKE tapped fingertips together and pursed his lips in thought.

"It seems to me," he said slowly, "that inasmuch as this Werner and his cohorts condemned Lommel to death, they'll try to carry out the sentence. What do you think?"

"I agree. So does Lommel, himself. The fact is, Bob, I've already ascertained that Lommel is to be spirited from the F.B.I. offices in about two hours. They're taking him to a safer place, but Lommel says he won't live half an hour once he is outside the Federal Building."

"If those four madmen are as clever as they're reputed to be, perhaps he won't," Bob Clarke mused. "Look here, Warrick, hunting down those men isn't going to be easy. We've got to make them come to us. The old-fashioned red herring which they'll sniff."

"If you ask me," a fresh voice said, "you might use some strong cheese to bring them out. That usually works with rats."

Clarke jumped up and stretched both hands toward Sandra Grey, much better known as "Sandy." Warrick greeted her with a great deal of pleasure also. He knew how valuable an operative Sandy could be.

"Seeing you two together"—Warrick sighed—"makes me wonder why on earth you devote your lives to hunting down criminals. You belong in a rose-covered cottage."

"Some day we'll have it," Sandy said. "Right now, everybody has other little jobs, like winning the war. Fighting these disciples of a modern-day, earthly Satan is enough to handle. Well, when do we start gunning for those four men?"

"We were just discussing it," Warrick said. "Bob, I had an idea you were about to suggest something. Remember, you implied these men must be baited and brought into the clearing."

"Exactly, and at this moment *Herr* Lommel offers the best lure of all. Is the F.B.I. sure of him, Mr. Warrick?"

"If you could hear the man talk, you'd be convinced, Bob. I would vouch for him personally."

"Good. That makes things easier. I'm sure the F.B.I. will work with me on this. Go back and have a talk with the man in charge. I want to take Lommel's place."

"Take his place!" Warrick and Sandy gasped.

"That's suicide if they carry out their plans!" Warrick objected. "They intend to kill Lommel."

"But I don't intend that they shall kill the Crimson Mask," Clarke said firmly. "Listen—this is what you must get the F.B.I.'s consent to...."

He talked for ten minutes, outlining carefully Sandy's part in this deadly game. Then Warrick hurried off to prepare the ground. Half an hour later he called in an okay.

"Get started, Sandy," Clarke told her. "Don't forget the signals, and keep a sharp eye out for trouble. I'm going to beard Dave Small downstairs and tell him he's out of the game temporarily. He isn't going to like that."

CHAPTER III

LOAD OF TNT

LOMMEL, UNDER constant guard, was rather amazed when F.B.I. men took him from a well-protected office in the Federal Building and led him to another room closer to the entrance of the suite. Lommel sat down and he was left alone. That, too, was both disquieting and dangerous. He began to fidget nervously, and he smoked cigarettes chain fashion.

The room was dimly lighted except for the spot where he sat. A rather bright light was suspended almost above his head.

Twenty minutes passed. He arose and started to pace the floor. Then he noticed an open door leading into another office. There was someone coming through it. Lommel backed up slowly, seized the swinging overhead light and turned it directly on this figure.

For a moment or two he was sure his eyes were playing tricks on him, until the stranger smiled broadly. For Lommel was looking at an exact counterpart of himself.

"Sit down, please," his double said. "Did I do a good job of it?"

"You mean," Lommel exclaimed, "that you have made yourself look like me? A good job? I thought I was going mad."

"I could hope for no more favorable criticism. I'm the Crimson Mask, Mr. Lommel. When it's time for you to be taken to another refuge, it will be I who shall go out in your place. That's why I applied make-up to resemble you. Now, there is little time to lose. Do you firmly believe they will attack you?"

"Any moment," Lommel answered. "By now they probably suspect me of telling the F.B.I. where our headquarters were. That is a lie—at least if you take it in a practical way. I did know F.B.I. men were following me, and I made little effort to throw them off my trail."

"Why are you so sure they'll try to kill you?" the Crimson Mask persisted.

"Because of their ego. You cannot realize the vastness of a Nazi's ego. I was condemned to death. Unless they execute me—murder would be a better word—they will lose face. Goebbels' propaganda thrives on stories telling how the great Nazi agents operate against all manner of circumstances. Killing me would make a marvelous broadcast."

"Then they'll never make it," the Crimson Mask vowed. "Climb out of your clothes. We're going to exchange."

When two F.B.I. agents, with Ted Warrick in tow, entered the room they just stared from one man to another. The Crimson Mask laughed. If his disguise could pass the scrutiny of these men, it was good.

"I'm the Crimson Mask," he said. "Is everything quite ready?"

"Yes," one of them answered. "My name is Nolan. I'm taking you away. As soon as we gel clear of this area, the real Lommel, with enough agents to guard him, will be whisked to an internment camp not too far from here."

The Crimson Mask frowned.

"You boys usually know what you're doing—but is it safe to put Lommel into a camp full of Nazi sympathizers?"

"The way we've arranged things, it is," Nolan replied. "You see, Lommel isn't well-known among Nazi sympathizers. He's always worked more or less under cover. He'll be sent to the camp under an alias and with a solid story as to why he was arrested. *Herr* Werner and his trio will never think of looking for him there."

The Crimson Mask glanced at his watch. "We've got to kill five minutes and then I'll be ready. Good luck, Lommel."

"And good luck to you," Lommel clasped the Crimson Mask's hand firmly. "I don't deserve such kind treatment and if I could do so, I would not permit you to risk your life for mine."

NOLAN AND the Crimson Mask walked slowly toward the entrance of the building. When it was time, the Crimson Mask stepped up to a window overlooking the street and glanced at a business building across the way.

He carefully counted eleven windows from the north and four stories up. As the second hand of his watch touched the arranged moment, a tiny light began to wink.

Unless one looked deliberately for the light, it could hardly have been seen. It kept on winking for about four minutes. The Crimson Mask's facile mind turned those signals into words. He nodded grimly and turned to Nolan.

"I suppose your men have been covering the area. Someone has been helping me, too. A car pulled up about twenty minutes ago and it nosed out from the curb. There is only one man in it. A patrolman, who seems to be a stranger on this beat, put in an appearance about the same time. He stepped up to this car as if on official business, talked to the driver for a few moments, then strolled away. He's still within shooting distance."

Nolan whistled. "We'll nab that fake cop. Don't worry about that. What'll we do about the car?"

"Nothing. We've got to make them show their hand. Perhaps none of the four men we want is in that car. We can't be sure. Therefore, we'll compel them to act. That is, if you don't mind, Nolan?"

"If you don't, why should I renege? I'll get someone to grab the cop."

"Better than that," the Crimson Mask said, "tell the driver of the official car in front to handle the cop. If a squad goes out now, the rats may smell the trap and spring it before we're ready. Just you and I will travel in the car."

"Right." Nolan grinned. "I've heard several times that the Crimson Mask doesn't know what fear is. I guess those stories were right."

"Well you're coming too, without whimpering about it, aren't you? Lay off the hero stuff. There's a job to be done and we're the boys for it. Let's go, G-man."

The F.B.I. car was parked directly in front of the building. They walked up to it. The Crimson Mask, in his pose as Lommel, kept looking about furtively. Nolan spoke to the driver who nodded, got out and began walking casually down the street in the direction of a uniformed patrolman.

The Crimson Mask slid behind the wheel, wriggled further over in the seat and Nolan drove. He sent the car away from the curb and headed directly across town. He intended to reach the avenue, which would be fairly quiet at this time of night. If an attack came there, the chances of bystanders being hurt would be much less than in the congested areas.

The Crimson Mask kept looking over his shoulder. Sandy had delivered that message and when she suspected a car as being ready to follow, she knew what she was talking about.

"Nolan," the Crimson Mask said softly, "that car I was suspicious of is coming after us. Keep a steady speed, obey all lights, and don't let them know we're wise "

"What if they start shooting?"

THE CRIMSON MASK'S right hand moved fast and a gun appeared in his fist.

"According to the information I have, only one man is in the car. If he opens fire, I'll show him what real shooting is like. Say—that driver isn't ready to strike yet. When you stopped for this traffic light, he stopped, too, and well behind us. Maybe it's only a tail."

"That would be my luck," Nolan growled. Then he added, hopefully, "Maybe he won't try anything until there's a clear path for a getaway. I'll reach the avenue soon. It's only five blocks further on."

They proceeded across another block passed it, and the Crimson Mask gave a start of amazement.

"Of all the fool things! That driver just turned off. He's left our trail, Nolan. That doesn't make sense, he didn't follow us just for the ride."

"I'd better keep right on as though we are unaware of him," Nolan said. "I've got a hunch he'll soon be back, but he'd better hurry. There's the river just ahead."

They reached a point one block from the avenue and stopped for a traffic light. When they started up again. Nolan saw a car coming his way. It was a oneway street and this man was clearly in the wrong. The man's car started to pick up speed, too.

"Keep out of his way," the Crimson Mask said quickly. "That's our man, Nolan. He's trying for a head-on collision. Look! See how he's weaving? Let him get fairly close, pull over to the left and see if you can miss him. I'll take over from there."

The Crimson Mask opened the door of the car and put one foot on the running board. His right hand clutched the heavy automatic and, he was tensed for a dangerous move.

The oncoming car veered crazily. Nolan was no slouch with the wheel how ever. Just as it seemed the car would crash head-on, Nolan gave the wheel a sharp twist and the F.B.I. car swerved aside. There was no more than a foot of space between the two cars.

As they passed at no great speed, the Crimson Mask was on the running board and he deftly transferred from one car to another. He clung to the spy sedan, yanked the door open and a pop-eyed driver gaped at the business end of the Crimson Mask's gun.

The Crimson Mask slid into the scat.

"You can stop the car now," he said. "Or would you rather have me do it—after you are dead?"

The driver was Karl, one of the vaunted New Order breed, but his face was white with terror now. He looked ahead, gave the wheel a spin and barely avoided a double-parked truck.

"Lommel," Karl said, "what is wrong with you? We engineered your escape, did we not? How did you get that gun?"

"I borrowed it." The Crimson Mask smiled. "Stop this car, do you hear me?"

Karl gulped and let up on the gas. The car kept right on going. The Crimson Mask reached for the ignition key, tried to turn it and the key broke off. The car kept on rolling along at about twenty miles an hour.

Karl let out a wild scream.

"It is Werner's work! He is responsible. Jump, Lommel, jump! We are doomed."

Karl started to open the car door, but the Crimson Mask's automatic dug into his ribs.

"Slay where you are. What do you mean, doomed?"

"The car—it is loaded with explosives. The fenders, bumpers and radiator are wired so that contact with anything will set off the blast. It was my job to drive right into your car, Lommel."

"Take the next corner," the Crimson Mask snapped. "Take it wide, too, and keep your horn blowing like blazes. If you even seem as though you are ready to hit anything, I'll shoot!"

CHAPTER IV

THREE TO GO

WHEN THE car veered around the next corner, beads of sweat were standing out on the Crimson Mask's forehead. Karl was half frantic with terror. None of the false pride and heroism he had displayed on the meeting hall stage was evident now. He was just an ordinary man, afraid of death.

He took the next corner too, and the next. Always that gun kept prodding his side.

"Why not jump?" he half screamed. "We could save ourselves. I will say you displayed courage worthy of another chance, Lommel. Werner will take you back. You can be one of us again."

"Where is Werner?" the Crimson Mask asked, speaking in perfect German. "How can I believe you?"

"I do not know where he is," Karl bleated. "We separated. Gottfried and I were to arrange this. He watched for you in front of the building."

"Dressed as a policeman?" the Crimson Mask demanded.

"Yes. How did you know? We took the uniform away from another policeman and enticed the one on the beat in front of the F.B.I. building, away. How did you know—"

Karl glanced at the man beside him and gave a yell of alarm. It was no longer Lommel who sat there, but a man who wore a crimson mask over his face.

Karl took the next corner crazily. For a moment the Crimson Mask wondered if he would deliberately drive into something and blow both of them up.

But Karl was by no means eager for death. Despite all his boasts, he wanted to live. The threat of just brushing a fender or bumper against another car was bad enough, but that gun in the hands of the crimson-masked man was almost as bad.

"When you turn the next corner, head west," the Crimson Mask ordered. "You'll see the river straight in front of you. That's where this car is going."

"But we shall be killed, too," Karl wailed. "It would be better to break loose wires to stop the car."

"And have someone bang into it and get blown to bits? It's the river, my friend, and if you don't do the job, I will, but then you'll be very dead."

Karl gulped and obeyed. In his smug little mind he began to wonder why on earth he had ever undertaken such a bad scheme. Werner had said the explosion must come in a congested section where it would blast people and buildings, besides disposing of Lommel. Werner had given Karl a Nazi salute, a quick, firm handshake, and had watched him drive off—to death.

Karl had planned to jump as soon as he was sure both cars would collide. Now he realized that Werner had arranged things so that this was impossible. Werner tolerated no errors and he did not mean to have Karl make one.

"Unspeakable fiend," Karl said in German.

"Double that if you're thinking of Hitler," the Crimson Mask said. "I... look out for that car!"

They passed through a red light and were moving across the avenue when a car flashed past them with only inches to spare. Karl wilted behind the wheel. The Crimson Mask grabbed control of the car, driving with one hand. He could not slow down, but he was able to maneuver the vehicle at twenty miles an hour without too much trouble.

He saw the pier loom up. The tires rolled over its wooden surface. The Crimson Mask opened the door beside him.

"Get ready to jump," he told Karl. "When you land, lie still, or I'll start pumping lead at you."

KARL SEEMED astounded that he was getting a break. He opened the door, gave a leap and vanished from sight. The Crimson Mask prayed there would be no string piece across the end of the pier. If there was, that pier and probably himself with it, would be blown to atoms.

He could not afford the time to make sure. It was time to jump himself. Be got onto the running board, still guiding the car in a straight line with one hand. His attention was on the pier and the possibility of that string piece. When he jumped, his attention was too much on this matter and he lost his footing.

Unlike Karl, who rolled over a couple of times and then jumped to his feet, the Crimson Mask fell heavily and was knocked senseless.

The car, however, rolled to the end of the pier and dived nose first into the river. There was no explosion. The impact was not hard enough to set off the mechanism and the water shorted whatever ingenious arrangement Werner had incorporated into the car.

The Crimson Mask was in no danger from that, but there was an added peril. This section of the city was descried. Nobody saw the car roll off the pier nor the two men jump out of it. Karl became aware of that a moment after he started to run away.

He looked around, saw the Crimson Mask sprawled out on the pier and decided to do something about it. Once danger had passed, he was his old arrogant self. He reached into a pocket, drew out a knife and started hurrying back to where the Crimson Mask lay.

Making sure he was still unobserved. Karl's lips parted in an inhuman smile He raised the knife and poised it above the man who apparently lay so helplessly at his mercy. The knife started to descend. But the Crimson Mask was not helpless now. He had quickly come to his senses.

Through slitted eyelids, he saw Karl approach, and he saw the knife. He did not move because his nerves and muscles were still shocked into weakness by the force of his contact with the pier.

But when the knife started down, he raised one leg and kicked out. It hit Karl in the pit of the stomach and sent him hurtling backward. He did not fall, but the pain he suffered made him go slightly mad. With a wild oath he rushed forward again, intent on finishing off this crimson-masked interloper before he could get on his feet.

Karl made a dive and brought the knife down. It slashed into the wooden pier instead of the Crimson Mask's heart, because the Crimson Mask had quickly rolled over.

Now he got to his feet. Karl was bent over, yanking the knife free. As he straightened up, the Crimson Mask made a lunging dive for his legs. Karl crashed to the pier, wriggled desperately and got the knife arm free. He jabbed with it and the Crimson Mask uttered a gasp of pain as the blade sliced through the fleshy part of his shoulder.

He gave a tremendous upsweep with the other arm and the heel of his hand slammed against Karl's chin. The spy lost his final chance to bury the knife deep in some more vulnerable spot. Yet that did not stop him from trying. He attempted to drive the dagger upward to impale the Crimson Mask's throat.

A hand shot out, grabbed Karl's wrist and twisted it hard. Karl gave a wild veil of agony as bones snapped. Weakened, he fell heavily and the point of his own knife slid between ribs and buried itself in his heart. Karl shivered once and was quiet.

HEADLIGHTS BATHED the scene before the Crimson Mask could get up. He tensed, ready to leap off the pier if these were Karl's friends. But a trim figure slid from behind the wheel and Sandy Grey ran toward him.

"Bob—you're hurt!" she cried.

"It's nothing," he told her. "Watch out for trouble while I search this man."

"Is he one of those—"

"There are only three left now," the Crimson Mask said grimly. "I'm hoping to find something which will lead me to the others."

The Crimson Mask turned Karl over on his back and transferred the contents of Carl's pockets into his own possession. Then he faced Sandy.

"We'd better get out of here. As soon as we reach a quiet corner where there is a store, I want you to phone the F.B.I. Tell them one of the spies is on this wharf and that a car, wired to blow up on contact with any other object, is at the bottom of the river. They had better get it out and be careful doing it."

"Your arm is bleeding badly," Sandy said. "Bob, it must be taken care of. Come on."

He jumped into Sandy's car. She stopped to telephone, then proceeded straight back to the neighborhood of the drug-store. They parked the car and hurried through devious alleys until they reached the rear of the drug-store.

Two minutes later Sandy was applying antiseptics to the wound. She bandaged it neatly. The Crimson Mask removed the disguise and became Bob Clarke again.

Downstairs, Dave Small was busy locking up a little early. He knew the Crimson Mask had returned and he was eager to find out what had happened.

Soon after, the three of them were in the laboratory while Bob Clarke explained the events which had almost cost him his life.

"The sheer devilishness of Werner's plans is enough to make a man's blood run cold at first," he told them. "Then it will boil, as mine is doing now. Werner not only meant to kill Lommel, but tried to make sure it was done in a spot where a lot of other people would suffer. If that car had blown up where Karl meant it to, the whole block would probably have been blasted to bits."

Small whistled. "Boy, those Nazis certainly don't care if they get killed murdering other people, do they?"

"The one I got was afraid. His kind usually is afraid when death comes at him, and believe me, this Nazi was no hero. Now we'll have a look at this man's stuff... Ah, a wallet. His name was Karl. That indicates he was one of the quartet."

"Which leaves only three," Dave Small said.

"I'm not so sure." Small looked over at Sandy. "What happened to the Nazi who swiped that cop's uniform and paraded up and down in front of the Federal Building?"

"I don't know," Sandy replied. "I saw the driver of your car walk toward him. Somehow the Nazi must have realized things were not just right because he turned around and streaked for it. I heard a couple of shots and that's all. I had my hands full following you."

CHAPTER V

VISITORS AT DAWN

B **OB CLARKE** phoned Warrick and got the complete answer. The fake patrolman had planned his getaway well. He hadn't even been recognized.

"The police and G-men are already at the pier," Warrick informed. "We're all grateful that you reduced their numbers from four to three. Any line on the others?"

"Not yet," Clarke admitted. "I'm going through the dead man's effects now. Call me if anything develops."

"But it has already," Warrick groaned. "A freighter, half-loaded with supplies for our allies, caught fire. Incendiary all right, and one of the spies was seen in the vicinity. The gangling one called Paul. They're still at it, Bob. Heaven knows when they'll stop."

As Bob Clarke hung up, Small gave a shout of triumph. Among Karl's possessions he had found a much worn, forgotten bit of paper which had been tucked in a pocket.

"It's a cash receipt for goods that were delivered to him from a delicatessen. There's no address on the receipt, but that store would know where he lives."

"Good," Clarke said. "That's your part of the job. Go up to the vicinity of the store. Maybe you'll find it open. A lot of delicatessens in that neighborhood are all night places. Phone them, give Karl's name and ask for a bill of goods to be sent C.O.D. Trail the delivery clerk—and you've got it. Let me know as soon as you get there."

Small hurried away, eager to be of help. Sandy was preoccupied and worried looking.

"Bob, I've been thinking of this Lommel. You told me he was married and had a child. Now if Werner or any of his bandits were after Lommel, wouldn't they try to harm him by striking through his family?"

Clarke nodded. "I was just getting around to that. The F.B.I. may be watching them. I don't know. At any rate, you'd better get up there. See what the wife knows—especially about Werner, Gottfried and Paul. Pose as a newspaper woman. Stay with her and watch yourself for trouble."

"Is it all right if I question her about reasons why those men want to murder her husband, Bob?"

Bob Clarke frowned. "What makes you ask that? Lommel was tried and convicted of being a traitor to the Nazi regime. He was sentenced to death and those men will try to carry out the sentence, that's all."

"Is it?" Sandy asked. "I didn't question the fact much even before they really did attempt to blow him to bits. Now why couldn't they have merely shot him as he left the Federal Building?"

Sandy stopped talking, and shuddered. She looked over at Clarke and her eyes were filmy.

"That would have meant you'd be dead, Bob. Didn't you ever think of the risk you took?"

"Sure I did. What's more, I was reasonably certain that they would not attempt to shoot Lommel. You see, often a man who is shot doesn't die too quickly. Especially when the assassin is forced to fire from a distance. They wanted Lommel to die instantly."

"Then you believe as I do—that there must be some other reason for the importance of Lommel's instant death," Sandy said quickly. "Something more than just the fact that Nazi agents will carry out a sentence of death merely to inflate their ego."

"That's right." Bob Clarke smiled. "And it proves I pick my assistants well. Not even the G-men have thought of that. Lommel's death, just because he was regarded as a traitor, is almost inconsequential compared to the things those bums could do with no more risk than polishing off Lommel."

"Maybe he'd talk," Sandy suggested.

"That is odd." Clarke frowned. "He was so darned honest about everything else. I just can't see him holding anything back—unless he isn't aware of the secret he holds. I may visit him, but right now it's more important to dispose of his enemies—and ours."

SANDY WALKED to the door.

"I'll see Mrs. Lommel at once. It's past midnight, but I have an idea she'll lie awake after what's happened. And Bob, I didn't tell you this before because you have enough to worry about, but I may have been seen leaving those offices from which I signaled you."

Bob Clarke bit at his lower lip a moment.

"That's bad. What makes you think so, Sandy?"

"Well, I entered that suite of offices with the pass-key you gave me. I watched, saw what happened and signaled you. Perhaps Karl and this phony patrolman were not the only ones on deck. It's possible that either Paul or Werner were also there and also saw the signals. At any rate, I left the offices as soon as you drove away. When I came out, someone ducked around a corner of the big corridor. I didn't see him—only his shadow."

Bob Clarke opened a drawer and took out a small, flat automatic. He handed this to Sandy.

"You're a crack shot with one of these," he said. "Keep it handy and use it if necessary. Remember, always, that the men we are trying to wipe out are brutes without an iota of mercy."

She took the gun and hurried away. Clarke lit a cigarette, leaned back and relaxed while he tried to figure out what Werner's next step might be. He studied newspapers for leads, but found so many that it was impossible to sort them out.

Shipments of precious cargo were leaving for England and Russia every hour. Troop trains were rushing across the continent continually. Important men, like General Thomas, who was more or less a secluded figure but commanded a branch of the Army which had seen little action yet—the Chemical Warfare Service—must be taken into consideration. General Thomas, Clarke knew, probably was in a key position to combat any attempts by the Axis powers to use gas or other vicious, banned types of warfare.

All of these things were important enough to call for attentions on the part of the three surviving spies. They might strike at these or a hundred other objectives. The trail was barren of any leads so far. Bob Clarke pinned hopes on what Dave Small and Sandy would discover.

While he waited, Clarke sat down before a triple mirror and applied light make-up with deft hands. He changed his appearance by using a disguise he frequently adopted when on the trail.

Under no circumstances must anyone discover that Bob Clarke and the Crimson Mask were the same person. If that news leaked out, he could expect to have a bomb lobbed through the front window of his store or meet a hail of hot steel any time he walked out on the street.

He changed his clothes, slipped two heavy guns into especially created pockets, then sat back to wait. No more than fifteen minutes went by before he got results. Dave Small phoned in.

"Meet me at the corner of Prentice Avenue and Whiteacre Place," he said briefly. "I've run the little Nazi's nest down."

It was a cozy little nest at that, as Clarke shortly discovered. Karl may have believed in the iron discipline and the so-called simple living ways of the Nazis, but he liked comfort.

Dave Small led the Crimson Mask to a fourth-floor apartment fitted up with overstuffed furniture, a thick rug and swanky decorations. There was a liquor cabinet against one wall. Small opened it up and called the Crimson Mask over.

"Hey, take a look at this. A shortwave radio set hidden behind the liquor cabinet front. It's only good for receiving, and the dial is set for Berlin reception. I'll see what's cooking over there, huh?"

WHILE SMALL listened to the excited sputterings of a German announcer, the Crimson Mask searched the apartment. He concentrated most of his attentions on a big desk, but Karl apparently had been careful. There was nothing lying around to give the slightest hint about the plans of this gang.

In a spacious clothes closet, fitted up like a photography lab, the Crimson Mask found a roll of film. It had been hung up to dry. He held this to the light and frowned. Only a dozen shots had been taken and the rest of the film was blank.

In its 35 mm. size it was difficult to determine the subject, so the Crimson Mask went over to an enlarger, inserted the film and projected a large picture of the film. One by one he slipped the frames through and studied each photograph.

The pictures were all taken of the Hotel Viceroy, a swanky midtown spot. Each side was shown clearly and there were even angle shots taken from the roof of some higher building. He rolled up the film and put it into his pocket.

Then he went back to the desk. A memo pad caught his eyes. There were indentations on the blank surface of the top leaf, indicating that Karl had used a heavy hand in writing.

The Crimson Mask searched a drawer, found a soft pencil and carefully moved it across the surface of the pad until he brought out the words which had been written on a page Karl had torn off. He read:

White coat, size 36.

"Now what in the world would Karl be doing with a white coat?" he wondered. "The size would fit him all right. Maybe fit Gottfried, too, the other member of the gang who resembles Karl in size."

"There are millions of white coats," Dave Small said, "and if Gottfried is in one of 'em, we've cut ourselves a sweet job trying to find him."

"The pictures were of the Hotel Viceroy," said Clarke. "Turn that radio down, Dave. I'm using Karl's telephone."

The Crimson Mask called the hotel and got a night desk clerk. He gave his identity as that of a reporter for one of the big papers.

"I'm just wondering if any important guests showed up today," he said. "Like to interview 'em in the morning. With a good mention of the hotel, of course."

"Well—a couple of Hollywood actresses checked in this morning," the clerk informed him. "The papers carried that story tonight, so you know about that. We have a couple of British officials here to meet General Thomas, who checked in today also. Then somebody who won a pie-making contest—"

"Thanks," the Crimson Mask said. "None of them are up my alley."

He hung up and called Small over.

"General Thomas!" he exclaimed. "He's a pretty important man in this war, Dave. Werner made a statement to the effect that it wasn't hard to polish off important men. He's right, too, because our generals don't go around protected by a lot of Gestapo agents. I wonder if they are planning to do something with him."

"What gives you that idea?" Small asked.

"Because those pictures I found were of the hotel where the general and his retinue are stopping. There's a chance they were taken to help plan a getaway. Of course, Karl's death is probably already known to those other three spies so they'd be apt to carry out their plans without the use of these pictures."

"Maybe we ought to have a look," Small suggested. "Wait until I turn off this doggone radio."

BEFORE HE reached the instrument, the announcer switched to English and immediately plunged into a colorful description of the imaginary panic Werner and his men had created.

"In our former broadcasts," the announcer said, "we told about four agents who are no longer interested in their own lives, but are willing to die for the New Order. That is the type of men we create here. Word has reached us that a traitor to our cause was sentenced to execution by *Herr* Werner. We call upon him to carry out that sentence. It must be accomplished above all other things. No traitors can be permitted to live. And so we greet our four glorious comrades in arms who are fighting a battle against the entire resources of the United States. We call upon Werner and Gottfried and Paul and Karl. Wipe out the traitor!

"Show those soft Americans what men are really like. Destroy their fortifications, their arsenals and factories, if you can. Go down fighting if need be, for you shall become the inspiration of our young people. *Heil!*"

"He'd better send one of those *Heils* down to Satan's stronghold, because that's where Karl is," Dave Small grunted as he started to yank wires loose from the radio. "I'll fix this thing so it won't carry any more phony propaganda."

"That was only part propaganda, Dave," the Crimson Mask said. "It contained an open order for Werner and his satellites to execute Lommel. I wonder why. The announcer stressed it so much that there must be a good reason—a better one than we know—now. I'm going to find out what it is as soon as I settle this affair of the Hotel Viceroy."

"Do I go along?" Small queried anxiously.

"No. There's another job for you. One of those spies will be busy with General Thomas. That leaves two on the loose and they might concentrate on Mrs. Lommel."

"But Sandy is there," Dave argued.

"I know she is," the Crimson Mask admitted, and I also know the calibre of these three spies we're after. It may take more than Sandy to stop them. You get up there and keep watch. At least until Sandy is satisfied nothing is going to happen."

CHAPTER VI

THREE DEVILS PLAN

LEAVING KARL'S apartment, Clarke and Dave Small separated outside. Small hurried to Mrs. Lommel's address and took up an advantageous point from which he could watch the windows of her apartment. Once he saw Sandy pass and glance out. Small felt better then.

The Crimson Mask, meanwhile, subwayed downtown and reached the Hotel Viceroy. It was almost dawn when he checked into the place, paid for a room in advance because he had no baggage, and sat down to rest and think.

He had to reach General Thomas and talk to him. More and more the Crimson Mask believed there was more to this scheme of things than appeared on the surface. That Nazi announcer had been just a bit too insistent upon Lommel's execution.

The Crimson Mask lifted the phone and asked to be connected with General Thomas' room. A sleepy voice answered him.

"Hello, Mac," the Crimson Mask said jovially. "I just got into town and—"

"You've got the wrong room," Thomas answered gruffly. "My name isn't Mac."

"I wanted Fourteen-ten," the Crimson Mask said. "That's you."

"This is Sixteen-thirty-seven. Now will you allow me to hang up and go back to sleep?"

The Crimson Mask murmured an apology and waited twenty minutes more. He slipped out of his room, climbed the stairs to the sixteenth floor and made certain he was unobserved. He already knew what kind of locks were on the doors of this hotel and it took him only a couple of minutes to open General Thomas' door.

He stepped inside quietly, moved along a short hallway and into a living room. Through a door he could see a man sound asleep in the next room. He drew his red mask over his eyes, stepped up to the bed and turned on the light.

Thomas sat up with a jerk, rubbed his eyes and then started to leap out of bed, startled by the sight of this man he believed to be a masked burglar.

"Hold everything," the Crimson Mask chuckled. "I'm no thief."

Thomas blinked a fen times more and then uttered a long gasp of astonishment.

"That red domino. You're the Crimson Mask! I thought you were more or less of a legend."

"You might find that to be the truth after all, General Thomas. However, there isn't much time to lose. Your life is in danger. Did you know that?"

"My life—in danger? Why, I don't know who'd want to kill me."

"I may have made a mistake," the Crimson Mask went on. "If so, it will be serious for the person who is really threatened. Yet I think I'm right. They are after you."

"They? Whom do you mean?"

"Three Nazi spies. You've read about them, undoubtedly. The men who have sworn to wreak as much damage as possible upon us before they are captured."

"Oh, yes, of course. You say three. I thought there were four."

"There were, until a few hours ago. I made the count three—most definitely. General. The man who died had taken photographs of this hotel from every angle. It looked to me as though they intended to pull a job here and were planning a getaway."

"But I can't understand why they would want to murder me," Thomas said. "I am a ranking officer. I do know many secrets of the Chemical Warfare Service, but good heavens, so do a lot of my subordinates and some of my immediate superiors! Killing me wouldn't cripple the branch of service to which I belong."

THE CRIMSON MASK thought for a moment. "Is there anyone else in the hotel whom they might go after?" he asked.

"Nobody of any great importance. Of course, there is always the chance that those men will murder ranking officers merely for the prestige of saying they did so."

"No, there is always method to the madness of dictators and their agents. Why did you come here, General? Is your mission of any great importance?"

"Absolutely not. I really consider it a brief vacation. You see, a new radio station opens tomorrow night. I'm to take part in the inaugural broadcasts. Ralph Fellows and George Brown own the station. They are prominent in Washington affairs and I have known them for a couple of years."

"Maybe we're getting some place," the Crimson Mask said. "Such a broadcast would involve the presence of many distinguished people. If the spies could wipe them all out—"

"Impossible," General Thomas declared. "The station and studio will be guarded. There will be a distinguished body of men present, true—British officials, the Chinese attache, some South American representatives, and a famous Dutch official. Only the British officials are staying in this hotel. The others are to arrive just before the broadcast and depart immediately afterward."

"Which pins it down to you or the Englishmen," the Crimson Mask said. "Those spies intend to move in on this hotel. I'm sure of it. There was nothing about any radio studios."

"We'd better notify the F.B.I.," Thomas declared. "There is no use in taking chances."

"No, those spies may know a lot of F.B.I. agents. If they show up, our men will run for it and I intend to get them. One by one, or in a group. I don't care which, so long as they are either dead or locked up. That kind are the only good Nazis."

"Admitted, sir," Thomas agreed. "But just how do you intend to arrange this?"

"Very easily. I've rented a room on the tenth floor. You get dressed and go there. Remain inside. I'll stay here and take your place."

"I can fight my own battles, you know," Thomas argued.

"Who is to doubt that, General? But why should you take chances? I know how to deal with men like those spies."

Thomas nodded. "All right. I can see the logic to that. Spies... good heavens, who'd have thought I'd run into them again! You see, during the first World War, I was a member of the Black Chamber. Pretty good at deciphering those German codes, too, if I do seem to be bragging. There wasn't one I didn't master. The job became a passion with me. Then I switched to the Chemical Warfare Service because I thought I'd get more action."

"You may have that yen satisfied yet," the Crimson Mask said, and smiled. "Let's not lose any more time."

BEHIND THE doors of a seedy-looking pool parlor, Gottfried, Paul and Werner met for a conference. The pool room had closed up long ago, but its owner was a Nazi sympathizer who was quick to aid the men who were on the way to becoming Nazi heroes. A rather thick wad of currency also helped him to believe in these three.

Werner was pacing the floor of the dark room and cursing softly under his breath.

"I have learned enough to realize we were killed," he finally said. "Karl is dead—killed by a detective who wears a crimson mask and has the reputation of a Robin Hood. Bah! Karl always was stupid. Gottfried, some of the blame rests upon you, too. Your position as a patrolman walking up and down in front of the Federal Building should have given you an opportunity to observe that it was not Lommel who got into the car."

"But it was!" Gottfried insisted. "I saw him with my own eyes."

"And what about you, Paul?" Werner asked. "Has it come to the point where I cannot trust either of you?"

Paul unwound his lanky form from a chair.

"*Herr* Werner, it was not my fault nor Gottfried's. Probably not Karl's either. You may not know it, but the Crimson Mask has the ability to disguise himself perfectly. It was he who lured Karl into a trap. It was he who came out of the Federal Building disguised as Lommel."

"Then why didn't you do something?" Werner demanded.

"There was no time—and I didn't know it was not Lommel then. According to plan, I remained hidden. I happened to see a signal lamp winking a message. Naturally, I went to investigate. From the offices where that signal originated, I saw a young woman emerge. I think she may have seen me, too. At any rate, by the time I reached the street again, Karl was gone and Gottfried was running away from one of those cursed G-men."

Werner hurled the butt of a cigar into the corner and faced his two aides.

"Very well, I accept your excuses. We shall carry on without Karl. You heard the short-wave broadcast from Berlin tonight? We all know that Lommel must be silenced. But first, there is another matter. That of General Thomas."

"He is mine." Gottfried drew himself to attention. "We drew lots, *Herr* Werner. I shall kill the general."

"Good." Werner nodded curtly. "I am glad to see your spirit, Gottfried. Yes, it is your task. Unfortunately, Karl was to lay all the plans, and there is no time to create new ones. You will have to take your chances. Is that clear?"

"*Ja, Herr* Werner. It is clear. We have the white coat which Karl furnished. I managed to have the name of the Hotel Viceroy embroidered upon the lapels, exactly the way it is done on the white coats of real waiters."

"Very well," Werner said, "you are ready then. The Hotel Viceroy provides a complimentary breakfast for all its guests. You will slip into the hotel, steal a tray and go to General Thomas' room. You will arrive there early, so that no other waiter will have preceded you."

"And then—a knife. It is a quiet way and I should like to see an American general writhe in pain." Paul licked his lips in anticipation.

"Paul," Werner said, "you will first of all attend to Lommel's wife and son. You know the usual method of handling such women. Take her and the child to the prepared place. This must be done in time so that you may be in the vicinity of the Hotel Viceroy at seven-thirty in the morning. That is when Gottfried will emerge if he is lucky. You are to aid his escape."

"It is clear." Paul sat down. "I know just what to do about *Herr* Lommel's wife."

BY THE look on Paul's face he was an expert in these matters, but had not enjoyed a task of this kind for a long, long time.

Werner spoke further.

"Meanwhile, I shall take care of Lommel, himself. If I cannot reach him, he will soon learn that his family is being held and that will close his stupid mouth if he guesses what we are up to."

"But Lommel has been taken somewhere," Gottfried said.

"And I know where he has been taken," Werner smiled. "He is locked up at an internment camp not too far from here. The G-men do not know that from their headquarters I have secret information. So I know that they hold Lommel, and relate a false story of being picked up at sea after a submarine he commanded was lost. That is a very good story—for the work I intend to do."

"I cannot understand," Gottfried began.

"Idiot. As a submarine officer he will be placed with other interned officers of our undersea fleet. Oh yes, the Americans have sunk some of our submarines. Too many, curse them. The prisoners they took are at Camp Marigold. The officers occupy an old hospital there, the crew and interned aliens live in barracks."

"You are going to enter the internment camp?" Paul asked in awe.

"Why not? It is simple. They do not look for people who seek to enter such a place. I know a way. For your own information and peace of mind, I will admit that I have had a great deal of help.

"Now get to work. Paul, your mission must be completed before Gottfried begins his. I am going at once to the camp."

CHAPTER VII

SURPRISE FOR A NAZI

PAUL DEPARTED immediately. Werner left half an hour later, and Gottfried was alone.

He spent some time in oiling and cleaning his gun. Then he tested the sharpness of a short, wide-bladed dagger. He dozed after that, his mind filled with the glory that would be his when he returned to Germany.

Killing a general on the battlefield rated an Iron Cross. To dispose of one while on enemy soil, was an even more glorious task. There would be oak leaves with Gottfried's iron cross. Perhaps a promotion to even outrank Werner. Gottfried would have enjoyed that. Werner was a hard task-master.

When it was time, Gottfried slipped out of the refuge and began walking rapidly along the quieter streets. Twice he ducked out of sight when patrolmen appeared, but Gottfried was not unduly worried. Nobody knew what the three men who were so badly wanted, really looked like.

Reaching the employees' entrance of the Hotel Viceroy, he consulted his watch, stalled a little longer, then boldly walked in. Along the deserted corridor, he pulled the white coat from under his clothes and donned it. The garment fitted perfectly around his suit coat. Werner had been insistent about that. A coat that was too small or too large might arouse suspicions.

Gottfried tossed away his hat and entered the kitchens. A glance showed him what was expected of a waiter. The place was a bustling madhouse of activity. There were more than sixty waiters, all busy preparing breakfast trays.

Gottfried seized a tray and some napkins. He planked a sugar bowl and a cream pitcher on the tray and edged his way out. He covered the tray with a napkin. There was a satisfied grin on his face. The tray contained no breakfast, but he was certain that General Thomas wouldn't care much—not after he digested his meal of cold steel.

Thorough-going Werner had supplied Gottfried with the number of General Thomas' room. He stepped into an elevator and was whisked to the proper floor. He walked slowly down the hall, balancing the tray clumsily. Once more he checked his watch. Paul would have completed his mission by now and at any moment he would park outside the employees' entrance. Everything was prepared.

As Gottfried's knuckles rapped on the door, a thought entered his mind. He would give the dying general the Nazi salute before he left. That would be something to tell them when he was decorated for this.

A voice called an order for him to enter. Gottfried smiled contentedly. Leave it to the foolish Americans not even to lock their doors. He turned the knob, entered, and closed the door softly behind him. He let the sugar bowl and creamer clink to indicate he was really a waiter.

"Breakfast, sir," he called out. "Shall I place it on the table?"

"Of course," a voice called from the living room, but Gottfried couldn't see anyone there.

He was half-way across the room before he noticed a high-backed chair pulled up before the windows. A column of cigarette smoke curled lazily ceilingward.

This, Gottfried decided, was going to be easier than he thought. He placed the tray down and rattled the dishes again. Then he reached under his coat, drew the knife and slowly advanced toward the chair. Before the victim would know what happened, the knife would flash before his eyes and be buried hilt deep.

He stole closer and closer to the chair, knife held high. The figure in the chair did not move and yet Gottfried suddenly found himself covered with cold sweat. There was something wrong. He could feel it. His eyes flashed around the room for a second, came back and then opened wide in horror.

GOTTFRIED HAD not noticed it before, but there was a mirror between the two windows and he was reflected in it as perfectly as if focused there by a movie camera. Not only that, but Gottfried could see the man seated in the chair, too!

It was no man dressed in a general's uniform, but a slender figure with a crimson mask over his eyes. And—a gun in his hand! Gottfried gave a shrill cry and tried to get around the chair for a quick thrust with the blade he held.

The gun lashed out, its barrel collided with his arm and the knife fell from fingers gone limp under the impact of the weapon. Gottfried licked his lips and forgot all about medals and honors. The one thought predominant in his mind was Paul, who would wait just so long and then come in to find out what had happened.

Gottfried moved back until he hit the wall. There he stood, one arm dangling limply, the other half raised. The Crimson Mask arose and kept his gun pointed at the spy.

"You must be Gottfried," he said pleasantly, "from descriptions I've heard. You resemble Karl in build, while Paul is tall and rangy and Werner happens to be a rather small man. Like your *Herr* Goebbels and with the same kind of a ratty mind, no doubt."

Gottfried didn't answer. His tongue refused to move, but mentally he wished he had joined the infantry instead of the spy network. There was a gun in his pocket, but he saw little chance to use it. This crimson-masked man was too sharp-eyed.

"Well—are you Gottfried?" the Crimson Mask asked.

The spy's head wagged up and down. It didn't even occur to him to try and bluff it out.

"Good," the Crimson Mask said. "Now we can get down to business. I'm going to ask you a question. Just once. If you don't answer, or you lie, I'll give you the same treatment Karl got and—well, he didn't survive, if you know what I mean. Why did you come here to murder General Thomas?"

Gottfried's paralyzed tongue loosened up a bit as he saw the eyes behind that crimson mask narrow.

"I—I do not know. I—I only followed orders. They do not tell us reasons. Let me live and I shall tell you everything. Everything!"

"Thanks," the Crimson Mask said drily, "but it's too late now. You lied, Gottfried, and you know the penalty. I'll give you one more chance to tell the truth about General Thomas."

Gottfried hung his head and managed to get a glimpse of his wrist-watch. Paul should be here at any moment now. He was fervently thankful that he had thought to leave the door unlocked. Paul would come right in. A minute or more—that was all the time he required.

The Crimson Mask suddenly lowered his gun, kicked a chair closer and sat down. Gottfried could hardly believe his eyes. The man was actually off his guard. Gottfried's piggish little eyes contained an iota of hope now.

"You have promised that I will live," he said slowly. "Very well then. I shall talk. General Thomas is an important man. Wait—I'll show you. I have a dossier on him."

Gottfried took a long chance then. He depended on the seeming negligence of this masked man, on his eagerness to know the truth about General Thomas. Gottfried's fingers closed around the butt of his gun.

HE SCREAMED an imprecation and drew it. There was a single shot. Gottfried felt white-hot lightning stab his arm. He felt blood seeping down across his fingers which no longer held a gun. There was a smile on the masked man's lips. To Gottfried it spelled death.

With a wild yell, he lurched across the room, past the chair placed before the windows and hurled himself through the glass pane. The Crimson Mask had not expected that. He dropped his gun and made a grab for Gottfried's legs—and missed.

One look out of the window told him that Gottfried was really a good spy—a dead one. He had landed on a roof extension eight stories down. There was no excitement anywhere below. Nobody had seen that dive.

The Crimson Mask reached up to strip off the domino and then hesitated. There was a click at the front door. He heard it open and he bent down to retrieve his gun.

Light footsteps approached. The Crimson Mask's jaw dropped a notch. There was a boy, about eight years old, standing in the doorway. His face was the color of chalk, but there was resolution in his eyes. He moved forward a couple of steps.

CHAPTER VIII

THE NAZI MANNER

S ANDY FOUND Mrs. Lommel to be a pleasant, worried woman of about thirty-five. Her eyes were red from weeping. At her side stood a boy, her son, bright and alert. He was spotlessly clean in a white shirt, corduroy pants and a bright red sweater.

"What else can I say about my husband?" Mrs. Lommel looked up at Sandy. "There have been many reporters here today. Eric was a good man. At first he believed in those monsters over there—in Germany. Then he changed. Little Curt helped to unravel his mind. Curt was born here. He is an American."

The boy smiled shyly, but said nothing. Sandy asked more routine questions and found Mrs. Lommel highly co-operative. Sandy prided herself on her judgment of people and this woman seemed to be as patriotic and honest as any one she had ever met. None of her husband's former fanaticism had entered her mind.

Sandy decided to take a long shot. She hunched her chair closer and dropped her voice.

"Mrs. Lommel, I haven't been honest with you. I'm not a reporter, but—well, sort of a detective. Now wait before you condemn me. My whole idea is to help you and your husband. I do not suspect you of anything. All I want is information."

"About what?" Mrs. Lommel was stunned by the news. "What do I know that could help?"

"Perhaps more than you realize. Didn't your husband ever confide in you? Didn't he even hint about the plans made by the spy organization?"

"Not one word," the woman said flatly. "At first he was proud to be working for the New Germany, but later on, after the war began and the cruelty inflicted upon conquered nations was made known, he changed. He never talked about this undercover work at all."

"Not even after Pearl Harbor?" Sandy insisted.

Mrs. Lommel smiled a bit. "After that happened, he became mad. Fighting mad. He wanted to help this country, but he didn't dare do a thing. They would have killed him at the first sign of treachery. Just as they want to kill him now. And they will. They will. I know how those devils work."

"Mrs. Lommel," Sandy said, "we think there is another reason why those men want to murder your husband. Something beyond the fact that he is regarded as a traitor to the Nazis. Have you any idea what it may be?"

Mrs. Lommel didn't have a chance to reply. Some one rapped gently on the door. Instantly, the boy hurried to let the caller in. He opened the door and suddenly vanished, as if he had been yanked out of the room.

Sandy and Mrs. Lommel jumped up, then stopped short. The boy reappeared. Behind him was the rangy, cruel-faced Paul. He held the boy with one hand and pressed a gun muzzle against his head with the other.

"Curt!" Mrs. Lommel screamed.

"Silence, you idiot!"

Paul kicked the door shut. He eyed Sandy, and recognition seemed to dawn in his eyes.

"One more sound from either of you and I'll blow this boy's brains out. You—there. What are you doing here?"

"I'm just a friend," Sandy said. "I came to see Mrs. Lommel."

"You are a liar. You work for the Crimson Mask. It was you who signaled him so that Karl died. I am glad you are here. Very glad. You will lay that purse on the table and then both of you back against the wall. Hurry! Do you want to see this boy killed before your eyes?"

MRS. LOMMEL obeyed quickly. Sandy hesitated only a moment or two. She knew a cold-blooded killer when she saw one and this Paul was supreme in that category. His finger was white against the trigger of the gun.

Paul emptied the purse, appropriated the money in it, and also the small automatic, which made him laugh derisively. Still holding onto the boy, he gave further orders.

"There is a car directly outside the door. Both of you will walk out of here and enter that car. I shall follow, with Curt. If you signal anyone or raise an alarm, he dies. Now start. There is little time."

Sandy did not move her head when they reached the street, but out of the corner of her eyes, she saw someone lurking in the doorway of a store across the street. That would be either Dave Small or the Crimson Mask. Sandy's hopes rose high.

"It's better to do just as he says, Mrs. Lommel," she advised. "I hardly doubt but that he would murder your son."

"Silence!" Paul commanded.

They got into the back seat of the car. Paul dragged Curt with him into the front seat and drove with one hand. The car hit a cross artery, followed it to a speedway and turned north. Paul maintained an even speed so as not to attract any attention, and always that gun was ready to shoot at the boy.

Curt whimpered a little at first, but then he sat stonily silent, staring through the windshield. Mrs. Lommel sobbed.

Sandy kept raising her eyes to peer in the rear view mirror. They were being followed—at a considerable distance—and now and then the headlights vanished, but Sandy knew all the tricks which Small or the Crimson Mask could pull. They merely shut off their lights and gave the impression that nobody was following. When they were turned on again, it looked as though another car had just turned out of a side street.

Finally, Paul turned sharply to the left and bumped across a rutted road. No headlights trailed him down that narrow lane. He stopped beside a single-story house which was hardly more than a shack.

At his orders, Sandy and Mrs. Lommel got out and walked into the house. It was dusty and forlorn. Paul forced Sandy to tie Mrs. Lommel to a heavy chair, then he strapped Sandy into another.

"Excellent," he said. "Werner will be delighted to meet an agent of the Crimson Mask. Remember—if you try to escape, the boy dies. Now, Curt, you and I will step outside and wait for the clever person who thinks I do not know he was following us. It will be the Crimson Mask, without question. Come, Curt."

He gave the boy a hard shove out of the door. Sandy's heart sank. Perhaps Paul was smart enough to trap the Crimson Mask.

Outside, Paul cuffed the boy until he began to cry. Then he hit him again, hard. The boy tripped and fell. When he got back on his feet, Paul had disappeared. Curt began running through the darkness and headed straight back toward the house.

Suddenly a man stepped out and checked him. Curt skidded to a stop. A hand grasped his arm and he waited stolidly for more punishment. But this man spoke in a kindly voice and Curt saw that it wasn't Paul.

"Don't make any noise." It was Dave Small who spoke in a whisper. "Just take me to where your mother and the other lady are."

A gun butt crashed down on Small's head. He fell to his knees, made an ineffectual attempt to reach his own gun, but another blow sent him flat. When he woke up, he was securely tied and lying on the floor between the chairs which Sandy and Mrs. Lommel occupied.

DAVE SMALL groaned and sat up. He grimaced at Sandy.

"What happened? Where's that rat—and the boy?"

"Gone," Sandy said. "He took the boy with him. If any of us are missing when he returns, the boy will be killed. Dave, if the New Order breeds such monsters as that, give me a nice congenial head hunter or a cannibal every time."

"I'll settle for a knife to cut myself loose with," Dave Small grunted. "Where did that jerk go?"

"After the Crimson Mask. He took the boy along to insure our staying here—and to intimidate the Crimson Mask. It looks hopeless, Dave."

It was within only moments of Sandy's despairing cry that, in General Thomas' suite in the Hotel Viceroy, the Crimson Mask was staring at the boy who had entered so unexpectedly. He saw the terror that shone in those bright young eyes, but for a moment the Crimson Mask was taken aback. He started to walk slowly toward Curt.

Suddenly Curt spoke.

"Paul is here. Paul has come with me."

The Crimson Mask heard a rasping oath, the sound of moving feet, and suddenly the boy ducked, whirling around and hurling himself at the feet of the advancing man behind him. He spoiled Paul's aim.

The Crimson Mask's gun cracked. Paul fired twice, but missed. He kicked at the boy, turned the muzzle of his gun down. The Crimson Mask fired again. This time Paul was half whipped around by the force of the slug that burned through his shoulder.

He wheeled and darted down the hallway to the open door. The Crimson Mask went after him, but Paul had plotted his getaway well. An elevator was at the floor, its door wide open and the operator huddled in a heap in one corner of the lift. Before the Crimson Mask could reach it, the doors slid shut and the elevator dropped.

The Crimson Mask rushed back to where the boy stood, shaking a bit and still as pale as paper.

"Who are you?" the Crimson Mask asked.

"I am Curt. Curt Lommel. My mother is in a house. A nice lady and a man are with her. Paul tied them up."

"Look!" The Crimson Mask dropped to one knee and grasped the boy by both shoulders. "You're a smart boy. You stopped me from walking into a trap where Paul would have killed me. Now I'll help you—but you must try to remember where your mother and those other people are being held."

"Oh, I know that," Curt said promptly. "All the way from the house to this hotel I watched."

"Good!"

"The Crimson Mask ripped off his domino, took Curt's hand and they raced from the room. Only three minutes later they were in a speeding taxi. The Crimson Mask did some explaining to the driver. The cab driver drew a hard breath as he listened.

"Nazi spies!" he said grimly. "Them Huns who said they'd wreck the city before they were caught?" He squared his shoulders. "Brothers, count me in! I'll make this wagon travel like one of them Airacobras. Hang on!"

CURT GAVE the necessary directions and they were soon streaking along the highway he indicated.

"Make the driver slow up," Curt said finally. "I have to watch the numbers of the telephone poles. When Paul brought us, he turned off this road, but his headlights hit a pole and I remembered the numbers on it."

"Good boy." The Crimson Mask put on his domino again. "Paul hasn't too much of a start and he'd hardly expect a boy like you to remember where he went. I guess men like him don't believe American boys are smart, eh, Curt?"

"No, sir. But they're the ones who aren't so smart. Please—you won't let him kill my mother?"

The Crimson Mask shook his head from side to side, but he was far more worried than his expression indicated. Paul might simply leap from his car as soon as he reached the house where his three prisoners were held, turn a gun on them, and run for it. The man was desperate.

Curt suddenly leaned forward.

"I remember the next corner! It was so sharp. Two or three minutes past it and we'll find the road."

The driver slowed down and Curt checked the numbers on telephone poles. He gave an excited cry and pointed out the half-hidden entrance to the lane. The driver turned into it, paying no heed to the ruts that threatened to break every spring in the car.

Soon they saw the outlines of the shack in a little valley before him.

CHAPTER IX

PRISON CAMP

C **URT HAD** no more than pointed out the shack than the Crimson Mask saw it, also. He saw Paul's car, too, and some one was running toward the house.

They were close enough to recognize Paul's spare figure and the Crimson Mask saw him hurl something through the door, then race away. Before the cab ground to a stop, smoke was seeping through chinks in the house.

The Crimson Mask leaped out, began running. A gun cracked and the bullet whined uncomfortably close. As he dropped flat he instantly realized what Paul's strategy was. The spy lurked somewhere in the brush, ready to kill anyone who approached the shack.

The Crimson Mask felt Curt wriggle up to him. Curt spoke in a strained voice.

"It's a funny old house. I looked around when I was there. It's got only one door—that one in front. All the windows are boarded up except a little window at the back. I could get through it, but you couldn't."

The Crimson Mask heard the taxi driver blundering around. Suddenly he let out a scream which was doubled with the spang of Paul's gun. The taxi driver sat down fast, nursing a wounded thigh. He was out of the battle.

Smoke was coming from the house thicker than ever and flames were beginning to shoot out of cracks beneath the front door. The Crimson Mask drew out a knife and banded it to Curt.

"This is your party, Curt," he said grimly. "Your job is to rescue your mother. I'll keep Paul busy while you get to the back of the house. Break in the window, cut your mother and the others loose. Hurry! And don't let Paul see you."

Curt wriggled away. The Crimson Mask rose to his full height and began to walk slowly toward the path which led up to the front door. Paul fired twice. The Crimson Mask was untouched, and he pumped a bullet in Paul's direction. His aim must have been good because he heard Paul scamper to another hiding place.

Still, the Crimson Mask kept on going, completely exposed. Paul fired again. The slug burned past the Crimson Mask with no more than an inch or two to spare. Paul couldn't have too many bullets left, unless he carried an extra gun or ammunition. The Crimson Mask had to risk that.

He was in the clearing in front of the house now, as perfect a target as Paul could have wished for. The spy's gun cracked only once this time. That bullet found a mark, but only a minor one and the Crimson Mask kept right on advancing, heedless of the burning sensation from the flesh wound in his side.

Paul was retreating. The Crimson Mask could hear him crashing through the underbrush. Then the window at the rear of the house caved in with a loud noise. Paul moved faster, intent on reaching the rear of the place. He must have guessed what was happening.

The Crimson Mask broke into a run, too. He sent a slug whanging in the direction of Paul's course. That stopped the spy for a second or two, but it also drew an answering shot.

Some one gave a yell from the front of the house. It was Dave Small. He was carrying Mrs. Lommel as he staggered toward Paul's car parked nearby. Sandy followed, holding Curt by the hand.

Paul suddenly broke through the curtain of underbrush and streaked madly toward Small. The Crimson Mask was after him in a flash. Paul, heedless of the danger involved, raised his gun, centering it on the limp burden in Small's arms.

THE CRIMSON MASK'S gun rapped twice. Paul lurched sideward. His finger had been tight against the trigger and the gun exploded, sending its bullet into the ground at his own feet.

Paul started reeling toward the brush again. Apparently this time he had only escape on his mind, but there was a crimson-masked avenger rushing toward him. Paul's breath came in wheezes. He trembled with panic, staggered behind a bush and crouched there, automatic ready.

He saw the Crimson Mask approach, still shielding Paul's former prisoners. Paul leveled his gun, took careful aim, and squeezed the trigger. The mechanism clicked on an empty cartridge chamber.

Paul's mind snapped then. He whipped out a large clasp knife, opened the biggest blade and charged straight across the clearing.

The Crimson Mask fired three quick shots. Paul stopped in his tracks and stood there, his features red in the light of the fiercely burning shack. He seemed to have turned into granite for half a minute, then he toppled forward like timber crashing to the ground.

Instantly Sandy was at the Crimson Mask's side.

"Bob!" she whispered. "You've been hurt again. Bob, is it—?"

"Are you all right?" he demanded hurriedly. "How about Mrs. Lommel and Dave?"

"Yes, yes—we're all of us all right. Curt got us out of there just in time. Paul threw several incendiary bombs into the house… Your side is bloody, Bob. You've got to take care of that wound."

"Later. Come on. I've got to talk to Mrs. Lommel."

Mrs. Lommel answered the Crimson Mask's questions eagerly.

"No, I haven't the slightest idea why I was being held except that Paul hinted it might be to keep my husband from talking."

"That is the only answer," the Crimson Mask said. "The fourth spy, Werner, has not put in an appearance and I've an idea that was intended. Somehow your husband had to be told that you were a prisoner. Such information would be hard to smuggle into an internment camp, so Werner must have gone there to handle your husband personally." He turned to Sandra Grey. "Sandy, take Mrs. Lommel, Curt and the taxi driver home. Dave, you come along with me in Paul's car."

The Crimson Mask drove back to town furiously while Dave Small told the story of his capture.

"You can't be blamed, Dave," the Crimson Mask said. "Paul was a rat, but clever enough to realize that so long as he had the boy at the point of his gun, all of you were stymied. He even sent the boy into General Thomas' suite so all my attention would be focused on him, while Paul blasted me."

"Curt's a great kid," Small said. "Say, if Werner has gone to that camp, what can you do about it?"

"I can go there, too," the Crimson Mask said firmly. "However, it's broad daylight now. Werner won't dare strike until night. The only way he could get into that camp is by stealing in, so he'll have to lay low until darkness helps him. The other prisoners will hide him. Meanwhile, I've got to make certain arrangements that may take time."

"You're really going into that camp?" Dave Small asked slowly. "Into a nest of Nazi sympathizers and even captured sailors, who'd kill you in a second if Werner gave the word?"

"I'm going, Dave. From here on it's my party."

NIGHT WAS drawing near when a slow local puffed its way upstate. The last coach was sealed and well guarded. In it were aliens assigned to internment for the duration. They were all glum.

Among them was the Crimson Mask, who was much more worried than he looked. It was beginning to get darker by the minute. Werner would hardly wait long. The deaths of Gottfried and Paul were already in all the newspapers and Werner might have knowledge that he alone was left.

He would know that Mrs. Lommel was free, and that Lommel might have been given that good news. Therefore Werner would strike hard and quickly—to silence Lommel forever.

There was a clever disguise on the Crimson Mask's face. It made him look like a stolid, angry Nazi. He had been locked up with these others and routed for the prison camp as soon as the authorities could get the plan working.

Officials at the prison camp had not been warned to search for Werner. Such an act might drive the spy to such desperation that he would risk everything to get Lommel before he was caught.

The Crimson Mask knew what he was walking into. He would be locked up behind a high fence, among sworn enemies. Werner would be literally in command of the Nazis there and they would obey him to the letter. Once the Crimson Mask made his identity known, he would have to fight the whole pack.

The train stopped at a station not on any time-table. The last coach was unhooked and left there. Several big vans were waiting. The prisoners were herded onto the platform and two military policemen called off names.

The Crimson Mask answered to the one he had assumed and joined six others in a small group. They were escorted to a van and loaded aboard. The others were still standing on the platform when the van rolled away.

"What is the meaning of this?" the Crimson Mask demanded in the perfect German of which he was master. "Why are we taken from the others?"

A Nazi prisoner laughed.

"It is just the foolish way Americans have of doing things," he scoffed. "Those of us in this van were all connected with the German or Italian embassies. Not officially, of course, but we seem to outrank the others in this party of prisoners. Therefore we go to an old hospital which has been turned into comfortable quarters for captured officers. We are rated as officers."

"Is it easier to get away from the officers' quarters than the regular camp?" the Crimson Mask queried.

"Are you crazy?" his companion asked scornfully. "Why should we try to get away? It would only mean that we would be forced to serve the spy ring here or do some other dirty work for the glory of the New Order. Bah! I have had enough of such glory. I intend to settle down and be an example to the other prisoners."

"But it will be difficult in the quarters to which we are assigned," the Crimson Mask said. "As I understand it, captured submarine officers and important Nazis are held there. They will be forever planning an escape, and if we do not join—well… Is there need to explain further?"

"No. Yet it will make no difference so far as I am concerned… Well, we have arrived. Such a place! It looks like a resort hotel."

They were mustered out of the van, lined up and inspected. Guards searched each man once more and finally they were led to a huge dining hall. It was about half filled, and none of the guards interrupted when the new arrivals were greeted with yells and even Nazi salutes.

The Crimson Mask sat down and let his eyes rove across the room. He saw Lommel, seated alone at a corner table. There were, of course, no signs of Werner. If he were here, he would be under cover.

CHAPTER X

MURDER STALKS THE CAMP

AFTER A surprisingly good meal, the Crimson Mask found that he was free to stroll around the grounds. A quick inspection showed him how easy it would have been for Werner to slip over the fence. There were guards enough, but their attention would have been fastened on the prisoners, not on someone breaking into the camp.

The Crimson Mask spotted Lommel, walking slowly along. He was unaccompanied. The Crimson Mask fell into step with him.

"Good evening, *Herr* Lommel," he said in German.

Lommel turned pale and licked his lips. He kept walking though, and studied his companion in the fading light.

"So it has finally come then," he said in a tired voice. "Werner sent you, of course, to carry out the execution."

"What makes you think so?" The Crimson Mask had a smile on his face which Lommel could not fathom.

"Because I am not known here by the name of Lommel," he said. "You recognized me, so—"

"You are wrong, *Herr* Lommel. The last time we met, I looked like your twin brother."

Lommel stopped dead and stared.

"The Crimson Mask!" he muttered softly.

"That's right. We'll keep on walking. If anyone catches up with us, don't talk. Lommel, Werner had your wife and son kidnaped yesterday. Now wait! They have been freed and unharmed."

"Thank heaven for that!" Lommel said fervently. "I suppose you were responsible for getting them free. I owe you much, Crimson Mask. I wish there was some way I might repay you."

"There is. That's why I came here, posing as an interned alien. Lommel, your wife and son were taken as hostages. Why? There must be some reason. Something you know which might be dangerous for the Nazi spy ring if you talk. What is it?"

Lommel looked squarely into the Crimson Mask's eyes.

"I swear that I do not know. Lately I was not trusted much and was told little. I had a feeling my sentence of death had been planned long before I spoke up at that meeting. Werner merely seized upon that chance as a golden opportunity."

"Karl, Gottfried and Paul are dead," the Crimson Mask said. "There is nothing to fear from them. But Werner—it may be that he is here, in this camp."

Lommel stopped walking and his eyes lit up.

"Then that must be it! Until today, everyone was friendly to me. The other internees walked with me, ate with me. But today, I have been avoided as though I suffered from a plague. Yes, that is Werner's work. He has told the others. That means—death."

"If you are telling me the truth, that you have no idea why Werner is so bent on exterminating or silencing you, I'd better arrange to get you out of here."

"No. Werner would only follow. Perhaps he will not kill me at once. Usually he likes to torture a man by telling him what is to happen. If I could get him to talk, to say why I am doomed—"

"Are you really willing to risk as much as that?" the Crimson Mask asked.

"I would risk even more," Lommel declared fervently. "Anything to atone for what I have already done to a nation like this one. You must let me alone. I'll draw Werner out. Never mind what happens to me. But get Werner. He is a madman, yet a genius. For many years he was trained for just such work as this. Now—leave me. If the others see us talking, you will be suspected, too."

"Wait a moment." The Crimson Mask checked him. "What's your program for tonight? I've got to know, so I can stay close."

"In a few minutes we go into an assembly hall and listen to radio programs. The programs are censored for us, so we listen only to what the officials here direct. No small radio sets are permitted, naturally. Be careful, my friend. Most of the others here are fanatically loyal to the Nazi regime."

LOMMEL HURRIED away then. The Crimson Mask walked slowly back to the quarters, entered and found most of the men on their way to the assembly hall. He stepped aside, made certain none of the guards saw him, and watched every man who entered. He had an excellent description of Werner and was sure he would recognize him, but the man made no appearance.

Soon the big doors were closed. A loud-speaker began to broadcast music. The Crimson Mask realized that the entire area around the building was practically empty of guards. They were all in the assembly hall, except those on duty at strategically placed posts. If Werner ever intended to get in his work, he would be on the prowl now.

As the Crimson Mask stole away, he could still hear the radio. An announcer was telling about a new radio station, dedicated with this program. General Thomas spoke and the Crimson Mask smiled. At least, none of those four men of murder had succeeded in carrying out any of their important plans.

He reached the rambling porch, stole down it and slipped over the railing. Making his way forward, he reached a thick bush beside the walk leading to the building. He crouched there to wait.

Suddenly the entrance doors of the building were opened and Lommel appeared. He was in a hurry, and there were no rules which compelled him to stay in the assembly hall if he didn't wish. He came down the steps two at a time and began running.

Suddenly Lommel vanished from sight. The Crimson Mask moved toward the spot where he had last seen him. He heard low voices, a groan of agony. Someone spoke in German. The Crimson Mask realized it must be Werner.

"So, *Herr* Lommel, you heard the broadcast and you know, eh? Talk, traitor, or I shall drive this knife slowly into your heart. Speak softly, do you hear me?"

"Yes, I know," Lommel answered. "When I was recalled to Germany, the whole plan was described to me. Somehow, you planted men in that new radio station, men who very carefully prepare its programs, so that every word they utter has a double meaning. It is the new code, worked out at the end of the last war. A code that was never used until now. So that is why you wanted to kill me! You were afraid I'd talk. You were right, Werner. If I had known, this whole plan would have been blown wide open."

"Ah, yes. Just as you'll be opened up, with my knife. The foolish Americans believe I am busy trying to sabotage. They do not realize that every move I made was to reach you. And Lommel, it may make your death harder if you know that Paul has your wife and child. They will be killed, too."

"You are mistaken," Lommel said stonily. "Paul is dead. So are Gottfried and Karl. You will join them soon."

"How do you know this?" Werner demanded. "Speak up, dog! Speak, and I promise not to harm your family after I get out of here."

The Crimson Mask rose slowly and started moving forward. There was a rush behind him and two heavily built men came hurtling out of the darkness. Unarmed, completely surprised, the Crimson Mask was brought down with a crash. A hand was clapped across his mouth, then he was dragged into a small clearing.

Lommel gave a cry of horror. Werner smiled coldly.

"I am beginning to understand," he said. "This man is the Crimson Mask. Of course that is how you know about Paul and the release of your family, Lommel. It is good work. Now I shall kill both of them."

THE CRIMSON MASK saw Werner approach. He was held by the two internees who had been watching for guards. Struggling did no good, and he was unable to cry out. Werner's knife was blood-stained. Lommel had suffered already.

The doomed man lay on the ground, apparently too weak to move. Werner paid no attention to him, concentrating everything on the pleasure of killing the Crimson Mask.

"You are the Crimson Mask," he said softly. "Why not admit it? Why not acknowledge that I have defeated you? Karl and Gottfried and Paul were idiots. It did not require much cleverness to trap them. But I am Werner. You cannot trick me."

The Crimson Mask made one final desperate effort to shake off the grasp of the two men who held him. It failed miserably and the knife started creeping toward his throat.

Suddenly a yell broke the silence. Lommel was on his feet. His face was smeared with blood, his eyes shining in pain. He lurched forward. One hand clawed at Werner's face.

The spy whirled and raised the knife. Lommel threw himself directly at Werner. For a moment it seemed he might beat the spy down.

One of the men holding the Crimson Mask let go to join in the fight. The Crimson Mask was ready for that. He swung a mighty fist. It connected with the man who still held him.

Rushing forward, he got an arm-lock on the second internee, swung him back and let go. As the man swooped in, the Crimson Mask stepped aside lightly and let go with a straight arm jab. It connected with such force that pain shot up the entire length of the Crimson Mask's arm.

He heard shouts all over the camp. Then a scream. Lommel staggered backward, a knife sunk to the hilt in his chest. Werner looked around, saw the Crimson Mask approaching and started to give ground. He waved one hand before him and shouted for mercy. He read correctly the look in the Crimson Mask's eyes.

"No—no—I surrender! I give up, do you hear? Don't—don't—"

The Crimson Mask smashed a blow to Werner's middle. The spy howled in agony, doubled up and took a score of sharp, savage punches to the face. When the guards reached the spot, Werner was on the ground. His features were puffing out rapidly and he kept moaning and begging for mercy.

It required a lot of telephoning before the internment camp guards were satisfied that the newly arrived prisoner was really the Crimson Mask.

"And don't stare at me that way." The Crimson Mask laughed softly. "You will never see this face again. Naturally, I'm disguised."

The officer in charge gestured toward Werner, who was handcuffed to a chair and still moaning.

"I think you plastered a disguise on that guy's face too. His best friend wouldn't recognize him. If rats like him have friends. We'll cool him all right."

Werner looked up and some of his old defiance rose within him.

"You can do nothing to me. You cannot prove a thing."

"What do you call using that knife on Lommel?" the Crimson Mask asked.

"Lommel was a soldier of the Reich." Werner straightened up in his chair. "He was traitor and I carried out the order of a court-martial. In war, an execution is not murder."

THE CRIMSON MASK sat down on the edge of a desk.

"Werner," he said coldly, "your nerve is colossal. I know why you stalked Lommel to kill him. Lommel had been told in Germany about the code which was used tonight over the new radio station broadcast. You were afraid he would talk. Well, for your benefit, that radio broadcast has already been cut off and the owners of the station placed under arrest.

"It was a clever scheme. You and agents like you have accumulated a great amount of information which would interest the Reich. It was intended to broadcast it in code over this station, especially created for that purpose. Other stations might have changed the script and ruined the whole thing.

"Sooner or later your trick would have been discovered—especially if General Thomas were allowed to live. You tried to kill him because he could break this code. He learned it somehow, during the last war. Your campaign of terror was a blind to throw us off the real scent."

Werner shrugged. "What difference does it make? You can still only keep me locked up."

"Listen!" the Crimson Mask said firmly. "What you call carrying out the sentence of a court-martial is termed coldblooded murder here. You won't be tried as a spy. You'll face a jury for murder and be convicted as surely as you are sitting there right now. We're not interested in you as a spy any longer—only as a killer. And we have a most uncomfortable chair in our prison for your kind. It will send you where Karl and Gottfried and Paul and millions more of your sort have gone. One of these days you'll have a happy reunion down there—when you *Führer* arrives in style. It won't be long now, Werner."

The spy began whimpering. That turned into loud pleas for mercy, and finally Werner cracked. The Crimson Mask turned away.

"It's funny how men who are bred on deceit and treachery, on murder and violence, can never understand they have to take what they give," he said icily. "Iron men? Hah! They're like slinking rats inside. Real men couldn't stomach such a way of existence. Men like Lommel, for instance, who gave his life so that that treacherous broadcast would be stopped in time. Such men see clear through Nazi teachings, right to its rotten core. And blubbering in that chair is a typical example of the kind of men the New Order breeds."

The Crimson Mask turned away from the nauseating sight. His work here was finished, but when more enemies of his country tried to get their taloned claws into its defenses—he would be ready.

THE DANGEROUS
GAMBLE

CHAPTER I

REFUGEE SHIP

THE BIG liner was nearing New York. Her twelve hundred passengers were showing the strain of the long voyage that began at Hong Kong, proceeded to Portuguese East Africa and thence across the Atlantic to New York.

They were showing a great deal of enthusiasm too, every one of them, waiting for the moment next morning when the Statue of Liberty would break through the haze and tell them beyond any doubt they were back home.

The passengers aboard this liner knew what privation and suffering meant. They'd spent long weeks as Japanese prisoners, living on watery soup and rice. The dining room had done a colossal business all the way over, yet left them unsatisfied. This wasn't an American ship and the passengers all wanted good old ham and eggs, apple pie and coffee that tasted like the real thing.

In the dining room four men occupied one table. They'd become friends during the long journey and each had stories to tell that would have curled the hair of a ventriloquist's dummy.

Philip Adrian, drug salesman for an American concern, was the oldest. His gray hair had grown long while he was a prisoner and he permitted it to remain this way. It framed his clear cut features attractively. Adrian was the least talkative of the quartette.

John Marcy, publisher of an English-Chinese newspaper, was about forty-five. His clothes were loose because he'd lost more than twenty-five pounds, but he was still cheerful and his face glowed with a broad smile. His left arm was unnaturally stiff and the hand was always gloved. It was a false limb.

Warren Fenwick, manufacturer of staples in Hong Kong, before the Japs decided to take over his business, was the bean pole of the group. He usually wore a bowler hat, carried a cane and affected spats. Somber of face and attitude, he was still liked by the others.

Wylie Wilson leaned across the table and swirled ice and whiskey into a miniature whirlpool in his glass.

"If they don't consider me too old and decrepit," he said, "I'm going to enlist in some branch of the service and fight those rotten Japs. Most particularly, I'd like to come face-to-face with the officer who slapped me for three hours until my cheeks were raw and bloody. I'm no bloodthirsty individual, but if I could sink a bayonet into that two-legged beast, I'd feel better."

"You never told us why they persecuted you that way," Phil Adrian said.

Wilson grimaced.

"I was a chemist. Had my own business and doing well until they blasted their way in. They wanted dope—cocaine with which they meant to feed the Chinese. They thought I had a large supply of it and wanted me to tell where it was hidden. I couldn't tell them something I didn't know because that cocaine existed only in their imaginations."

John Marcy said, "We all feel bitter, Wilson. We've a right to. I'm going to do what I can to help defeat those yellow beggars. I think we all will. But let's forget that now. We're getting close to home. Dreams we've had for months are coming true."

"Marcy is right," Fenwick grunted. "We Should forget our troubles and try to make up for lost time. Well, I think I'll turn in. I want to be one of the first to spot that old lady with the light of liberty welcoming us. See you gentlemen in the morning."

PHIL ADRIAN arose too, finished his drink and walked slowly around the deck once. There was a deep frown creasing his forehead. He chewed on a cigar nervously and then hurled the mutilated butt away. He walked rapidly to his stateroom.

It was shared with two missionaries who paid scant attention to him. Adrian sat down at the small desk, drew paper toward him and wrote a message, a very careful message in which every

The Crimson Mask saw the blade hurtling toward him

word counted. He folded this, jammed it into his pocket and went back on deck.

It was late. Most of the passengers had gone below for sleep so they'd be able to welcome the dawn and New York Harbor. Adrian paced the deck until it was almost barren of life. Then he made his way forward, scurried down a companionway ladder and approached the radio room. Its door was closed but light streamed beneath it.

Adrian looked over his shoulder nervously, extracted the folded piece of paper and slipped it under the door. Then he rapped on the panels twice and raced down the corridor to his cabin.

The radio operator opened his door, peered out and shrugged. He was sure there'd been a knock. He stepped into the corridor and looked in both directions. A shadowy form was just disappearing aft. The radio operator opened his mouth to call the man back, thinking he wanted to send a message, but believed the radio room closed because of the late hour. The figure disappeared.

Then the operator turned back. He crossed the threshold, bent down and picked up Adrian's piece of folded paper. He opened it, read the message and whistled in amazement. Seizing his cap, he locked the room and hurried on deck. He proceeded straight to the bridge knowing the captain was there.

The radio operator saluted.

"Sir... someone I did not see slipped this note under my door. Apparently, it is a message which the man wishes sent because there is also a ten dollar bill pinned to the paper. I don't know whether or not to send the message, sir."

The captain took the note, stepped over beneath a light and read it.

MOST URGENT THIS MESSAGE BE SENT. TO F.B.I. NEW YORK: AXIS SPY AMONG PASSENGERS. HAS INSTRUCTIONS AND DETAILS OF GIGAN-TIC PLOT HARMFUL TO UNITED NATIONS. CHECK ALL PASSENGERS. IF UNSUCCESSFUL, I WILL COME FORWARD WITH NECESSARY INFORMATION ALTHOUGH IT MAY MEAN MY DEATH. CANNOT SIGN. TOO DANGEROUS. BUT TAKE MY WORD CLEVEREST MAN IN ORIENT ABOARD.

The captain rubbed his chin and stared into space for a moment or two. Then he took the radio operator aside.

"We are a neutral ship carrying diplomats and refugees. We are not supposed to act for either the Axis or the United Nations. However... we have no argument with America or its allies. Neutral or not, we can't allow a clever spy to reach shore to murder and destroy. Send the message, but... don't tell a soul, do you hear?"

"Yes, sir." The operator saluted smart. "I knew you'd say that, sir. Hoped so, anyway. I'll send it immediately."

He hurried back to the radio room, locked the door and sat down in front of his instruments. The message went through promptly and he received an acknowledgment. The operator leaned back and thanked his lucky stars that he worked for a captain who could place conscience above such things as strict neutrality.

Outside, in the corridor, a man walked slowly toward the radio room. He darkened the corridor by the simple expedient of loosening the electric light bulbs. When he knew he was protected by the gloom, he rapped on the radio room door.

The operator jumped up, thinking this might be the mysterious sender of the message. He unlocked the door, yanked it opened and saw no one. He looked vainly for another message under the door, then stepped into the corridor.

A STRONG arm wound around his throat, shutting off the scream he tried to let out. He was held like that until his senses were spinning. Then he was thrust against the wall, a fist collided with his jaw and he became unconscious.

The attacker eased him to the floor, entered the radio room and found the message promptly. He lit a match, held it to the edge of the paper and watched it burn until his fingertips were seared. He dropped it then, let the remainder be reduced to ashes and ground these underfoot.

For a moment he hesitated and seemed ready to smash the radio, but decided against this and departed as silently as he had come.

But he'd been too late and knew it. The message had been sent. Only one thing was in his favor. Phil Adrian was afraid to come into the open with his accusations. The spy cursed the so-called efficiency of the Japanese and especially cursed Phil Adrian.

The next morning a coast guard cutter stopped the liner. A ladder was dropped and twenty G-men swarmed up it. In charge was Bill Blane, slender, agile and bright-eyed. His men went to work. By the time the ship dropped anchor they had sorted the passengers, questioned some of them and hadn't the vaguest clue as to who had sent the message.

Two hundred F.B.I. men came aboard to help. Now they really went to work, taking one passenger at a time. The F.B.I. men were possessed of information that astounded the passengers. They knew everything about them, down to second cousins.

Phil Adrian was examined in his own cabin. The missionaries had already been allowed to go ashore. Adrian answered questions promptly, permitted a scrupulous search of his possessions and person, and was allowed to pass through.

John Marcy grinned amiably at his questioners.

"Say—you fellows are worse than the Japs," he said. "But I see your point all right. I'll bet this false arm of mine made you suspicious. Quite a way to carry information, eh?"

"Quite a way." Bill Blane smiled. "I'm glad you're taking it pleasantly. Sorry too, that we had to ship your false arm ashore for a laboratory examination. It will be returned to you shortly. Now about this gruesome statue here. Don't tell me you intend decorating a mantel with that?"

Marcy chuckled and picked up the statue. It was made of the finest porcelain—the figure of a kneeling Chinese with a garrote drawn around his neck. The artist had created each little detail of the figure's agony. It wasn't an appealing work of art, but it was delicately done and as perfect as anything could be.

"Ghastly thing, isn't it?" Marcy smiled. "This piece is as rare and valuable as stuff from the Ming Dynasty. I procured it for next to nothing from a Chinese who was getting ready to flee into the interior before the Japs came. I intend to present it to a museum."

"We'll have to look it over," Blane said. "Please go back to your cabin and stay there. We hope to allow you to go ashore very soon."

MARCY NODDED agreeably, stepped out and grinned at Fenwick who was going in next, laden down with all his baggage.

"Fenwick," Marcy said, "they're going to ask you two million questions about that Chinese document you carry. Better have your answers ready."

Fenwick grinned.

"I'll let them read it. Nobody else ever could, not even the Chinese, because it was written a thousand years ago in some unknown dialect of Northern China."

Fenwick submitted to the same intense questioning. He explained about his document, produced it and Blane promptly impounded the thing.

Then Wylie Wilson entered. He went through the same routine and he also had an unusual possession, a lavishly decorated and embossed Chinese music box. He played it for them and the tune

The Crimson Mask lashed out with a vicious punch

was some outlandish conglomeration of notes which would have made American jive sit up and take notice.

Bill Blane was getting quite an assortment of these things. Most passengers possessed some relic they wished to keep with them.

Gradually, however, the passenger list was whittled down to a hundred and twenty-three persons still regarded with suspicion. These were slated for at least temporary internment at Ellis Island.

Blane went to the captain's quarters.

"About this message," he said. "I haven't mentioned it before because we've all been too busy. I'd like to see it."

The captain shrugged.

"I am very sorry. Within two or three minutes after the message was dispatched, my radio operator was attacked and the message burned to ashes, then powdered underfoot. My operator saw neither the man who delivered the message nor the one who stole it.

"I would prefer," he said, "that this business not be mentioned at all because we are a neutral ship without right to interfere between warring powers. It would do me no good back home if this news leaked out."

Blane nodded.

"Nor in Japan if you were sent back there for more exchange prisoners. I'll keep it quiet, Captain, and thank you very much for this—ah— unneutral co-operation."

The captain shook hands.

"A man's country may be neutral, sir, but an individual can possess a personal viewpoint on what is right and what is wrong. I hope you trim the shirts off those Japs and exterminate the Nazis!"

Phil Adrian hurried ashore. No one met him and he wasn't sorry for this. He had an idea that he was a marked man and anyone who was close to him might also be the object of an Axis spy's revenge. Adrian looked around and saw no suspicious characters watching him. He hurried toward the nearest taxicab and gave orders to be driven to a small downtown residential hotel.

He checked in there, demanded a room on the top floor and promptly locked all windows and the door. Without removing his hat or coat, he hurried to the telephone and made a call.

The number he called was that of a telephone in a quiet drug store in one of the toughest parts of town.

CHAPTER II

LAST WORDS

THAT PARTICULAR drug store was an odd place as far as drug stores go. It was old fashioned, had colored bottles of water in the windows and on the door was the name and license number of the owner. It read Robert Clarke, Ph. G.

Here was no soda fountain, no lavish display of perfumes, coffee percolators, clothing, or sporting goods. The shelves were stocked with the best of patent medicines. A large section was reserved for the prescription department and there were counters displaying instruments for the sickroom.

An apple-cheeked, somewhat rotund man was behind the counter wrapping a bottle of medicine. He handed this to a woman who was poorly dressed and whose reluctance to accept the package was obvious.

"I don't like to charge this, Mr. Small, but I haven't any money and Patsy is so sick…."

"Forget it," Dave Small smiled. "Big shots with lots of dough have bills sent and pay 'em when they feel like it. That's what you do. The price is sixty cents."

"Sixty cents!" the woman gasped. "But last winter, when I had the same bottle filled, it was a dollar eighty. The cost can't have gone down that much."

"Your boy is in the Army, isn't he?" Dave asked. "He volunteered right after Pearl Harbor. Since then, the price of medicine has gone down because that boy is helping us get the drugs we need. Oh, yes… wait until I get a bag."

Dave opened a large glass container and dumped out a bagful of hard candy.

"Take this home to Patsy with our compliments. We like to do things for good customers. Thank you very much. Good-by."

Dave walked to the back room. Robert Clarke was studying a recent work on criminology and without looking up, Clarke spoke.

"I heard you out there. Soft hearted! You know doggone well it cost us more than a dollar to make up that prescription and you also know her son isn't helping to get drugs from the Far East. He's on a sub chaser in the Atlantic."

"Oh, sure, I know," Dave protested weakly. "But it doesn't hurt to let her think… oh, shucks Bob, you give away more medicine than you sell. You keep charge accounts and forget to mark charges down. Can I help it if I'm getting soft like you?"

Bob Clarke laid the book down and grinned broadly.

"It's okay, Dave, I'm just kidding. You can forget to mark down that sixty cents too."

Dave straddled a high stool beside the prescription counter and lit a cigarette.

"You're a funny guy, Bob. Of all the places to start a business, you pick the poorest section of the city, but it's your store so why should I kick? In fact, I like it. I… there goes the phone. Somebody else's kid is sick. Lots of colds going around this year."

DAVE HURRIED to the booth and then called Bob.

"For you," he said. "Some man and he sounds pretty excited."

Bob Clarke stepped into the booth.

"Who did you say it was? Adrian? Phil… Phil Adrian from China! Man, am I glad to hear from you! Last I knew, you were in a Jap prison camp."

"I might as well still be," Adrian replied nervously. "Bob… I need someone I can trust. Your father and I were very close friends. You're like him and now I need you badly. I'm at the Alton House, not very far from your store. Get here as quickly as you can. Don't announce yourself. Just go directly to Room One thousand twenty-five. It's urgent, believe me."

"Depend on it," Bob said. "I'll be there."

He hung up, hurried out of the booth and began stripping off his white coat.

"What's up?" Dave asked.

"I don't know," Bob replied. "An old friend of my father's just got back from China where he was being held by the Japs. Says he has to see me about something important and believe me, he certainly sounded scared."

"Maybe a job for the Crimson Mask?" Dave asked hopefully.

"It could be almost anything, Dave. Call me a cab, will you? Doggone, where's my hat?"

Bob Clarke fidgeted nervously as the taxi made its slow way along the narrow cross street. Bob Clarke wondered if Phil Adrian really was in danger.

If so, it concerned the war because he'd just returned from a war zone and perhaps knew something detrimental to the Japs. But why on earth hadn't he gone directly to the police or F.B.I.? For a fleeting instant Bob wondered if, by any remote chance, Phil Adrian had discovered that Bob Clarke was the Crimson Mask.

He rejected that idea quickly. Only three people knew that Bob Clarke had another identity. Dave Small, of course, was aware of it. Then there was Ex-police Commissioner Ted Warrick, through whose help Bob Clarke had turned to fighting crime. Lastly, there was Sandra Grey, familiarly known as Sandy. She had discovered Bob Clarke's secret and joined his little band.

There was an obvious reason why it was dangerous for Bob's dual identity to be made known. As the Crimson Mask, he raided the underworld, fought crooks who lived like kings, brought justice to murderers who planned carefully and carried out their plans with bloody ruthlessness. These people would have given a lot to learn the identity of the man behind that crimson mask.

It began when Bob Clarke was still studying pharmacy in college. His father, who'd been a police sergeant, was shot in the back by crooks. As he died, Bob Clarke determined to avenge his death and battle the elements which caused such conditions to exist and flourish.

A strange thing happened just before Bob's father passed into a coma. His face became suffused with blood. It formed a perfect domino mask around his eyes. This, Bob Clarke duplicated in velvet by fashioning a crimson mask which fitted over his eyes and concealed his features.

He'd gone into the thing with determination, studying all angles of crime detection. He knew how to disguise himself, how to alter his voice. He became a crack shot with any kind of gun and built up the ability to move about with no more noise than a ghost.

Behind the prescription department of his drug store, he maintained an elaborate criminology laboratory equipped with all manner of devices for tracking down crooks. No one in that poor neighborhood would have dreamed that kindly Bob Clarke could be the Crimson Mask. His role as a slum district druggist was a perfect shield.

BOB DISMISSED the cab in front of the hotel, walked past the desk and entered an elevator. He was taken to the tenth floor, checked room locations and went to the one furthest down the left wing. He rapped on the door. There was no answer. He tried, again and then he pressed an ear against the panels. Very faintly, he heard someone groaning.

Bob dipped a hand into his pocket and brought out a set of peculiar looking keys. In less than half a moment he had the door open. He stepped into a small, comfortable living room. A distinct groan came from the bedroom and he hurried there.

Phil Adrian lay across the bed, his face perfectly white, his fingers curled in agony. He tried to raise himself as Bob entered, but there wasn't that much strength left.

Clarke raised him and supported him against a pillow. He reached for the phone, but Adrian stopped him.

"No time, Bob. No time. Ordered dinner… food poisoned. Oriental stuff. Done for. Must talk. Listen carefully. Three men and myself came aboard ship… water, Bob. Get me some water."

Clarke sped to the bathroom and returned with a filled glass. He held Adrian's head while the man sipped it gratefully.

"Eases burning… in stomach," Adrian said. "At Hong Kong—I was a prisoner. Ship made special stop for me and three others. I… tried to escape one night. Did too, but I… heard plans being made to send a spy over here on the ship. He… is one of the three men. One of three, Bob. Get him!"

"Which three men?" Bob asked tensely. He knew the futility of calling a doctor. Adrian's face was already turning gray and his eyes were filming.

"John Marcy, Warren Fenwick and Wylie Wilson. One is a spy. Suspect them all. Tried to find out... impossible. Too clever. I notified F.B.I. by radio. Gave no name. Thought they'd find out which one was... spy. They tried, but couldn't. Water, Bob. More water."

Adrian talked again, his voice growing weaker and weaker.

"Has plans... to disrupt United Nations efforts. Something big. Got to stop him. Got to, Bob. Very clever man. Pick of spy system. Bringing in plan some way."

"How?" Clarke asked. "He can't get it past the F.B.I."

"Already has... I think. Find him, Bob. Find him and... kill him. It's the only safe way. Kill him."

"I'll take care of things," Clarke said. "Who poisoned your food?"

The message burned until his fingertips were seared

"Don't know. Spy suspected I was on to him. Knew I sent message to F.B.I. Had to get rid of me. Bob... Bob, I'm slipping. I'm going out. Get help. You can't do it alone."

Bob bent over the man.

"Phil... I can do it alone. I'm the Crimson Mask and I'll never rest again until this spy is captured or dead."

"Crimson Mask... heard of you. Even the... Chinese heard of you. Good, Bob. Played hunch and it worked. Knew you were reliable. Get him, Crimson Mask. Get him and kill him. Wish I could stay around and see...."

ADRIAN'S BREATH became labored. He closed his eyes like a very tired man. Clarke knew the signs. He was going into a coma from which there'd be no awakening. Bob sped to the telephone and asked for a doctor and an ambulance. Then he spent about three minutes looking over Adrian's possessions. He discovered a notebook which he slipped into his pocket.

It was time to leave and for more reasons than one. Clarke hurried into the hall, ran down to the seventh floor and used the elevator the rest of the way. He left the hotel lobby, ran around the corner and entered a drug store. He called Dave Small on the phone.

"Close up if necessary," he said. "Adrian is dying, but he told me enough. Get Sandy. Have her go to the dock where that refugee liner arrived this morning. She has newspaper credentials. Have her check on three passengers. Here are the names. John Marcy, Warren Fenwick and Wylie Wilson. One of those three men is a very important Axis spy."

"Right," Dave said. "Sandy can find out where they are staying. Then what are the orders?"

"Have Sandy watch one of them and you take another. The third we can't do much about right now. Get busy, Dave, and don't make any slips. These spies play for keeps."

Bob hung up, dashed out of the drug store and assumed a leisurely pace as he turned the corner and headed toward the hotel.

An ambulance was backed to the curb. About a dozen pedestrians waited to see the patient brought out. Bob waited too, eyeing each person carefully.

More than half were women who chatted to one another and clucked their tongues sympathetically as the stretcher was carried out. Three of the men turned away. Two remained to observe the proceedings. One of these finally resumed his walk, but the other didn't move until the ambulance had pulled away and vanished.

This man was slight of build, wore rimless glasses and had a sharp, thin face. Bob Clarke saw him smile in self-satisfaction and then idly stroll north. Clarke followed at a respectful distance. He'd been fairly certain someone would be on hand to make sure Adrian was either dead or dying.

CHAPTER III

ONE OF THREE

IT WAS almost dark as Bob Clarke set out after the man who had aroused his suspicions. Trained in the art of shadowing men, Bob kept the trail easily, but more and more he began to wonder whether or not the man he followed wasn't leading him into a trap.

In the first place, the man started circling back and stopping suddenly. Twice he darted into doorways and came out again almost instantly. Bob fell for none of these traps. By maintaining a respectful distance he wasn't even tempted.

These spies must not get the slightest idea that Adrian had talked to anyone, must not know that an independent force was working on the case. They'd pull in their necks and retire from active work until the heat died down. Bob wanted them out in the open where he'd have a chance to crack down.

The slender man turned a corner very fast. Clarke stopped cold. In a few seconds, the spy emerged again and retraced his steps for half a block. He saw Bob, even passed within two feet of him, but paid no great amount of attention. Clarke strolled idly along in the opposite direction. He passed, looked into a store window and was just in time to observe the spy give one last glance around and then plunge into an alley.

Clarke waited two or three minutes. Then he ambled up to the alley also, passed by it once and turned back. He darted into the darkness, stopped and took the time to extract a crimson mask from his pocket and draw it over his eyes.

He patted a hip pocket where an automatic was ready at an instant's notice. There were no signs of the man he'd followed. The Crimson Mask kept going until he came to a rear door. It was open about half an inch and faint light streamed out of the aperture.

The Crimson Mask sensed a trap, but an opportunity like this to land that spy was too good to turn down. He decided to take a chance. Moving without noise, he stepped inside what seemed to be the kitchen of a deserted restaurant. Rusty pots and pans hung from hooks. The floor was littered with refuse and a single, low watt bulb illuminated the place. The sound of someone walking across a bare floor came from the front.

The Crimson Mask drew his automatic, moved the safety to off position and proceeded to stalk his prey once more. It must be the man he followed because the alley was blind and this was the only door in it.

The front of the place was empty except for a dusty table and upended chair and a phone booth against a side wall. All other tables, chairs and decorations had been removed. The man he'd followed stood at a tiny desk attached to the phone booth and was running his finger down the page of a phone book. He used a flashlight to see by.

The Crimson Mask, protected by darkness, made no move to attack. If this man wanted to make a phone call, that was excellent. The Crimson Mask might overhear enough to give him a lead. The spy stepped into the phone booth, carrying the book with him. He dropped a coin into the slot and while the nickel made its usual racket on the way down, the Crimson Mask moved closer.

He heard the man dial, heard him ask for someone, but in a voice so muffled he was unable to hear the words. He edged still closer. Now he could hear.

"Yes, yes, everything is good. Adrian is dead by now and he did not talk. The poison would not permit its victim to speak. I saw him crawl to the bed and try to reach the telephone. I observed this from a window across the way. Then I watched the hotel entrance and an ambulance came. He was taken away, but I saw his face. Already gray with death and his jaws were rigid. We have nothing more to fear from him."

THERE WAS a moment of silence while the spy listened. Then he merely agreed with the person at the other end, hung up and started from the booth. As he did so, the Crimson Mask moved forward.

"Stop where you are," the Crimson Mask called out. "One more step and I'll bring you down with a bullet."

The spy gave a wild shriek of terror, whirled and raised both hands shoulder high. The Crimson Mask approached cautiously. Somehow, he didn't trust this slip of a man. He seemed to have all the slippery qualities of an eel.

"Whom did you just phone?" the Crimson Mask demanded. "Talk, you rat, or I'll squeeze the truth out of you."

"It... was only to a plumber. Yes, a plumber. I have bought this restaurant. There is need of repairs. Take my money. I will not resist. It is foolish to argue with an armed man."

Grimly, the Crimson Mask moved closer. He was no believer in forcing the truth out of anyone by physical violence, but Axis spies failed to come up as high as the lowest category of crooks. They were wanton killers and destroyers and their intent was to enslave the entire world. Such men as these neither gave mercy or expected any.

Suddenly, the little man's right arm snapped down. As it did so, a knife slid out of his sleeve and into a position for throwing. The Crimson Mask saw it start hurtling toward him. He dropped to his knees and the blade whizzed above his head.

The spy had turned and was running madly toward the back door. The Crimson Mask's gun blazed once. He aimed for the spy's legs and the Crimson Mask rarely missed. The spy let out a yowl of pain, stumbled a couple of more steps and then crashed to the floor.

At almost the same instant, someone banged heavily on the front door. The Crimson Mask glanced that way and saw a policeman's cap outlined against the opaque glass. He groaned, for of all times to have a cop happen by, this was the worst.

In a moment he knew, the glass would be broken. He scurried over to where the spy had fallen, bent over and rapped a hard blow to his jaw. Then he searched the man and found nothing. The cop was banging again.

The Crimson Mask took a long chance. He sped toward the phone booth and, as he hoped, found the telephone book jammed beneath the little counter and the coin box. It was opened to the page which the spy had checked.

He tucked this under his arm and went catapulting toward the rear door. Just as he disappeared, the front door opened and the uniformed patrolman entered. His flashlight swept the empty store, centered on the spy. The cop closed the door quickly and locked it. Then he ran over to where the small man lay.

WITH A glance at him, the cop sped to the rear door, looked out and then closed and locked this too. He returned to where the small man was sprawled out, clucked his tongue at the sight of blood and raised the man into a sitting position.

The spy opened his eyes and groaned. Then he started to swear.

"We were wrong. That was no F.B.I. man. *Ach* no. He wore a red mask over his eyes and at first I thought he was just a holdup man."

"A red mask? Are you sure?" the cop asked. "There can be no mistake?"

"I saw him, didn't I? But not while he trailed me. No—he was cleverer than anyone I ever knew. Yet, I went through with it because those were the orders. You happened along none too soon, Otto."

The cop grimaced.

"I had trouble getting a uniform to fit. The policeman I selected was tough. I had to use a knife on him. But this man with the red mask—I have heard of him. He is known as the Crimson Mask."

"Bah, Otto, what can a mask do? Make a man invulnerable? If you had not been late, we should have had him, mask and all. As it stands, things worked well. He saw me telephone, heard me talk. I... hurry—look and see if he took the telephone book."

The cop ran noisily to the booth, returned and said that the book was gone.

"Very good. Excellent. I would like to have that man at my mercy for a moment or two. I know ways to make him suffer for what he did to me. You had better get the car, Otto—bring it to the front door and then carry me out. Leave your uniform on and I shall pretend to be drunk. These foolish Americans will never know the difference."

"As you say," Otto agreed. "Still, I do not understand this. You pretended to make a call, you marked the phone book. What is it getting us? Why should we risk so much to accomplish so little?"

"I do not know. Only *Herr* Ehrlich knows and he does not tell us. We should not ask questions and, Otto, do not get too curious about *Herr* Ehrlich. He is the most important man ever sent here and the smartest. He helped to talk the Japanese into attacking Pearl Harbor and now he is here to aid us in creating confusion.

"Come, what are you waiting for?" he snapped. "Carry me out! This leg hurts and I must have a doctor. Take me to headquarters. We have several doctors on our lists who will help."

"Very well," Otto grunted. "First, I get the car. It is only around the corner."

"Wait," the slender man snapped. "Carry me to the phone booth. While you are gone, I shall really make a call. This one is not part of any trap."

Two minutes later the small man braced himself against the back of the phone booth and dialed.

"This is Froebel. I carried out my end as instructed. You were right. Someone did follow me. An F.B.I. man? No—they were not around. I purposely acted suspiciously in front of the hotel so if anyone was there, I'd be noticed. This man who followed me is very clever. Do not underestimate him. He wears a red mask which Otto seemed to be afraid of...."

"The Crimson Mask!" The man at the other end gasped. "That is not good, Froebel. He is worse than the F.B.I. We must be especially cautious now. The Crimson Mask is aggressive. He shoots quickly...."

"He shot me through the leg," Froebel grunted. "What you tell me is not news. But he will be taken care of. I'm not impressed by a red mask. How did the others make out? We are protecting *Herr* Ehrlich and there cannot be any mistakes."

"Everything is fine. You will have your leg attended to and then wait for further orders. Good-by, Froebel. Good work!"

Froebel hung up and scowled. "They should tell me what this is all about," he grumbled half aloud. "Just throwing suspicion upon someone is not work for a man like me. And why should we risk so much to throw suspicion on some fool?"

There was an answer to that, but Froebel didn't have the slightest notion of it. Nor did he recognize the vast importance of the job he'd just completed successfully.

One man did. That was *Herr* Ehrlich, Nazi agent supreme. The message which Phil Adrian had managed to send from the refugee liner had spoiled excellent plans. It required Ehrlich to adopt new ones and they had to be exceedingly good because the slightest slip would mark him with an inevitable result—the electric chair! Ehrlich knew what had happened to saboteurs who landed on United States soil.

He was still surprised that the Americans had become tough. That wasn't in the Nazi bible nor among Nazi plans. Americans were supposed to be soft, tender-hearted. They'd almost worshipped criminals not so long ago. Ehrlich didn't see why they wouldn't also worship spies.

CHAPTER IV

FALSE CLUES

STRIPPING OFF his domino, the Crimson Mask emerged from the alley, glanced at the restaurant door and saw it closed. He didn't stop to investigate. If the shooting had attracted one policeman, a drove of them soon would be converging on the scene.

He walked briskly down the street and hailed a taxi. He snapped on the tonneau lights, laid the telephone book on his lap and looked at the two open pages. He tilted the book a little and noticed that the spy had marked a telephone number with his thumbnail. It was the connection at the Hotel Ardmore.

"Stop at the next drug store," Clarke ordered the driver. "I have a phone call to make."

He entered the booth and called the Ardmore.

"I'm looking for three men. One may be registered at your hotel. Will you see if a Warren Fenwick checked in? Or Wylie Wilson or a chap named John Marcy?"

Clarke hung on for a moment. The answer came promptly.

"We have a John Marcy registered, sir. He checked in late this afternoon. Shall I connect you?"

"No. No, thanks. I—want to surprise him. Please don't even mention the inquiry."

Bob Clarke returned to his cab and was driven back to his own drug store. It was locked, indicating that Dave was still out on the job. He let himself in, walked to the back room and sat down to wait. He smiled a little and decided he could afford to look triumphant. His first move as the Crimson Mask had uncovered the spy. John Marcy was due for a surprise all right. One he wouldn't like.

Sandy returned first, highly elated. She was as tall as Clarke, strong and straight. Her eyes were steady and blue, her lips perfectly formed and almost always smiling.

Bob welcomed her with outstretched arms. For a moment neither spoke and then Sandy made her report with enthusiasm.

"Bob—it was simple. I found out where those men lived. Marcy lives alone in a hotel. Fenwick is a bachelor too and owns a big home on Longacre Lane. Wilson is married and was going home to a new apartment on Allerton Drive which his wife leased and fixed up. I took care of Fenwick. Dave went to see about Wilson."

"All right," Clarke smiled at her, "but what did you find? What makes you gloat that way?"

"The case is finished before it begins," Sandy answered. "Fenwick went straight to his home. I arrived soon afterwards, rang the bell and asked for an interview. A butler let me in and, Bob… he had the thickest Heinie accent you ever heard. He told a maid to ask Fenwick if I could see him and she had an accent just as gross. She came back and told me Fenwick would see no one. Why, that pair did everything but give me the Nazi salute… and boot."

"Now wait a minute." Clarke pushed her into a chair. "Just because Fenwick has a staff of German servants is no reason to pin him down as the spy. As *Herr* Ehrlich. That's the name of the man we're after."

"Bob—imagine yourself being held prisoner by the Japs for months and months. Locked up in some filthy prison with nothing to eat. Knowing all the time that behind the Japs are the Nazis.

"Then imagine being released, sent back here. Would you hire a gang of German servants? I'd clout the first Nazi I saw and believe me, those servants were Nazis. They looked at me as though I were scum. The butler walked and acted like a Kraut colonel."

"You may be right," Bob said. "We'll wait and hear what Dave has to report. I had some luck too. Trailed a spy, heard him make a phone call and I even discovered whom he called."

"Fenwick, I'll bet," Sandy stated.

"No—John Marcy. At least, the spy called Marcy's hotel. He is the only suspect living there. I… here comes Dave. Now we may be able to organize our information."

DAVE ENTERED breathlessly. He hurled his hat on a chair and gave a whoop of delight.

"Bob… Sandy… I've done it. Absolutely and positively. Wylie Wilson is our man. I can just about prove it. Listen… I went to his apartment. His wife came to the door and told me Wilson was too tired to see any reporters. That was a nice brush-off, but I didn't quit.

"Instead, I talked to employees who work in the building and you know how those people are. No less than three of them told me that Wilson's furniture was moved in only today. That they saw the covering of a big picture, whipped loose by the breeze and… the picture was that charming skunk Adolf Schicklemickle. Yep—a beeootiful picture of the big boy himself.

"Also… and get this, my friends… there were two short-wave radio receivers brought in. Two, no less. Sets fully capable of picking up Berlin at any time."

Sandy and Bob looked at one another in amazement. Dave eyed both of them.

"Hey, what's wrong? You act as though that information wasn't worth a plugged dime."

"Maybe it is and maybe it isn't," Clarke said wearily. "All I know is that the three of us have been sadly duped. One of those men must be *Herr* Ehrlich. We'll concede that. But all three of them can't be Ehrlich. Sandy and I picked up concrete evidence against Marcy and Fenwick, too."

Dave Small gasped.

"I don't get it. As you said, all three of them can't be spies."

"Consider this angle," Clarke said. "Ehrlich, whoever he may be, knew that Phil Adrian suspected all three men. He also was aware that Adrian sent a warning radiogram to the F.B.I. and that it was certain a very thorough investigation would be carried out. They'd be watched, their movements checked. So the man who is Ehrlich proceeded to throw suspicion on all three men, including himself. Enough suspicion to cloud the whole issue."

"I'm beginning to understand," Sandy then said. "It's not so good, Bob."

"For my money," Clarke said, "Ehrlich just took the first five innings of this game and made chumps out of us. He must even be aware now that the Crimson Mask is fighting him, too. These steps we uncovered were meant to confuse the F.B.I., but they backfired on us, too. We haven't progressed an inch."

"Why not pick up all three of them, put them in some nice snug hideout and work 'em over?" Dave Small suggested.

"Oh, no, Dave. The F.B.I. did that practically, and they got nowhere. Ehrlich is one of those three men—yes—but he knows how to protect himself."

"Bob," Sandy asked thoughtfully, "do you think Ehrlich took the identity of one man, perhaps having him murdered? Or is it possible that Ehrlich has posed as this man both in the United States and China for years and years?"

"Most likely the former idea," Bob answered. "He stole the identity of the man he is supposed to be. In fact, from what Adrian told me before he died, I'm sure of it. Dave—take care of the store. Sandy, you stick around in case things break. I'm going to pay the F.B.I. a visit—but not as Bob Clarke."

BOB REMOVED his coat, sat down before a triple mirror and opened drawers in the table. He took from them creams and dyes. He altered the color of his hair, changed the contour of his face and darkened the skin slightly. Cleverly created lines gave his features added age. Within ten minutes there was no resemblance to Bob Clarke, slum district druggist.

He went into another room, opened a locker and selected clothing from a complete assortment of garments that ranged from the rags of a vagrant to the swank evening clothes of a night-clubbing youngster with too much money.

He slipped an automatic into a hip pocket, folded his crimson domino and stowed that away. Then he left the store by a rear door, proceeded through a confusing series of courtyards and alleys until he reached a street a block away from the drug store. He purchased a newspaper at the nearest stand, read the whole story of the arrival of the refugee ship and noted that William Blane headed the F.B.I. detail in charge of questioning the passengers.

Blane, the Crimson Mask found, lived in a modest neighborhood where he occupied a one-story house. The Crimson Mask went there directly, studied the place and saw that it was dark. He

Sandra Grey

slipped around to the rear, opened a door without much trouble and went in. Nobody was at home so he settled down in a comfortable chair and waited.

There in the darkness and silence he was able to think deeply, but no matter how hard he pushed his brain, there seemed to be no answer to his question. Which of three men was the spy?

The man's cleverness was displayed by the way he'd thrown confusion into the ranks of the investigators. By including himself among the suspects, he became practically immune. Such a man wouldn't make many slips. He'd plan far ahead, plot every move and be certain there were no loopholes.

An hour passed and then there were footsteps on the porch. A key was inserted in the lock and the door swung open. Lights flashed on. Bill Blane of the F.B.I. scaled his hat onto a chair, yawned and walked into the living room. Then he stopped dead and started to reach for his gun.

Before him sat a man who wore a crimson mask. There was a smile on his lips as he arose.

"Please don't draw a gun, Blane. I'm here to exchange information which may help us nail down that spy who slipped ashore today."

"The Crimson Mask!" Blane grunted and then he laughed. "I don't know whether to make a pinch or shake your hand. I'll compromise by doing neither—just yet. What's on your mind?"

"A man named Ehrlich who may be either John Marcy, Warren Fenwick or Wylie Wilson. I took it upon myself to become interested in the case. Up to now I have confined myself mostly to running down crooks, but we're at war, Blane. Every last man, woman and child of us must get into the scrap."

"How much do you know?" Blane asked.

"Not a great deal. Phil Adrian was murdered. He radioed you people that one of those three men was a spy. I can tell you a bit more about that. Adrian was imprisoned at Hong Kong. He actually escaped one night, but voluntarily returned to his cell when he overheard plans being made to send a spy here aboard the refugee liner."

Blane sat down.

"Okay—I'm satisfied that you're on the level. Always thought so anyhow. We're not releasing the fact that Adrian was murdered. We're keeping a close check on the three suspects, but we're getting nowhere."

THE CRIMSON MASK chuckled.

"Especially when you have discovered that Fenwick has a staff of German servants and Wilson keeps a picture of Hitler and two short-wave radios in his home."

Blane whistled in amazement.

"Nothing gets past you, does it? Yes, we did find that out. Marcy, however, seems to be in the clear. Almost too obviously so."

"Ah, but he is not. One of Ehrlich's spies allowed me to trail him, permitted me to overhear him make a telephone report and even arranged that I could determine whom he called. It was Marcy, so he is in it, too. Blane, it's clear to me that Ehrlich is confusing the issue by throwing suspicion on all three suspected men, including himself."

"I was getting that general idea," Blane admitted. "Now that you have told me about Marcy, I can see your point. You've been honest with me and I don't doubt that you may be able to help.

Heaven knows we need all the assistance we can get. Therefore, I'll tell you something. Each of those three men carried with him an object that is of especial interest."

"For instance."

"Well—Marcy has only one arm. Claims he lost his left up to the elbow in a Jap bombing raid. He wears a false arm, made of aluminum. We took it away from him for study.

"Marcy also had a very valuable antique statue of Chinese origin. A rather bloodthirsty little thing depicting a man's execution by strangling.

"Fenwick had an ancient foolscap. It's lettered in little-known Chinese script which we have been unable to translate.

"Wilson carried an elaborate music box that plays a Chinese tune."

"You have examined these things, of course," the Crimson Mask said.

"For hours. We've treated them for all known brands of invisible writing. We've baked them, put them under ultra violet rays. Every expert we could round up has had a crack at them with no results at all."

"I expected that," the Crimson Mask said. "Where were those objects picked up by the suspects?"

"In Hong Kong. What makes it so darned suspicious is the fact that they paid incredibly small sums for them, claiming the owners fled into the interior and were willing to take anything. Those pieces are of historic value, especially to the Chinese."

The Crimson Mask arose.

"It's possible that two of the suspects—the innocent ones— were tricked into accepting those objects so that Ehrlich could take along a third bit of art work which really meant something. Blane... will you hold those objects in custody until I ask you to release them?"

Blane nodded.

"Of course, provided the owners don't raise the roof."

"They won't," the Crimson Mask assured him. "Especially the man who is Ehrlich. My idea is that the spy is carrying certain instructions here. Orders too detailed to trust to memory. So long as you have custody of those objects, one of which probably contains those orders, Ehrlich will be unable to act. We can hold him down just as long as you keep those articles."

Blane offered his hand.

"I'm glad you're in this, Crimson Mask. Some of the stories going the rounds indicate that you don't exactly adhere to the letter of the law in tracking down criminals. That's quite all right with me. Unofficially, of course. This time you're working against spies and you have a right to be as ruthless as they. Good luck. Contact me at any time."

The Crimson Mask walked out, stripped off his mask halfway down the path to the sidewalk and turned north. He moved along briskly, his mind made up to tackle the three suspects directly and without kid gloves. Blane would be unable to hold those valuable art objects very long and before their release, Ehrlich must be uncovered.

CHAPTER V

THE ROAD TO PERIL

WYLIE WILSON occupied an apartment in one of the better buildings in town, where there were doormen, many elevators, soft rugs and rich furniture in the lobby. He was in the seventh floor front, one of the most expensive suites in the place.

The Crimson Mask, minus his domino, ambled through the lobby and entered an elevator. He was taken to Wilson's floor and approached the apartment door without hesitation. A trim, uniformed maid let him in and the Crimson Mask indicated somewhat ambiguously that he was from the F.B.I. He entered a spacious living room, sat down and drew the mask over his eyes.

Wylie Wilson came in, tying a monogrammed bathrobe around him. He saw the red mask and gave a start of amazement.

"Don't be alarmed," the Crimson Mask said. "Please sit down. You're pretty much under suspicion of being a spy, Mr. Wilson. Did you know that?"

"I… guessed it from the going over I got aboard ship today," Wilson admitted. "You're the Crimson Mask. I've heard of you. Can I be of service?"

"Indeed you can. Mr. Wilson, traveling with you from Hong Kong were three men. One of those is a spy. One is dead—murdered. I'm assuming, of course, that you are not the enemy agent. Did you see anything to make you suspicious?"

Wilson shrugged and reached for a cigarette. He proffered the box to the Crimson Mask and then held a lighter for him. Wilson drew deep on his cigarette. He was a fast, heavy smoker. His fingers were stained yellow from tobacco tar.

"I can't say any of them acted like a spy," he said. "Come to think of it, enemy agents try to act as normally as possible, don't they?"

"Yes, but all men of that type—crooks or spies—make little slips. I thought you might have noticed something. Please understand I must also suspect you. Therefore, the questions…."

"I don't know that I should answer them," Wilson said sharply. "After all—how do I know who or what you are? A man who hides behind a red mask doesn't exactly inspire confidence. However, ask away. If the questions don't get too personal, I'll answer."

"Good. How long were you in the Orient and what were your connections there?"

"I'm a chemist—a salesman of drugs. Being trained in that profession I can handle my business better. My employer is the Gerard Drug Corporation. I've worked for them eight years, six in China and Japan."

"You brought back a certain music box of Chinese origin. What made you buy it?"

"Say," Wilson looked up suddenly, "thanks for reminding me. The F.B.I. took my music box away. I'm going to get it back. Why did I buy it? Man alive, the Chinese merchants sold it to me for two hundred dollars Mex. It's worth four or five thousand in solid American money. I don't turn down chances like that."

"Naturally." The Crimson Mask snuffed out his cigarette. "Were you approached with the offer to buy or did you seek out this merchant?"

"He came to see me. I can't understand what this is all about. Why don't you come here man to man? Remove that silly mask and let me see whom I'm talking to! Until you do, I won't answer another question. In fact, I'm inclined to call in the police."

"And tell them how it happens you have a picture of Adolf Hitler in this house and two powerful short-wave radios, Mr. Wilson? I don't think you will. Now about that picture and the radios…"

WILSON FLUSHED.

"All right, you win. Nobody will believe this, but I can't explain how that picture or the radios got mixed up with my furniture. I smashed the picture. It's thrown into one of the big closets. I don't know what to do about the radios. Certainly I won't listen to that blather enemy propagandists keep pouring at us."

"I'll look at the picture." The Crimson Mask arose. "You don't mind?"

"I do," Wilson grunted, "but there doesn't seem to be much I can do about it. One word of this to the F.B.I. and I'll be on Ellis Island before I catch my breath. Come along."

Wilson led him through the apartment. The maid who let him in, glanced out of the dining room, saw the red mask and started back in alarm. Wilson threw open a closet door, turned on lights, and the Crimson Mask saw what was left of Hitler's portrait.

"I put my foot through it," Wilson explained. "Later, I intended to burn it. Now are you satisfied?"

"Quite," the Crimson Mask smiled. "I'm sorry to bother you this way, but it's very necessary and, in the long run, you'll appreciate it because if you are not *Herr* Ehrlich, I'll clear you. Goodnight, Mr. Wilson."

The Crimson Mask closed the apartment door behind him, removed his mask and rang for the elevator.

"Oh—I'm sorry," he told the elevator operator. "Forgot something. Go back down… I'll ring when I'm ready."

The doors closed with a thud that could be heard in Wilson's apartment. The Crimson Mask stepped into the stairway, propped the door open half an inch and waited. Five minutes went by and no one emerged. He knew that Wilson could have used the telephone to warn his agents, if he was the spy. Yet that was risky because Wilson would suspect that the F.B.I. might have tapped his wires.

Two floors below, the Crimson Mask again rang for the elevator and was taken to the lobby. He ambled out, mentally noting the half dozen men who were standing idly around.

Reaching the street he turned west. Fenwick was next on his list and he hoped for more success than he'd had with Wilson.

Reaching the corner, he saw a medium-sized van approach and start to slow up. At almost the same instant two men crossed the street toward him. Another followed the route he'd been taking and a fourth came in from the opposite direction. The Crimson Mask was trapped.

The four men closed in rapidly, each with his right hand deep in his coat pocket. The Crimson Mask had an idea that if he went for his gun, he'd be riddled.

"You will please remain just as you are," one of the men said softly. "If it becomes necessary, we shall kill you right here. Otherwise, you may have a chance to live."

"Didn't take Wilson long to work, did it?" the Crimson Mask said sharply.

ALL FOUR of the men chuckled as though it was a good joke. The truck pulled to the curb. The door opened and the Crimson Mask was ordered to climb into the seat. He hoisted himself up and stared at the muzzle of a drawn gun in the hand of the driver. He also noticed that the back rest of the seat had been swung back to gain access to the van proper.

"Get in back," the driver said. "Make it fast, you stupid clown, who wears a red mask. Hurry, or the mask you will wear will be blood."

The Crimson Mask crawled over the seat, lowered himself into the back of the van and two men clambered in after him. The back of the seat was raised into position and a small light turned on.

"Sit down," one of the spies ordered. "We have a question to ask and then we shall leave you. Remember—both of us are crack shots. The Gestapo teaches its students to shoot fast and accurately."

"Among other things, including murder and rapine," the Crimson Mask retorted. "Ask away, but if you think I'll talk, you're crazy."

"How were you brought into this case? We know you work independently and the police or G-men could not reach you. Come now, be sensible or shall we unloose that stubborn tongue of yours?"

The Crimson Mask eyed the pair closely. They were beady-eyed killers, highly trained in the art of murder. They were men who deserved to die as much as their friends who had ravaged most of Europe.

"Why are you so sure I'm the Crimson Mask?"

"What nonsense! We watched Wilson's apartment just in case something like this happened. You shot and wounded one of our men, but not before he saw and recognized the mask. Well—do you answer?"

"No," the Crimson Mask snapped.

Instantly a gun was shoved against his chest. The second spy searched him, removed his gun and then slapped him heavily across the face. This same spy crawled back a bit, fumbled in a burlap sack in the truck and fished out a camera and synchronized flash gun.

"First," he said, "we take your picture so that all our agents will know what you looked like without the mask. Watch him, Franz. After the picture is taken, we shall show him how strong we of the Reich can be."

The camera was held at eye level and aimed carefully. The gunman moved away so as not to impede the picture. The Crimson Mask grew tense. When that flash bulb went off in this small, dark space it would affect the eyes of the two spies as much as his own. For a fraction of a second they'd be blind and in that space of time he had to work if he expected to get out of tins alive.

He placed the positions of both men so that he could reach them even if he was blinded. Then he drew a long breath. The camera steadied. The Crimson Mask saw the spy's finger slowly push down the shutter button. He closed his eyes tightly just as the flash bulb went off.

OPENING THEM again, he could see little. The powerful light had penetrated his eyelids, but it had blinded the two spies badly. The Crimson Mask reached for the position where he knew the gun was held. His fingers grasped it, yanked it away. With his other hand, he lashed out a vicious punch. Knuckles met jaw bone and the Crimson Mask grinned crookedly.

He gave a savage leap toward the man with the camera, knocked him down and got a grip on his throat. He was slowly strangling him into unconsciousness when the first spy managed to hoist himself up on his knees. Still groggy from the blow, he waddled forward on his knees.

Before the Crimson Mask realized the man was awake, an arm curled around his throat. Then the spy beneath him raised his arms and pushed. Combined with the strength of the other, the Crimson Mask was forced back.

He let go the spy's throat and rolled back. Both his hands flew up to grasp his attacker. He grabbed hair and tugged. The spy let out a dismal yowl. But it was hopeless. The one called Franz, got to his feet, stepped back and kicked out with perfect aim. The Crimson Mask took that shoe squarely under the jaw and went limp. He wasn't unconscious, but nerves and muscles were definitely paralyzed.

Both men stood over him now, muttering curses. Franz drew a gun and slanted the muzzle downward. Through slitted eyelids, the Crimson Mask saw this, but he couldn't move an inch.

"No, Franz," the other man cautioned. "We go through with the original plan. No one knows he is the Crimson Mask but us. When his body is picked up, they will say death was accidental.

Come—we climb into the driver's compartment and leave this idiot to die."

Franz kicked the Crimson Mask a couple of times in the ribs, growled a curse and then rapped on the back of the seat. The driver opened it and Franz climbed out. The other spy slapped the Crimson Mask experimentally and grinned. He was confident this strange spy fighter was quite unconscious. He seized a small iron ring on the floor, yanked it and a little trap door opened.

The spy drew on a heavy glove, reached down and pulled up a section of pipe. Almost at once, the odor of the exhaust assailed the Crimson Mask's nostrils. The spy climbed into the seat and the back was closed.

CHAPTER VI

LISTENING EARS

THE CRIMSON MASK closed his lips tightly and fought to regain strength. Gradually, it came back and his muscles worked again, but now he had to breathe. His lungs were bursting. Fetid, strangling air entered his throat and he coughed. The van was rapidly being filled with carbon monoxide. He had three or four minutes before the stuff would rob him of his senses and begin the quick job of killing him.

He tried to grasp the section of exhaust, but the pipe was too hot. Fingers could not grip it and the thing was cleverly arranged so that plenty of strength would be required to move it back into position so the little trap door could be shut.

The truck came to a stop with squealing brakes. The Crimson Mask moved to the rear door and tried to open it. The doors didn't budge an inch and they were padded so that his poundings and kicks made no noise.

His wits reeled, for the concentration of gas was becoming serious. He ripped off his coat, wrapped part of it around his hand and tackled the exhaust pipe again. All he did was burn a hole through the cloth.

The truck was in motion again, rumbling along some fairly busy street for the Crimson Mask could hear traffic and also the muffled sound of voices. There were probably hundreds of people who might help him, no more than a dozen feet away and blissfully unaware that murder was being committed inside that innocent looking truck.

The Crimson Mask kicked at the feed pipe, but even that refused to budge it. He ripped his coat sleeve off, rammed it down the pipe, but knew that wouldn't stop the gas completely and there was almost enough of it inside the truck now to have lethal properties.

He kicked ferociously again at the pipe. His foot slipped off it and splintered the wood around the opening in the floor. He bent down, grasped one of the boards and summoned every ounce of strength he possessed. The board creaked, loosened a bit. He had to rest for a moment, but knew that if there had to be many such moments he'd pass out and sink into a coma from which there'd be no release.

Bracing himself, legs planted quite far apart, he tugged again. Muscles welled into whipcords. The board creaked again and this time some of the bolts let go. He worked once more until finally a two-foot length of the floor came away.

He dropped flat, thrust his mouth and nose into the opening. Even the dust-laden air he breathed from beneath the truck was like nectar. His wits cleared rapidly. The truck was crossing a bridge and now the air he breathed became even better.

He stood up finally. Soon now they'd believe he was dead. Obviously, they intended to either fling his body into some clump of brush or else steal a car and rig a fake suicide.

Reaching up, the Crimson Mask removed the small electric light bulb from its socket. Then he lay down again, nose and mouth pressed against the opening in the floor. Fifteen minutes went by. Sounds of traffic had ceased and they were on some fairly lonely road on Long Island. He was pretty sure of that.

Finally the truck slowed, made a careful turn onto a narrow dirt road and stopped. The Crimson Mask lay flat, covering the aperture in the floor, apparently limp in death. The trick seat-back was dropped and Franz looked into the van.

"He is done," Franz said. "If we could only tell the world how we killed the Crimson Mask. He is supposed to be very ruthless. To me he seemed as easy to kill as a baby. I will go back and make sure he is altogether dead and not just unconscious."

Franz scrambled into the van proper, bent over the Crimson Mask and seized his shoulder. The limp form turned. Two hands shot up and grasped Franz by the throat. They were strong hands and the fingers buried themselves deeply into the spy's neck.

The Crimson Mask maneuvered those fingers deftly, seeking a certain nerve which would paralyze Franz. He found it and the spy went limp. The Crimson Mask hastily arose and now there was a gun in his hand. The other spy turned in the seat, saw the coat-less figure standing there and tried to reach his gun. The Crimson Mask shot him through the head.

The driver opened the cab door and jumped out. He began racing down the road. The Crimson Mask leaped out, too. His gun leveled and blazed once. The spy slowed up, threw both hands into the air and tried his best to turn around and bring his own gun to bear. He didn't quite make it and toppled over on his face instead.

The Crimson Mask hurried up to the man, saw that he was dead and searched him. He found nothing of any value. He lifted the body, carried it back to the truck and stowed both dead men in the back. He dragged Franz out into the air.

The section was lonely and the shots had attracted no attention. In a few moments Franz came out of it, shuddered and sat up. He looked into the muzzle of a gun, so close to his nose that he could smell the cordite. Behind that gun was a grim-faced man.

"Your two friends are dead," the Crimson Mask said. "If you want to join them, that's your privilege. Otherwise, you'll talk. Which is it?"

"I'll… talk," Franz said. "I—I can't tell you much. We know little."

"Who is *Herr Ehrlich?*"

"I don't know—for sure. I swear that is the truth. Orders come from higher up and we only obey."

"How did you get on my trail so quickly? What higher up gave you those instructions? The truth, now, you wormy disciple of the New Order. I'm as tough as you or any other Nazi and all I ask is an opportunity to prove it!"

Franz shivered violently.

"One of our group met us at the corner around that building where Wilson lives. He said the Crimson Mask would come out and we were to seize you. I do not know how he found out you were the Crimson Mask, but he described your clothing and size."

"You were sent here not so long ago," the Crimson Mask said. "Of course, part of your training was received in some of those conquered countries. A toughening period, perhaps. Am I guessing right?"

"Yes. Yes, I served in Poland and in Czechoslovakia."

"As a Gestapo man who came after the troops blazed the way, or were you in the front lines?"

"I was of the Gestapo. We… cleaned up…."

"Thanks," the Crimson Mask said. "That makes what I have to do a much greater pleasure. Stand up, Franz. I'm going to show you that Americans are tough. Stand up, you sniveling rat!"

Franz gulped, half rose and made a desperate lunge for the Crimson Mask's legs. They danced away. A hand seized him by the scruff of the neck. He was yanked into an erect position and shoved back into the truck. He saw a fist caroming toward his nose and squealed. The squeal turned into a loud wail. The fist hammered again and again, until Franz wilted.

THE CRIMSON MASK hurled him into the back of the truck, climbed in himself and tied Franz securely. Then he searched him. In one pocket he found a cash receipt, one of those bits of cardboard that slide out of a cash register. It was numbered and the amount was for two dollars and thirty-one cents. The name of the store was on it. The Etude Shop. That meant a music store.

The Crimson Mask put this trophy into his trousers pocket. Then he arranged the exhaust pipe so it would no longer deliver a lethal flow of gas and drove the vehicle back to town.

He stopped not very far away from his own drug store, locked the truck and hurried through alleys and courtyards to the rear door. Dave Small and Sandy were waiting.

"Dave," the Crimson Mask said, "you'll find a medium-sized moving van parked around the corner. There are two dead men and one damaged Nazi in back. Drive it to Bill Blane's house. I'll give you the address. Park it in his driveway, and then get out fast. Coast in if you can. Phone me here and I'll do the rest."

Dave grabbed his hat.

"I'm on my way. This is one job I like."

The Crimson Mask took Sandy's arm and piloted her into the laboratory hidden behind the prescription counter. There he sat down before the triple mirrors and removed the disguise.

"Boy," he chortled, "are those Nazis methodical! They even took my picture, but I wrecked the camera. Here—take a look at this cash receipt. Know anything about the Etude Shop?"

"Yes, Bob. It's a music store and I've bought records and sheet music there."

"Good. Keep that receipt. As soon as the store opens tomorrow, go there and try to find out what this receipt was for. The amount is odd. Maybe one of the clerks can remember."

She tucked the slip of paper into her purse.

"I'll let you know as soon as I find out, Bob. But what happened tonight? Your coat is gone, your hands—why they're burned!"

Bob Clarke grinned.

"I went to visit Wylie Wilson, found him to be a fairly decent sort, but not given to answering questions very well. When I left, four of Hitler's hoodlums got the jump on me and I was taken for a ride... in the back of a moving van which was rigged so that exhaust fumes escaped into it. I burned my hand on the pipe. Nothing much and Sandy—am I in this man's war! Nailed two of those monkeys and fixed a third so that Bill Blane will be able to roast him."

"Then you think Wilson is the spy?" Sandy asked quickly.

"No. In fact, I wonder if *Herr* Ehrlich would allow anything to happen quite so close to his residence. I think Wilson was being watched from some window across the street. Before I went out, the trap was set.

"Now I intend to awaken Mr. Warren Fenwick, if he has gone to sleep already. It's after twelve. First though, I'll change this disguise a bit. Just in case some more of *Herr* Ehrlich's stooges spotted me without the mask."

Bob Clarke became the Crimson Mask again in an entirely new guise. He looked like a swarthy Latin-American, well-dressed and intelligent. As he finished donning his clothes, Sandy called him to the phone. It was Dave reporting the truck parked in Blane's driveway.

The Crimson Mask hung up, waited a moment and then dialed Blane's number. A sleepy voice answered.

"This is the Crimson Mask," Clarke said. "I just brought a load of garbage into your driveway. Three Nazis, my friend. Two of them are very good Nazis and I take the blame for killing them. It was done in self-defense. The third is alive and ready for your tender care."

"I'll go right out," Blane said. "If those dead men were spies, don't worry about killing them."

"I'm not worried!" the Crimson Mask laughed. "By the way, is Wylie Wilson's telephone tapped?"

"It is. Fenwick's and Marcy's are also tapped. We're not taking any chances. Why?"

"Just curious. If Wilson made a call tonight about eleven-five, and gave orders to, trap the Crimson Mask, you can pick him up for *Herr* Ehrlich. Meantime, I intend to see about the other pair. Good-night, Mr. Blane."

CHAPTER VII

DEATH TRAP

A **LIGHT CAR** which the Crimson Mask used was kept stored in a private garage near the drug store. Fenwick lived rather far out.

The Crimson Mask reached the neighborhood and saw that Fenwick's home was still illuminated. He parked the car, entered the miniature estate around Fenwick's house and took a preliminary glance through a window.

Fenwick was on the telephone and the Crimson Mask heard his voice easily through the open window.

"Never mind the hour," Fenwick was saying. "I've paid you to handle my legal matters a long time and now I'm insisting you do something for me at once.

"The Federal Bureau of Investigation took away from me a certain relic I brought here from China. It's a papyrus—foolscap—or something, and has a lot of Chinese writing on it.

"I want that back tomorrow, understand? They said it had to be examined for invisible ink... think I'm a spy. I just received a splendid offer for the article and I need it quickly."

Fenwick hung up with a bang, growling something about idiotic attorneys who earned their fees doing nothing. Very suddenly he was aware of an elongated shadow on the floor beside him. He looked up and shrank deeper into the big leather chair he occupied.

The Crimson Mask moved closer.

"Sorry if I startled you, Mr. Fenwick. I'm the Crimson Mask. I'm working on this spy case in which you are involved. I didn't use an orthodox way of calling on you because of the servants you employ."

Fenwick tried to bluster.

"Now see here! I've been put through a third degree by the F.B.I. and I don't intend to submit again—to a masked man, anyway! As for the servants—they were hired for me by an agency. I'm firing the lot of them tomorrow."

"Then you don't like Nazis?" the Crimson Mask smiled.

"Like them?... I detest their breed! They're the same type of brigands as the Japs. Perhaps you believe I like Japs, eh? Well—look at this."

Fenwick jumped up, pulled his trousers leg high and displayed an ugly deep wound in his leg. It was healing slowly, but had been serious not so long ago.

"Do you know what caused that? A whip! Those Japs lashed me for hours. This wound opened up and they concentrated on my leg until I thought they intended to cut it off with their blasted rice whips! Then they let me rot in a cell, refused me medical attention until just before I was repatriated. You're suspecting the wrong man if you think I'm a spy."

"I hope so," the Crimson Mask said noncommittally. "About this ancient document you want back from the F.B.I. Is there anyone who can decipher it?"

"Not so far," Fenwick said. "But this business received a certain amount of publicity in the papers. I had a visitor tonight who described the relic rather well. He said he could read it and that the thing was of immense value."

"All right," the Crimson Mask said. "Now tell me this. When you were locked up in Hong Kong, did you see Marcy or Wilson around the prison?"

"No. I saw no white people at all. Not until just before we sailed. Then I met them all."

"I see. You purchased this ancient document for a song, I suppose? A dealer came to you with an offer?"

"Yes," Fenwick frowned. "How did you know? Why are you here anyway? I'm no criminal or spy. I'm as patriotic as a mother with ten boys in the armed forces."

"One of you—Marcy, Wilson or yourself, is a spy," the Crimson Mask said. "That much is quite clear. I'm merely visiting all of you so that I can get an idea of your characters. In fact, I shall see Mr. Marcy immediately upon leaving you."

THE CRIMSON MASK stood opposite a glassed-in portrait and it reflected the doorway faintly. He could see someone listening, probably one of the planted servants. The Crimson Mask gave no indication that he noticed this.

"In fact," he went on, "I'd appreciate it if you would phone Mr. Marcy and tell him I'm coming. He lives in a hotel. Naturally, I can't wander about with this mask on. Tell him I shall come directly to his suite and be there in... half an hour."

"Very well," Fenwick grumbled. "I don't owe Marcy any favors, but neither do I want him scared out of his wits by a man in a red mask."

The Crimson Mask turned suddenly and heard faint footsteps disappearing across the hall. He walked to the front door. None of Fenwick's servants came to let him out. He thanked Fenwick, who had accompanied him to the door, and departed.

He drove downtown to where Marcy lived, but lounged in the car until about forty-five minutes had elapsed. The Crimson Mask knew the Nazi proficiency for setting traps. If anything happened at Marcy's, he could be reasonably certain the former Chinese-American newspaper publisher was part of the spy ring. The servants planted at Fenwick's were bound to report his intended visit. Fenwick wouldn't necessarily be involved.

Minus the mask but amply concealed by disguise, Clarke entered the hotel and went directly to John Marcy's suite. Marcy himself came to the door and let him in. The Crimson Mask indicated his identity and Marcy showed no surprise.

"Fenwick phoned," he said. "I expected you'd be wearing a mask. However, it makes little difference. I'll cooperate in every way I can."

"Good," the Crimson Mask glanced at Marcy's false arm, gloved and stiffly held by his side. "I see the F.B.I. returned your artificial arm. You know why I am here."

Marcy nodded.

"You think I may be an Axis spy. I'm sure I can prove my innocence, but strange things have happened since I returned. Things I simply can't account for. Like the package I received about two hours ago. It contains an oriental vase inscribed with fantastic symbols, similar to the document which Fenwick bought in Hong Kong."

"Who sent it?" the Crimson Mask asked quickly.

"I haven't the least idea," Marcy answered. "Want to see it? The crate and all is in that room over there...."

He raised the false arm an inch or two, let it drop back stiffly and pointed with the right. The Crimson Mask noticed this although he didn't show any indication of it. Marcy's arm wasn't false. The fingers had moved a bit, the wrist seemed supple. This man was not the real Marcy.

The Crimson Mask approached the closed door that had been indicated. He stopped and faced the spurious publisher, while his hand grasped the door-knob and turned it slowly. He didn't open the door.

"You know Chinese art, Mr. Marcy. Is this vase which was sent you so mysteriously really valuable? How big is it, measured against this door, say?"

"It is worth a fortune," the fake Marcy said. He stepped closer to the door and indicated with the ungloved hand a point several inches above the knob. "It is about that high. I..."

SUDDENLY THE Crimson Mask seized the fake Marcy by one arm and propelled him violently at the door. It had been moved only enough to release the catch so that when the spy hit it, the door flew open.

"No... no," the spy screamed wildly. A shot drowned out the rest of his yell. He staggered backward a step or two, closed his eyes like a very tired man and pitched headlong to the floor.

Automatic ready, the Crimson Mask risked a quick look into the room. Enough light streamed in so that he could see the death trap set for him. It was a pistol trap, with the gun fastened to the back of a chair and aimed straight at the door. When the door opened, the trigger was pulled by a cleverly arranged cord.

The Crimson Mask mopped his forehead with a handkerchief. If he hadn't noticed the fake Marcy move that supposedly artificial arm, he might have walked straight into this trap. It certainly proved that Fenwick's servants were spies—if Fenwick himself hadn't arranged this.

The man who impersonated Marcy was dead. The bullet had torn through his chest. His pockets contained nothing of consequence. Apparently, this hotel suite was soundproof enough so that the shot had not been heard. The Crimson Mask began to wonder about the real John Marcy.

He searched the suite and in a small bedroom at the rear he found a locked closet door. He opened it with one of his skeleton keys. Inside was the real Marcy. His right arm was tied to a clothes hook, his lips painfully gagged, his ankles securely tied. His left sleeve was pinned to the coat.

The Crimson Mask cut him down quickly and helped him over to the bed. Marcy gratefully took a drink of water.

"You must be the Crimson Mask," he said. "The real Crimson Mask, even though you are not wearing the red domino. Fenwick phoned me to expect you. Not ten minutes later someone arrived, identified himself as you and then slugged me. I don't know what happened after that although I think I did hear a shot."

"Come with me," the Crimson Mask said. "The shot killed a Nazi spy. Look at him and see if he is the same man who posed as me."

Marcy looked and nodded.

"That's he all right. Fooled me neatly. What in the world is this all about, Crimson Mask? I thought my troubles were over when they let me out of that stinking cell in a Jap prison."

"I don't think your troubles will be over until after this war is ended," the Crimson Mask shrugged. "We'll all have plenty. Sacrifices, danger... the war brought to our doorstep perhaps. We cannot deny the fact that our enemies are strong, daring and clever. Just how clever has been exhibited to me for the last several hours. Have a cigarette, Mr. Marcy?"

Marcy took one, sucked smoke deep into his lungs and sat down, relaxed.

"You can't imagine how good these taste. The Japs wouldn't give us any, although some of the guards had a habit of blowing smoke into my cell to tantalize me. That was one of their minor tortures."

"Didn't they even permit you to take along whatever tobacco you had when arrested?"

"Those lice," Marcy grunted, "even took my cuff links away. I know you think I may be an Axis spy. Protesting my innocence won't do any good, but I can say this.

"A lot of people aren't in this war up to the hilt. They haven't dug deeply enough for War Bonds, they haven't made sacrifices, learned how to live like a Spartan. Yet our enemies have done exactly that and have been doing it for years, just preparing for this moment.

"We can't starve those Japs out, Mr. Crimson Mask. I don't even think we can bomb them out. Deprivation won't do any good because they haven't known a single luxury in many, many years.

"The only way to lick those yellow beasts is by crushing them, smashing them into bits, and that can only be accomplished by making sacrifices of men, money, materials."

THE CRIMSON MASK nodded.

"I think most of us understand that, Mr. Marcy. We also know that there is another enemy, just as powerful and ruthless on the other side of the globe. They'll both be crushed no matter how much we must sacrifice to do it. You haven't been home long enough to find out what is really going on. You'll see—and feel comforted."

"I hope so," Marcy sighed. "Oh, what am I talking about? We Yanks always came through and this time it's no different except for the scope of the thing and the utter seriousness of it. I saw how those yellow dogs acted in Hong Kong. They're not human beings.

"They're murderers, wolves without an iota of mercy or decency! And you think I may be one of them! That is probably the grossest insult I've ever experienced."

The Crimson Mask laughed.

"No doubt, Mr. Marcy. I'll apologize now, but I'll take back the apology if you turn out to be *Herr* Ehrlich."

"Who is he?" Marcy asked bluntly.

"The Axis spy who was planted on that refugee liner. The man who sent someone here to dispose of you, to trick me into facing a death trap."

Marcy nodded.

"I think what happened here rather lets me out, don't you? After all, it wasn't necessary that I get anyone to pose as me to kill you."

"Not unless you are the spy and were afraid the trap might fail. Then you'd have an alibi. No, Mr. Marcy, suspicion has not been removed from your name. Even that vehement and apparently sincere blast against the Japs doesn't prove anything. *Herr* Ehrlich would be smart enough to put over an act like that."

Marcy extended his one arm in a gesture of resignation.

"I see what you mean. Don't blame you either, but I wish I could prove my patriotism some way. It's not pleasant being suspected as a spy."

"You might answer a few questions," the Crimson Mask suggested. "For instance—did you ever see Fenwick or Wilson around the prison where you were held?"

"Never. I was not permitted any exercise. They never let me out of the cell."

"And the statue you purchased—the one the F.B.I. is holding in escrow—how did you get that?"

Marcy frowned.

"You know, it did strike me a bit odd. The Japs announced that I was being exchanged and would be sent back to the United States in twenty-four hours. They were overnice about the whole affair.

"Two guards took me to the shopping district to buy fresh clothing and some toiletries. On the way, this Chinese stopped me and asked if I'd be interested in purchasing the statue. The price he named interested me, but I had no money. The Japs had taken it all.

"Then one of the guards suggested I be allowed to visit the bank where I did business and draw my money out. I thought they'd confiscated it. The Chinese followed, the deal was made and I took the statue along."

"The whole thing was a frame-up," the Crimson Mask opined. "Either to confuse the F.B.I. when the ship reached port or to make you innocently carry a message of some kind incorporated into that statue. No one has approached you and offered to buy it since you've returned?"

Marcy shook his head.

"No, but I'm sure I can sell it at a handsome profit if the F.B.I. ever turns the thing back to me. I won't ask for it. If there is the least suspicion that it is part of a spy scheme, they can destroy the thing with my blessing."

The Crimson Mask arose.

"I'll contact Mr. Blane of the F.B.I. and explain what happened here so you won't get into any trouble over that body in the next room. Meanwhile, your best bet is to sit tight. Keep thinking back to your trip from Hong Kong. Perhaps the real spy made a slip you may remember. Contact Blane if you think of anything."

CHAPTER VIII

THREE TRAILS TO DANGER

L ATE THE next morning, Sandy arrived at the drug store and went to Clarke's hidden laboratory behind the prescription department.

"I visited the Etude Shop," she said. "One of the clerks did recall that cash register receipt. A man purchased a box of reproducing needles. You know... the needles they use on recording machines."

Clarke whistled softly.

"That may help us, but at this moment I don't exactly see how. We still have our three suspects and every one is putting on a splendid act. The one who happens to be *Herr* Ehrlich must be in contact with the spy ring, but he can't really act until he gets back the object which the F.B.I. took from him. I think I'll ask Blane to release Fenwick's Chinese document, Wilson's music box and Marcy's statue."

"But isn't that risky?" Sandy objected.

"Sure it is. One of the biggest gambles of my career, I guess. Yet it must be done. I'll phone Blane later, tell him to ship the things back to their owners and then we'll determine just which one of these articles our spy must have to finish his work here. Or perhaps I should say, begin it."

"Just how can we go about this?" Sandy asked.

"I don't know yet," Clarke told her. "I did say it was a gamble, but a necessary one. If we fail, catastrophe may result so... we cannot fail. We've got to load the dice for this gamble, Sandy. Suppose you come back just before dark tonight. Things will be set by then."

At seven o'clock Dave Small stuck a neat sign in the door of the drug store announcing that it was closed for the evening. Then he put out all lights in conformity with the dim-out regulations and went to the laboratory behind the store.

Sandy and Clarke were there and Clarke was just replacing the telephone on its cradle.

"I called Blane just now," he explained to Dave. "Told him to send back the articles and also to make sure the men who have tapped the telephone of each suspect are on the alert.

"Sandy, you're to take Marcy. Go to his hotel and watch his suite. If he has a visitor, follow the visitor, especially if he comes out with a package.

"Dave, you take Fenwick and do the same thing. When you find out where the visitors go, come back here and wait."

"I get it," Dave said. "You think whichever one of those articles is essential to the spy ring will be called for by an Axis agent who will then take it to their headquarters. Boy, if we ever let that man get away though!"

"We can't," Clarke said slowly. "Just keep in mind the fact that failure means the sacrifice of many innocent people, of property and goods that are vital to our war effort. If you get stuck and can't contact me, notify the F.B.I. and let them clean up. Don't take stay chances."

Sandy went off first. Dave Small changed clothes and donned a dark suit while Clarke applied disguise to his face. He handed Dave a gun.

"Use it if necessary," he said. "Sandy is packing a weapon, too. If you have to shoot... shoot to kill. That's what those spies will do and if you hesitate, they'll know you're weak."

Dave spun the cylinder of the revolver.

"Funny," he said, "I never thought much of killing anyone, but right now I'd enjoy planting a bullet in the hide of *Herr* Ehrlich."

"You won't get a chance," Clarke grinned. "Ehrlich will stay put. He knows he's being watched and won't take any chances. He'll simply send the instructions to the spy ring and let them handle the rest. Until the heat dies down, Ehrlich won't make a move and that is precisely what has stymied us. Get going now and remember how important your mission is!"

DAVE DEPARTED immediately. Clarke donned dark clothing which in darkness would make him almost invisible. His shirt was a deep gray, his hat black and his necktie very dark. He took along a pair of guns this time and some extra clips of ammunition.

Half an hour later, he was posted in the corridor of the apartment house where Wilson lived. A full hour went by and his worries increased as he spent this time thinking of the dire consequences if his hunch went wrong.

There would be explosions, trains derailed, ships sunk, fires started and assassinations. The Axis powers were no longer rolling along gleefully from one conquered area to another. They were gradually being checked and time meant everything to them. In order to gain more time, they'd resort to any sort of measure.

Then the elevator stopped and a slim man emerged. He had a briefcase tucked under one arm and proceeded straight to Wilson's door. A servant opened it. The Crimson Mask was close enough to hear the visitor's words.

"I am from the Gerard Chemical Company. Mr. Wilson phoned that he had reports to send over for our board meeting in the morning. I was sent to get them."

The servant let the man in. Not more than four minutes went by and the visitor emerged again. His briefcase was thicker now and he carried it by the handle.

The Crimson Mask raced down two flights of stairs and managed to catch the elevator on its way down. He stepped in, lined himself up beside the messenger and calmly lit a cigarette. Outside the building, the messenger went off in one direction the Crimson Mask in another.

Not for long though. Before the messenger was a block away, the Crimson Mask was on his trail. Oddly enough, the man preferred to walk and made no motion to hail a taxi. Once more, the Crimson Mask's skill in shadowing was put to a test.

The messenger headed east, across town. He walked directly up to the main entrance of a medium-sized brick factory building. Over the door was a sign indicating that the building was occupied by the Gerard Drug Company—Wilson's firm.

No suspicion could be attached to Wilson for this. He logically could have dispatched reports on the Chinese situation to his firm. The messenger showed neither suspicion nor caution in his movements.

The Crimson Mask watched him unlock the door, turn on some lights and then vanish. The Crimson Mask crossed the street and took up a position in a doorway opposite the entrance to the drug firm.

Soon a car pulled up and a stocky man got out. He marched up to the door and rang a bell. The messenger let him in with a respectful nod.

During the next ten minutes four more cars pulled up. Four more men entered the building. Presently the Crimson Mask saw a third floor office become brightly illuminated.

Then still another car pulled up. Its occupant got out, took a package from the front seat and held it somewhat gingerly. He was also admitted by merely ringing the bell.

A SHADOWY form came slinking down the street, close to the building shadows. It was Dave Small. The Crimson Mask hissed a signal. Small came over and stood in the doorway with him.

"I followed the guy who went to see Fenwick. He bought that Chinese document, wrapped it up carefully and brought it here.

I watched the whole transaction through a window. If Fenwick is involved, he certainly takes no chances. I even saw the cash passed."

"Good," the Crimson Mask nodded. "At least, we guessed right about this. I trailed a messenger who visited Wilson. I'm certain he didn't take away the music box though because Blane told me it was a pretty bulky object. I wonder where Sandy is? According to plan, she ought to arrive soon on the heels of another spy."

"What are they doing?" Dave queried. "Buying up all those objects which were brought over?"

"Naturally," the Crimson Mask replied. "That way, suspicion will still be fastened upon three men. I imagine someone came to Wilson's and got his music box. I… Dave… another car. Get back into the shadows."

This car stopped directly in front of the door. One man got out and kept a hand plunged into his side coat pocket. Then, both the Crimson Mask and Dave gave low groans. Sandy emerged from the car. Behind her came a second spy. They took her arms and she was hustled up to the door and shoved inside.

"They've got her," Dave said excitedly. "Maybe they'll just shoot her. We've got to do something quick."

"They'll ask questions first," the Crimson Mask said. "That gives us a short time. Let's take a look around the back of the building. If there is no other entrance, we'll shoot our way in."

They crossed the street, slipped into a very narrow passageway between two buildings and came out near a loading platform at the rear. A fire-escape led up to the roof. The Crimson Mask warned Dave to keep a sharp eye out and climbed the fire-escape to the roof.

He saw light coming from a skylight, crawled up to it and found that he could look down into what seemed to be a meeting room. There were ten men assembled there.

The room was luxuriously fitted. A long table with chairs placed all around it occupied the center of the room. At the front end were large windows framed by thick drapes and… an electric phonograph.

Sandy stood at the head of the table, her back only three or four feet from the phonograph. Two men stood close beside her and it was apparent that she was being questioned.

The Crimson Mask bit his lip as one man stepped up to her and slapped her brutally across the face. Another seized her arm and twisted it cruelly. There was no outcry from Sandy, not even a whimper. She faced them with her head high and her chin stuck out determinedly.

The Crimson Mask crawled noiselessly back to the fire-escape, climbed down it and met Dave.

"Go back to the street. Around the northeast corner from this factory you'll find a business district wide open for business. There's a music store halfway up the block. Buy a phonograph record. Anyone, just hurry. Sandy is being mistreated and any moment they may decide to shoot. Meet me on the roof when you get back. Remember, seconds may mean Sandy's life."

CHAPTER IX

ROLL OF THE DICE

D AVE CAME creeping across the rooftop a few minutes later with the record in one hand. He lay down beside the Crimson Mask and peered through the skylight.

Sandy still stood at the head of the table. One of the spies was idly driving the point of a knife into the smooth surface of the wood.

The Crimson Mask put his lips against Dave's ear.

"She has courage, Dave, but those rats have decided to kill her. They're giving her one last chance to talk and I saw her refuse them. We have to work very fast.

"I found a rope on the loading platform while you were gone. It's tied so I can slide over the edge of the roof and reach that window directly behind Sandy. Now look closely. See that phonograph? It stands close to the heavy portieres that mask the window.

"When I signal, you smash this skylight and jump down. Here—put this crimson mask on your face. Stick those men up, Dave. Shoot if any one of them makes a move. Then you will follow these instructions…"

One minute later, Dave watched the Crimson Mask slide off the edge of the roof and lower himself toward that window. A faint whistle reached his ears and Dave promptly kicked in the skylight. He jumped through it and landed in the middle of the table not very far below. There was a gun in his hand.

"Stay where you are!" Dave barked. "Every one of you!"

"The Crimson Mask," one man shouted.

Another moved forward aggressively.

"I thought this girl was associated with the Crimson Mask! It is just as well. We have him also now."

"This gun says the opposite," Dave roared. "Lift your hands, all of you!"

"Bah!" the closest spy cried, "you have a gun with six bullets. Perhaps you could kill six of us before we shoot you. What of it? We are more than six and we are prepared to die."

"Perhaps," Dave told them. "However, before the shooting starts, I might add that while you hold this girl as hostage, I also have a hostage of my own. His name is Ehrlich'!"

There were gasps of astonishment and then the spokesman derided the idea.

"You do not even know who *Herr* Ehrlich is. If so, the F.B.I. would have arrested him long ago. This is a bluff."

"I can prove it isn't," Dave said. He reached under his coat and extracted the phonograph record he'd bought around the corner.

"On this record is the voice of *Herr* Ehrlich with instructions to all of you and… an admission that he is slated for quick death if the girl and I do not walk out of here safely within the next thirty minutes. Kill us and you kill the man who has come from around the world to act as your leader!"

"And if you do prove this—if we do let you go, then what?" the spokesman demanded.

"We start over again," Dave said. "You don't have to take my word for it. Let me play this record and you'll see."

Dave jumped off the table, backed toward the phonograph and gave Sandy a confident smile as he passed close to her. Dave didn't exactly feel as confident as he looked. This trick depended upon supreme perfection and the least slip would mean exposure and... death.

THERE WAS a record already on the phonograph. Dave removed it, placed it to one side and placed the one he carried into position. All the time he faced those spies with gun leveled. He turned on the mechanism and the motor hummed. Then a voice spoke.

"You will do as this red masked man orders. I am his prisoner. Two men are with me and have orders to kill me at precisely nine-thirty. I have the word of the Crimson Mask that we can break this stalemate only by letting any prisoners go free.

"I am making this record as he watches me. He has forced our hand and there is nothing left to do but get away. You will quickly assemble all records, divide them among you and go into hiding until you hear from me. If I am not released, then you will carry out the instructions on the recording I delivered to you.

"If you fail, I will be killed and all of you hunted down. The entire organization will be broken up at a time when it is needed most. Do as the Crimson Mask orders. It is our only chance."

Dave reached for the starter switch and snapped it. The spies he faced were no longer belligerent. The spokesman was pale, nervous.

"You heard what *Herr* Ehrlich has ordered. Otto—Hans—Eugen, you will get all papers at once! Bring them here. Hurry—we are not granted much time!"

Three men fled from the room, were gone about ten minutes and returned loaded down with books and papers. They placed these on the table. The group of spies clustered around them.

Then, from behind the portiere, came a second man who wore a crimson mask. He held two guns in his hands.

"We'll take over," he called out loudly. "Remember, there are more bullets here now. There are two Crimson Masks. Line up against the wall, all of you! Face it and keep your hands as high as you can reach."

One of the men made a wild grab for his gun. An automatic in the Crimson Mask's hands blazed once and the spy toppled across the table, slid off and fell limply to the floor. The others backed up and obeyed orders.

Sandy stepped close to the Crimson Mask while Dave moved forward to search the prisoners and disarm them. The Crimson Mask whispered to her.

"Find a telephone. Call Blane and have him send enough men to take care of these rats. Also have him assemble our three suspects at Wilson's apartment. Hurry!"

When a strong detail of G-men arrived, they found only one Crimson Mask waiting for them. Blane led the squad. He checked over the papers on the table while his men handcuffed the prisoners and led them away.

Blane looked like a small boy with four ice cream cones and six large bags of candy.

"Crimson Mask—I don't care how you accomplished this, but you've cleaned out one of the most dangerous spy nests in the country! These papers give names, addresses. They list plans and victims. If they ever went through with this, I shudder to think of the results!"

"What about Wilson, Fenwick and Marcy?" the Crimson Mask asked.

"All will be at Wilson's apartment by the time we reach it. Want to tell me about it now... or at Wilson's?"

"We'll wait," the Crimson Mask said. "Take me to Wilson's place now."

Just before they left, the Crimson Mask went over and picked up the phonograph record which Dave had removed from the machine. Blane watched him with a puzzled expression on his face.

"This record will do the trick," the Crimson Mask said. "The one on the turntable means nothing. I used it to fool this band of spies. Let's go."

The three suspects were seated in Wilson's apartment and guarded by four G-men. Fenwick looked his anger. Marcy was cool, but kept smoking one cigarette after another. So did Wilson, who didn't seem very disturbed about it all.

The Crimson Mask faced them. Blane laid the horrible little statue of Marcy's on a table and beside it he placed the ancient Chinese document which Fenwick had brought over.

The Crimson Mask said:

"Wilson… where is your music box? We might as well assemble all the evidence."

Wilson shrugged, walked over to a desk and took the music box from a drawer. He wound it up, started the music and grinned.

"I thought Mr. Blane and his G-men examined these things and satisfied themselves that none were being used to convey a message."

"We checked them," Blane admitted. "Just the same we'll listen to what the Crimson Mask has to offer."

THE CRIMSON MASK spoke clearly. "Wilson… the drug firm for which you work is really a spy ring. Every last man of the spy group has been arrested. That news should make one of you gentlemen begin squirming. I might add that for the last few hours, I've been pretty sure which of you is *Herr* Ehrlich. Now let me finish before the questions start.

"First of all, one of these objects brought over as relics does carry a message. It is so complicated a message that Ehrlich couldn't trust it to his memory. In order to divert suspicion, Ehrlich arranged that each one of you be allowed to purchase an object which might be regarded with suspicion.

"In that manner, no great amount of attention would be bestowed on the article which really contained the message. It might be incorporated into the Chinese symbols on that foolscap. It might be part of the design on the statue or the inscriptions on the music box."

"Then why were those things not checked?" Fenwick demanded irritably.

"They were—thoroughly," the Crimson Mask said. "Therefore, we must look to some other means. The foolscap carries no secret message. The statue might have something inside it though that seems rather impossible. The music box might give a message through those wild notes it plays."

"I don't think so," Blane put in. "We X-rayed the statue and..." he coughed, "... we sawed it in half. Patched it so the cut can't be noticed. We listened to that crazy music by the hour. It means nothing."

"It means something to Ehrlich," the Crimson Mask said. "Wilson—while you were a prisoner of the Japs, they treated you no better than Fenwick or Marcy, which means very badly. You were deprived of all luxuries, fed poorly, allowed little or no exercise and no cigarettes. Is that right?"

"Indeed it is," Wilson said. "People here simply cannot imagine what conditions existed there. Ask Fenwick and Marcy. They were through the same thing."

"I've already asked them," the Crimson Mask said. "They quite agree with you. How long were you under arrest?"

"More than six months," Wilson answered. "Six months of hell."

"And it took about two weeks to reach the United States after your release. You have been here only a couple of days. Wilson—if you were permitted no cigarettes in Japanese custody, if you were deprived of them for six long months, how does it happen your fingers are so stained with tobacco tar? Fenwick and Marcy are inveterate cigarette smokers too—yet they have no such stains."

Wilson looked up sharply. His eyes traveled from the Crimson Mask to Bill Blane of the F.B.I. Then he looked at his fingers for a moment.

"Perhaps," he said, "it is because of the brand of cigarettes I smoke. Sorry—I can't give you any reason for the stains."

"Then perhaps you can explain why one of those short wave radio sets so mysteriously sent here was, in reality, a reproducing instrument. Perhaps you can explain why you sent Nazi agents to buy reproducing needles from the Etude Shop. Why you made a recording of the music from that Chinese music box and sent it to the Gerard Drug Company where a band of spies were in session. Perhaps you can tell us what that wild jumble of notes from the music box means!"

WILSON CALMLY reached for a cigarette and lit it with steady hands. He made no comment.

The Crimson Mask went on.

"The recording of those notes means nothing if played at normal speed, but if played slowly, some notes stand out. If played fast, other notes take precedence. These notes become a code. They deliver to the spy system here, certain instructions. How about it, Wilson?"

Wilson smiled.

"You have nothing on me, Crimson Mask. Nothing!"

"Perhaps we have," the Crimson Mask said. "Suppose we produce the real Mrs. Wylie Wilson?"

"You can't do that," Wilson snapped. "She is...."

"Dead? I thought she must be. Odd, how a man who suffered in a Japanese prison, who had been away from home so many years, wasn't even greeted by his wife upon returning.

"There was a woman posing as your wife, yes. One of your stooges. You're not Wylie Wilson. You are *Herr* Ehrlich, one of the Nazis who worked undercover to induce Japan to commit suicide.

"You came here to head the spy system, came with detailed orders carried in the music of that Chinese music box. You had Phil Adrian murdered, you tried to kill me. You maintained contact with your men by signaling from a window."

"Prove it," Wilson said almost pleasantly.

The Crimson Mask faced Blane.

"The telephone wires of all three suspects were tapped. Did Fenwick or Marcy call anyone about selling their Chinese objets d'art?"

"No," Blane said. "They didn't."

"Then how does it happen that those men who offered to buy the objects learned they had been released by the F.B.I.? The only persons who knew were the three suspects themselves. Wilson—

or *Herr* Ehrlich—signaled the news and had his agents try to buy those articles to cast continued suspicion upon two innocent men.

"Oh yes, Ehrlich—the messenger who came here for your report to the drug company, also carried away a recording of your music box. He is arrested and he has talked."

The false Wilson crushed out his cigarette very slowly. His hand shook a bit now and the still lighted cigarette butt fell to the floor. He bent down, automatically and started to pick it up. Suddenly his hand flashed toward a shoulder holster. A glittering gun appeared. The muzzle raised.

There was a single shot. Ehrlich sank back into the chair, looking rather surprised, particularly at the sight of blood that seeped between the fingers of his hand, pressed against his chest.

"You cannot... prove..." he started to say. Then he tumbled out of the chair.

The Crimson Mask stowed away a smoking gun.

"I hoped he'd do that. I made a promise not so long ago—a promise to see this case through and to kill Ehrlich. Blane, by questioning those prisoners, you will discover one who will talk willingly. There is always one like that. Make him tell who murdered Phil Adrian. Send the killer to the chair."

"It will be a pleasure," Blane said grimly.

The door closed. Blane turned around. The Crimson Mask was gone.

In the security of the lab behind Bob Clarke's prescription counter, Clarke chuckled as he told Sandy what had happened.

"Dave put a record on the phonograph, but he didn't play it. I was behind the portiere. When Dave jumped through the skylight, all attention was focused on him and I slipped through the window.

"I knew Ehrlich was posing as Wylie Wilson and I imitated his voice so that the spy group believed they were listening to a record which Ehrlich had made. It was a gamble, but it worked.

"Ehrlich's plan to throw complete suspicion on two other men and also upon himself, fooled us for a time, but while Hitler's agents may be highly trained and very clever, they still slip."

"I'm glad you killed Ehrlich," Sandy said quietly. "He was a monster, Bob."

"They're all monsters," Bob countered. "Nazis, Fascists and Japs—they are beasts. They don't know the meaning of mercy or fair play. Now they will be fought on those same terms. They made the terms, but wait until you hear the rats squeal! That kind never can take it!"

THREE MEN OF EVIL

MEN OF MURDER

THEY WERE an incongruous trio. The dumbest patrolman on earth would have suspected there was something wrong with the three men if he had seen them assembled, but they were careful that no one observed them.

André Aumont was the tallest of the three. He wore a Chesterfield coat, a derby, a white muffler of the finest ilk and carried a cane inside of which a rapier was hidden. André Aumont was the dandy. His black eyes sparkled with a peculiar sort of venom and he had slim white hands that were deceptively strong.

Jean Bovy was the shortest, and as commonplace as red clay. His face was plump, friendly, and his attitude more or less meek. He might have been selected as a typical small merchant or assistant office manager. His clothing was ordinary and reasonably neat. The hair at his temples was tipped with gray.

Victor Chantel, the third man, was the most outstanding in his massiveness and the cruelty etched on his features. An ugly scar that ran from the left corner of his mouth to his left ear was a souvenir of a Paris sewer fight. His arms were ungainly, his shoulders abnormally broad. It was said in Paris that Victor Chantel could actually tear a man's head off his shoulders.

As usual, André the Magnificent, now assumed the role of spokesman as he pointed toward the mouth of the alley which shielded the three men from observation. Directly across the street was a five-story loft building, on the second-floor windows of which was the name of the Paris Metal Working Company.

"This will be very easy," Aumont said to his companions. "There is one old man who watches the place. They are doing good business over there and should provide us with considerable loot."

BOVY, THE commonplace man, frowned.

"*Bien*—but do you not see the sign? It says 'Paris Metal Working Company.' Without doubt, the owners are French as we are. It does not seem right that we should rob our own countrymen."

"Bah!" Chantel thrust his ugly face closer to Bovy. "What does it matter? If there are things we want. The Boche will pay good money for it. Have we not always taken what we want and to the devil with those who oppose us?"

"That is true." Aumont adjusted his gloves, drew out his cane sword about ten inches, then snapped it shut again. "We cannot call ourselves Frenchmen. We are men of the world—soldiers of fortune. If the accursed Boche pay us to work for them—then we do as they command. And, Jean, have you forgotten they did not execute us as they did so many others?"

"I know." Jean Bovy still frowned. "We are valuable to them and therefore we were allowed to live. They shipped us here by submarine. Since then, we have worked faithfully and been well paid. But now the devils have overrun all of France. They broke the armistice. They will break us, too, when we are no longer of service to them."

Bovy relaxed. "Very well. We have always worked together, we three. In the days when Paris was Paris we drove the gendarmes crazy. Even the Deuxieme Bureau sought us and never even came close."

"Good," Chantel the Ugly approved. "If they could not get us, how can these Americans put us into prison? They do not even know we are here. Come, let us get this over with. *Herr* Shugg was impatient the last time because we did not secure enough of what he wishes. André, you will lead the way, eh?"

Aumont thrust his cane under one arm, smoothed his gloves by pulling them tightly, then he walked briskly toward the street. Bovy was next, and he plodded along the street to a side entrance of the building they meant to raid.

The Crimson Mask plastered the traitorous French crook twice on the jaw

Chantel, who brought up the rear, wore a seedy cap. He had never worn any other kind of head gear. The sewers of Paris were low and a hat only made him duck, so Chantel swore by his cap. As he passed beneath a street light, it was plain that he still belonged in those ancient sewers from which the Nazis had routed him.

Aumont marched straight up to the front door of the building, found a night bell and pressed it. He saw the gleam of a flashlight and gave a covert signal. Bovy, at the side entrance, saw this signal and went to work at once. He picked the lock, pushed the door open, and something caught. Bovy cursed. The door was fitted with a stout burglar chain.

He drew nippers from under his coat, gave a covert look around and saw Chantel nod that everything was serene. The nippers closed around the chain, but Bovy didn't have the strength to cut that stout defense. He hissed, and Chantel hurried up.

The huge brute of a man took the nippers, braced himself and applied pressure. Muscle cords bulged along the entire length of his shoulders. There was a sharp click and the chain was cut. In a second, both men were inside.

Aumont, meanwhile, held the attention of the gray-haired watchman.

"But it is impossible that the owner is not here," he protested. "I had an appointment with him. I am to consult with him about government work. I am a busy man, which is why I had to meet him after hours. Have you a telephone?"

"Yes, sir." The watchman nodded. "We've got a phone all right, but you can't come in to use it. Sorry, Mister, but rules are rules. There's been a lot of robberies of places like this the last month, and if I let anybody at all in, I'll get fired. You wait here and I'll phone the boss."

"Very good," Aumont said. "You will please hurry."

THE WATCHMAN closed the door, shook his head doubtfully, and breathed easier when the heavy steel bar held the door closed. He walked briskly across a shipping room, turned into the office of the small plant and barely sensed that there was danger present. It was a shadow he saw, but the maker of that shadow moved fast.

Chantel, with a grin of anticipation, whipped a narrow silk rag around the watchman's throat, shoved a knee into his victim's back and held him until the watchman grew limp. Chantel kept up the pressure another minute or two, judged then that the watchman was dead, and let him fall to the floor.

Bovy, meanwhile, hurried to the main entrance, opened the door and let Aumont inside. So far they had been entirely unobserved. The few pedestrians who had passed paid no attention. There had been nothing to attract them. These three adroit crooks of another nation were smooth, and operated perfectly.

Aumont nudged the watchman's body with his foot and glanced at Chantel.

"He is dead—never fear," Chantel grunted with considerable pleasure. "Have you ever known me to fail, André? My little scarf has had plenty of practice. Now we must find the things we came for."

Upstairs, they passed through a workroom filled with small benches where master craftsmen assembled expensive jewelry, alloyed metals, and prepared certain items listed as military secrets by the government. The intruders advanced on a huge safe, glistening dully in the light that came through a window.

Bovy took charge now. His sensitive fingers tested the vault dial, his trained eyes gauged the thickness of the door, then he went to work. A small drill with a diamond point bit into this supposedly burglar proof steel. Forty minutes went by. Chantel and Aumont kept moving around the building, but Bovy held strictly to his part of the job. When he had four of these holes created, he nodded in satisfaction, unplugged the drill and stowed it into a kit of tools he carried around his waist.

Then he took out a slim vial, removed the glass stopper and with the aid of what seemed to be a minute medicine dropper, he squirted some of this liquid into the tiny holes. Four tenuously extremely slender wires went in also, then he plugged the holes with a mixture that looked like metal which was malleable in a cold state.

He connected the four wires to a larger one. To the end of this was an ordinary electric light plug. He carried this wire to the nearest fixture, removed the bulb and replaced it with the plug. Then he called to Chantel and Aumont.

"I am ready," he said. "Eleven times I have done this and not yet have I ceased to marvel at the explosive those Boche created and gave to me. Such a small amount is needed—but the havoc it creates! Sometimes, I think men who can prepare such things as this should be masters of the world."

"So long as we work for them and they pay us well," Aumont commented dryly. "Get on with it, Jean. Every wasted moment makes our danger greater."

Bovy grinned, turned and grasped the light switch that controlled the current. Then he gave a yelp of alarm.

"André—Victor! The watchman. He is no longer on the floor! He... There he is! Get him—quickly!"

CHAPTER II

THE CRIMSON MASK

THE WATCHMAN, who had acted well enough to pretend he was dead, stood beside a small red box which he had already opened. The celluloid collar around his neck had saved him. Chantel's garrote had become twisted in the collar and all the pressure he had exerted had not been enough to choke the watchman to death.

Gamely, the old man had crawled away while the intruders were busy. The nearest method of raising an alarm was a fire-box and he had this open before they spotted him.

Chantel, cursing in French, reached over his head and his fingers closed around the haft of a knife snuggled down the back of his neck. He drew it, reversed the weapon and held it by the point. He flung the blade—and Chantel never missed.

It hit the watchman between the shoulder-blades. He groaned, started to sag, but he was not quite finished yet. He managed to insert his finger through the loop of the fire-alarm lever. As he sagged toward the floor, his own weight pulled the lever down.

Instantly, a terrific clamor arose as four huge bells began to strike. Chantel reached the watchman, jerked his knife free and looked around like a trapped panther.

Bovy kept on working methodically. They had come this far and he meant to get that loot. He turned the light switch. There was an explosion and the whole door of the safe was blown off its hinges. Aumont rushed up to it and both of them hurriedly stripped the safe of what they were after.

There were shouts outside. People drawn by the clamor of the bells believed the explosion to be the result of a fire they couldn't see yet. Sirens were wailing in the distance.

"We separate," Aumont said hurriedly.

He was stuffing small bars of shiny metal into his pockets. Chantel and Bovy were similarly engaged. The weight of their loot barely topped twenty pounds and when it was distributed between the three, it created no bulk and would not impede their haste in making their escape.

Aumont raced downstairs, reached the side door and let himself out. He saw Chantel emerge, then. Both of them flattened themselves against the wall and waited. When the fire apparatus arrived they hurried to the street and mingled with the crowd.

Bovy had taken longer, for he had been engaged in assembling his burglar apparatus. This done, he ran between the rows of benches toward the stairs. It was dark, and Bovy didn't see the small pile of scrap filings on the floor. His foot landed on them and he did a somersault. When he landed, one foot was curled beneath him, and beads of sweat shone dully on his forehead.

He got up, put some pressure on his left leg and it started to buckle. His ankle felt as though ten million red-hot needles were being inserted through it.

Downstairs, he heard axes being used on the door. Bovy hopped toward the dead watchman, hastily removed the man's cap and put it on his own head. He unslung the time-clock the watchman carried, put this over his shoulder, and hopped toward the stairs. Before he descended, he set fire to his own handkerchief and his hat. They burned quickly and emitted a lot of smoke.

He was on the main floor when the firemen broke through. Bovy could not speak much English, so he just pointed at the steps. Smoke was filtering down them. The firemen rushed toward the stairway with extinguishers ready, while others dragged in a length of hose.

Bovy moved to the door. Nobody attempted to stop him and the pain in his ankle had died down now so that he could put a little weight on it and limp painfully along.

THE CAP and the watchman's time-clock formed a good disguise and he reached the fringe of the crowd unhindered. He wished he could run, but that was impossible, so he limped away with what haste he could. Reaching an alley, he went down it. There were no signs of Aumont or Chantel. Trust them to put plenty of distance between the scene of the robbery and themselves.

Chantel flung the weapon and it hit the watchman
between the shoulder-blades

By the time Bovy reached the end of the alley, he could hardly walk. His ankle was swollen and threatened to buckle under him with each step. Finally he came out on a narrow, dismal street. It was dimmed-out in accordance with war regulations, but he was attracted by dimly lighted windows and a sign that read:

APOTHECARY

Bovy resolutely made his way toward the drug store. He did not dare visit a doctor, but a druggist might help him without asking too many questions. He hobbled up to the door, read the name of the owner and decided he must take a chance. He opened the door and light illuminated the words printed on the glass panel:

ROBERT CLARKE, Ph.G.

Jean Bovy knew little of American customs, so he did not realize that this was an odd drug store for the current day and age. It had no soda fountain, that almost indispensable prop of the average pharmacy. There were no counters laden with glittering boxes of candy. No women's hose, percolators, cosmetics, and sundry articles that are so usual to a business of this kind.

The showcases contained nothing but essential materials for the treatment of sickness. Only the best of prepared medicines were on display, and a good part of the premises seemed to be taken up by a large prescription counter that was almost as clean as an operating room.

Robert Clarke, the owner, looked up and saw Bovy enter and drag himself over to a chair. He hurried from the prescription department, realizing that this customer was hurt.

Bovy was not capable of expressing his feelings in the English he knew, so he hopefully turned to his native tongue. His eyes lighted up when Bob Clarke answered in fluent French.

"M'sieu," Bovy said. "I have had an accident. My ankle—it is hurt. I could find no doctor—"

"Let me look at it," Clarke said. "I may be able to reduce the swelling, but you had better see a doctor as soon as possible. There may be a fracture."

He helped the man into the back room, seated him on a high stool, and carefully removed shoe and sock. The swelling was pronounced. Clarke applied a soothing agent, and had started to put on a loose bandage when he saw something glitter brightly at the man's trousers leg. The druggist brushed at it, and a couple of metal shavings fell to the floor. He picked these up without Bovy noticing it.

There was something else, too—a smear of cream-colored paint on both trousers legs.

Bob Clarke was engaged in completing the dressing when he heard the bell tinkle, and glanced up to see the door open. The man who entered was pudgy, eager-eyed and obviously excited. He hurried to the rear of the store and Clarke nodded to Dave Small, his assistant.

Clarke arose hurriedly. He was acting on pure hunch now, but sometimes his hunches were too strong to be ignored, and this was one of the times.

"Hello there, Dave!" he greeted heartily. "I expected you earlier. You want the usual, I suppose?"

HE WALKED from behind the prescription counter, reached up and picked a bottle off a shelf. He proceeded to wrap this while Dave Small stared at him as if he had gone suddenly mad.

Clarke spoke to him quietly, his lips barely moving.

"I've got a funny case back there. Man with a sprained ankle. I noticed he wears some kind of a bulky affair around his middle. Looks like tools to me. That's not all. Tell you about it later."

"Okay," Small said. "Maybe he had something to do with what happened about a couple of blocks from here. The Paris Metal Works was robbed, the watchman murdered. One of those robberies where the crooks take nothing but rare metals. When shall I come back?"

"Stick around outside. When this man leaves, trail him. Be sure he doesn't see you. Then hurry back."

Dave Small handed over a dollar bill, gravely accepted some change, and tucked the wrapped bottle into his pocket. He walked out and Bob Clarke returned to his patient.

"You are very good," Bovy told him in French. "My ankle feels better already. Perhaps now I can be on my way, *oui?*"

"There is no reason why not," Clarke told him. "I wouldn't walk much though, and you'd better see a doctor as soon as you can, as I told you."

"*Merci*. And what do I owe you, *M'sieu?*"

Clarke shrugged. "I can't charge for treating a case. I'm no doctor of medicine. All I did was apply an emergency dressing. There is no charge."

Bovy thanked him profusely. As he left the store, limping slowly toward a taxi stand, Bob Clarke saw Small take up the trail. Clarke went back to his prescription department, carefully placed the two tiny bits of shining metal on the table and studied them. He lit a Bunsen burner, picked up one sliver of metal with a pair of tongs, and held it in the colorless flame. The metal became dark red, then strangely turned different shades between green and violet.

Clarke shut off the burner and leaned back. He had recognized this metal. It was palladium, a very rare metal, but the type which some band of thieves had been stealing all over town. This sliver indicated that Bob Clarke's customer had been in a place where palladium was used, and that a shaving had adhered to his leg. Dave Small's report of a burglary and murder at the Paris Metal Works tied the customer to the robbery and killing.

Clarke tried to figure out just why these crooks were so actively in need of three rare metals—palladium, rhodium and iridium. True, they were expensive, far more so than gold or platinum. Yet alone they would be hard to dispose of, and could be easily traced.

Bob Clarke's strong young face clouded slightly, as it always did whenever he first came upon any fresh sign of crime or criminals. He had an active interest in these for, unknown to but three people in the world, he was the Crimson Mask, an eerie hunter of criminals and desperately feared by them. Naturally he was forced to work under cover, and when abroad on his work he wore the crimson domino which was his identifying mark, and which had given him his pseudonym.

Because of his outstandingly successful activities, many men would have given every dollar they owned to know who the Crimson Mask was, so that they might send trained killers to dispose of him. His life was in constant danger whenever he operated against crime, but he knew how to take care of himself.

BOB CLARKE had entered this work right after he had opened his drug store. In fact, the store itself was a camouflage for his unearthing of criminals, a work in which all the ramifications had been carefully thought out.

His lifework was a dedication to the memory of his father, a sergeant of police, who had been shot in the back by crooks, and Bob Clarke's inexorable hounding of all criminals was the son's method of avenging his father. It had been as the elder Clarke lay dying, that a strange thing had happened which was responsible for the character that now had been assumed by the son on his vengeance trail.

A rush of blood to the dying sergeant's face had created an almost perfect red mask, and young Clarke had taken this as a symbol. So when his work against crime had begun he had, wearing a crimson domino that was reminiscent of his dying father's face, invaded the haunts of the underworld and tracked down the men who had murdered his father.

But he had not stopped there, even though the satisfaction had been great. Through a man who had been one of his father's closest friends—Theodore Warrick, who at that time had been police commissioner—Bob Clarke had come to realize that the police were often handicaped because of red tape, the activities of shyster lawyers, and sometimes a bit of crookedness within their own ranks. An outsider was needed, a man who could take chances—a man who could shoot when it was necessary, who could break any and all laws if by so doing he solved the case at hand.

That was how the Crimson Mask had come into being, and Bob Clarke had thrown himself into the role with enthusiasm. He learned all the possibilities of its varied phases, even to the point where he could now perform as well as the best safe cracker or second-story man, if necessary. He had made an intensive study of scientific criminology, and behind his prescription counter in the drug store was another laboratory which his customers never saw. It contained all the equipment essential to tracking down clues and criminals.

Painstakingly, Clark had learned how to disguise himself. His methods, however, were never elaborate, for in each role he undertook he depended largely upon his acting. He studied those roles carefully—unless they had to be adopted in an emergency—and lived them to the hilt. He spoke several languages, could imitate voices and accents. He was a crack shot with any kind of a weapon, and knew fighting from judo to straight punching.

Bob Clarke was greatly indebted to former Police Commissioner Warrick for his advice and encouragement at all times, from the first moment the commissioner had urged the young man to try the work. And now Warrick always stood by, to help in any way possible. His connections with the Police Department enabled him to find out many things which the Crimson Mask would have found impossible.

Dave Small, Clarke's assistant in the drug store, and an old college friend, also knew the identity of the Crimson Mask, and frequently took part in the forays against crooks.

Then there was a third person in on the secret—a girl named Sandra Grey, but who more usually was called "Sandy." Clarke's secret was safe with her because of her love for him, and his for her. She was a first-class aide to Clarke, too, which might not have been expected of a girl like Sandy, only five-feet-three, and with her Dresden china beauty.

But she could fight—and fight furiously—because she knew how to handle a gun as well as any expert. Also she had brains, and an amazing coolness that made her invaluable to the Crimson Mask in a crisis.

With these three incomparable aides—the only three people in the world who knew that Robert Clarke was the Crimson Mask—the work of the Nemesis of crime had been devastating to the underworld of law breakers.

And now he would soon call on them again, for his hunch that was rarely wrong told him he was facing a new, and particularly dire menace to the good of humanity.

CHAPTER III

STRANGE POSSIBILITIES

B **OB CLARKE** waited impatiently for Dave Small's return. He was gone about an hour and by the expression on his face when he did get back he didn't have much to report.

"Looks like we picked the wrong fellow that time, Bob," he said. "His name is Jean Bovy. He came here from France just before Schikelgruber blew into power. He lives at the Hotel Pierpont in an inexpensive room and works for a man named Vilette who runs a store uptown. Kind of a ritzy place selling perfumes, silks and novelties. Been in business for years. Bovy seems to be head man there, next to the owner, of course."

"We didn't pick the wrong man," Clarke said firmly. "Not by a long shot. Bovy was in the metal working plant tonight. He must have sprained his ankle running away from the cops. Dave, I know I'm right because there were shavings of palladium stuck in his trousers legs. Shavings of that metal would be found nowhere except in a place where it was used a lot. The stuff is very rare."

"Maybe we ought to clamp down on the guy," Small suggested.

"No—not yet. I imagine the same gang that have been busy all over town raided that metal works. It makes about a dozen jobs to their credit, and all they ever take are stores of three rare metals. I want to find out why. There's a lot more to this case than its surface indicates. Stay here while I run over to the metal plant and have a look. Be back soon."

Clarke put on a coat and hat, made his way to the plant and was there in time to see the murdered man being carried out. Bob Clarke was well-known to everyone in this vicinity and just as well-liked. Patrolmen waved at him and smiled. People who clustered around curiously also greeted him.

He had purposely selected this rather cheap neighborhood in which to establish his business, not only because it gave him a staid cover, but because he felt it needed a reliable drug store. And he had soon discovered he was right. The people quickly came to trust him, for he was fair in his dealings and never lacking in understanding of their problems.

As a result, his business was large. The profits involved were small however, but he didn't care. More often than not, he charged a needy family less than the drugs cost him. This paid dividends though. He was accepted everywhere, and at this particular moment, he not only could ask questions, but be escorted inside the plant.

"You read about the other robberies, I suppose," one patrolman said to him. "Well, this is another of the same. Boy, whatever those guys use to blast a safe open is sure powerful stuff. The boys from H.Q. never heard of anything like it."

Clarke walked between the rows of work-tables. The place was brightly illuminated now and he saw the tiny pile of metal shavings into which Bovy had stumbled. He also noticed that the legs of some work-tables had been freshly painted a cream color—the exact shade of the paint which had stained Bovy's trousers legs. That cinched it. Bovy had been here. He was a part of the murder mob.

"Did they get much?" Clarke asked his patrolman guide.

"We don't know yet. The owner is on his way down. But it will be just like the other jobs, take it from me. These guys must have a swell market for certain metals that are used in alloying jewelry... See you later, Bob. I'd better get over there and help the lieutenant."

BOB CLARKE had seen enough. He walked downstairs and had reached the main office when a man of medium build, about forty-five, and obviously worried, hurried up to him.

"You're a detective, of course," he said, and gave Clarke no time to deny this. "My name is Devlin. George Devlin. I own this place. Your man phoned me, said the safe was blown open and looted, and that my watchman had been murdered. This makes the twelfth job these crooks who have been looting metal businesses have pulled. When are you going to run them down?"

"Now just a moment," Clarke interrupted. "I'm not—"

"We pay the Police Department to protect us!" Devlin burst out.

He was a nervous, irritable type with a tendency to take it out on the first person he met. Bob Clarke just happened to be the goat this time. Clarke gave up trying to deny he was a plainclothes officer.

"Did you have much in the vault?" he asked.

"About twenty thousand dollars worth of iridium, a few ounces of rhodium, and a little palladium. Perhaps a pound or two. Will you tell me why this gang of crooks only seeks those metals?"

"Not even if I knew," Clarke answered with a grin. "Now should you want to see a policeman, you'll find them upstairs. Good-by, Mr. Devlin."

Bob Clarke returned to the store and Dave Small met him with consuming curiosity. They retired to the back room from which point the store itself could be watched.

"More than twenty thousand dollars' worth of loot taken," Clarke said. "As usual with this particular gang, it was those three rare metals. Twelve jobs—as expert pieces of work as I have ever heard of—just to get a lot of metals it's highly improbable they could sell. What's behind it, Dave? There is the big question."

"Well"—Dave Small thought back to his college days—"the three metals in question are used in alloys of which jewelry is manufactured. Maybe those gorillas have a plant where they make things like that, can't get much on account of priorities, and are stealing the stuff."

Clarke grinned. "Did you ever hear of jewelry makers being expert cracksmen? Dave, whoever blew that safe knew his business inside and out. Furthermore, he must have been provided with not only the best tools, but some new kind of explosive. However, I do think you may have unconsciously hit the nail on the head."

"I don't get it," Small said, somewhat ambiguously. "But I'm glad it works out."

"Look," Clarke told him. "There must, as you suggested, be priorities on those three metals. But they're not only used in manufacturing jewelry—they're needed for making spark plugs for bombers. Each metal, among other things, is also used as a catalytic agent in the manufacture of poison gas. The metals are rarer than gold or platinum. No nation, inimical to the Allies, has any of them. Or not enough, at any rate. Dave, I think this is an international plot!"

"Run by the Nazis?" Small's eyes opened wide.

"Why not? Don't you think they'd stoop to hiring robbers and killers to get what they wanted? The Nazis are plain robbers and murderers themselves. They'd only be in good company by associating with professional killers. That *must* be it, Dave!"

"You forgot two things," Small argued. "First of all, realize that these metals are unusually valuable. Iridium, for instance, is worth about a hundred and ninety dollars an ounce. Rhodium, about one hundred and sixty-five. Palladium is the cheapest, at somewhere around thirty dollars the ounce. That's inducement enough for any band of crooks."

"Perhaps," Clarke agreed. "But you forgot the methods of this gang—and the fact that they use a new and exceptionally powerful and effective explosive. Every safe job would be handled that way if gangland knew of the stuff. What's your other alibi?"

SMALL GRINNED.

"I guess you're right, Bob. Usually, you hit the jack-pot. But this Bovy, he's as French as Paris. Why would he be helping the rats who conquered his own people?"

"You answered that one yourself, 'As French as Paris,' you said. But Paris is no longer France, but Berlin. My idea is that the Nazis picked up some of the best crooks in France—and believe me, some clever ones operated there. They got them to this country with orders to steal—but only palladium, iridium or rhodium. I intend to find out."

"How?" Dave Small asked bluntly.

"By calling upon my lame customer—Bovy. I rather think he'll talk, especially when I inform him I know he was mixed up in the murder of the watchman and the robbery of Devlin's place of business."

"Maybe I ought to go along," Small said hesitantly. "There happens to be more than one monkey tied up in this."

"We've got to keep the store open, Dave," Clarke said slowly. "You'll have to stay. Oh, yes, when Mrs. Squillaciote comes for her husband's medicine, it's wrapped up over there. Charge her seventy cents."

"Seventy cents?" Small cried. "Why, I know what went into that stuff. It's worth about three and a half. I... Okay. Okay, seventy cents. That family is a good customer. They've got seven kids. When they grow up and pay the bill, oh boy, what pennies from heaven!"

"Now"—Clarke grinned—"you're showing sense. You might call Sandy, too. When I get back, perhaps we'll make some plans as to how to outwit this band of crooks, if I can get a lead on them."

Bob Clarke entered his secret laboratory, opened a desk drawer and took out a telephone. It was a direct wire to ex-Commissioner Warrick's home. Warrick was usually on tap, and he needed the former police head's advice now.

"Good to hear from you, Bob," Warrick said when the connection had been made. "Finally got a track on those iridium bandits you've been interested in?"

"They pulled another job," Clarke said, "and included a bit of murder. One of the crooks sprained his ankle and came into my store for treatment. Dave trailed him and I'm paying the gentleman a visit. Mr. Warrick, what do you know about George Devlin, who owns the metal works which was robbed tonight?"

"Devlin? I do know him. He's quite popular. A little gruff at times, but willing to help in any worthy enterprise. Financially, he's okay. Came here from China where he had spent a lot of time. Do you suspect him, Bob?"

"In a case of this kind, I suspect everyone," Bob Clarke answered. "Get me a list of the other robberies if you can, will you? Especially the amounts of each metal stolen. This might turn into something bigger than we expect, so I'll depend on you."

"I'll get it," Warrick answered. "Good luck, Bob."

Robert Clarke put the telephone away, walked over to a triple-mirrored make-up table, and sat down. He applied a disguise that was simple, but highly effective. He parted his hair differently, put on shell-rimmed glasses and made his complexion a trifle ruddier. These things, properly done, altered his appearance to an amazing extent.

He changed into a dark suit, armed himself with a .38 automatic and then, after a final glance at himself, he left the premises through a rear door.

This brought him into an alley and he crossed courtyards, climbed fences and finally reached the street behind the drug store. Bob knew this path like a book. By means of it, he could come and go as he pleased and never be seen.

He was using this back way now because he wanted no one to guess he was on his way to the Hotel Pierpont—making a call as the Crimson Mask.

CHAPTER IV

MASKED VISITOR

WHEN BOB CLARKE reached the Hotel Pierpont, it turned out to be a modest family residence hotel. He got the number of Bovy's room by simply asking a desk clerk for Mr. Bovy's mail, indicating that he was a friend.

The desk clerk looked into Box 732. There was no mail. Clarke thanked him, walked to the elevator and was taken to the seventh floor. He located Room 732, made a trip to the other side of the hotel floor, and when he was satisfied that no one observed him, he returned to Bovy's door.

There he removed the glasses, took a crimson mask from his pocket and adjusted this over his eyes. Pulling down the brim of his hat, he hid the mask fairly well. Then he tapped on the door.

The voice of the man who had been in the drug store answered him. The Crimson Mask mumbled something. Bovy limped across the room and told him to speak clearer. Clarke tried a long shot.

"Monsieur Bovy," he said, "this is the hotel doctor. I am told you injured your foot. It is my duty to treat your injury. Without charge, of course."

The door opened instantly. The Crimson Mask had recognized the avarice in this man when he had been at the drug store.

Bovy saw nothing wrong with the man who stood before him. He couldn't see the crimson mask. He stepped aside and the Crimson Mask walked in.

Bovy closed the door, turned and began blinking slowly and almost stupidly.

"I—do not—comprehend," he said, in fair English.

"You will." The Crimson Mask spoke in French. "Sit down, *Monsieur*. We have certain things in common, you and I."

"But there must be some error," Bovy cried. "That mask—you are a thief!"

"So are you, even though you wear no mask," the Crimson Mask said tartly. "Sit down, *Monsieur* Bovy, or I shall be compelled to knock you down. We shall be frank. I know you took part in a murder and robbery earlier this evening. A robbery I had planned myself, but you beat me to it. Now I want a share in the loot."

"Madness!" Bovy sounded a little weak, although he put on a good act. "This is utter madness. I do not know what you are talking about. I shall call the manager—"

"Go right ahead," the Crimson Mask invited. "Won't he be surprised when I tell him how you sprained your ankle leaving the Paris Metal Plant in such a hurry."

"What do you want?" Bovy asked. "Not that I do not still think you are crazy, but if a few dollars will send you away—"

"Fine. Excellent." The Crimson Mask inclined his head a trifle. "I am interested in about ten thousand dollars. That is half of the loot, I think. Ten thousand dollars, or should I change it to francs and make it sound like more?"

"It is not necessary," Bovy answered stiffly. "I shall call the manager."

He limped over to the telephone, removed the instrument from its cradle and dialed. There was a quick response.

"This is *Monsieur* Bovy," he said. "There is a man who wears a red mask in my room now. He demands ten thousand dollars' blackmail. Yes, blackmail. If I do not pay, he will have me arrested for some robbery and a murder he has dreamed about, apparently."

Bovy hung up and turned around to face the Crimson Mask. Instead of seeing a man ready to flee, the Crimson Mask now smoked a cigarette and smiled quite calmly.

"They are coming right up," Bovy said sternly. "The manager and some detectives. Blackmail me, will you?"

"*Monsieur,*" the Crimson Mask said slowly, "the phone in your room has a direct connection with the outside. It does not go through the switchboard. You didn't phone the manager of the hotel because if you had, it would have been necessary to speak in English. You spoke French. How long will it take before your friends arrive?"

Bovy went a bit mad then. He seized an ash-tray and hurled it. The Crimson Mask was up and out of that chair before Bovy's pass was completed. He ducked beneath the missile, bobbed up close to the French crook and plastered him twice on the jaw.

Bovy dropped instantly. The Crimson Mask bent over, searched him and found nothing except a plentiful supply of cash. He rolled Bovy under the bed, made a hurried exit, and tapped on the door across the hall. There was no answer so he used one of a set of keys on the lock. It didn't fit, but the third key he tried did. The Crimson Mask stepped inside and waited.

In less than ten minutes an immaculately dressed man, carrying a cane, approached Bovy's door and listened outside it a moment. The Crimson Mask observed this by quietly opening the door of the room he had commandeered and peering through the crack.

The caller knocked, got no answer, and hastily fished keys out of his pocket. He selected one which apparently had been furnished by Bovy and unlocked the door. The Crimson Mask heard him gasp, and then the door closed quickly.

The Crimson Mask removed his mask, donned the horn-rimmed glasses again and quietly made his way to another floor. There he took an elevator to the lobby, went outside and posted himself across the street.

Bovy and his sleek friend emerged in a few moments and walked rapidly west. The Crimson Mask followed at a discreet distance and was certain he was not observed, for he was a past master at the art of shadowing.

The two men kept walking until they reached a particularly dark part of town, a section given over to small manufacturing plants, all closed at night The only illumination came from the street lights which were radically dimmed.

The Crimson Mask saw them make a quick turn into an alley. He hesitated a moment. This was going almost too well. His original idea had been to force Bovy's hand, make him call at least one of his allies in this campaign to steal all the iridium, palladium and rhodium possible. That had seemed to work to perfection, but now the Crimson Mask had his doubts. What if that sleek man had brains enough to guess the Crimson Mask's plans and was leading him into a trap?

The Crimson Mask made up his mind. If he stopped now, he might lose track of his only clue. Bovy was bound to change his residence. The Crimson Mask switched the automatic to his side coat pocket, kept his finger curled around the trigger, and resolutely entered the dark alley.

At the far end of it, barely outlined, he could see Bovy and the sleek man talking. The Crimson Mask advanced cautiously. Perhaps they were waiting for someone.

Then he discovered, with a rude shock, that someone was waiting for him. It was Chantel, the brawny killer who came hurtling out of the darkness, his murderous strip of silk ready to be slapped around the Crimson Mask's throat.

There was no time to draw the automatic, not even time to shoot accurately. The Crimson Mask was almost bowled over by the force and speed of the attack. He recovered his balance, lashed out with his one free hand and clipped Chantel across the jaw.

That only served to enrage the killer. He made an attempt to get that bit of silk in place, failed because the Crimson Mask weaved out of his way. Chantel started using his feet. This was an unexpected form of attack, and it sent the Crimson Mask hurtling back with waves of agony shooting through his system.

HE MANAGED to draw the gun. Chantel saw it dimly and stopped. He half crouched and kept maneuvering cautiously. Then he stopped and breathed venomous curses.

The Crimson Mask bit his lower lip. He knew what this meant. Chantel was holding his attention while the other two closed in from behind. The Crimson Mask was trapped unless he put a bullet through this giant of a killer at once.

His finger squeezed trigger. Chantel was hurled back by the force of the slug that ripped through his forearm. The Crimson Mask half turned to face his other attackers, but he was just too late. He felt something prick against the small of his back. It was a sword or knife of some kind and sharp enough to administer excruciating pain. He let go of the automatic and raised his hands.

"All right," he said in French, "I know when I have met better men."

Chantel came forward slowly. His left arm hung limply, but his right was poised for a knockout blow.

"Not too hard, little one," the man standing behind the Crimson Mask warned. "We wish him alive for questioning."

There was no ducking that blow. It was well-aimed and collided with the Crimson Mask's jaw. He fell sideward, hit the wall of the building, then slowly sank to the ground.

They picked him up promptly and carried him down the alley. Chantel ran ahead and in a moment or two drove a cheap sedan to the curb. The Crimson Mask was loaded aboard. Bovy and Aumont jumped in and drove off before an inquisitive patrolman, attracted by the shot, appeared at the mouth of the alley....

An hour later, the Crimson Mask had a somewhat rueful expression on his face. He had been defeated and the fact that it must have taken an inordinately clever man to out-think him rendered no comfort. He gazed at the three men who stood before him. Chantel had crudely dressed his wounded arm and he kept running that bit of silk between his fingers as if he couldn't wait another instant to use it.

Aumont, the sleek one, lit a cigarette and even offered one to the Crimson Mask.

"You are French?" Aumont inquired pleasantly.

The Crimson Mask was not fooled. Aumont was the smartest and most cruel of this trio. The voice seemed friendly, but the eyes were brittle and crafty.

"I do not wish to talk—yet," the Crimson Mask replied in perfect French.

"You have friends then? Whom you hope will rescue you?"

"Perhaps." The Crimson Mask puffed on his cigarette.

"Bien," Chantel snapped. "The more I can garrote. Talk—talk, you wearer of a red mask, or I shall show you how we make people talk in Paris! We found the mask in your pocket."

The Crimson Mask did not reply. He knew none of these men had even heard of the Crimson Mask. That proved they had been in the country only a short time and most certainly had not contacted the local underworld. They worked independently, which made them all the more dangerous.

He looked around and saw that he was in a modest living room. The windows had all shades drawn, but the section seemed to be a quiet one. There was a familiar odor to the place. It smelled like his prescription room. Somewhere in this house was a laboratory of some kind.

"COME NOW," Aumont said, "we are all French here. Perhaps you came on the same mission as we did. The Boche tell us little."

"The Boche," the Crimson Mask half snarled. "Even crooks should be faithful to their own country and not help to sell it into slavery. If you work for the Nazis, I will never talk."

"Ah, but we only seem to work for them," Aumont said suavely. "They pay us handsomely to steal certain things. The articles are naturally worth a lot of money. We turn the loot over to them, yes, but when there is enough, we rob them too. See how easy it is? Now let us have this out, *mon ami.* You must be a thief like us. Otherwise, why the mask? Who are you?"

The Crimson Mask leaned forward.

"I am not at liberty to say, gentlemen, but what you have told me alters the situation. I am—a certain other party, believed you were working closely with the Nazis. If that is not so, there is no reason why we cannot join forces."

"He is wasting time," Chantel growled. "Why should we join someone else anyway? Our profits will only be divided among more and we all get less. I say let me garrote him and get this over with. We have not much time left."

"No!" Aumont waved a hand impatiently. "Our friend interests me greatly. I have a feeling he can help us."

"We should inform *Herr* Shugg," Bovy declared placidly.

Aumont whirled on him, his eyes burning in wrath.

"You were instructed to mention no names, you offshoot of a stupid dog! It is dangerous to mention names. One more word and I shall... Well, use your own judgment, Jean. You are important to us, but not that important. Don't forget it."

Aumont signaled Chantel who moved forward quickly and with an open display of eagerness.

"You will use the silk, Victor. At first gently, until our friend finds he must either talk or die. If he does not talk, increase the pressure until he is dead. Go to work."

CHAPTER V

DEATH'S WINGS BRUSH

C HANTEL'S WOUNDED arm did not seem to bother him much although the Crimson Mask could see that it still bled a little. Chantel advanced closer, the silken cloth ready. Aumont seemed to sense that his prisoner was no ordinary man and he drew the sword out of his cane and held it ready.

"Perhaps," the Crimson Mask said, "I should talk. I am beginning to think that perhaps the three of you are worthy to meet the man I work for."

"Worthy?" Aumont put plenty of sarcasm into that word.

"Yes—just that. You see, Jacques Poncet is in this country."

"Poncet?" the three chorused. Aumont stepped closer. "Are you sure? This is no lie to save your miserable life? Poncet is the greatest crook Paris ever produced. We know he disappeared months ago. If he is here, he could be of inestimable value to us."

"He is here," the Crimson Mask said. "In return for sparing my life, I shall tell you where to find him. Of course, I must have your word that I will not be killed."

"You have it," Aumont declared eagerly. "Poncet is the man for us. We must get him to join us. Chantel—step away. Do you not understand? This man works for Poncet and he is entitled to our respect. Now, where can we find Poncet?"

"At the Alonzo, one of the finest hotels. He is not alone, you understand?"

Aumont winked knowingly. "Poncet has never been known to operate alone. It is a blonde—*oui?* What room, quickly? We need him at once. There is the biggest job of our careers ready and it is ticklish to handle."

"I can't tell you what room nor what name he goes under," the Crimson Mask said. "I meet him in the lobby at seven-ten o'clock in the evening. Always on the dot. You know him, of course?"

"But yes." Aumont showed his elation. "I have seen him. We are not friends, but I would recognize him anywhere. Now we have you to dispose of."

"Me?" the Crimson Mask cried. "I thought I—"

"We do not need you, and neither does Poncet. You see, *mon ami,* if we allowed you to go free, you would tell Poncet how we treated you. That would be fatal, because Poncet is a hot-tempered man. Therefore, we see to it that you disappear... Chantel, that is your job, but it must be done without the garrote cloth. Come here... Jean, watch our prisoner well."

The Crimson Mask's heart sank. He had hoped that fiction about Jacques Poncet would gain him nothing short of freedom. Poncet's name had occurred to him on the spur of a desperate moment. That French crook was without a doubt the wiliest, most dangerous man the sewers of Paris had ever produced. The Crimson Mask's criminal files contained pictures of the man and his complete history. Few others were aware of what he knew—that Jacques Poncet was dead. Even the Nazis had realized he was too clever to be trusted and they had secretly lined him up with other prisoners and shot him down.

Chantel listened to Aumont's instructions and kept nodding eagerly. This man, the Crimson Mask realized, was almost a homicidal maniac. It was just plain luck that many other people than that watchman tonight had not been murdered as these three had performed their robberies.

Chantel took the Crimson Mask's own automatic from his pocket and leveled it. Bovy and Aumont hurried away. For some reason this had to be done quickly. Chantel gave terse orders. The Crimson Mask obeyed because he could do nothing but wait for a break.

HE WAS marched out of the room, gun muzzle snugly fitted into the small of his back. He was forced along a short hallway to a back room. The house, it appeared, was a fairly large bungalow and the section where it was located was a quiet one, for the Crimson Mask heard no sounds at all.

He opened the door at Chantel's direction and stepped into a long, well-fitted laboratory. An experimental lab by the looks of the apparatus and the chemicals. The Crimson Mask sat down on a high stool.

Chantel seemed to know just what he was supposed to do and where things were. He opened a drawer, took out a leather case of hypodermic needles and with gloved hands, inserted one needle into a small brown bottle. The Crimson Mask could see its label. It was a violent poison. Administered directly into the bloodstream it would kill in a matter of seconds.

Chantel held the needle in his right hand, the heavy automatic in the left. His left arm still bled. The Crimson Mask saw that his sleeve was soaked through and glistening with fresh blood. The heavy gun wobbled just a bit. That meant Chantel's damaged muscles were getting tired. Even his immense strength could not control the damage done by the Crimson Mask's bullet.

"We could not talk this over on a business basis?" the Crimson Mask asked.

Greed showed in the French crook's eyes.

"What kind of business, eh?"

"Cash. I have quite a little. Working for Jacques Poncet is always profitable. The money is hidden. I could tell you where to find it if you spared me."

Chantel laid the syringe on the lab bench.

"But of course I am willing to talk business. Where is the money? Tell me and I shall let you go."

The Crimson Mask took a long breath. At least, death was no longer breathing down his neck. If he could stall until Chantel's gun hand became too weak to pull the trigger, he would improve that chance. Chantel was too eagerly engrossed in the prospects of gaining a small fortune to think about transferring the gun to his sound hand.

"I must draw a map," the Crimson Mask explained. "It will not take long. There is a pencil in my pocket and paper before me. With this map you may easily locate my share of profits from Poncet's American enterprises."

"Draw it hurry!" Chantel cried. "We have not much time."

The Crimson Mask slowly extracted the pencil from his pocket, began making a crude map and stopped now and then to reflect and chew on the end of the pencil. His eyes watched the gun in Chantel's wounded hand. It was shaking harder than ever.

Chantel suddenly picked up the hypo and gestured with it. He was getting impatient. The Crimson Mask drew some more. Then he said:

"Tell me—since we are to be friends—what you and the others are after here? How did you reach this country? I must know, otherwise how can I trust you?"

CHANTEL, IN his extreme eagerness, talked.

"The Boche hired us. We were sent here via submarine. Our mission is to steal certain metals which are essential for the war against the Allied Nations. The Boche pay us handsomely because we are such good thieves. That is all there is to it."

"But who pays you? To whom do you deliver the stolen articles?"

"Get on with the map," Chantel growled. "We deal with a man we know as *Herr* Shugg. We never see him except in a dark room or when we are blindfolded, but he pays us every time we deliver."

"And is there a chance for me to join you and pull one big job? You know, Poncet never trifles with anything unless the profits are large."

"There will be a big job soon," Chantel said impatiently. "But the map—it is ready, *oui?*"

"It is ready."

The Crimson Mask shoved the paper across the table. To pick it up, Chantel had to lay down the hypo. This he did and, as his eye flashed to the fake map, the Crimson Mask jumped from the chair.

Chantel tried to raise the gun. Only when his muscles refused to work as rapidly as his brain directed, did he realize that the Crimson Mask had played a trick on him. He did his best to transfer the gun to his right hand, but there was not time and his finger refused to pull the trigger. There was no strength left in it. The gun started to sag.

At that moment the edge of the Crimson Mask's hand struck Chantel's wrist and the gun clattered to the floor. The Crimson Mask kicked it away, ducked a little and bored in, with both fists flying. Chantel made an ineffective attempt to grab the hypo, but the Crimson Mask was fighting for his life and gave him no chance.

Chantel swung his right fist in a long, wide arc calculated to knock the Crimson Mask's head off. It missed, and Chantel was flung half around by the energy he put behind the blow. He turned back and a fist collided with his nose. He became dazed. It seemed to him that this ex-prisoner was possessed of as many limbs as a spider and they were all being employed to deliver shattering punches.

Chantel staggered backward. He got out his strip of silk, but by now his left arm was paralyzed and the silk garrote became useless. The Crimson Mask planted two hard ones to the pit of Chantel's stomach. When he doubled up, the Crimson Mask straightened the man with a haymaker that originated close to the floor. Chantel fell backward and lay still.

The Crimson Mask did not waste any time. He found the box containing hypos and selected an empty one. Then he checked the supply of chemicals, found a narcotic and injected some of it into Chantel's shoulder. That would keep the big man out for hours.

That done, the Crimson Mask rushed to another room and used the telephone. He was dialing when he realized he had not the vaguest idea where he was. So he hurried outside, established the address and then called Dave Small.

"Close up," he ordered quickly. "Take the sedan and drive to Sixty-five Prospect Avenue. I've got one of the French crooks here. I'll tell you what to do when you arrive."

"Shall I bring Sandy?" Small asked. "She's been here since right after you left."

"Have Sandy begin an investigation of the man for whom Jean Bovy works. The owner of that perfume and novelty store. She may not be able to get much at this time of night, but it wouldn't hurt to try. Step on it, Dave."

DAVE SMALL arrived in twenty minutes, pulled up in the driveway beside the house, and they carried out Chantel.

"Take him to the cellar under the drugstore," the Crimson Mask ordered. "I gave him enough morphine to last until dawn. Just before then, give him another shot. He must not wake up or realize where he is. That's your job, Dave. Now get him away from here. I'm going to find out who owns this house and why there is a chemical laboratory here."

In the house, the Crimson Mask replaced the domino mask which he had taken from Chantel's pocket. He also checked his own automatic, then inspected the premises. Apparently, a man lived here alone. The place was neat, the lab expensively supplied. The name on the door was "Otto Renner."

"German," the Crimson Mask grunted. "Maybe he's *Herr* Shugg. At least, he should know something."

The Crimson Mask sat down to wait. It was not long before he heard a key inserted in the front door. A slender man wearing thick glasses came into the room. The Crimson Mask turned on the lights and arose.

"I wouldn't move or shout for help," he said sternly. "Just sit down, Mr. Renner, and we'll talk this over."

Renner's astonishment left him. He obeyed the order and slumped into a chair.

"I thought we had finished with this nonsense," he said flatly. "I still refuse to have anything to do with Nazis."

"Oh, is that so? To whom have you spoken, Renner?"

Renner gave him a peculiar glance.

"How should I know? You are masked. The other man—I was told to call him *Herr* Shugg—talked to me while we were in a pitch-dark room and I was tied to a chair. If my refusal means death—go ahead and shoot. I would rather be dead than helping Nazis."

The Crimson Mask lowered his gun.

"Suppose I'm not a Nazi and, perhaps, on your side."

Renner half arose with ill-restrained eagerness.

"If that is the truth… But no, it is just another trick. One of those psychological things which Heinrich Himmler believes can crack the minds of anyone. First, I am taken away to a place I could never find because I was blindfolded. Then I talk to a man in utter darkness. Now I return home and face a man who wears a red mask. Himmler's terroristic methods may work with some people, but not with me. I have lived in a free country too long. I know the meaning of liberty and happiness. Shoot! I can't stop you, but you will never make me work for Hitler!"

CHAPTER VI

POSSIBLE SUSPECT

IF RENNER was acting, he was superb. The Crimson Mask knew this. He sat on the edge of a table and thrust the gun into his pocket.

"Look, Renner," he said, "I think I know just what happened. They took you away, tried to intimidate you, then released you.

That would be dangerous if they didn't have some scheme to keep you quiet or even join their ranks. Only a few moments ago I was held prisoner here by three men who were in a vast hurry to kill me. Two left. The third—well, he left too, but not of his own volition. I was to be murdered by some of your poison and with one of your hypodermics. The blame would have been thrown upon you. Just how, I'm not sure, but someone will call soon."

Renner blinked owlishly. "Then you—are not against me? You are not a Nazi?"

"I'm an American," the Crimson Mask said. "I wear this mask as a protection. Have you ever heard of the Crimson Mask?"

"Yes—yes. Oh, that is good. I know you will help me. They demand that I use my laboratory to create explosives, poisons. They want to create terror here when they are ready to act. I—"

The doorbell rang. Renner jumped up and before the Crimson Mask could stop him, he had the door open and was delivering a tirade to the amazed man who stood there. The man took one look over Renner's shoulder, whirled, and disappeared into the night. The Crimson Mask uttered a groan.

"That did it," he said. "Renner, you're probably a good scientist, but as an aide to a detective you smell. That man came here to threaten you, to help you locate my body. Now he knows I am not dead. He knows you are still in the clear. That places you in danger and spoils my plans."

"I am—sorry," Renner apologized. "I did not think. I am a fool."

"And that," the Crimson Mask agreed, "is the gospel truth. You pulled such a dumb stunt, Renner, that sometimes I wonder if it wasn't meant to be that way. Perhaps you are smarter than you act."

"I swear it was a mistake!" Renner implored. "I am not used to—to this. My place is in a laboratory where I understand things."

"Well, you'd better get away from here fast," the Crimson Mask warned. "Once *Herr* Shugg's messenger returns with the news, they'll come gunning for you. You know too much. Pack a bag. I'll take you to a hotel where you must lay low. If you don't, Renner, I'll know you're a Nazi, too, and you will be watched. Get going."

Renner threw some things into a valise. The Crimson Mask stripped off his domino. The disguise was still intact. Aumont and his men had never even noticed it.

At the corner he hailed a taxi and rode with Renner to a quiet uptown hotel. He had to risk this. If Renner was *Herr* Shugg, the Crimson Mask was playing right into his hands. But if he was on the level, then Renner's life was being saved. It was worth the gamble.

Later, the taxi dropped the Crimson Mask near a subway station. He paid off the driver, rode downtown in the subway, and then switched to a bus. Finally, he faded into the darkness of the street behind the drugstore. From there he moved fast.

Dave Small and Sandy were waiting for him in the private lab. The store was closed up and darkened. Sandy hurried toward him, though he looked little like Bob Clarke in his disguise. Neither spoke for a moment and he held her closely.

YOUR GORILLA pal is sleeping it off okay," Dave Small said then. "I'll give him a shot in about two hours. Bob—is that all I'll have to do with this case? Playing nursemaid to a Parisian punk?"

"You'll get your fill of the case." Bob Clarke removed the disguise and sank wearily into a chair. "Dave, go through the files and get everything we have on Jacques Poncet. He was a famous Parisian crook who disappeared after the Nazis came. I know he is dead, but you'll make him live again if my memory serves me well."

Small padded away. Sandy curled up in a chair beside Bob Clarke.

"I couldn't do much checking on Vilette," she told him. "He's the man who owns that perfume and silk and goods store where Bovy works. Vilette has been in business there for years, and still has a stock of stuff he got from Paris before the war. He's high-priced, travels in society. Bovy has worked there only about six or seven weeks."

Clarke frowned. "So Vilette mingles in society, does he? That means he comes into contact with men—and the wives of men—

who may hold important government positions. Maybe Vilette is *Herr* Shugg."

"I think he is," Sandy said. "Of course, I haven't the faintest idea of who *Herr* Shugg may be, but I don't like the name anyway. You see, Bob, Vilette has the strangest clientele. His stock is terribly expensive, and yet a small all-night restaurant across from his store reports they see cheaply dressed men, obviously not Americans, going in and out all day long."

"Ah!" Bob Clarke cried. "Now we're getting somewhere." He looked around. "Dave, you have the papers, I see. Before we study them, let me tell you what this case is about. First of all, there are three Paris crooks working for the Nazis. They seem to be specialists in safe cracking and robbery. They steal nothing but palladium, iridium and rhodium. The loot is turned over to a man known as *Herr* Shugg whom nobody has seen—not even the thieves themselves. These rare metals are being piled up for shipment to Berlin where they will help create poison gases or special alloys used in planes, tanks and subs. I mean to see that the Nazis don't get these metals."

"Look," Small said, "we've got one of the French crooks in the cellar. Through him we can locate the other pair and grab 'em. That will end it."

"True, but it won't get us back the stolen metals," Bob Clarke countered. "Neither will it land us this *Herr* Shugg who is much more important than the French crooks who've sold out to Berlin. No, there must be another way."

Dave Small shrugged. "Anything you say, Bob. But when it comes to fighting Nazis, I want to be right in there slugging away."

"Well put." Clarke grinned. "We'll accommodate you. Let me see that dope on Jacques Poncet...."

An hour later, Bob Clarke looked from a full length rogue's gallery picture of Poncet, to his double standing before him in the lab. Dave Small was perfectly disguised.

"Your job will be dangerous," Clarke said. "If those other two crooks ever get wise you're a fake, they'll not hesitate to kill you. I'd do the job myself, but Poncet happens to be just your build. The Nazis have kept the news of his execution a secret."

"I thought I was in on this too," Sandy said.

"You are," Bob Clarke told her. "That's another reason I hate to take such risks. Poncet was famous for the fact that he always kept a blonde around. Said they were good luck. You are the blonde. Put on some frills and plenty of make-up. Both of you speak French well enough to get by, because Poncet was known as a silent man, talking only when necessary and then grunting his orders."

DAVE SMALL began peeling off his clothes and disguise.

"Let me get this straight," he said. "Tomorrow at precisely seven-ten in the evening Sandy and I are to walk through the lobby of the Hotel Alonzo. There the two French crooks will pick us up."

"Right—and from then on both of you are on your own. Remember, the idea is to find out where they meet Shugg. That's most important. Also, where the rare metals are cached, although I doubt anyone but *Herr* Shugg knows that. Run along home now, Sandy, and get some sleep. The same applies to you, Dave. You'll need your wits about you tomorrow."

When he was alone, Clarke glanced at a clock and saw it was almost dawn. Yet he didn't hesitate to phone Warrick on the direct wire. Warrick always stood by when the Crimson Mask operated.

"We're on their trail," Clarke said to the former commissioner, and went into a detailed explanation of the case. Then he added, "Mr. Warrick, I believe that George Devlin, whose place was robbed last, kept an unusually large amount of those rare metals on hand. I want to find out why, and all about his current contracts for work. At the same time, you might also get me the name of the biggest local user of those metals. Can do?"

"Call me tomorrow afternoon at two," Warrick said. "I'll have your information. Watch it, Bob. I've an idea you're dealing with some pretty desperate people."

Bob Clarke laughed. "You should see the sample I've got in my cellar. Talk about Paris sewer rats! This one is a representative example. Thanks—and I'll phone at two."

He hung up, leaned back and lit a cigarette. His mind went over the case, particularly the men involved in it. The French crooks were merely stooges, a means to an end. He was after bigger game.

Otto Renner intrigued him. The German chemist seemed honest about things, but *Herr* Shugg would be a past master at the art of deception. Therefore, Renner remained high on the list of suspects.

Then he considered Vilette, the French merchant who employed Jean Bovy. The man whose customers appeared to be people of moderate means, and whose merchandise would attract only those with wealth. Vilette was due for a thorough check-up.

There was even a possibility that George Devlin could be behind the scheme and have ordered the three French crooks to rob him. Certainly, they had obtained their largest amount of loot at his place.

Bob Clarke snuffed out the cigarette, yawned, and realized he needed rest. There was a couch against the wall and in three minutes he was sound asleep.

The next morning, Clarke opened the drugstore while Small went into the cellar and treated Chantel so he would sleep quietly for several more hours. After a generous breakfast in a nearby restaurant, Bob Clarke returned to the store and donned a single disguise, different from the one he had used the night before.

"You take charge until I get back," he told Small. "Tonight it will be your turn to howl while I stay here and mix cough medicines for the neighborhood kids. You know, Dave, that doesn't sound like so much, but it's as important as running down these Nazi beasts. We save valuable lives here. Did you realize that?"

"So do a lot of other druggists," Small commented dryly. "Only they make a good living at it while you give away half the stuff. Take Mrs. Squilliciote last night. I told her the medicine was seventy-five cents and she told me I was a liar. Seems the doc said the stuff would cost plenty. I had to argue with her, and why? To gyp you out of a couple of dollars. It's not right, Bob."

Clarke grinned. "Mrs. Squilliciote is raising some pretty darned nice kids. They're not old enough to work. Her husband makes barely enough to buy food, and she deserves a break. We'll soak somebody else. She gave you the seventy-five cents, of course?"

Dave Small colored. "Well—yes, and no. A couple of the kids were with her and one of 'em was hollering for some ice-cream. She—er—didn't have the money so I... Oh, doggone it, I told her to spend the seventy-five cents on ice-cream for the whole bunch. I'll pay it myself."

Bob Clarke roared and smacked Small on the back.

"Forget it, you gelatin-hearted tough guy. Seriously though, I'm going to pry into the affairs of Vilette, Otto Renner and George Devlin. Maybe Devlin has nothing to do with this, but I'm playing a hunch. See you this afternoon."

CHAPTER VII

DEVELOPING CLUE

SHIELDED BY his simple disguise, the Crimson Mask first visited the hotel where he had lodged Renner, and discovered that Renner had not left his room. He phoned to make sure and when Renner answered, he mumbled something about a wrong number and hung up.

From there, he proceeded to the rather fashionable section where Vilette had his business. It was a lavish store, hung with expensive draperies and silks. The windows contained rare perfumes and exceptionally well-done wood carvings. In the middle of the larger window was a wooden statue of Joan of Arc holding aloft a flag bearing the Cross of Lorraine. The flag of General DeGaulle and Free France.

The Crimson Mask stood beside that window for half an hour. Twice he saw two different men sidle up to the window, study its contents a moment and then, with a quick look around, enter the place.

The Crimson Mask entered also, almost on the heels of the last man. Jean Bovy came forward to meet him and for a moment the

Crimson Mask almost exclaimed in alarm. Then he recalled that his disguise was different.

"Something I can do for you, *M'sieu?*" Bovy asked.

"Just looking around," the Crimson Mask said. "When I find something interesting, I'll call you."

Bovy bowed and moved away, but he kept his eyes on the Crimson Mask. After fifteen minutes of stalling, the Crimson Mask saw Vilette himself emerge from a back room. Of the men who had entered the store, there was not the slightest sign.

The Crimson Mask made a purchase and left. There was certainly something suspicious about the place. Where had those men gone? Who were they? Obviously not customers.

The Crimson Mask's next stop was at a Government bureau where he posed as a manufacturer of jewelry. An official talked earnestly with him.

"We need all the help we can get, especially that of someone who knows precious metals," he was told. "Give me the address of your plant and no matter how small it is, I'll send a man there to see if you can handle a subcontract at the least."

"Thank you," the Crimson Mask acknowledged. "What about my getting supplies of metals through? Like palladium, iridium and rhodium?"

"You will be given priorities. Enough will be sent so you can carry on. Of course, it is impossible to get those metals in any other way. What do you say?"

"I'll be back." The Crimson Mask shook hands with the man. "First, I want to finish up a couple of small orders, then clean the place so it will pass your inspection. In a couple of days I'll let you know."

He walked slowly away from the building, his mind actively concerned with the fact that it was impossible to obtain such rare metals as those stolen by the gang except by priority. Yet the gang knew just where to go to rob. There was a leak somewhere, but so far, the Crimson Mask could not see how any of his three suspects could possibly acquire such information. It was almost two o'clock and he decided to visit Warrick personally rather than phone.

Theodore Warrick was a slim, gray-haired man with a militarily erect figure. He eyed the visitor who was admitted to his home and showed no sign of recognition.

"I must be improving," the Crimson Mask said, "to fool you."

"Bob!" Warrick ejaculated. "I've been waiting for your call. Come into the study. I'd never have known you and yet—now that I do know—I wonder how on earth I failed to recognize you."

THE CRIMSON MASK grinned.

"It's the simplicity of it, sir. The F.B.I. believes in disguises as practical as this one I wear. No false whiskers or puffed-up cheeks. They aren't necessary. Now, what about George Devlin?"

Warrick sat down.

"Well, as I told you before, Devlin seems to operate a successful and honest business. Since the war he has gone into defense work whole-heartedly. Even to the extent of sacrificing big profits. He makes a particular kind of spark plug out of those rare metals. They are used in a new type of plane."

"Hmm," the Crimson Mask muttered. "Hitler makes poison gas out of them. Now who is the biggest user of those metals here in town?"

"James Morgan and Company. Morgan is an old hand in the business, and I guarantee he is to be trusted. What's it all about, Bob?"

"The use of some vicious Parisian crooks by Hitler to steal rare metals which he needs so badly. It's as easy to explain as that, Warrick. I even know the French crooks—have one a prisoner, in fact—but I don't know the identity of the Nazi agent with whom they deal."

Warrick nodded slowly. "They'll probably pile up all of those rare metals they can get before attempting to ship the stuff abroad. Could be done by contacting an Axis U-boat or even by smuggling the stuff to South America. Bob, we can't allow the Nazis to get that stuff. It might mean the difference between life and death for thousands of our boys. Hitler will make poison gas from it. When he get desperate, he may release the stuff. Without those metals, his efforts will be cut in half. If it comes to a choice between capturing the spy leader or getting the cache of metals, I think you know what to do."

The Crimson Mask did. He thanked the former commissioner and made a quick taxi trip to the firm of James Morgan and Company. This was a plant about twice as big as Devlin's. Morgan proved to be a white-haired old man who listened to the Crimson Mask's reasoning and agreed to help in every way.

"Of course," he said, "you come here and represent yourself as the Crimson Mask. I have no way of knowing whether or not that is the truth, but I am a judge of men, and I believe I can trust you. I've known Devlin for about eight years—ever since he came here from China. I don't think he is involved in any gang of crooks. After all, his own place was looted and his watchman murdered."

"Perhaps"—the Crimson Mask took a new tack—"we might get somewhere by determining just who could have known that Devlin possessed such an amount of the metals. Is the news broadcast throughout the trade, Mr. Morgan?"

Morgan smiled. "Of course it is. We're a tightly-knit bunch, we rare metal workers. In fact, a trade journal we all take announces it whenever someone lands a good contract."

"Like the one you hold now?" the Crimson Mask asked. "I know about it, you see. Devlin bid on that job too, didn't he?"

"Came out second best." Morgan rubbed his hands in glee. "I'll lose money on the deal. Devlin would have, too, even with his higher bid, but I determined to get the job and I did. Now what shall I do to protect my supply of the metals? That's your province, I think."

"Do nothing more than usual," the Crimson Mask said. "I doubt you could keep news of any special protective measures being taken from this gang. They're smart. Meantime, I'll do what I can, and the police will also try to protect you. You've been very helpful, sir. Thanks."

The Crimson Mask went back to the drugstore then and became Bob Clarke. He took care of business while Dave Small altered his identity to fit that of the dead Jacques Poncet, thief extraordinary. Sandy reported shortly before it was time for them to leave, and she had accomplished a good job on herself.

Her soft complexion was roughened. There was just a trace of too much rouge and her lipstick was a shade too red. Her clothes also, were meant to attract attention.

While he worked, Dave Small kept studying a French grammar to refresh his pronunciation and vocabulary.

Clarke came back to wish them luck and, during a moment when the store was empty, he led them through it to the door. They walked out like two customers....

AT PRECISELY seven-ten, Dave Small and Sandy paraded through the lobby of the Hotel Alonzo. Sandy was especially surprised when she saw Aumont. She had expected a rough-looking person with crude manners. Instead, Aumont was the height of fashion and elegance.

"My name," he told Dave, "is André Aumont, late of beloved Paris. I am sure I've seen you somewhere before. The cafés, perhaps? Monte Carlo?"

"I have never seen you before in my life," Small declared bluntly. "Get out of our way."

Aumont showed no embarrassment over the curt dismissal. He merely stepped a little closer and dropped his voice to a whisper.

"But, *mon ami*, surely you have heard of Jacques Poncet?"

Dave Small played the part well. His eyes suddenly became hard, the corners of his mouth drew down. Sandy tugged at his arm as if she wanted to get away quickly.

"It is an unusual name, I suppose," Small said. *"Monsieur* is French, perhaps lonesome in an alien land. I shall be happy to see you at my suite. *Au revoir!"*

Aumont bowed politely and returned to his chair. Sandy and Small saw Jean Bovy waiting there and the pair of them talked rapidly in whispers. Small led the way to the elevators and in a few moments they were safe in the suite which had been rented that morning by telephone.

"Think we can put it over?" Small ran a finger around his collar.

"I hope so," Sandy declared, with a sigh. "Dave, that man is dangerous. Did you see his eyes? They're like the eyes of a snake.

Cold—calculating. I'm more afraid of him than I would be of the toughest American crook."

"You should see the monkey we've got on ice in the drugstore cellar. Think we should contact Bob and tell him how things stand?"

"No," Sandy decided swiftly. "Aumont may have an in, and our telephone could be tapped easily. We'd better just let things happen of their own accord."

CHAPTER VIII

DANGEROUS GAME

AUMONT GAVE them plenty of time. It was nine o'clock before he tapped on the door. Dave Small let him in. Aumont bowed again, especially in Sandy's direction. Then he coolly helped himself to one of Small's cigarettes and sat down.

"I think," he said, "we should understand one another. I worked Paris for all it was worth in my day, but I never hoped to come up to you, *Monsieur* Poncet."

"You know me then?" Small sighed. "I knew it would happen one day. No matter. If I understand you, I have little to fear. That is true? I am not a man to tamper with."

Aumont smiled. "How well I know that. Your reputation was on a par with the greatest criminal France has ever known. Of course, you would be interested in a little proposition?"

Small merely inclined his head. He wanted to speak as little as possible. Sandy sat down across the room, as if this were no affair of hers.

Aumont blew smoke toward the ceiling.

"What do you think of the Nazis?" he asked.

"Accursed pigs," Small said vehemently, and meant those two words.

"Ah, yes. You may be a crooked Frenchmen, but you are a true Frenchman, is that it? What if I told you we might profit handsomely by Nazis who are in this country and need our services?"

"How much is in it?" Small asked promptly.

Aumont laughed. "It is true then? We shall work together. I have need of your services. Especially since one of my own men vanished most mysteriously a short time ago. The odd part is that I left him with one of your men and he has never returned."

Dave Small nodded. "I know. Little escapes me, Aumont. You treated my assistant rather poorly last night. You doublecrossed him too, but let me assure you, when you deal with me or my aides, such stupid tricks will not work. Your man is dead. Mine is alive, and none too friendly toward you."

Aumont flushed. "Oh, come now, it wasn't as serious as that. When your man told me who he was, I became eager to find you. We did not intend to harm him and anyway... Didn't you just say your man won?"

"We always win," Small declared pompously. "Now what is this business? Perhaps I will deal with you, perhaps not."

Aumont drew his chair closer and lit another cigarette from the butt of the first.

"You have undoubtedly read about the robberies of various jewelry manufacturing plants? Of course. I am the man who engineered the robberies. Clever, eh? I work only with two men. One, now that Chantel is dead. You must tell me about that some day. Chantel was strong and smart. At any rate, you could help me undertake several more of these robberies. A certain Nazi agent pays double the market value of the metals and iridium, for instance, is one hundred and ninety dollars an ounce on the market."

"Who is this agent?" Small asked.

Aumont shrugged. "That I cannot say, because I do not even know. I have a certain method of contacting him, and we meet in a darkened room. Will you agree to help?"

"Yes," Small answered slowly, and then set his trap. "However, I must first meet this agent you speak of. And I insist that I direct the scheme once I decide to work with you."

"But that is impossible!"

"Then there is no deal. And remember—you know who I am and you could reveal me to the American police. But I also know you and what you have done. We are stalemate. Good-night, *M'sieu*."

"No—wait!" Aumont held up his hand. "Perhaps I can arrange it. In two hours I will be back. I shall have a final answer then. Think it over, Poncet. There is much money to be made. What do we care if we get it by helping the Nazis? Were our own people kind to us? Every *gendarme* in France sought us. This is a chance for revenge and for profit, too. In two hours, then."

AUMONT LEFT in a great rush. Sandy wrinkled her nose.

"Imagine that! A Frenchman who sells out and commits murder and robbery for the hyenas who overran his own nation and holds her in slavery. Dave, open a window. The room reeks of skunk."

"Yeah"—Dave Small grinned—"and we'll reek of embalming fluid if anything goes wrong. Listen—I'll refuse to take you with me. When we're gone, trail us. Notify Bob where I'm taken and leave the rest to him. Once I get close enough to this *Herr* Shugg, I'll hang onto him plenty tight."

"I wish you didn't have to meet *Herr* Shugg," Sandy mused. "These Nazis aren't fools. I've never underestimated them. They've studied so many crooked angles that they can spot one being worked on them a mile away. But we've got to chance it, Dave. It's the only way to contact Shugg and land him."

Dave Small spent the next two hours alternately pacing the floor and smoking cigarettes chain fashion. He gave a start when the door buzzer sounded. It was Aumont, grinning in delight.

"It is arranged," he said. "You are to come at once. Before morning, we shall be at work. Tonight's profits, *M'sieu*, will be as great as those the night you stole the necklace of that fat viscountess. Your coat and hat. We must not delay."

Sandy quickly drew a fur scarf over her shoulders, picked up her bag and stepped to Small's side. He glared at her.

"This is not for women," he growled. "Stay home and keep quiet until I get back."

She said nothing—just sat down and watched the two of them leave. After a full quarter of an hour, she hurried to the door, made her way to the lobby and sauntered out to the street. There she turned left and headed toward a luncheonette. As she started to enter the place, a man rudely brushed past her and got to the lone telephone booth first. Sandy waited. She saw the man hang up and stepped to the booth to enter the moment he left.

As the door opened, the man faced her with a smile. He spoke, and his French was thick with a German accent.

"*Mademoiselle* wishes to use the telephone, yes? Ah, good, but wouldn't *mademoiselle*, rather accompany my friend and me? It would be a pity to spill the blood of so pretty a woman in such a cheap place as this."

Sandy seemed just as stolid as ever. She started to turn, and the man in the telephone booth stepped out. Suddenly, Sandy whirled and before either he or the stodgy-looking man behind her could act, she was inside the booth with the door shut.

She raised the receiver and watched the pair, wide-eyed. They could only see her head and shoulders. With her free hand she held a lipstick and was rapidly fashioning words on the wall of the phone booth. Then she felt the door pushed in and placed her foot against it.

She found a coin, dropped it into the slot and dialed the number of Bob Clarke's private telephone. One of the men removed his hat, shoved a gun into it and hiding the weapon this way, silently threatened Sandy. She heard the automatic system put through the call. Then she nodded slowly and turned away from the phone. She still clutched that lipstick though and gouged the soft end of it into the space between the telephone hook and the phone. Enough lodged there to keep the hook up.

Then she opened the door. Instantly, both men aligned themselves beside her.

The man who had spoken before nodded and smiled, but his voice was cold.

"You were wise not to speak. Had your lips moved, I would have shot you at once. Prepare to tell us whom you called. Now make no outcry and do not attempt to get away."

Sandy marched between them and felt as if she were being led to a gallows. If they were wise to her, then they knew that Dave Small was a fake, too. They might even know the identity of the Crimson Mask. She shuddered and then winced as the grip on her arm tightened.

As Sandy walked along with those two men, fully conscious that she probably was being led to her death, in a distant part of town a tiny red bulb glowed on and off beneath Bob Clarke's counter in the drugstore. That meant his private phone was ringing. He could not answer quite yet. A doctor was engaged in writing a prescription and giving additional verbal orders.

Clarke knew that Dave Small and Sandy might be in trouble at any moment and they would use that phone to call him and he was on tenterhooks.

He wished there was some way to hurry this physician along.

But he had to listen and it was comforting to notice that the light kept flashing. That meant that whoever was calling was still on the wire. Finally, Clarke got rid of the doctor and sped to his lab. He answered the phone anxiously, received no reply, and began to sweat. He shouted into the phone, for he knew the connection was open.

After what seemed a long time a rough voice answered.

"You just called this number," Clarke said. "What's the matter?"

"I didn't call you, Mister," a man said. "This is the Pickwick Luncheonette on Grand Avenue. The receiver is stuck. Party who dialed your number must have gone away. A girl and two fellows, if I remember."

"Thanks," Bob Clarke said. "Thanks very much."

He hung up, hastily ran to the store and locked up. Then, as quickly, he applied a disguise, shoved a gun and the red mask into his pocket. He left via the front door this time. He had to take risks now, but fortunately no one observed him.

He hailed a cab and had himself driven to the Pickwick Luncheonette. Entering, he went straight to the phone booth and closed the door. He saw the smear of lipstick and knew what Sandy had done. He peered around, lit a match, and spotted a few scrawled words on the wall.

"Dave—me—trapped. Shugg. Aumont."

That was all, but it served to announce that the Crimson Mask's plan had backfired. Then, in horror, he remembered that one of Shugg's men had seen him with Renner and must have guessed that Chantel had been killed or made a prisoner. Yet that alone would not have made Shugg suspicious of Dave Small, in his role of the French crook, Poncet. There was something else.

The Crimson Mask made up his mind swiftly. Nothing could be gained by wasting time waking Chantel up. He would never talk. And Bovy would not be available—that was certain. Clarke had no idea where Aumont lived and, anyhow, that suave French crook was bound to be actively engaged in the kidnaping of Small and Sandy.

Everything rested on the three suspects whom the Crimson Mask had singled out. He dropped a coin into the slot and called the hotel where he had tucked Renner away. Renner did not answer. The Crimson Mask's eyes narrowed.

He phoned the store of Vilette and there was no answer there, either, so he checked through a phone book, located the Frenchman's residence address and, instead of phoning him, decided to go and see the man. He also found out where George Devlin lived and noted this address down.

The Crimson Mask was ready to take action.

CHAPTER IX

THE NARROWING TRAIL

DEPOSITED IN front of an ornate apartment house by his taxi, the Crimson Mask swiftly located Vilette's suite. He took a firmer grip on the gun in his pocket and punched the bell.

Vilette himself answered. He backed away in fear when he saw the masked man. The Crimson Mask stepped inside and kicked the door shut.

"Who else is here with you?" he demanded shortly.

"I am alone. I—I do not know what this means."

"Where is *Herr* Shugg?" the Crimson Mask shot out.

That question brought unexpected results. Vilette staggered to a chair and sat down heavily. He covered his face with his hands.

"It makes no difference what happens to me," he half sobbed. "But the others—you have no right to take reprisals against their people. It is not humane. But who could expect the Boche to act like human beings?"

He stood up defiantly, bracing himself as if he expected the Crimson Mask's gun to blaze.

"I'm no Nazi," the Crimson Mask said. "In fact, I'm hunting one right now and I thought you might help. I am the Crimson Mask."

"*Oui*—I should have known," Vilette cried eagerly. "I thought it was the finish of me and my plans. Many of the men I helped have heard that their sisters and brothers, their wives and sweethearts, their parents, have been executed in revenge."

"Revenge for what?" the Crimson Mask demanded.

"Then you do not know?" Vilette queried. "I—I should not talk. I have no right—"

"This is a free country, and you can say what you please. Listen, Vilette, certain friends of mine happen to be in the hands of a Nazi spy ring. I've got to find them. I came here because I suspected you. Jean Bovy, one of your clerks, is involved with the Nazis."

"Bovy!" Vilette half screamed. "He—there is the black traitor! Bovy! I shall slit his throat! I shall—"

"Stop talking about what you'd like to do," the Crimson Mask ordered. "Tell me about Bovy. Why do you hate him, now that you know he is a traitor?"

"For months now," Vilette said, "I have been helping Frenchmen get into the armies of Free France. Men who escaped from France before the Huns came, and who had reached America. These men want to fight, but they have people over there and the Huns execute the families of any Frenchman who joins DeGaulle. These men have come to me for help. Sometimes I arranged to have food sent to their people. Sometimes I advised them to change their identity and join the forces of Free France. Lately though, some of them have suffered. I knew a spy was in our midst, and now I know it was Bovy!"

"We'll take care of him," the Crimson Mask said grimly. "I guess I can cross you off my list of suspects. Carry on that good work. I'll help if I can."

The Crimson Mask rushed out of the place and removed his mask in the corridor. Vilette's explanation was coldly logical. Those men visited his place of business for help, and got it. Vilette was just a loyal Frenchman.

Now Renner and George Devlin remained. The Crimson Mask was driven to Devlin's place. It was a private home, large and comfortable looking. He hurried to the rear of it and peered into a window. Devlin sat at a desk, apparently busily engaged. That seemed to let him out, for if Devlin was *Herr* Shugg, he would be with Dave and Sandy right now.

THE CRIMSON MASK went to the window of another room, got it open silently, and crawled through. Devlin saw him a moment later as he stood in the doorway, gun in hand, red mask gleaming in the light.

"The Crimson Mask!" Devlin jumped up.

"Sit down and keep your hands on top of the desk," the Crimson Mask ordered. "I can't afford to trust anyone. Not even the man whose robbery I am investigating. I want information, Mr. Devlin, and I want it fast."

"Yes—of course," the man said eagerly. "Anything you say. I—I know you're on the side of law and order. Listen! I've been sitting here thinking. My factory was robbed only of rare metals which are essential to making war. I believe some Nazi plot lies behind it."

"Then your thinking is straight," the Crimson Mask commented. "Who knew you had that amount of iridium and the other metals on hand?"

"Why, lots of people. It was no secret. I had to get a priority to obtain the metal. Others in the same line bid against me. Plenty of people knew about it."

"That's what I was afraid of," the Crimson Mask said. "The loot stolen from your place was almost ten times as large as that taken in any previous haul. Have you been home all night, Mr. Devlin?"

"Yes. Why?"

"Any visitors?"

"Yes. I'm getting more iriduim and I'll be ready to start work soon. My chemist disappeared and a fellow called on me tonight looking for the job."

"His name?"

"Why—I'm not sure." Devlin picked up a piece of paper. "Yes, here it is. Otto Renner. Looked like a good man to me. Obviously German, but he claims to have fled from Germany in fear of his life before the war began. Do you know him?"

"I do," the Crimson Mask said. "But not quite well enough. Thank you. I believe you have helped me tremendously. Good luck with your contract and I hope to land the people responsible for the loss of your indispensable metal."

The Crimson Mask backed out of the room and hurried to the front door. His hand twisted the knob, and his nostrils quivered slightly at a sweetish odor he detected. And the knob was moist.

Outside, the same sweet smell persisted, and his face grew cloudy. He looked back at the house, shrugged, and hurried to a cross street where a taxi would be more apt to roll up than here.

He got one and was driven to the vicinity of Otto Renner's home and laboratory. It was dark. He paid off the driver, went up to the front door and tried it. The door was not locked, but instead of entering, the Crimson Mask quietly released the knob and walked off the porch without making a sound. As silently he moved to the rear of the house.

The back door was locked, but it opened readily when he found the right key among those he carried. There was no chain inside. The door gave way before him and he stepped into the kitchen.

Moving slowly, gun held ready, he crossed the kitchen, went through the dining room, put his back against the wall, and edged toward the hallway door. He could see faint light streaming through the window in the door. Suddenly, that light was blotted out. Someone inside was peering out through the window.

The Crimson Mask felt for the light switch, found it, and snapped on the dining room lights. As they illuminated the hallway, the man at the door spun around. There was a gun in his fist. He was Jean Bovy.

BOVY'S GUN flamed, but as the French traitor pulled trigger, the Crimson Mask was in action. Bovy's slug missed him because the French traitor shot too hurriedly. The Crimson Mask was deliberate about his own shot. Bovy took the slug through the center of his forehead. He was dead before he hit the floor.

The Crimson Mask turned on more lights. He knelt beside the crook and rapidly searched him. In a vest pocket he found a small piece of paper with a phone number written on it. Hurrying into Otto Renner's living room, he sat down at a table and used the phone.

When he had dialed the number on that bit of paper, a man's voice answered. The Crimson Mask spoke in French.

"It is done. Well done, *M'sieu.* The danger is ended."

"Excellent," came the reply. "Most excellent. You know your orders from here on. Get busy."

The Crimson Mask hung up slowly, his gaze on a folded newspaper that lay beside the telephone. It was open to the want ads and someone had encircled one ad with a pencil. It was a notice that a chemist trained in metallurgy was wanted. The ad gave only a box number.

The Crimson Mask stuffed that paper into his pocket, put out the lights and hesitated at the door for a moment. The shots seemed to have been well muffled, and apparently had not alarmed any neighbors.

He recalled that there was a garage at the rear of Renner's place and he ran there. A cheap sedan was installed in the garage. The Crimson Mask got behind the wheel. ...

In the meantime, neither Dave Small nor Sandy Grey were having an easy time, after their kidnaping.

Small, in his disguise of Jacques Poncet, submitted to a blind-fold when Aumont stopped his car on a quiet street. Bob Clarke's assistant tried to determine where they went from there on, but it was impossible. Finally he was led onto a porch and into a house. There was a soft rug on the floor and the odor of an aromatic cigar in the air.

Aumont took him into some room just off the hall and pushed Small down into a chair. The blindfold was whipped off, but for a moment or two he might as well have gone blind. Total darkness met his eyes.

Then a gruff voice spoke. "You are Jacques Poncet?"

"Yes," Small replied simply. "I do not like this mystery. I am used to meeting men face to face."

"In due time," the man in the dark said. "You are noted as one of the most clever crooks ever developed in Paris. Perhaps you are so clever you can tell us how you escaped a German firing squad on the morning of September twelfth, Nineteen Forty-one?"

Dave Small started to arise, but felt the prick of a blade against the back of his neck, and heard Aumont laughing softly. The man in the darkness spoke again, triumphantly.

"Perhaps you are a ghost, *Monsieur* Poncet. Who knows? But ghost or not, you failed to trap me by trusting in the fact that I must be quite isolated from my own nation here in America. The fact is, I have a short-wave radio. By a series of transmissions that have never been traced, I can communicate with German officials in Paris. Naturally, I checked on you—and I find you are dead. What is the explanation?"

"You admitted I am a clever man," Dave Small countered. "Must I go into explanations? I might need to escape in a like manner some other time."

NO ANSWER came to that. Minutes crawled past and no one spoke. But that needle-pointed blade at Small's back had a language all its own. Then he heard a door open, heard a feminine voice cry out, and he slumped deeper in his chair. Sandy!

He and Sandy had walked into a trap. One which even the Crimson Mask could not have foreseen. *Herr* Shugg checked everyone, and possessed a means of communication with the Nazis in Paris. Aumont had known, when he had come to escort him here, that Dave Small was a colossal fake.

The lights were turned on. Small blinked, and looked for *Herr* Shugg, but there was no one in the room except Aumont who held his sword cane ready for action. Then Sandy was brought in. She shrieked imprecations in French.

"It's no use," Small told her dully. "They've got us cold."

Two other men were in the room now. Their sullen faces and manners branded them as Nazis. Aumont stepped in front of Small and Sandy.

"I wish Chantel was here to make you talk," he said. "Myself, I cannot stand blood. Anyway, there is no time. It is my opinion that you are agents of the Crimson Mask. I did not know of him until *Herr* Shugg explained. I nearly made a fool of myself. Now we are all going on a little trip. Perhaps you wish to know where?"

"It might be interesting," Dave Small answered, with a slight shrug.

Aumont waved the sword. "Of course. We are all going to rob a certain safe of more iridium, rhodium, and—I hope—a quantity of palladium. But we shall be most unfortunate after the robbery is complete. Some of us will be caught. Trapped by armed guards with orders to shoot quickly. It will be too bad—the headache the police will get when they try to determine who you are, and how you came to be mixed up in this. But they are paid for such head-aches. Are you ready?"

Dave Small grasped the arms of his chair, prepared to leap at Aumont, sword or no sword. He never got the chance. The two Nazis moved rapidly beside him and he was hauled out of the chair and his wrists tied behind his back. Sandy was also bound.

Aumont flipped Small's throat with his cane.

"You are, of course, the Crimson Mask. The girl is your accom-plice. I accused you of being the Crimson Mask's aide, but you did not respond, so I know you are that one himself. Very nice. Now if you make a sound or wriggle in any way, this little blade of mine will be thrust through the throat of the girl. Remember, if you try anything, she dies."

Sandy still clutched her purse in one fettered hand. She managed to get it open, reach inside and take out a tiny vial of perfume. She got the stopper off and as they led her toward the door, she turned the vial upside down in her palm.

On the way out she suddenly swayed and fell against the door. Her fingers closed around the knob for a second, then they dragged her away. A car waited outside. Both Small and Sandy were forced into the rear. No attempt was made to blindfold them this time, but neither of them recognized the neighborhood, nor placed the house in which they had been trapped.

CHAPTER X

THE TRAITOR

O NCE MORE the car in which the kidnaped pair rode, stopped, this time deep in a dark alley. But as they turned down this, Dave Small caught a glimpse of a sign on the building adjoining the alley. Here was the factory of James Morgan and Company, metal workers. Aumont was going to rob it and try to plant the blame on Small and Sandy.

Gags of adhesive tape were quickly applied, then they were led into the building across the alley. On the top floor, Aumont prodded Dave Small with the point of his sword cane and forced him to climb a ladder to the roof.

Between buildings, one of the Nazi agents had already created a shaky bridge of a wooden plank. Sandy crossed it first with Small coming up shortly. Now Aumont went ahead while the two Huns guarded the prisoners who saw Aumont seize a loose end of tar paper with which the roof was covered. He drew this away, grasped a bit of cord and raised what seemed to be a newly fashioned trapdoor in the roof.

Aumont removed his shoes, dropped through the trap and was gone for ten minutes before things started popping. They were announced by three quick shots that came unexpectedly. One of the Germans rushed over to the hole in the roof and dropped flat, to reach down and grasp Aumont's wrists. He hauled the treacherous Frenchman out.

The second Nazi forced Dave Small and Sandy toward the still open trapdoor. They could hear a steady pounding as if someone were trying to crash into the room below. Aumont had a thick piece of cloth into which the loot had been dumped. He could hardly lift the bundle and hastily made three portions of it. As he worked, the two Nazis hastily bound the arms and legs of Small and Sandy.

Then Aumont's sword cane flashed again. He grabbed Sandy roughly and pushed her through the trap. Small was similarly treated and he landed on the floor beside Sandy. One of the Nazis dropped down to pick up Sandy and toss her on an old couch, but before he could reach the ladder to the trap again, it closed, and all three of them were in darkness.

The door of this room was being rapidly demolished. Sandy and Dave Small, gagged and tied as they were, could do nothing; could not make a sound. And they knew that in a moment the guards outside that door would break in and start shooting.

The door gave way, but for an instant no one came through it. The trap was lifted slightly, and through it a gun barked twice. Bullets smashed into the door, but there were no answering shots. Then the trap slammed down, and footsteps were scampering over the roof-top.

A flashlight cut the darkness then, as someone came in through the smashed door—not the expected guard, but instead the Crimson Mask was peering down at Small and Sandy as they were revealed in its beam. They knew him at once, though he wore no mask, for both of them had seen him in this particular disguise before.

The Crimson Mask leaped to Sandy, as she lay on her side on the old couch. His gun was in his right hand as he drew out a penknife with his left, laying his flashlight down on the couch.

"So I've got you!" That was the growling voice of the Nazi who had had no opportunity to escape. Another flashlight gleamed— one in the hand of the Nazi—full on the Crimson Mask and Sandy. "Now you all die!"

In the flashlight's beam the Crimson Mask caught a glimpse of a Nazi ring on a finger of the hand in which the man held a Luger.

Instantly the Crimson Mask's automatic roared. The Nazi's gun roared, also, but sent its bullet up into the air as the man died from a bullet in his heart.

THE CRIMSON MASK worked swiftly then. Leaving the dead Nazi where he lay, he freed Dave Small and Sandy, ripping the tape from their lips, and within a few minutes all three of them were in Renner's sedan which the Crimson Mask had commandeered. He talked as he drove.

"We're going after Shugg," he said. "I'm mighty sorry about what happened to you two. Shugg got wise to you, eh?"

"He checked by short-wave radio with Paris and found out that Poncet was dead," Dave Small explained. "That tore it."

"They took me to some house—I don't know where." Sandy clung to the Crimson Mask's arm. "I was blindfolded. Dave was there—I could hear his voice. And, Bob, I thought it was really the end."

"Then maybe there were three minds with that same thought," the Crimson Mask said. "Shugg set a trap for me, too—with Bovy ready to shoot me down. I got him. In his pocket was a telephone number which I called, and Shugg answered. Then I looked closer at the piece of paper and saw that it had been torn off some business stationery of James Morgan and Company.

"And that's when I guessed the robbery was all but completed already. So I went to the Morgan place as fast as I could get there, to be in on the finish of the robbery. I got in—no matter how, though maybe you can guess—and was prowling when I heard a thump in that room next to the roof. I had a hunch what that was, so big a hunch that I didn't wait for anything, but got busy bursting the door down, and—"

"Lucky it was you," Small said. "They planned to take the loot which was ready for them in that room, then to arouse the guards and, as they broke in, to fire at them. The guards would have shot back, naturally, and their targets would have been Sandy and I."

The Crimson Mask chuckled. "I'm sorry about those guards. Had to slug 'em, but this was an emergency, and I may have saved their lives, at that. Now you two stay in the car. I'll be back shortly."

The Crimson Mask who had stopped the car, walked straight toward a big house. Inside it, Aumont was piling up the small ingots of rare metal and gloating proudly. George Devlin nodded in full approval of the loot.

"Bovy called and said the Crimson Mask was dead," Devlin told Aumont. "You took care of his aides, so that is that. Our haul makes the cache big enough to send abroad and I will signal for a submarine to meet a certain fishing boat. Possibly, now that this mission is complete, I shall receive further orders. I hope to begin active sabotage. We shall have no more trouble with Renner, because he is safely dead in the loft of his garage."

"If there is money in it for me," Aumont said airily, "I am willing to blow up the City Hall."

"And if your face was a little darker, a little coarser, and looked more like that of a braying donkey, I would be willing to call you Laval instead of Aumont," a voice said.

Devlin jumped up and reached for a gun. He never even touched it. A bullet plowed through him, high in the shoulder and he dropped, writhing in pain.

Aumont's sword flashed. His face was as white as paper.

The man facing him wore a crimson mask and the smoking gun he held threatened Aumont. The French traitor looked into those eyes glittering through the mask. He shuddered, slowly released the sword and raised his hands. He tried to move, but his knees trembled and he lost all control of his legs.

The Crimson Mask kept him covered.

"**WHERE IS** the other Nazi who got away with you?" he demanded.

"He—he is not here. Give me a chance. I will expose the whole thing. I will—"

"You'd sell out to Satan's lowest imp," the Crimson Mask said, and picked up the telephone.

"Hello—listen closely," he said, when somebody answered. "This is the Crimson Mask. Go to the home of George Devlin. You will find him and a French alien waiting for you. Devlin is no American. He's a Nazi, sent here long ago in preparation for the day Hitler knew we would be at war. He went into the jewelry manufacturing business to get gold and other rare metals legally. These were shipped to Hitler.

"Since the war, those metals have been needed more than ever. So Devlin stole them. He even went so far as to bid on Government contracts requiring the use of the metals he wanted. He bid far below any reasonable price, got the contract and priorities for the metals. When the metals were delivered, he had himself robbed.

"Tonight he burglarized James Morgan and Company who just had a delivery of several pounds of the metal. You'll find it in Devlin's house and also the rest he stole these last few weeks.

"You might also notify all police to watch out for a big, brutal-looking man who answers to the name of Victor Chantel. He's dangerous but when your men find him, he'll be sleeping on a park bench. He's a murderer and an associate of Devlin's. Oh, yes. At the home of Otto Renner, you'll find another man—dead. I killed him in self-defense. Renner is also dead, hidden in the loft above the garage, a victim of the Nazis he refused to aid."

The Crimson Mask hung up, slowly put his gun away and then leaped at Aumont. The fight lasted about one minute and Aumont went to the floor, his suave features swelling all out of shape. The Crimson Mask hit him with the butt of his gun for luck and repeated this treatment on Devlin. Then he went back to where Dave Small and Sandy waited in Renner's car. They stayed there long enough to see police cars drive up.

"Sure it was Devlin," the Crimson Mask told them. "He came from Germany via China years ago. Sandy, I smelled the perfume you managed to smear on the door of his house when I visited him, but even before that I was sure Devlin was our man. He could keep track of deliveries of the metal, get priorities to obtain fairly large quantities of it himself. Aumont, Bovy and Chantel were sent here to help him so there wouldn't be the slightest suspicion that Nazi agents were involved if anything happened. I imagined Devlin's orders were strict on that score. Hitler wouldn't want us to know he was starved for those metals.

"Devlin tried to pin the blame onto Otto Renner because he was a perfect stooge. When Renner disappeared under my orders, Devlin ferreted him out by inserting an ad for a chemist of Renner's type in every newspaper. He knew Renner needed work and would respond. When he did, Devlin killed him.

"Aumont helped to throw suspicion on Vilette, too, with the aid of Bovy. Vilette happens to be just as patriotic a Frenchman as Aumont is a traitor. Now let's go back, give Chantel another shot and lay him on a park bench. The cops will know what to do with him."

"And then?" Sandy asked.

"I think," the Crimson Mask said, "I'd like to sit in the park, too. With you, Sandy. I feel the need of fresh, clean air. Contact with traitors like Aumont and murdering Nazis like Devlin, fouls your lungs. Also it's warm. The park is dimmed-out and—"

"And we haven't had a date in days," Sandy said, smiling.

Dave Small touched the Crimson Mask's shoulder.

"Stop the car and let me get into the front seat and drive," he said. "Good gosh, I don't have to watch you two make love, do I?"

FIVE CLUES TO MURDER

MINOR VICTIM

THERE WAS light enough to see by, but not much more. The grass beside the highway was still heavily covered with dew and the sun gave promise of becoming uncomfortably hot before long.

The highway ran alongside a large farm. In the fields a man was applying a hoe to a row of vegetables. The farmers were at work earlier than ever these days, trying to perform an impossible task of feeding millions with a serious shortage of help—and doing it too.

Coming along that lonesome ribbon of concrete was a solitary small figure. At first glance it was impossible to determine just what manner of man this was. He seemed to be half smothered in the clothes he wore. A closer look would have revealed the thin face of a boy no more than ten or eleven years old.

The trousers he wore were men's, with the cuffs rolled up into a bulky mass. The shirt looked as if it had been created for a giant. The coat was ragged, dirty, and the shoes flopped with each step and threatened to fall completely off the boy's feet. He had to shuffle along to keep them on.

His face was a mixture of eagerness and terror. He kept looking over his shoulder nervously. The farmer in the field attracted his attention for a moment and he slowed up, as if to approach him. He changed his mind apparently, for he continued to shuffle along.

The boy tenderly rubbed a small, lean jaw that was swollen and discolored. Another mark across his forehead could have been made by some kind of club. His hair was matted, his hands dirty, but there was sheer determination in every move he made.

The Crimson Mask's hand wrenched the gun from the crook's grasp in a flash

He heard the distant purr of a car and turned quickly. His eyes lighted up and that seemed to change his whole face. He became a boy again, not a little old man. He moved to the side of the road and stood there waiting for the car to approach. He raised his arm and moved a small thumb in a familiar gesture.

The car slowed too, but only for a short distance. There were four men in it.

The driver muttered an imprecation. From the back seat an overfed hulk of a man who seemed to be in charge leaned forward and squinted against the rising sun. His cheeks were inflated and his shoe-button eyes seemed drowned in flesh. His thick, fat lips were curved in a sardonic grimace at the moment as he stared ahead, a grimace that showed a row of uneven yellow teeth.

"There he is, the little rat!" he growled. "Hinch, fix him up good, you hear me? I mean good."

The driver hunched over the wheel.

"Okay, Kraus, I'll fix him all right. Hang on! This is going to be good."

THE DRIVER pressed his foot down hard on the accelerator. The heavy car shot forward in a sudden burst. The boy, almost off the road, saw it suddenly veer toward him. A grown person might have realized what that meant in time to leap out of the way. The boy just stood there, fascinated.

The car hit him with a crunching sound. The boy's body was thrown into the air, a distance of about twenty feet, and it came down on a pile of brush. He lay sprawled across this, motionless.

The car came to a stop with screeching brakes. It backed up. The man Kraus, who had given the orders for this crime, got out and ran to where the boy lay. He turned him over on his back, looked at two glazed eyes. Roughly he thrust a hand over the victim's heart and left it there a few seconds. He was preparing to carry the boy away when a shrill hail from the farmer made him rush back to the car alone.

"Let's get away from here!" he said roughly. "The kid is dead as a door nail. Smashed up plenty around the face too."

"Step on it!" one of the others warned. "Some hayseed in the field saw it. He's coming over. Maybe I ought to give him a few slugs, huh, Kraus?"

"No," Kraus snapped. "The way it looks now the kid was hit by some hit-and-run guy. If we plug the hick, the cops will figure there is another angle. Hinch, will you get this crate going?"

The car shot away and rapidly disappeared into the distance. The farmer broke into a run. He had seen the boy struck and was certain the man who got out of the car had not picked the boy up.

The farmer found the victim quickly enough, and gasped in horror. He knelt beside the boy and raised his head gently. Like Kraus, the farmer was pretty sure the boy was dead, but he took more time to be certain of this and he discovered a heartbeat.

He picked the boy up, cradled him in his aims, and started running toward the farmhouse.

His wife took over there while the farmer got on the phone and called the police.

"They're sending an ambulance from the city," he said when he hung up.

"Thank heaven, we're not so far out. How is he, Martha?"

His wife shook her head slowly.

"He's unconscious. I don't know—not so good, I'd say. Takes a lot to kill a boy like this though."

The farmer mopped his face with a huge red handkerchief.

"Now who'd want to kill a nice little kid like him?" he wondered. "I saw it happen. When the boy first attracted my attention I thought he might be one of the kids sent from the city to work on the farms. But his hands are smooth—too smooth to have done that kind of work."

"Richard," his wife chided, "this boy isn't any more than ten years old. Half starved, by the looks of him. Did you get the number of the car?"

"No. It got away too darned fast. Like I said, the boy was deliberately run down. Do what you can. I'll go out to the road and make sure the ambulance doesn't pass the house."

Martha was right about the vitality of a small boy. The doctor who came with the ambulance made a quick examination, didn't wait for a stretcher to be brought in, but carried the boy out to the ambulance.

"Got to work fast," he told the farmer. "He's pretty bad. Looks like a skull fracture, among a lot of other things. Tell your story to the police when they arrive."

The ambulance turned around, opened its siren, despite regulations to the contrary, and burned up the road back to the city. The run to the hospital was more than half an hour and would have been longer except that traffic obligingly opened its ranks for the swift white vehicle.

AT CITY HOSPITAL capable hands took over. It was noon before the boy was wheeled out of the operating room. His face was completely swathed in bandages except for the closed eyes and the small, blue-lipped mouth.

The surgeon in charge motioned to a slim, blond girl who wore the uniform of a nurse's aide.

"Miss Grey," he said, "you'll have to sit beside him. Take his pulse every ten minutes. If it becomes thready, send for me at once. You can handle this. I've seen you work and we're so terribly short of trained nurses—"

"I'll handle it, Doctor," Sandra Grey said. "Poor kid. Do you think there is much danger?"

"Yes, I'm afraid so. We repaired a fracture of his skull and mended a broken arm. There were contusions all over his body. Between you and me, Miss Grey, the boy didn't get all those contusions from being struck by a car. Some were much older than the fresh ones he got today."

Sandra Grey's blue eyes became cold and extra shiny.

"You don't mean he was beaten? A boy like this?"

"That's what I mean. After you've been in this work a little longer, you'll find there are some people who will never die of heart disease. They can't get that illness because they don't have hearts—nor brains that are human and kind. Remember—let me know if he wakes up or if his pulse gets weaker or more unsteady."

Sandra Grey, more usually called "Sandy" by those who knew her best, quietly sat a chair beside the head of the bed and took the boy's pulse. It was fairly good.

She sat there for two hours watching those eyelids of the boy. They flickered a bit. His lips moved. He was trying to say something.

No words came and the eyes did not open. He was still affected by the anesthetic. Sandy made him more comfortable, examined his pulse again and found it a trifle stronger. There was but little fever.

Then the eyes opened. The boy moved and whimpered. His left arm was in a cast, but he tried to move it anyway. His right arm came up, fighting the bed covers.

He spoke fragments of sentences. Sandy listened intently.

"No—no, leave me alone. Please—don't—no! No, I won't be still. I will—I will run away again. I will, too! Wait—and see. No—don't—don't hit me—"

Sandy said something a trifle unladylike under her breath.

The boy tried to sit up and she had to exert considerable pressure to keep him quiet. He kept talking, uttering those hardly understandable fragments, and it was clear that in his delirium the past reached his mind and made him frightened. He twitched and tossed. Finally, he became quiet and lay back, exhausted.

It was another hour before he opened his eyes again. This time they were clear and alert, although there was something vague about them, too. Sandy smiled at him.

"Don't be afraid," she said soothingly. "You're all right, son. Nobody here is going to hurt you."

"Where—am I?" the boy asked.

"In a hospital. You were hit by a car. Don't you remember?"

"I don't remember anything," he said weakly. "Who are you?"

"Just consider me your friend. Let me ask you just one question and then you must be very quiet. What's your name?"

"I don't know," the boy answered with the open honesty of his youth. "I can't remember—"

Sandy gave him a few sips of water and made him remain silent. The boy kept looking at her. Finally his right hand came from beneath the covers. Sandy took it gently. The boy smiled and went to sleep. Sandy sat there, holding his hand, until she thought her back would crack.

LATE IN the afternoon he awoke again. He seemed to be a bit stronger and the surgeon was satisfied that there was no immediate danger.

"He'll do," he told Sandy. "Tomorrow we'll move him into the children's ward. I don't like to, but we don't know who he is or who can be financially responsible for him. Hospital rules, you know."

"Yes, Doctor," Sandy said. "I've talked with him a bit. He can't remember his name. How can we reach his people?"

The doctor whistled softly and bent over the boy. He asked him a few questions and drew only that stock answer— "I don't remember."

"Amnesia." The doctor frowned. "No question about it. He's old enough to have an active memory. The skull fracture, of course. This condition may persist indefinitely."

Sandy smiled at the boy. "We'll try to bring that memory back. Meantime you must have a name, son. How'd you like to be called Jimmy?"

The window smashed as the crack of a gun sounded,
and the man straightened up with a shrill cry

"Sure." The boy managed a smile. "I like Jimmy. I like you, too. You're my nurse and you won't leave me, will you?"

"Not on your life," Sandy declared stoutly. "Doctor, is it all right if I try to help him think back?"

"Yes, of course. Might do some good, in fact. He's your patient, Miss Grey. Until tomorrow, at least. Call me if he begins remembering things."

Sandy went to work then. She questioned the boy over and over again. It was no use. He remembered the car, walking along the road and—

"There were a lot of mice," he told her. "They squealed. You know."

"Mice that squealed?" Sandy asked. "Oh, yes, of course. Were they in a barn? Did you come from a barn?"

"I don't know," the boy answered.

He went to sleep shortly afterward. Sandy called another nurse's aide to relieve her and she walked slowly to the elevators. One took her to the basement of the hospital and she made her way along a corridor marked with an arrow and a sign:

PHARMACY

CHAPTER II

SERENADE

A MAN, HARD at work in the pharmaceutical lab of the hospital, was a clean-cut man of average height and build, with clear eyes, a firm chin and he had strong, capable hands.

His name was Robert Clarke and he had a Ph.G. after his name.

He owned a drug store, too. A rather odd place for it he had selected, too, for Robert Clarke could have established himself in a far better section of the city, behind the flamboyant glitter of a modern pharmacy. Instead, he preferred one of the poorest sections of the metropolis and a much smaller, most sedate store. Here he sold drugs and medical supplies only. That is, he sold some. He gave away plenty to needy folks in the neighborhood. In some cases he was paid in due time, but whether he was or not, always he remained happy.

With the war he had offered his services gratis to this hospital because there was an acute shortage of pharmacists. Sandra Grey, one of his three closest friends, had followed him into the hospital as a nurse's aide. Bob Clarke's drug store was still open, and now in charge of apple-cheeked Dave Small, always cheerful assistant to Bob Clarke and another of the three nearest friends who shared Clarke's complete confidence.

Sandy slid onto one of the high stools at the lab bench. Clarke swung around to face her.

"Something wrong?" he asked.

"I don't know, Bob," she said soberly. "I think so. It may seem trivial, but you could help."

"Me?" Clarke raised a graduate to eye level and measured out a quantity of a brown fluid. "Or the Crimson Mask?"

"Both, probably. Bob, you've fought criminals for years now. Your father fought them, too, before he was murdered. Ever since, you've been involved in an almost endless battle against murderers, thieves, cheats and even enemy agents. Always the cases have been important ones. This one isn't. At least it doesn't seem so on the surface."

Bob filled a medicine bottle, corked it and applied a label. He called an orderly and sent the medicine upstairs. Then he closed and locked the lab door.

"Let's have it, Sandy," he said then.

She smiled faintly. "It really seems so—so terribly small. Bob, it's a boy who was brought in early this morning. He was hit by a car and nearly killed. The doctor tells me there were marks on his body which indicated he had been beaten before the accident. Now he's lost his memory. Amnesia."

"And just where do I come in?" Bob Clarke asked. "Me, and the Crimson Mask?"

"I want you to find out who the boy is," Sandra said. "Where he belongs. Bob, don't you see, his parents must be frantic? There wasn't a thing on him to help identify the boy."

"Look, Sandy," Clarke said, "if the boy had been beaten, his parents won't be weeping their eyes out for him. He's better off here."

Sandy shook her head slowly. "You haven't seen him. He's so thin—half-starved, I'll bet. But, Bob, the boy is intelligent and brave. He's not just an average kid from some slum area. I know. I can tell, and I'm just as sure it wasn't his parents who beat him. Won't you go up and talk with him?"

"If you want me to," Clarke answered, "of course, I will. Let me warn you, though, that I can't see anything about the case which would make me drop all this important hospital work. If it is amnesia, the boy will come out of it and tell the whole story sooner or later."

"Sooner or later." Sandy's voice was faintly derisive. "Bob, think how his parents must feel meanwhile. Please—let's go up right now."

CLARKE NODDED, arose, and unlocked the door. They went to the elevator and were soon walking toward the boy's private room.

"They're going to move him into a ward tomorrow," Sandy said. "I wish they wouldn't."

Bob Clarke made no comment. He entered the room and a few minutes later the boy opened his eyes. They rested first on Clarke and the boy gave a whimpering cry and tried to hide behind the covers.

Sandy quickly comforted him. "Jimmy, this is a friend of mine. Are you afraid of all men?"

"I don't like them," the boy exclaimed. "They hurt me!"

"I'm not going to hurt you," Clarke said gently. "I want to help you. Think hard now. You have a name. You must remember it."

"I don't remember anything except the mice that squealed. There were millions of 'em. They squealed like anything."

Clarke sat down beside the bed and patiently went to work on the boy. After ten minutes he gave up. It was clear the boy's memory went back just so far and then stopped abruptly.

Gradually, however, Bob Clarke did draw some meager results and they were astonishing. The boy was willing to answer questions so far as he could recall things, but almost everything was filmed with the haze of a faulty memory.

"There was music, too. A great big orchestra played 'Serenade.'"

" 'Serenade'?" Clarke said, surprised. "You mean Schubert's?"

"Yes. It goes like this."

From beneath the bandages that covered his whole face, came a muffled whistle. Schubert's "Serenade," rendered somewhat off key, but the melody was there and even some of the tricky arrangements.

Bob Clarke looked at Sandy. "You're right about him. He's no ordinary kid. He knows music—the best. He's had darned good musical training for his age. He must come of a good family."

"I told you so," Sandy declared.

"What about this music?" Clarke asked the boy. "Where did it come from?"

"I don't know," he answered. "I couldn't see anything. I think I was blind. I just heard the music when the car stopped."

Clarke edged his chair closer. "Let's talk about the squealing mice first. Now you were blind. Okay—but you could smell just as you could hear. What did it smell like when you heard the mice? Like fresh hay? Or was there a lot of smoke? Or—"

"Gasoline!" the boy broke in quickly, as if the thought had entered his brain and he spoke before he lost it.

"Squealing mice and gasoline." Clarke frowned. "Now the music. What about that?"

"Just music. Just Schubert's 'Serenade' is all. I was awful hungry and I got hungrier while the music played."

Bob Clarke's eyes narrowed. There was much more to this than appeared on the surface. A ten-year-old boy. For Clarke's money the boy had been blindfolded. That was what had made him think he was blind.

"You're doing very well," Clarke encouraged. "Now what else? The last thing you heard was the mice, then the music. Before that there must have been something else."

"Boat," the boy said promptly. "It whistled.

"How long did the boat whistle before you heard the music?"

"I don't remember. Not very long, I think. And there was a ghost that screamed. That was in between the boat whistle and the music. The boat whistle happened right after we left."

Clarke blinked in sheer amazement. "A ghost that screamed? How do you know it was a ghost?"

"Because it scared the men. It scared me, too. It sounded like a ghost. We were in a house, I think."

BOB CLARKE wrote down this sequence of events and turned to Sandy.

"This boy was taken in a car," he said. "That's clear. He doesn't remember from where nor what his destination turned out to be—if there was any other destination besides this hospital. First, he heard a boat whistle soon after a ghost that screamed. Those two ideas sound wild, but they aren't. There is an explanation of them somewhere. Then he heard Schubert's 'Serenade' and finally a million squealing mice associated with the smell of gasoline."

"Bob," Sandy said, "you're going to try and help him—us?"

"Yes. How could I refuse? Maybe it will all turn out much worse than we expect. For the boy, I mean. But he does come of a good family, good people who like music, and have trained the boy to like it, too. The punishment inflicted on him was not done by his parents, or whoever brought him up. People who like that kind of music aren't the type. Keep talking to him. See if he can remember any other little details, no matter how crazy they may seem. I'll talk to the doctor, then see if I can check back."

Clarke arose. The boy's eyes smiled, deep beneath the layers of bandage.

"You're a pretty good guy," the boy said.

Clarke grinned. "You're not so bad yourself, old-timer. I'll call you Jimmy, too—okay? Good. Just one more thing. Lately you've been afraid of men because they hurt you, made you cry—"

"I didn't cry," Jimmy said promptly. "I wouldn't cry."

"Great. Think carefully now. Have you always been afraid of people? Did someone always hurt you?"

"I—don't remember," Jimmy answered weakly. "I don't think so. I—"

"He's tired," Sandy said. "Let him rest. Bob, I hate to drag you into this. It may be nothing at all."

Clarke looked down at the helpless figure under the bed covers. His face was grim.

"Somebody," he said softly, "hurt that boy terribly. The auto accident didn't give him amnesia or he wouldn't remember anything beyond that point. He was so badly punished that he lost his memory before, but since it happened, he remembers a few things. Take good care of him."

Bob Clarke walked out of the room and proceeded to the surgeon's office. It did seem odd to become so interested in the problems of a ten-year-old boy he hadn't known until a few minutes ago. Usually Clarke, as the Crimson Mask, handled only important cases, mysteries which puzzled the police and taxed the ingenuity of both. So far as ingenuity went, this particular job he had just taken, would require plenty to break it. Bob Clarke had never worked on flimsier clues.

The Crimson Mask whom Bob Clarke had become to wage his private war against crime was an almost legendary figure who appeared whenever some serious crime was committed. He had always been interested in crime and criminals. His father had been a police sergeant, which in past accounted for the interest, but there was more—much more.

When young Clarke had been in college, his father had been shot in the back by thugs. As he lay dying, there had been a strange rush of blood to his face. It had formed a perfect mask—a crimson mask. The son had never forgotten. He had gone through school, established his drug store and then had promptly begun studying criminology. He had been helped by ex-Police Commissioner Warrick who had been a close friend of his father's, and who had been present at that never-to-be-forgotten deathbed scene.

GRADUALLY THEN, Bob Clarke had moved to prevent crime or to see that criminals were properly punished. He had realized that his life would be in danger if the underworld knew his identity, so he had adopted a crimson mask as a disguise, a mask that was a replica of that phenomenon he had seen on his father's face before he had died in the hospital.

In a short time this crimson-masked investigator had become well-known to the police, but even they had no idea of his true identity. Few would have associated the daring of the Crimson Mask with the gentle kindness of Bob Clarke, Ph.G.

Warrick knew his secret, of course, and was often extremely helpful. He had influence that went to high places. Dave Small, Bob's assistant, was also in on the secret and frequently offered his active aid. Sandra Grey had slipped into Clarke's life when he had been investigating an important case and she had stayed. They were completely in love, but so long as he followed the dangerous avocation, both realized it was better if he remained free. Sandy worked with him, too, and she was competent and courageous.

Now, it seemed, the Crimson Mask was on the trail of a ten-year-old boy's past. A vague, indefinite trail replete with what might easily be the wild imaginings of youth. Squealing mice, a masterpiece of music, a boat whistle that sounded miles from the water and finally, to top them all, a screaming ghost.

Bob Clarke smiled wryly as he entered the surgeon's office.

CHAPTER III

THE SQUEALING MICE

THE DOCTOR leaned back in his chair.

"So you're interested in the boy, too," he said to young Clarke. "Of course, I expected it. You're interested in everyone, Bob. Stop blushing—I know all about the work you do in that drug store. Work you often don't get paid for and you know it when you hand out expensive vitamins and concentrates. Yes, this boy is suffering from amnesia. There is no question but that he had been very badly abused. I found a fairly recent near fracture of his jaw. Made before the accident. There were contusions about the head and face, too, not made by the car which struck him."

"Do you think that amnesia could have been caused before the accident, Doctor?" Clarke asked.

"Quite possibly, although such a thing seems incredible. The blow on the jaw might have been responsible and there were some wallops on the head, too. They left scars. Yes, the amnesia may have been present before the accident. Did I say accident? The police tell me it was clearly an attempt at murder."

Bob Clarke closed his eyes slowly.

"There are people in this world who don't belong here," he said grimly. "People who would half-kill a boy like that. Doctor, I want to help him. There isn't much I can do, but don't move him to a ward. I'll accept financial responsibility and see that all the bills are paid. Do what you can for him. Poor kid—can't even remember his parents."

"I'll take care of everything," the doctor said. "In fact, you and I will share the expenses, eh? Only don't broadcast it. I've a reputation here as a hard-bitten old man. It gets results."

Clarke grinned, offered his hand, then went out. He proceeded to the garages behind the hospital and talked to the ambulance driver who had brought the boy in. From him he got the location of the farmhouse where the accident had happened.

Clarke waited for his relief to show up, then left the hospital. He filled his car with gasoline, using his precious ration coupons. In a short time he was driving along the highway toward the farmer's house. In a secret pocket of his coat was a crimson mask which he could don if necessary. He opened a compartment in the car and took out a .38 automatic and slipped this into his pocket, too. Sometimes the unexpected happened and he wanted to be sure of things.

The farmer was quite willing to talk. In fact, he was eager.

"Never saw such a thing!" he declared. "There I was, in the lower field. I saw the boy first, then the car. The kid tried to thumb a ride and the car slowed. Then it speeded up and the driver deliberately aimed for the boy. Hit him an awful wallop. I heard it and my blood ran cold."

"Could you see how many men were in the car?"

"No. There were more than two, though, because one big fellow got out of the back and there was another beside the driver. This big one went over to the boy. I'll swear he started to pick him up, but when I yelled he ran away. Wish I'd got the number of that car. It was intended murder, that's what it was."

Bob Clarke thanked him, made inquiries about gasoline filling stations along the highway, and departed. In his mind he reasoned out that episode of the squealing mice and the odor of gasoline. The boy had been in a car,

Before the crook realized what was happening, the Crimson Mask landed on him

blindfolded. The car had stopped to refuel. Somewhere along this highway he would find those squealing mice—with luck.

He stopped at half a dozen gas stations and asked about three or four men and a boy in a black sedan. None of the attendants remembered anything like that.

FINALLY CLARKE rolled into another filling station, a frowsy-looking place with one pump. It was especially dark here, too, exactly the kind of place to which those men would have come for gas. The attendant was an old man, slightly deaf and watery-eyed.

"Nope," he said promptly. "Ain't seen no car with a boy in it."

"Maybe the boy was asleep on the back seat and you didn't notice him," Clarke urged. "How about a black sedan with three or four men in it? No boy, maybe."

"You expect me to remember every car that stops here? Mister, you ain't no cop or you'd have showed a badge. I ain't talking to you."

Bob Clarke sighed and got back into the car. His foot sought the starter button and froze there without depressing it. He heard a squeaking sound. It seemed to come from directly above his head. He closed both eyes, listening intently. The squeaking persisted and he realized a boy's active imagination might have construed it as the sound of mice.

Clarke got out of the car again and looked up to where a rusty old sign was being gently fanned by the breeze. It gave out those constant squeaks. Clarke walked briskly into the filling station.

"Now before you start threatening me," he warned the old man, "remember that I can call in the police. That car I asked you about did stop here just before dawn. You remember it because very few cars are on the road any time during the day and at dawn they come infrequently. Do you remember the car?"

The old man moved over as though to protect the ancient cash register on a bench. Clarke ordered him to open it.

"I'm no stick-up man," he said, "but if those men stopped here—and I know they did—you must have ration coupons from the car. Those coupons should have the numbers of the car written on the back. Produce—or, so help me, I will get police here."

"All right," the old man snapped. "There was a car like that. No kid in it—just four tough-looking guys. I—sold 'em gas without any coupons. Man has to make a living."

"Oh, sure," Bob Clarke said sarcastically, "even when it means selling gasoline illegally. But I'm no officer. My business is concerned with the car. Now describe the men—and did you look at the marker plates? What state?"

"I didn't see the markers. There was no tail-light. I only saw one of the men. Big fellow. He didn't ask me for gas without a coupon. He said if I didn't give it to him, he'd break my neck. He was about five feet eight or nine. Weighed about two hundred and thirty, I'd say. Thick lips and little eyes."

Clarke asked about the possibility of a boat whistle sounding just before dawn. The old man looked at him as if he thought him crazy.

Clarke left the gas station and drove back over the route which the boy's captors must have followed. There were side roads—plenty of them. They might have come out of any one, but Clarke stuck to the main highway. He still had a long way to go. The clue of the squealing mice was settled, but the other three offered even sterner difficulties.

He drove at about twenty miles an hour, trying to figure out how in the world a boat whistle could have been heard here. There was also that clue concerned with Schubert's "Serenade." That came before the boat whistle and it was highly possible that the car with the boy had stopped at some roadside eating place where there was a juke box.

BOB CLARKE stopped in four, examining the juke box record listings, if there were any. The fifth spot gave results. It was a squalid place advertising the sale of beer and food. He went in, ordered a sandwich and walked over to the ornate juke box. He felt like yelling for joy. Schubert's "Serenade" was listed.

He inserted a nickel and the record began to play. Clarke hummed the tune as he sat down at the counter.

"Nice music," he told the counterman. "Funny to find a record like that among all the jazz and jive. I'll bet it isn't played much."

"Oh, no?" The counterman swabbed with a dirty cloth dangerously close to Clarke's plate. "Lots of people like good music. Me, I like it hot. But you never can tell. I'm on a twenty-four-hour shift. This morning, before daylight, four guys walk in for hamburgers. One of 'em shoves in a nickel and out comes that tune. I guess maybe he didn't like it though, because he said something kind of rough about it."

"Four men," Clarke repeated slowly. "One of them was a burly sort of chap. Thick lips and squinty eyes. Right?"

"Yeah. Are you a friend of theirs? Are you from Craigville, too? Maybe I shouldn't have made no cracks about the music, huh?"

"You can crack all you want about it. They were not friends of mine. What makes you think they were from Craigville? That's in Connecticut, isn't it?"

"Yeah—mill town. There was a metal tag on the car with that name on it."

Clarke asked about the other three men and received descriptions that would have fit a million men. He left his sandwich, tipped the counterman handsomely and went out to his car. Now came the boat whistle. That seemed as impossible as the screaming ghost—but the mice that squealed and Schubert's "Serenade" had also seemed impossible.

Clarke was whistling the "Serenade" as he drove slowly along the highway. Things were progressing better than he had hoped for. The car in which the boy had ridden was from Craigville. Perhaps a stolen car, but still it was a clue.

He concentrated on the boat whistle next. It couldn't have come from a boat—that was clear. But there were other whistles. He saw a railroad crossing signal flash red, and slowed up. In the distance he could hear the roar of a train. He gave a grunt and stepped on the gas.

It seemed that he was trying to beat the train to the crossing. He switched on headlights, too. The engineer saw him and Clarke heard the peculiar throaty whistle of the streamliner. He stopped and let the train go by. He stayed there, bent over the wheel, thinking deeply.

The first thing the boy had recalled was the boat whistle which turned out to be the whistle of this train. There were plenty of the same type streamliners rolling by here every day. Right after the boat whistle it appeared the party had stopped at a house where the screaming ghost had developed. That had been shortly followed by the music. So that house was somewhere between the roadside restaurant with the juke box and this railroad.

CHAPTER IV

THE SCREAMING GHOST

BOB CLARKE turned his car around. It was about a mile back to the restaurant. He drove slowly, looking for houses.

He was twenty miles out of New York. This particular highway had once been an important one, but a new road had been built some years before and now the highway was a lonesome place. He saw one house, investigated, and found that it was deserted, broken down, and filled with dust and dirt that had not been disturbed for weeks.

Further along, he saw a weak light glittering from a window. He saw the house a little later—a bungalow set well back. He turned into the driveway and came to a stop beside the house. Shutting off the lights of his car, he got out and approached the front door.

A man appeared almost instantly. At first he acted as though he expected someone and then, when Clarke came into view, he gave a startled jump.

"What do you want?" he demanded.

"Have you a telephone?" Clarke asked. "I'm on my way to New York, but I've got to phone ahead. I'll pay—up to a dollar."

"Show me the dollar," the man said quickly.

Clarke produced a bill which was all but snatched out of his hand. The man led him into the house, a rather dirty place with old, partly broken-down furniture.

Bob Clarke sat down at a small table before the phone, called toll line and asked for the first combination of numbers that entered his head. Oddly enough, the operator did ring the exchange and number, but there was no answer. Clarke didn't mind. He began talking, carrying on a mythical conversation to the effect that he would be late and he was apologetic about it. Finally he hung up, turned around, and stayed seated. He offered the man a cigarette and eyed him closely.

He saw a thin, sparse-haired individual with a skinny nose and closely-set eyes. A man who would do practically anything for money, Clarke estimated.

"Kind of lonesome around here," he said affably.

"I like it that way." The man leaned down for a light. "I don't like people much. Most of 'em got too much money while I nearly starve to death. I'll show you to the door."

"But I'm in no hurry now and I'm tired of driving. Let me sit here and chin a while." He added hastily, "It's worth another dollar."

"Go ahead and talk," the man offered, and snatched the second dollar bill.

"Well"—Bob Clarke crossed his legs and grinned innocently—"I don't know what to talk about. Let's see—this place is lonesome, as I said. Any ghost's around these parts?"

"They never bother me, if there are," his host answered. "What is this? You don't act to me like a guy who just wants to kill time."

Clarke leaned forward, resting one elbow on his knee.

"You're a businessman," he said. "You appreciate the value of money. Now suppose you answer one question and if the answer is right, there's fifty dollars in it for you."

"What's the question?" the man asked cagily. "And you'll have to give me the fifty before I do any talking."

"Agreed. Now some particular friends of mine pulled a job recently. A neat job and I've been trailing them from Craigville. You know, the mill town in Connecticut. Now I want to know—"

The man suddenly jumped up and raced out of the room. When he came back, there was a shotgun in his hands.

"Get out!" he said. "You're some kind of a crook, that's what. I ain't having anything to do with crooks. You talk like a crook and doggone, you look like one. Mosey now, or I'll throw some shot into your hide."

CLARKE AROSE slowly. He half raised his hands and started backing toward the door. It began to look as if he had made a mistake. This man liked money, all right. So much so that the offer of fifty dollars might have caused him to give some kind of a vague answer to the question. Instead, he had run for a shotgun. Was that caused by his spoken theory that Bob Clarke was a crook, or was it caused by sudden panic?

If only there was something to warrant the boy's story of a screaming ghost. Certainly in this house there was nothing to make any sound like that.

"Get going!" the man yelled stridently.

From somewhere deeper in the house a shrill voice repeated the words and then added an unholy squawk that almost made Clarke's hair stand on end. He knew what it was—a parrot. This was what the boy had heard and it was no wonder he had been scared.

Suddenly Clarke dropped his hands and grabbed the barrel of the shotgun. He moved it out of range, then yanked it from the man's hands. He threw the gun onto a chair, grabbed the man by the collar and shoved him back toward a clothes closet. He got the door open, pushed the man inside, closed and locked the door.

"You can break out," he said loudly. "And if those punks come back, tell them there is more than me on their trail."

He hurried to his car. He had locked the man up so he couldn't read the marker plates. The plates identified the car as Bob Clarke's and he intended to return soon. And when he did, in another guise, the owner of the house might possibly assume that his recent visitor and the Crimson Mask were one and the same.

He drove well down the road, pulled off it, and worried the car between some trees and bushes. He sat there for more than two hours. Then he put on the crimson mask, made sure his gun was ready for action and started back toward the house on foot.

The place was ominously quiet, although a light still burned in one room. The Crimson Mask circled the house cautiously. He had given that man plenty of time to get in touch with his friends if he wished to. The Crimson Mask hoped he had done so.

Estimating the character of the owner of the house had been easy. He was tight-fisted, none too clean, and lived a hermit-like existence. The presence of the telephone indicated his house was being used by someone who was willing to pay. Certainly the owner would never have gone to the expense of a phone.

The back door of the house was locked, but it was a cheap affair and gave way easily under the urgings of the Crimson Mask's set of master keys. He stepped into the darkened kitchen, left the door open just long enough for weak moonlight to allow him to study the place. He closed the door then and silently walked toward the front of the house.

He had his gun ready. Not that he feared this man, but there might be others to form a more dangerous reception committee. The owner of the house was an abject coward. When he had pointed the shotgun two hours before, it had wavered badly and he had barely let his finger rest against the trigger. It had been easy to disarm him.

The Crimson Mask risked a quick look into the living room. The owner was there, seated in a chair and wringing his hands. He looked more worried than Mussolini, with the start of the invasion so near.

"Good evening."

The Crimson Mask stepped into the room.

THE MAN jumped up with a short cry of terror. He made one frantic move toward the shotgun propped against the wall. The

Crimson Mask's automatic swung with him and the man stopped. Then he stared, as if the crimson mask intrigued him.

"Who are you?" he demanded.

"My name doesn't matter," the Crimson Mask said. "I'm here about a ten-year-old boy. The one who visited you yesterday—last night. Tell me about him and you won't have the slightest trouble with me. Refuse, and there is no knowing what will happen to you."

"I—I don't know anything about a boy. What would a boy be doing here? You've—made a mistake. Yes—a mistake."

"But he remembers being here," the Crimson Mask said gently. "Think hard. Or perhaps if I skinned your ear with a bullet, it might help to restore your memory."

"No—no, don't shoot me! Don't! I'm an innocent man. I live here all alone. I—can't even see who you are. I'm going to move the lamp closer. Maybe you're a crook of some kind. Isn't that a mask?"

"A crimson-colored mask. I take my name from it. Move the lamp if you wish, but don't throw it. I'd only shoot you down and you'd burn to death when the lamp exploded."

The hermit picked up the gasoline lamp from a table and held it high. He backed away a step.

"The Crimson Mask! So that's who you are. Somebody is going to be awful surprised when they see you."

"So! Moving that lamp was a signal, eh? Well, I expected that. I'm ready. Get back—back against the wall. Put the lamp down and raise your hands. Back up—do you hear me?"

The man certainly did, if the expression around his mouth and in his eyes meant anything. He slowly stepped backward and he was in a direct line with a window.

That window smashed suddenly. The crack of a gun sounded— sharp and clear like that of a rifle. The man straightened up with a shrill cry, staggered to a chair and fell into it. He slowly slid off it onto the floor.

The Crimson Mask instantly ducked and crawled toward the window. He straightened up beside it, gun ready. In the faint moonlight he saw two men approaching.

The Crimson Mask fired one bullet. Both men turned and fled.

Moving fast, the Crimson Mask hurried to the other side of the small house. Two more were approaching and he sent these scurrying for safety with another slug. That would hold them for a short time.

If he stayed away from windows, they were unlikely to attack. They could sit it out and wait for him to collapse with fatigue.

He picked up the telephone. It was dead. They had remembered to sever the wires.

The Crimson Mask heard the owner of the house utter a low groan and sped to his side. He placed the man in a more comfortable position, but a quick examination showed he had only a short time left. That bullet had ploughed through his lung.

"Four of them—four," he mumbled. "One named Kraus. Bad—bad—"

"Keep talking," the Crimson Mask urged. "They knew that was you standing in front of the window. The light was in front of you. They could see all right and they shot you down, anyway. Who is the boy?"

"Don't—don't know. Never told—me. Used to let crooks hide out here—Kraus knew. He brought—boy. Then changed his mind. All I know. Everything—the truth. All the—truth—"

"Kraus must have said something about the boy," urged the Crimson Mask. "By talking you can redeem yourself for whatever you've done. Only speak quickly. There isn't much time."

"All I know. Nothing else to—tell. They stayed here five—minutes. I—I'm dying? Don't let me die. I've got— money. Don't let me—die!"

A BOARD squeaked on the small front porch and a shadow passed the window. The Crimson Mask fired hurriedly and missed, but the man who was trying to peer in raced away fast. The Crimson Mask eased the dead man to the floor and scurried toward the back of the house. Sure enough, the other two were approaching, in that direction.

He took deliberate aim through the window and then he pulled the trigger slowly.

One of the men gave a leap into the air and screamed shrilly, but he was able to stagger away into the night. His companion had a fond idea that his own skin was precious for he fled, too—without pausing to help his wounded pal.

The Crimson Mask knew this could not go on. The spot was isolated. There was little chance of a car passing at this hour of the night, and even so the shots might not be heard.

He had to get away and without any further delay.

CHAPTER V

ONE HAZY MEMORY

QUICKLY CHECKING, the Crimson Mask saw that the house was being watched on all four sides now and that the quartette was not too far away—barely out of pistol range. They could close in, one by one. He couldn't watch all four sides, and every moment that went by made his predicament that much more dangerous.

There was an attic to the house. The Crimson Mask recalled it plainly—and there was one small window at the front and another at the rear. If he could force three or even two of the men to make a concentrated attack on the front, he might find an opportunity of escape through the back.

The Crimson Mask sprinted to the front door and opened it about a foot. Instantly, the man on guard there dropped flat. The Crimson Mask fired a shot in the general direction of the killer and promptly drew return fire. He didn't have a surplus of bullets, but his position made it imperative for him to take risks.

He fired again. The men from the east side of the house crawled around to flank the door and sent two slugs smashing into the side wall of the house.

From the west came another attack. The Crimson Mask could not see the thugs, but they could watch him. He threw the door wide open. Instantly, three guns let go. He answered the fire until he had only one shot left. Then he quietly faded deeper into the house and ran up the narrow steps to the attic and sped to the rear window.

Luckily, it was in good shape and could be raised quietly. Downstairs, they sent a couple of more slugs through the front door. In a moment or two they were bound to charge.

The Crimson Mask leaned out of the window. Below, close to the back door, was the fourth thug. He watched the door and must have fully believed the man he was after was busy defending himself at the front. The Crimson Mask thrust one leg over the window sill, then the other, until he sat precariously on the edge.

Downstairs the men were on the porch, wondering why they drew no fire. In a moment they would guess. The Crimson Mask took a long breath and jumped. The window was high above the ground and the crook was directly below it. Before he realized what was happening, the Crimson Mask landed on him. The thug made a *whooshing* noise as he was flattened to the ground.

The Crimson Mask risked one precious second going through some of the thug's pockets. He got a pencil and some matchbooks for his pains. That was all. Running with all the speed he could muster, the Crimson Mask faded into the night as two of the thugs who had been in front came barging around the corners of the house.

They must have seen him for their guns opened up, but the Crimson Mask was running fast and bent low. The bullets zinged above and around him, but none came too close.

He kept on going in the general direction of his car. Now and then he heard the thugs prowling through the brush, but where they were clumsy, the Crimson Mask remained agile, avoiding dry bushes and utilizing the scant moonlight to study each advancing footstep. Speed was no longer necessary. Care was.

He reached the car, got in, and a moment later he was on the highway streaking back toward the city. There was no pursuit. Even if the thugs had heard or seen him drive off, their own car was probably much closer to the house and it would take them several minutes to reach it.

The Crimson Mask drove straight to a garage near his store and on the way he removed his mask. He put the car away and walked to the drug store. It should have been closed long ago, but Dave Small was still on the job, worried half sick over Bob Clarke's continued absence.

DAVE SMALL greeted him eagerly. They closed up and went to a back room where the pharmaceutical department was located, passed through it and into a well-hidden laboratory. There Bob Clarke sat down, with a long sigh, and lit a cigarette. He took from his pocket the meager possessions of the crook he had knocked cold.

"I know all about that boy at the hospital and what you're trying to do," Small said. "Sandy called no less than seven times in the last couple of hours. She wanted me to tell you that the boy is doing nicely."

"Good." Clarke nodded. "We don't know who he is, but the men who had him are willing to go to any lengths to get him back— probably to kill him, since they failed before. Or to stop me from finding out the truth about him. The boy himself is unusual. He gave me clues that led straight to one of the hideouts and I tangled with the four men who tried to kill the boy. I winged one—not badly because he stayed in action. I knocked another out and fished these from his pockets."

Dave Small took the three articles.

"An advertising pencil with the name of a barroom on it," he commented. "San Francisco, eh? And two empty books of matches, both with San Francisco ads. I guess there is no question but that the guy came from the West Coast."

"Those things point that way," Clarke said. "I'm going to call Sandy and assure her I'm okay. Then I'm contacting Mr. Warrick. I need his help."

Picking up the phone, Clarke made his call, and in short order heard Sandra Grey's voice over the wire.

"Jimmy is getting stronger every hour," Sandy reported. "I left the hospital at midnight. Tomorrow I'll do a double shift to be with him. Bob, you don't think they'll try to get him again, do you?"

"The monkeys behind this wouldn't stop at anything," Bob Clarke said. "By the way, is there any chance of photographing the boy without those bandages?"

"None whatsoever," Sandy answered quickly. "I mentioned that to the doctor and he flatly rejected the idea even if it meant the boy would be identified. There are too many stitches."

"Tough," Clarke said. "It would help a lot. Well—I'll see you in the morning. By then I may have some information."

He hung up, waited a moment, then dialed another number. He had to wait for some time before there was an answer and during the interim he spoke to Dave Small.

"My idea is that the boy was kidnaped. Just a snatch job with some unusual complications. Maybe Mr. Warrick can contact the West Coast… Hello! Mr. Warrick? I need your help. There is a boy at the hospital—"

"I read about him in the papers," Theodore Warrick answered sleepily. "Are you interested in that case?"

"Up to my neck in it. I didn't know the story had been printed, though. I located the men who are responsible for what happened to the lad. They got away, but I'm reasonably certain at least one of them came from California. San Francisco, perhaps. I want you to contact the police and F.B.I. out there. See if there is any record of a kidnaped boy, or even a missing boy about ten years old. Call me back as soon as you hear anything."

"It will take an hour or so," Warrick said. "Of course, the time element out there gives us some advantage. All record bureaus will still be open. Do the best I can."

Clarke hung up. "Dave," he said, "I'm going back to the hospital. Just a few things to ask the boy. If I'm not here when Mr. Warrick calls, take down all the dope."

"Right," Small said. "And I hope something breaks so you need me in this case. Kidnapers are the lowest breed of beasts that exist—especially when they pick on kids."

Bob Clarke put on his hat. "We're not even sure it is a snatch, Dave. If it is, Mr. Warrick will soon let us know."

AT THE hospital, Clarke was admitted without any trouble and made his way to the boy's room. There was a nurse on duty, but Jimmy was awake and he tried to raise himself on the pillow when Clarke stepped in.

"Would you mind?" Bob Clarke asked the nurse.

She smiled. "Of course not. Jimmy has been asking for you ever since he woke up an hour ago. I need a cup of coffee, anyhow."

Clarke closed the door, sat down beside Jimmy, and grinned at him.

"We'll soon restore that memory of yours, son. I found your screaming ghost. It was a parrot."

Jimmy was all attention. "Honest! Gee—it sounded awful."

"Scared the daylights out of me, too. Did you ever hear of Craigville? That's a town in Connecticut."

"No, sir," Jimmy replied.

"All right. How about Charleston? No? What of New Haven? You don't know that city either. Suppose we take Augusta."

"I never heard of it," Jimmy said.

"But you know about San Francisco, of course?"

"Oh, sure. That's... It's—I forgot. I'll try to remember."

"No, don't bother," Clarke said. "There is another city that is composed of two words. The first is Los—"

"Los Angeles," Jimmy broke in. "It's a big city."

"Do you live there?" Clarke interjected quickly.

Jimmy's eyes clouded over. "I—don't know, sir."

"Never mind," Bob Clarke said. "I'm sure you do know the Pacific Coast. You probably come from there. You never heard much about the East Coast."

"I wrote letters," Jimmy said half absently.

"To whom? Think hard, Jimmy. To whom did you write them?"

"I don't know. Honest, I don't, but I remember my hand got tired. Awful tired. There were so many of them."

"You're okay, Jimmy," Clarke said. "Is there anything else you want to tell me? Oh, yes—the boat whistle was on a locomotive. It sounded just like a ship. And I found your mice. The noise came from a squeaky sign at a gasoline station. The music was from a juke box. Nice number—'Serenade'."

"I can play it," Jimmy offered. "I—think so. Part of it. Did you find out about the airplanes and the air raid?" Bob Clarke held his breath. Perhaps this was the one clue he needed so badly.

"What air raid, Jimmy?"

"I don't know. I was blind when it came, but there were lots of sirens and lots of planes. They sounded like dive bombers. Then I wasn't blind. There was a word. It was red-colored. Like fire. It said 'Acme'. What does that mean?"

"It means the highest point. Perfection. Like the 'A's' you probably get on your report cards. That's enough for tonight, Jimmy. I'll drop in again tomorrow. So will the lady. Want to do me a favor?"

"I'll do anything, sir," Jimmy said eagerly.

"Tomorrow, when there's nobody else around, tell her I like her very much. Will you do that? Good. Now go back to sleep. I'll stay here until the nurse returns."

CHAPTER VI

SNATCH!

JIMMY WAS fast asleep in ten minutes. The nurse came back and Bob Clarke hurried to his store again. Dave Small was on the phone when he entered.

"Just a minute, Mr. Warrick," Small said. "Bob just came in… Bob, the F.B.I. and the police all over the West Coast have no records at all about any kidnaping. There are two ten-year-old boys missing, but the kid in the hospital can't be one of them. These two disappeared only yesterday."

Clarke took the phone. "No reports of any kind?" he asked. "That's odd. I could have sworn it was a snatch. It looks as if the four men came from the West and I assumed the boy did, too. I could be wrong. By the way, do you know of any nearby town that had a pretty realistic blackout test within the past week or so? Planes diving and all that?"

Warrick laughed. "As a director of the Air Raid Warden Service, I should know about it. Yes, a test of that kind was pulled five nights ago in a medium-sized manufacturing town in Connecticut. Craigville, I think the name was. Planes dived, searchlight batteries went into action, and pursuit ships from nearby airfields took to the air."

"Craigville," Bob Clarke said softly. "It ties in. Thanks—and will you keep checking on any kidnaping reports? I still feel I'm on the right track—just a question of getting the right geography."

"I'll keep in touch with Dave," former Commissioner Warrick promised. "Good luck, Bob. I'd like to see you restore that boy to his parents."

Bob Clarke closed his eyes wearily after he hung up.

"I'm going to draw a map," he told Small. "It will show where the bungalow is at which a man was killed tonight. Phone the State Police from outside somewhere and tell them to go there. The call must be anonymous."

"I'll take care of it as soon as you're in bed," Small said. "You need rest, Bob."

Clarke nodded. "I do—because tomorrow I'm going to Craigville. That boy was there. He remembers an air raid test which took place in that town five days ago. It shows Jimmy's amnesia began before that time although his memory is only fair even just back to that point."

"And where do I come in?" Small demanded. "Or do I just act as a messenger boy?"

"This time"—Clarke started removing his tie and shirt—"it's a one-man job. Maybe as we get deeper into it, I'll need you. The store has to stay open, you know."

Bob Clarke's sleep the next morning was interrupted by a phone call from Sandy which brushed away the cobwebs with her first words.

"Jimmy's grandfather came for him, Bob! He was at the hospital early this morning with a lawyer. They even had their own doctor and he ordered the boy removed to the grandfather's hotel suite."

"I'll be right over," Clarke said. "This can't be on the level! It's almost impossible."

But the impossible was true. Bob Clarke found that out by talking with Sandy and the surgeon who had operated on the boy. There was even a check from the grandfather reimbursing Clarke for the money he had advanced to pay the boy's bills.

CLARKE FANNED the air slowly with that check.

"So the boy's name is Paul Lockwood and his grandfather is Peter Lockwood," he mused. "Did he say where he was from?"

"Yes," the surgeon said. "Denver. He operates a mine or something out there. They were quite insistent on removing the boy. Naturally, since the grandfather brought along a doctor who assumed charge of the case, there was little I could do."

"Well, I guess that's that," Clarke said. "We tried to help, anyway. Were you quite satisfied with proof of relationship between the boy and this Peter Lockwood?"

"Positive. Lockwood brought along several photographs of the boy, from some five years back. You know, I saw him before the bandages were applied and I remember what he looked like. Those were pictures of the boy, all right."

"And did the boy show any signs of recognition?"

"Absolutely none. In fact, I don't think the lad wanted to leave. Said he had an important message from you to Miss Grey."

Bob Clarke smiled. "I did give him such a message. Thanks, Doctor. Just to satisfy myself I think I'll look up the grandfather and have a little talk with him. I became greatly interested in the boy, you know."

"You'll find Lockwood at the Hotel Elite. I think he intends to leave for the West as soon as the boy recovers sufficiently to travel."

Bob Clarke left the hospital and called a taxi. In a few moments he was using the house phones at the Hotel Elite. There was no answer from Lockwood's suite. Clarke went to the desk clerk.

"Mr. Lockwood went out a short time ago," he was told. "I think an attendant is in the suite, however. Maybe they muffled the phone so the boy wouldn't be disturbed."

"I'll go up," Clarke said. "What's the room number?"

The clerk looked over his shoulder. "I can do better than that, sir. Here comes Mr. Lockwood himself."

Bob Clarke turned quickly to face a tall, slender man of about fifty. He had iron-gray hair and a distinguished appearance.

"Mr. Lockwood?" Clarke said. "I'm Robert Clarke from the hospital. About the boy—"

Lockwood beamed. "Of course. I was going to look you up when I found time. A mighty nice gesture on your part—offering to pay the bills. Fortunately, I read about Paul in the newspapers. I'd been frantic for days trying to locate him. What do you think really happened?"

"I'm more worried about what's liable to happen," Clarke said. "I phoned your suite. The boy—Paul you said his name was—is there, isn't he?"

"Yes, with an attendant I hired. A male nurse. I couldn't have a woman in a bachelor's suite now, could I? Didn't the attendant permit you to come up? Sorry, but I gave him orders no one was to see Paul."

"He didn't even answer the phone," Clarke said. "That's what worries me. I think we should go up."

LOCKWOOD BLANCHED.

"At once. Come along."

They hurried to the elevators and were whisked to the ninth floor. Lockwood was taking keys from his pocket as they ran along the corridor. He got the door open promptly. They stepped into a well-appointed suite, passed down the foyer, and Lockwood gave a scream.

A man, wearing a white coat, lay in the middle of the floor. He was dead. Beside him was an empty bed, the covers of which had been torn off and thrown to one side.

Lockwood closed his eyes and moved his lips in either a prayer or an imprecation. Clarke didn't know which, because he was examining the attendant. The man had been stabbed through the heart.

"Phone the police!" Lockwood said. "I—I don't feel capable of anything. Paul is gone. He was kidnaped before, and now they've got him again. Or wait! Perhaps I shouldn't call in the police. There may be a note ordering me not to. I don't know what to do."

"It's out of your hands," Bob Clarke said grimly. "This is murder, besides kidnaping. Where is the telephone?"

The police spent two hours in the suite and asked uncounted questions. Lockwood gave them a description of the boy, stated that he, himself, had gone out for a walk, and upon returning had met Bob Clarke—and murder. He told about the first disappearance of the boy and stated over and over again that he had never received any demands for ransom.

"That's why I didn't report the disappearance," he explained. "I thought Paul had merely run away. He knew how to take care of himself. He was well-educated and traveled a lot. He had money, too. Then, when he didn't come back or send any word, I was afraid of kidnapers and I wanted to see if any word would come from such people."

After the police left, Lockwood covered his face and groaned.

"I'm an incompetent old fool. Paul's father was my son. He died a few weeks ago and Paul's mother died long before. I thought I could bring up the boy. Now look what's happened!"

Bob Clarke answered the clamor of the telephone. It was Lockwood's attorney. Clarke told him to come up.

The attorney's name was Edward Todd and Clark instinctively disliked him. He was too smooth, overly sympathetic, and he gave Lockwood advice which made Clarke's suspicions rise high.

"You told me not to report that I believed him to be kidnaped, when I consulted you yesterday," Lockwood said. "I should have. And I should have left the boy at the hospital where he'd have been protected."

Todd shook his head. "No, they could have taken him from the hospital just as easily. I was right the first time, too. Paul originally was kidnaped. Now he's been snatched again. This time you're bound to hear from the kidnapers. They commit crimes like this for only one reason—money. They'll approach you soon. My advice is to pay them off before you give any information to the police or the F.B.I."

"May I make a suggestion?" Bob Clarke interjected. "Mr. Lockwood might confer with the F.B.I., secretly...."

"Keep out of this," Todd snapped. "Who the devil are you, anyhow? Maybe you're even one of them. Lockwood, I think this man should be excluded from our conference."

Clarke got up. "I'm sorry, Mr. Lockwood. I was merely trying to help. If there is anything I can do, call on me. We all got to like Paul very much."

Lockwood just nodded. Bob Clarke went out and proceeded straight to the telephone booths in the lobby. He had overheard Lockwood telling the police where he lived in Denver, what his business was, and all pertinent facts about himself. Clarke phoned Denver, dumping a fistful of quarters into the phone slot when the connection was made.

He talked to a Denver newspaper, explaining that he was a New York reporter. From this source he secured a full description of Lockwood, and it fitted him well. Lockwood's reputation was excellent. He had left for New York some days ago on business.

Only one thing interfered with a full acceptance of Lockwood's story. Nobody at the newspaper office knew anything about a grandson.

CHAPTER VII

ATTORNEY WITH A PAST

CLARKE HUNG up, opened the phone booth door for some fresh air and stayed there, thinking intently. Then he made another call, to Theodore Warrick.

"Try to get police cooperation on this," he said, after explaining what had happened. "I want Lockwood out of his suite for a time.

Have the police send for him—and his lawyer. By the way, what do you know about an attorney named Edward Todd?"

"He used to represent more big shot bootleggers in the old days than any shyster," Warrick replied. "I wouldn't trust him. Not one bit. As for Lockwood, he'll leave his apartment soon."

"Good," Bob Clarke said. "I'll be over to see you. This time you'll take as active a part as I. We must find the boy and soon, too. He's sick. In the hands of some dumb mugs. He might die."

Clarke stayed in the phone booth until he saw Lockwood and Todd hurry through the lobby. Then he took an elevator to the ninth floor, stepped up to the door of Lockwood's suite and opened it with one of a set of master keys he always carried.

He spent ten minutes in the suite and found what he was after. He taxied to Warrick's house next and the ex-police commissioner greeted him warmly.

Warrick showed no real indication that he was beyond the retirement age. He was militarily erect, keen-eyed and bubbling over with eagerness.

"Now what in the world is this all about?" he asked when Clarke made himself comfortable.

"Just a boy," Bob Clarke said. "A helpless kid who is taking the brunt of the whole affair. It seems he is an orphan and Lockwood is his grandfather. A few days ago the boy vanished. Lockwood didn't think much of it, figuring the boy had just gone off some place. Funny attitude for a doting grandfather to adopt, but I understand the boy was used to traveling alone, even at his age. He was provided with money too."

Warrick nodded. "Lockwood is evidently a widower without the vaguest ideas on how to bring up a boy that age. Why didn't he call in the police when the boy was missing so long?"

"He explained that, too—and it's where Ed Todd comes in. Lockwood went to Todd and retained him. Todd advised against notifying the police on the theory that kidnapers might take drastic measures. He told Lockwood to wait."

Warrick lit a slim cigar and puffed on it slowly.

"Knowing Todd as I do," he observed, "such advice from him isn't astounding. Did Lockwood approach Todd or was it the other way around?"

"I don't know," Clarke said. "Anyway, the boy apparently got away from the men who held him, though he can remember nothing of it. He must have swiped those ragamuffin clothes he was wearing, too. The kidnapers located him along that highway and ran him down, with every intention of killing him. Something must have gone wrong with the kidnaping scheme, and they wanted him dead. A farmer saw it happen and ran up in time to prevent those killers from making off with what they thought was the boy's body."

"I know about that," Warrick said. "I talked to Sandy and she told me the whole yarn. What can I do to help?"

Bob Clarke took a studio portrait from his pocket. The picture of a handsome boy.

"Lockwood identified the boy with this and several other photographs," he explained. "They are authentic all right and it certainly makes out a good case for Lockwood, except for one thing."

"Let's have it, Bob."

"When Lockwood explained about the second kidnaping and the murder of that male nurse, he never mentioned the fact that he possessed photographs of the boy though he had shown some of five years back at the hospital. These later ones would have been of utmost importance. Maybe Lockwood deliberately refused to turn them over because he is afraid the kidnapers will retaliate against the boy. Anyway, when you lured him out of the suite, I went in and filched this one."

"Intelligent looking little fellow," Warrick grunted.

"He's smart all right," Clarke said. "Now I want you to take this picture to one of the newspaper syndicates and have them radio it to the West Coast. Have it printed in every newspaper there—the next edition, if possible. Tip off some of your friends on the police force to be ready if the picture draws any response, and if it does, here is the next step."

HE TALKED for fifteen minutes while Warrick took copious notes and kept nodding in full approval.

"Meanwhile, you'll be working on it?" Warrick asked.

Clarke headed for the door. "As the Crimson Mask. It's time to put these crooks on the defensive. I have one clue which leads to Craigville. I'm going to follow it right away."

He hurried back to the drug store, went into the lab and talked to Dave Small as he went to work. In front of a triple-mirrored dressing table, Clarke applied a light disguise. When he had finished, his skin seemed quite swarthy and his hair was a shade or two darker than natural. His teeth were stained, as if he smoked too much.

From a carefully prepared selection of various types of clothing, he selected a cheap, worn suit, a somewhat threadbare necktie and shoes that were run down at the heels. His shirt was none too clean either. He surveyed himself in a full length mirror.

Like the men of the F.B.I., Bob Clarke resorted to disguise only in emergencies and he depended much more on living a certain role than on the use of artificial devices to alter his appearance. In this disguise there was still some resemblance to Bob Clarke, but only his intimates would have recognized it.

He fished out a battered suitcase and filled it with cheap clothing.

"Tell Sandy she is to expect a call from Warrick," he told Dave Small. "She'll get her orders then. Your job is to take care of the store—without squawking. So far this is, as I said, a one-man job, Dave. Though as I also said, perhaps before I'm through, I'll need your help badly."

When Bob Clarke left through a rear door, he automatically became the Crimson Mask, on the hunt for a band of the most vicious and skillful criminals he had ever encountered. So far, they had dealt all the cards, struck when they wished, and were in full command of the situation at the present time. So long as they held Jimmy—or Paul—they could dicker.

The Crimson Mask took a bus to Craigville. The trip took only an hour and a half. There he checked his suitcase, went to a phone booth and ran through a book, taking notes of every business place operating under the trade name of Acme.

There were five places. Two were trucking firms and he temporarily crossed them off the list. One was a clothing merchant. The Crimson Mask walked to that address, but the place sported no red advertising sign such as the one he was sure the boy had seen.

The fourth place was a large laundry located in a manufacturing section. It had such an advertising sign, extinguished now because of the dimout regulations, but the Crimson Mask learned from a passerby that the sign operated from dusk until dimout time every day.

The Crimson Mask studied the neighborhood. Undoubtedly, the boy had seen that flashing sign from a window. Therefore, he must have been across the street. No further than that either, the Crimson Mask realized, because the laundry building was low and the sign was not high. Adjoining structures were much higher and would shut off any sight of the sign.

Across the street, buildings also towered well above the laundry. That sign was strictly for neighborhood advertising.

Most of the buildings across the street were factories—huge places working full blast. Certainly the boy had not been held in one of them. Then there was a single house, jammed between two of the factories and almost directly opposite the sign. It was a dreary-looking place, badly in need of paint and repairs. Dirty curtains hung in the windows and a "rooms for rent" sign was crookedly affixed to a porch pillar near the door.

HALF AN hour later the Crimson Mask was back at that rooming house with his old suitcase in his hand. A bleary-eyed, dirty-looking janitor with a strong gin breath let him in and assigned a room. The Crimson Mask left the door of his room opened wide and sat down to read a paper he had purchased at a newsstand downtown. It was a copy of a Los Angeles daily.

Now and then men passed by the open door and looked inside with open curiosity. The Crimson Mask never had obtained a good look at the four men who had stormed the farmer's house, but when one man ambled past the door with his arm in a sling, the Crimson Mask's interest mounted. Perhaps this was the crook he had winged during that gun battle.

Fully an hour later the Crimson Mask knew he had come to the right place. A hulking brute of a man stopped at the doorway. He had squinty eyes and thick lips—exactly as the gas station attendant and the counterman at the roadside restaurant had described the man they had seen.

"Hello," the Crimson Mask said. "My name is Carter. I just got a job at the Eastern Iron Mill. This certainly is a busy town. 'Way back on the West Coast I heard they needed hands here."

"Yeah." The big man entered the room. "I noticed you're reading a Los Angeles paper. Mind if I see it?"

The Crimson Mask folded the newspaper and handed it to the burly man.

"Are you from the Coast too?"

"Got a lot of friends there. Sometimes they get into the papers. My name is Kraus. I work out of town. How'd you happen to find this boarding house, pal?"

The Crimson Mask shrugged. "By hoofing it all over town. It ain't much of a place, but it'll do until I find a better one. The man who runs the house didn't want to rent me a room, but I told him I'd go to the government agency in town and make him. Say, I get that paper every night downtown. There's a newsstand sells out-of-town papers and I told 'em to save me one every day. You can have them after I finish."

"I'm in Number Thirty-seven right down the hall," Kraus said. "Just drop them outside my door. Thanks. I'll buy you a drink any time you say."

Kraus dropped one hand to the back of a wooden chair. His muscles tensed. The wood creaked and groaned and then cracked. The whole top segment of the chair broke off. Kraus looked at it with an amused expression on his big face.

"Well, what do you know? I don't even know my own strength, pal. See you later."

The Crimson Mask was unimpressed by that exhibition of brute power. Kraus was merely showing off, but it indicated he suspected the new roomer and wanted to emphasize the fact that he could handle himself.

Twenty minutes later the Crimson Mask left the rooming house. He departed quietly, but not stealthily. He wanted to find out if Kraus suspected him so much that he would put somebody on his trail.

The Crimson Mask strolled downtown, glancing in windows and acting just like a stranger who wanted to find his way around. And someone did trail him. A pipsqueak of a man who did a fairly good job of it.

The Crimson Mask proceeded straight to the newsstand and bought another West Coast newspaper. Finally, he purchased a ticket to a movie theater and went in. His shadow did the same thing.

The Crimson Mask passed the ticket taker, turned into the darkened theater proper, wheeled on one heel and as his shadow passed through one door, the Crimson Mask went out the other. It was done skillfully and so fast that the shadow hadn't the vaguest idea he had been tricked. The darkness helped some, but it was the Crimson Mask's talent for moving fast that really did the trick.

The Crimson Mask struck out for the boarding house. He wanted a chance to look it over. The boy might be there even at this moment. If he was, the Crimson Mask had determined to end the case at once—even if it resulted in a flaming gun battle.

CHAPTER VIII

THE TRAIL GROWS WARM

WHEN THE Crimson Mask let himself in, the rooming house was singularly quiet. He went to his own room first. Nothing seemed to have been disturbed—to the average eye at least, but the Crimson Mask was doubly observing because the life of that boy hung in the balance. He saw that his bags had been carefully examined. That didn't worry the Crimson Mask for they contained nothing to give him away as anything but a working man from the West.

He left the room and prowled the corridor first. Then he tried various doors. Some were not locked and those that were he opened with his own set of keys. Practically every one of the boarders was out. The Crimson Mask descended to the cellar and narrowly missed being spotted by the slovenly janitor. He found nothing there.

Instead of going straight back to his own room, he proceeded to the second floor and located the room directly below his own. It was not occupied and he went in silently.

Kraus and his tribe of hoodlums were also living on the third floor and the Crimson Mask possessed a strong idea that the janitor had assigned him a room on this floor so that Kraus could keep an eye out for him.

Naturally, they would be suspicious of anyone who came asking for a room and then demanding it, but the Crimson Mask had been required by circumstances to take such a risk.

He went to the window, opened it and leaned out. His own window was not far above. The Crimson Mask then pulled down the upper part of that window and left it that way.

Back in his room again he was sure that the boy was not here. Yet he was equally sure that Jimmy, or Paul, had spent some time in the house because many of the windows fronted that advertising sign which had impressed itself on the boy's memory.

The Crimson Mask returned to his own room, remained dressed, and sat down close to the door. In a short time he heard heavy footsteps. That would be Kraus. The big man banged on the door. The Crimson Mask let him in.

"Where you been?" Kraus asked. "I looked in a little while ago. Nobody here."

"Gosh, I thought I locked my door," the Crimson Mask said meekly. "I went down for another newspaper. A guy gets lonesome so far from home. Then I dropped into a movie, but I'd seen the darn thing before so I came back. Want something, Mr. Kraus?"

"No-o." Kraus prolonged the word. "I was just going out. Save the newspaper, huh?"

When Kraus left, the Crimson Mask closed and locked the door. He jammed a tiny bit of metal into the lock beside the key so that it couldn't be turned from outside, even with an especially made pair of pliers.

Next, he extinguished the light and lay down on the bed hard enough to make the rickety old piece of furniture squeak dismally. He was up in twenty seconds though and without making any noise. He tiptoed to the window, which was already raised.

Looking out, he saw Kraus across the street, pausing to light a cigarette. It was almost as if the man asked to be followed. The Crimson Mask hesitated for a moment. This might be just a plot on the part of that burly gang leader to find out, once and for all, if the new roomer really was a spy.

Yet the Crimson Mask could not afford to take chances. If Kraus was going to whatever hiding place they had for the boy, the Crimson Mask had to find it. Kraus was his only link.

KRAUS WALKED slowly down the street and turned a corner. The Crimson Mask quickly removed two heavy leather straps from his suitcase and buckled them together. He affixed one end to the radiator just below his window, dropped the rest of the strap outside and clambered down it agilely.

He reached the window below his room, slipped through and made his way softly to the door. In the hallway he glanced up at the sound of voices. Kraus had left men on guard to see whether or not the new roomer tried to follow.

Within two or three minutes after Kraus had disappeared, the Crimson Mask was taking the same corner and in time to spot Kraus before he made any further turns. The Crimson Mask dropped back then. The preparations which Kraus took indicated the importance of his mission and none could be more important than seeing to the boy.

The boy was in this town. The Crimson Mask was certain of that. Otherwise Kraus and his men would not be here. Finding him was the Mask's principal objective and the slightest misstep might result in catastrophe.

Kraus walked all the way and he frequently made abrupt stops or doubled back after turning corners. The Crimson Mask outwitted him every time, but he sensed that Kraus was no ordinary plug-ugly but a man with brains, and that behind him was a still smarter individual who might, so far, not even have shown his hand.

Finally, Kraus reached his destination—a small cottage on the outskirts. The burly crook knocked on the door and was instantly admitted. The Crimson Mask's hopes now arose to their highest point of the whole affair. Without much question, the boy was here.

Circling the house, the Crimson Mask paused long enough to adjust the red domino, draw his gun and carefully approach the rear door. It was locked. He crawled beneath a window which was open about half an inch. Through this slit he could look in. Kraus was talking to a squat, greasy-looking man.

The Crimson Mask began raising his gun and reaching to open the window wide and take them by surprise. Just as his hand touched the window, there was a shout behind him.

He turned fast. A man was running in his direction and he held a gun. Inside the house, Kraus instantly extinguished the lights. The Crimson Mask made a flying leap toward a lilac bush and got behind it as the gunman rushed up and looked around for the intruder he was sure he had seen.

The Crimson Mask circled the bush, reversed the grip on his gun and attacked. The gun came down, slugging the thug squarely across the back of the neck. He wilted without a sound.

The Crimson Mask left him there and raced back to the window. It was still open. He raised it. From inside, he could hear Kraus yelling indistinguishable commands. The Crimson Mask was through the window now and running in the direction of Kraus' voice.

Suddenly the burly crook stepped unexpectedly into the small hallway. He saw the shadowy form coming toward him and instantly took the offensive. He hurled himself at the Crimson Mask. They met with an impact that staggered both of them.

Kraus managed to secure a strong grip on the Crimson Mask's gun hand and gave it a savage twist. The Crimson Mask jolted a hard left to Kraus' throat, connected, and the big man reeled back.

He had remarkable powers of recovery, however, for a second later he was charging again. The Crimson Mask abruptly realized why Kraus was putting up this kind of a defense. From behind the house a car motor roared into life and tires ground against the cinders.

THE CRIMSON MASK ducked one of Kraus' wild swings, bobbed up and plastered the butt of his gun against the big man's chin. That put Kraus into a sitting position. The Crimson Mask made a dive for the door and was on the porch when the car made a quick turn out of the drive and rolled up the street to vanish from sight.

The Crimson Mask knew the taste of defeat then. The other thug had taken the boy away while Kraus held the fort. Kraus was clever enough to know that so long as he had the boy, he also held all the cards in the deck. The Crimson Mask wheeled at the sound of a slight scraping noise. He was just in time to meet another head-on assault by the big crook.

This time the Crimson Mask was thrown back by the impact and Kraus, with a growl of rage, started to follow up his advantage. There was some light on the porch and Kraus made out the color and shape of the mask on his opponent's face.

"Crimson Mask!" he shouted, "No mask scares me. I'll rip it off and pulverize your face. I'll—"

The Crimson Mask stood his ground. Kraus started to swing a blow that would have put his enemy away for an hour. It swished through the air—but the target had moved so fast that Kraus hardly noticed the act. He was thrown off balance by the swing, but the Crimson Mask knew this could not go on any longer. The thug he had knocked out behind the house would be recovering soon and the fellow still had a gun.

Taking Kraus prisoner was as hopeless as it was useless. The big man would never talk. Defeating him would have to be done by practical means and that meant only the recovery of the boy.

Kraus actually ran into the uppercut. It rocked his head, brought his teeth together with a painful snap and he fell backward across the threshold. A shout from behind the house warned the Crimson Mask it was time to leave. He sprinted away into the darkness.

Twenty minutes later he was inside the rooming house and reaching for the leather strap which hung from his own window. It was black and invisible in the darkness. He climbed it, slid into his room and quickly removed the strap.

Then he tiptoed to the door. The men were still out there. He could hear them whispering. He quietly removed the metal plug from the keyhole, concealed it, and hastily removed his clothes.

Kraus would not be unconscious long and he would at once suspect the new roomer of somehow having trailed him.

Kraus did return, not more than ten minutes after the Crimson Mask. He found his two guards in the hallway.

"But I tell you the guy never stirred," one of the men reported. "We watched that door every second."

"Did you look in on him like I told you?" Kraus demanded. "Listen—I was trailed tonight, by the Crimson Mask. He's a smooth article and if that new roomer is him, he'd put it over on you easy."

"We didn't open the door if that's what you mean," one guard replied. "We tried to use the pliers like you said, but they wouldn't work."

Kraus asked for the pair of finely pointed pliers, snarled a warning and his men drew guns. Kraus stepped up to the door, inserted the thin tips of the pliers and grasped the key in the lock. He turned it gently. He opened the door half an inch. Darkness greeted him. He opened it wider.

On the bed, the roomer stirred uneasily. Kraus stepped in, walked up close to the bed and peered down. Then he retreated, closed and relocked the door. He took off his hat and slammed it to the floor.

CHAPTER IX

HEADLINE TRAP

IN THE morning, the Crimson Mask yawned sleepily as he came out of his room. One man, sitting at the top of the stairs, glanced at him. The Crimson Mask walked out of the house and headed for the big plant where he was supposed to work.

He merged with the crowds of men and women, lost any pursuer easily and within a few moments he was on a bus bound for New York. His spirits were low and his brain frantically seeking some way of forcing Kraus to reveal where that boy had been taken.

He gave considerable thought to Edward Todd, the attorney with an unsavory record who was so eagerly coaching the boy's grandfather to keep quiet about the whole affair. Todd was perfect as the man behind the scenes.

Lockwood himself, as the boy's grandfather, seemed almost too amenable to Todd's persuasions. The Crimson Mask didn't cross off either of his meager list of suspects.

In town, he returned to the drug store, removed his make-up and donned fresh clothes. Briefly he told Dave Small what had happened, phoned Sandy, and told her to stand by for action.

Then he hurried for former Police Commissioner Warrick's house. Warrick was waiting for him.

"I muffed it last night," Clarke admitted ruefully. "The boy was all but in my hands and they got him away again. Until we have him, we're completely handicapped. Those mugs would no more hesitate to slit his throat than to light a cigarette."

"I've some better news, Bob," Warrick said. "As you suggested, the picture of the boy was radioed to the Coast last night and in time to be run off in the late afternoon and early morning papers. About half an hour ago a police chief phoned me."

"With news?" Clarke asked eagerly.

"Indeed—news of the best. The boy has been identified. His name is Paul Lockwood, all right. He was kidnaped during a visit to his grandfather—which puts the old man pretty well in the clear. His mother is dead. His father was killed on active service in the Solomons about three months ago. He left a considerable estate—well into the millions. An aunt is the guardian and executor."

"Did the aunt come forward with the information?" Clarke asked.

"Yes. When she saw the picture of the boy in the papers, she realized it was time to talk. Seems that after the boy was snatched from his grandfather she was approached by some member of the gang, and a huge amount of cash was demanded. She couldn't raise it because the estate was in probate. So she was told the boy would be held until she came through. Other than that, she has heard nothing."

Bob Clarke nodded. "And if she told the police, the boy would be killed. The old threat, the ancient method, but it still works. And they may have thought she had, until they found out different. Her hands are tied and so are ours—until the boy is found. What about the rest of my plan?"

"Working beautifully. Things will be all set for tonight."

"Excellent," Clarke said. "I hope you warned the boy's aunt not to phone the grandfather. If Todd is in on it, he'd find out about it and be on his guard."

"She has agreed to everything," Warrick said. "What's your next step?"

"Back to the drug store. Bob Clarke has to show up now and then. This afternoon I'll shoot back to Craigville in time to mingle with the workers from the plant. Sandy will contact you tonight."

BOB CLARKE returned to the drug store and relieved Dave Small until mid-afternoon. He was busily engaged in making up a prescription when Lockwood and Attorney Todd walked in. Clarke hurried to the front of the store.

"I hope you've come to tell me the boy has been found," he said earnestly.

"No—no, he hasn't," Lockwood replied. "Not a trace of him and, of course, we're afraid to see the police. I received a note this morning. It was shoved under the door of my suite. Read it."

Bob Clarke glanced at the brief message. It merely stated that if any further attempts were made to find the boy, he would be murdered. It advised that the probate court be urged to speed up the release of the money, the required sum prepared, and a blind notice be inserted in one of the evening newspapers. Clarke handed it back.

"I wish I had cash enough to help you meet their demands. By the way, Mr. Lockwood, it is my understanding that you are wealthy. Why don't you use your own cash to pay off these leeches?"

Lockwood laughed mirthlessly. "A fellow owns a couple of mines and he's put down as a millionaire. People don't stop to think that a mine owner probably has sunk every dime he could beg or borrow into the business. That's what I did. Unless I actually sold the mines, I couldn't raise a third of what those kidnapers demand."

"Tell him why we're here," Todd broke in.

"Oh, yes. We understand from the hospital that you and Paul had many talks. I hoped—forlornly, I suppose that he told you something which might help us to locate him. I'm ready to hire private detectives. Hire you also if you think you can help."

Clarke shook his head. "I'm sorry. You see, Paul was a pretty sick boy when I saw him. Frightened, too. He didn't talk much."

Lockwood sighed. "Then you can't help. Of course, I didn't hope too much, but Todd seemed to think you might know something. I'll see you again, under more fortunate circumstances, I hope."

Bob Clarke watched the pair walk out and wondered just why they had wasted time coming to see him. It sounded like Todd's idea and perhaps he merely wanted to find out whether or not there was a possibility that Bob Clarke might be the Crimson Mask, now operating in Craigville. There seemed to be no other answer.

That evening, when the big mill turned out its day shift, the Crimson Mask, in the same simple disguise, mingled with them as they passed through the gate. In a few moments he was back at the rooming house, armed with another West Coast newspaper.

He was reading it when Kraus came in. The burly man showed plenty of signs he had been in a fight. The Crimson Mask did not comment on them and Kraus offered no explanations. He picked up the newspaper and glanced at it. This edition contained no stories about the kidnaped boy. Kraus threw it down and stalked out.

"I'm getting another one later on," the Crimson Mask called after him. "I'll drop it in your room or outside the door if you like."

Kraus grunted assent. It was clear that he was worried, had almost reached the stage where he was beginning to lose his wits. The Crimson Mask mentally promised the brute another shock.

At seven-thirty the Crimson Mask went out. He was not sure whether or not he was being followed and took no precautions against such a move. He went to a cheap restaurant, ate leisurely and then ambled to the teeming center of this busy mill town.

HE SAW Sandy standing at a prearranged corner where buses stopped. The Crimson Mask stopped directly beside her. They seemed to be oblivious to one another, but Sandy spoke to him without moving her lips much.

"The paper is under my arm. It was flown from the Coast. No other editions will arrive until tomorrow, but the story is all over the West Coast right now. You'll have to work fast before local papers pick it up over the news wires."

"Good," the Crimson Mask replied. "You have the car? Meet me two blocks north of my rooming house. Be ready to travel fast."

She gave a barely perceptible nod. A bus pulled into the curb and Sandy started to climb aboard it. Her newspaper slipped from beneath her arm. The Crimson Mask quickly picked it up, switched it for one he held in his hand and turned away.

He returned to the rooming house as casually as if this were just an evening's stroll to get some of the factory dust out of his lungs. In his room, he proceeded to read the newspaper which Warrick had arranged to have printed and flown to the East.

Someone entered, climbed the steps and passed by his door. He looked up. That was undoubtedly the man who was detailed to shadow him.

"Hey!" the Crimson Mask stopped him. "If you see Kraus around, will you tell him I've got another newspaper? I'll leave it here on my table. The door will be open. I'm going to the movies."

"Yeah."

The crook gave him a funny glance and walked a little faster in the direction of Kraus' room.

The Crimson Mask seized his hat, hurried out of the house and popped into his car which was parked two blocks north with Sandy at the wheel. If Kraus was going to detail another man to trail him, it was too late now.

"Let's go," he told Sandy. "In another couple of hours we'll know who is behind this and we'll have Kraus where we want him—right behind bars, or on a morgue slab. Either one would suit me. Gorillas who snatch kids aren't worth the space they occupy."

Sandy kept the car at a steady speed. In lonely spots she let it out, but there was always danger of being picked up by motor cops. Speed laws were strictly enforced these days. In a short time the faint glow over the city was discernible.

"Unless Kraus knows some shortcut," Sandy said, "we've beat him to it. No cars passed us."

"I've been watching, too," the Crimson Mask said. "Maybe Kraus hasn't seen the newspaper yet, but something tells me he has. The man was eager to see if there were any stories about the snatch. The one he'll read in that paper I left will blow his hair off."

Sandy stopped not far from the swanky hotel where Lockwood had his suite. She took time to repair some damage to lipstick and rouge, adjusted her hat and nodded. "The concert artist is now ready. Shall we go?"

The Crimson Mask had removed the domino long before. He looked at the somewhat seedy clothing which characterized his part as a factory worker.

"You'd better go in alone, Sandy. I'll use the service entrance. Check your watch with mine. It's now nine-eighteen. At nine-thirty-five, start your performance."

They parted and the Crimson Mask made his way to the less austere entrance, entered a service elevator and went to Lockwood's floor. He made certain no one was around the corridors, adjusted the red mask, and walked up to Lockwood's door. He rapped hard.

LOCKWOOD OPENED it and started back in amazement and fright. The Crimson Mask stepped in and kicked the door shut.

"There's no need to be afraid, Mr. Lockwood," he said. "I'm the Crimson Mask. I know about your grandson and I came to offer my help."

"Oh, yes—yes, of course," Lockwood gulped. "Naturally, I've heard about you, but I never thought you'd interest yourself in a kidnaping case."

"There aren't many crimes more vicious," the Crimson Mask said. "Shall we talk it over?"

Lockwood could only nod, but he led the way to the living room and offered a chair. The Crimson Mask sat down and leaned back comfortably.

"I almost managed to rescue the boy last night," he said. "They had him in a town up in Connecticut."

"You actually saw him?" Lockwood asked. "Was he all right? Paul had been severely hurt, you know. He needed care. I—I…Do you mind if I have a drink? One for you, too, of course."

The Crimson Mask accepted. Lockwood went to a small bar which was part of the apartment fixtures. He pulled open a drawer, took out two napkins and placed them on a tray. Then he mixed two strong drinks, put the tray on a table and the Crimson Mask took his.

"How can I help you find him?" Lockwood said.

"By answering a few questions. For instance, how did you know those kidnapers actually had the boy?"

"Why—why, they approached his aunt. Naturally she told me. The child was kidnaped from my home."

"You received no other proof? Letters written by the boy, for instance?"

"No—no, I did not. Would you mind if I phoned my attorney? Perhaps he can offer some suggestions."

"I'm afraid any attorney would be quite superfluous, Mr. Lockwood," the Crimson Mask replied. "Tell me something about the boy's education. His hobbies—things like that."

"Why, he had none in particular," Lockwood exclaimed. "He was just a normal boy."

Suddenly the apartment rang to the notes of a piano played loudly. Lockwood gave an annoyed gesture, started to talk again and the piano blared out a melody.

"Confounded hotels," Lockwood snapped. "You never know what will move in next door. I'm under a strain and that playing isn't going to help me."

"It isn't so nice," the Crimson Mask admitted. "That selection being played happens to be a Chopin waltz, meant to be played softly and slowly. Don't you recognize it, Mr. Lockwood?"

"All I know is that it is driving me mad," Lockwood groaned. "I'll phone downstairs and have the management ask that tenant to stop."

"A good idea," the Crimson Mask said. "While you're at it, have the management also send for the police."

"The police? Why?"

"To make an arrest, of course. I'd name the man except that I don't know your name. It isn't Lockwood, of course. What have you done with the boy?"

CHAPTER X

MESSAGE TO SANDY

SLOWLY THE impostor leaned back, holding his half-emptied glass. For a moment it seemed he would try to bluff it out, but a look at the steady eyes glittering from behind the mask told him he would never put it over.

"So it's come to this, has it?" he snarled instead.

The Crimson Mask nodded.

"About time, too, don't you think? In a game like the one you play, the slightest slip means disaster. You slipped twice. The first time when you told me the boy never sent you any notes, indicating he was still alive. His aunt got none either and yet the boy wrote a lot of them. They were mailed to the real Peter Lockwood. To keep him quiet, of course."

"And the second mistake?" the impostor asked.

"The boy had been taught to love good music. One of his favorite numbers was 'Serenade'. It's being played right now. I arranged to have it happen at this moment because I felt sure you didn't know Schubert from Chopin or Cole Porter. Yet you claim to have brought the boy up, that he lived with you for years. Where else then would he get a musical education but in the home where he lived? And who would see that he was tutored in music except a man who loved it, as the boy does?"

The impostor smiled slowly.

"You're not underrated, Crimson Mask. When I heard from Kraus last night that you were on his trail, I really became worried. Now that we have the showdown, why not take off that mask and let me see who you really are."

The Crimson Mask chuckled. "I don't think so. Instead, we'll talk about the boy—and the real Peter Lockwood. Where are they?"

The impostor smiled again, drained his glass and placed it on the tray. He picked up the napkin and moved it toward his lips.

Halfway, the cloth dropped from his hand and he was holding a small but deadly automatic.

"It pays well to be always prepared," he said. "Now take off that mask or I'll put a bullet through it."

The Crimson Mask's voice was just as calm.

"Of course, you wouldn't hesitate at murder. You killed that attendant you hired to take care of the boy. That was skillfully done. Oh, yes, it reminds me of another little clue. I knew you had pictures of the boy. You showed them at the hospital. Yet I understand you did not turn any of the pictures over to the police even though they might have helped a great deal. You were afraid they might be printed and the boy's aunt might see them."

The impostor laughed sarcastically.

"Now I can shoot and not care whether or not you remove the mask. You are Bob Clarke, the druggist. I suspected that all along—ever since I found out the Crimson Mask was working on the case. Well, am I right?"

"You'll have to shoot first," the Crimson Mask told him, "if you wish to see what is behind the mask. And I wouldn't advise it. Police are all over the hotel. In a few moments they'll be at the door. You can't possibly escape."

"A likely story," the impostor derided. "You work alone, Crimson Mask. There are no police."

"We'll wait and see. I must compliment you on the way this job was pulled off. When the newspaper stories about the boy's rescue were printed, Kraus phoned you, of course. You promptly disposed of the real Peter Lockwood, took his papers and his place, came here where you were not known and established yourself in the hotel. Then you visited the hospital with an attorney, especially selected for his unsavory reputation. I even know why—because if anything went wrong, the police would suspect him first. You got the boy out of the hospital and brought him here.

"Playing the part of Peter Lockwood was easy, so you decided to play it out. You killed the attendant, sacrificing a man's life just to bolster an alibi. You smuggled the boy out of the hotel and then pretended it was all the work of the kidnapers."

"I'm a clever man," the impostor said. "I appreciate it in others, too. That's why I'm going to shoot you. I'll remove the mask, and destroy it and say you came here representing the kidnapers. They'll believe me—long enough for me to escape, anyhow. Competition of the kind you offer must be obliterated and so—"

THE GUN came up and centered. The crook heard the elevator door clang shut and heavy feet marching down the corridor. Then there was a terrific banging at the door. The impostor drew in a quick breath of anguish, glanced at the Crimson Mask and saw him serenely studying the tips of his fingers. The crook arose hastily.

"We're going out together. I'll keep the gun on you. If those cops interfere, you'll get the first bullet. Get up—walk toward the door."

The Crimson Mask arose slowly, while the pounding went on and the piano continued to play at an annoying tempo and crescendo. He walked to the door. The impostor commanded him to open it. The Crimson Mask grasped the knob firmly, flung the door wide and Kraus barged in.

For a second or two, both Kraus and the impostor were stunned by surprise. The Crimson Mask's right hand moved out in a flash. It wrenched the gun from the crook's grasp. The impostor went hurtling backward from a blow to the jaw. Kraus turned to run for it.

"Stop or I'll shoot!" the Crimson Mask warned.

Kraus stopped. He turned around, raised his hands and came back. Hand on his jaw, the impostor sat up shakily.

"Kraus, you ignorant fool, I told you never to come here."

"Yeah," Kraus roared, "but you forgot to tell me the old lady had crashed through with dough. A hundred and fifty grand. Sure, you forgot to tell any of us that and we did all the dirty work."

"You're crazy!" the impostor cried. "Am I?" Kraus hurled a ragged newspaper to the floor. "Read that. The headlines. They say the kid's aunt paid off a hundred and fifty grand, but the kid wasn't released—the kidnapers wanted more. You held out, and now look what happened."

"That's correct, gentlemen," the Crimson Mask said. "Look what happened. Mr. Lockwood—for want of a better name—if you say one more word, I'll put a bullet through you. Kraus, you know where the boy is. You probably also know where the real Lockwood is. Kidnaping happens to be a hanging offense now. There's a Federal law. Your one out is to produce the boy and his grandfather. Now—without waiting another moment. Otherwise, you'll swing. The Government usually uses the rope on kidnapers."

Kraus felt of his neck and turned pale. The impostor started to shriek a warning. The Crimson Mask turned the gun on him. Kraus licked his lips.

"I knew this wouldn't work out. We snatched the kid because we figured he had a lot of dough left by his old man. We didn't know it was in probate. Yeah, I'll talk. The kid is downstairs, in my car. The boys are watching him because I figured we were being double-crossed. The old man never was snatched. Orden, here—that's the name of the monkey on the floor—just ordered the old man to go to a hotel in Portland and register under a phony name. He was to stay there, even if it meant days, and the boy would be returned to him. Orden just busted into Lockwood's house, swiped clothes, pictures of the kid, and some money. He… Look out for the rat!"

The Crimson Mask swung to face Orden. Kraus darted out the door, slamming it after him. Orden started to get up. The Crimson Mask's foot lashed out and Orden fell back. Then the Crimson Mask ran out into the corridor.

KRAUS WAS at the far end already. He looked over his shoulder and saw the Crimson Mask standing there. Kraus had a gun in his hand. It came up and flamed once.

He missed because the Crimson Mask had fired just a fraction of a second earlier. The Crimson Mask's bullet did not miss. Kraus took it full in the chest. He folded up and fell heavily.

Sandy came out of the suite adjoining the false Lockwood's. The Crimson Mask whipped off the domino, grabbed her hand and they fled toward the staircase. Four floors below, they got into an elevator. In the lobby, the Crimson Mask stepped into a phone booth and called the police.

He left the hotel, looked down the street and saw a sedan bearing an auxiliary marker plate indicating it was from Craigville. He and Sandy stopped and waited. Two radio cars drove up silently. One shot in front of the parked car, the other blocked any hope of its backing up. Armed police got out.

More police arrived, finally an ambulance. The Crimson Mask saw the boy lifted from the car, saw three of Kraus' men climb out and reach for the stars.

Police were entering the hotel. Kraus, wounded, could not escape and the Crimson Mask's toes still tingled from the kick he had given the fake Lockwood. They would never escape.

He took Sandy's arm and they walked toward his car.

"You played Schubert like a disciple of boogie-woogie," he said, and grinned. "But it was loud enough to serve the purpose. Now let's get back to the hospital. Orden—the false Lockwood—will insist the Crimson Mask is Bob Clarke and I'd like to establish an alibi."

Sandy drove and the Crimson Mask quickly removed the make-up. His clothes were not the usual neat garments which Bob Clarke wore, but he quickly donned a lab apron that covered them well enough. Sandy hurried to the floor assigned to her.

An hour later she came down to the lab, her cheeks flushed, her eyes bright.

"Kraus didn't die, and he talked," she said. "He still blamed Orden for doublecrossing him. Mr. Warrick told me this. They telephoned Portland and the real Lockwood was found there just as Kraus indicated."

"And the boy?" Bob Clarke asked.

"He's upstairs, in his old room. They brought him here because every cop in town knew it's where he belonged. His memory is coming back, too. And, Bob—the boy had a message for me. His greatest worry was that he wouldn't be able to deliver it, but he did."

Clarke fussed with the pharmaceutical scales.

"Guess I'd better go up and see him," he said. "You don't mind?"

"He's asking for you," Sandy said.

Clarke grinned and walked away. Sandy stepped to the doorway.
"I left a message with him, too. Be sure to ask him—"

Bob Clarke's pace turned into a trot. He looked over his shoulder and smiled broadly.

TRAFFIC IN MURDER

CHAPTER I

VISITOR IN THE NIGHT

HE WAS a man of medium height, well-bundled up against the strong, icy blasts of an early winter. It was night but the street lights threw weird shadows against the snow that was falling fast. In the downtown areas, men were already working against time to clear up the snow before traffic started the next day.

The man seemed to be afraid. He kept looking over his shoulder as if he expected to see a dozen demons running him down. There was an expression of mixed horror and determination on his face. He was about forty, well dressed in arctics, a muffler, heavy gloves and a big overcoat, the collar of which was drawn well around his neck to keep out the cold and the driving snow.

He stopped beneath a street light and consulted a small piece of paper. He glanced at the sign beneath the light, made sure he was on the right track and began walking very fast up the silent, rather imposing street.

Here, only wealthy people lived, and the houses were big affairs, but neither rich nor poor were spared the fury of the storm. Doors and windows were tightly secured. A few lights burned in some of the windows.

The man was looking for a number. He hurried onto one porch, lit a match and found he was wrong. He half ran back to the sidewalk, kept going and counted houses in an effort to get the right one next time.

He finally paused for a last, long look around and saw nothing. It was difficult to see much farther than half a block anyhow because of the swirling snowflakes. He missed, entirely, the elongated shadow of a man who stood behind a thick tree trunk.

This man watched the hurrying individual run up the stairs of the big house. He saw the door open and then close. The watcher promptly headed for the nearest telephone.

Meanwhile, the frightened man punched the doorbell and waited impatiently. Above the bell was a neat nameplate indicating that Theodore Warrick lived here. Warrick himself opened the door. He was dressed in pajamas and a dressing gown.

"Are you Warrick?" the caller asked hoarsely. "The same man who used to be police Commissioner?"

"Yes," Warrick replied. "I'm that same man. What's wrong? Why, man, you're pale as a ghost. Come in out of the cold and tell me what's the matter."

"No—wait—I must be very certain," the visitor said. He dropped his voice to a whisper. "Are you also the man who can contact the Crimson Mask?"

WARRICK SEIZED him by the arm and practically yanked him inside. He closed the door, led the man into a study and sat down. The visitor didn't. He kept pacing the floor and Warrick saw little beads of sweat on the man's face, even though he'd just come in out of a raging blizzard.

The visitor finally stopped walking. He began to talk and the more words he uttered, the moister his face became. What he had to say made ex-Police Commissioner Warrick turn pale with horror.

"If what you are telling me is the truth," Warrick said, "it is vital that you see the Crimson Mask at once. If you told this story to the police, they'd begin a clumsy investigation which would wind up by these people covering their tracks so well nothing would ever come of it."

"Then take me to the Crimson Mask," the man said. "Unless we move fast it will be too late. I—forgot to tell you my name. It's Webb, Tony Webb. I'm not lying, Mr. Warrick. Even a confirmed liar couldn't think up a story like the one I just told you."

Tony Webb suddenly leaned against Bob heavily

"Wait here," Warrick said, "while I dress. We'll drive to see the Crimson Mask. It's very unusual, but so is your story. As you say, speed is positively essential so, to save time, I'll take you to him. Remember—I trust you not to reveal anything that happens. You will be left in my car, in a certain neighborhood. I'll go away and return shortly with the Crimson Mask. You understand, we can't risk revealing his identity to anyone, not even to you."

"Just hurry—please," Webb begged. "I had a feeling they were following me. I didn't see anyone, but they are very clever. There is someone who heads the organization. Someone who looks far beyond the present and if he isn't stopped, this is no telling what will happen. Ruined lives will be only a part of it."

Warrick hurried upstairs. He dressed with all haste and ran down the steps. He led Webb out the back door, across the yard now a foot and a half deep in fine snow, to the garage. They climbed into a sedan.

Warrick turned into the street and headed south. He made several other turns also. Far behind him, driving without lights, was another car and it was closely followed by still another. The passengers in these two cars were stony-faced men. Two of them had rifles.

Warrick finally entered an avenue which led downtown and he stepped on it. Gradually, the avenue changed. At the start it had been lined with large, handsome dwellings. These became two-story wooden affairs with cheap stores on the first floor. Even the road itself turned from smooth paving into cobblestones which were treacherously covered with ice and snow. Warrick skidded a couple of times, but straightened out successfully. He didn't speak. Neither did Webb who was tight-lipped and worried-looking.

ONCE WEBB removed his hat to mop perspiration from his forehead. This, in the face of a howling wind that got through the car windows and almost froze the moisture on his skin.

"We're almost there," Warrick said. "However, I'm as worried as you that we are being trailed. Tell me—how did you get away from those men?"

"It wasn't hard," Webb replied. "There were a lot of them and they were too sure of themselves. I managed to slip into a small supply closet which was provided with a window. Before they broke down the door or got men around to cover the window, I got through, jumped a story to the ground and escaped. It was almost too easy. I heard them searching for me and sometimes I wonder how in the world they didn't see me."

"Perhaps they did," Warrick grunted. "It's possible they let you go, but put men on your trail to see just what you intended to do about this ghastly business. Another five or ten minutes and we'll make it. The Crimson Mask will be able to help and in a case of this kind, he'll go after those buzzards with a vengeance."

"I was going to see the F.B.I.," Webb said, "but I thought they'd be too slow also. I... Warrick—there is a car right behind us."

Warrick glanced up in the rear-view mirror. It was true. A heavy sedan was no more than twenty yards to the rear and pacing them. Warrick looked down the deserted street for signs of a cop. He didn't see even a pedestrian.

Warrick was ready to pass an intersection and the traffic light was red. Here he could tell if the car behind really was trailing him. Warrick went right through the light. So did the car in back of him.

At the next intersection, Warrick got set to do a little fancy gymnastics with the wheel. He intended to turn the corner sharply, spurt down the side street and double back—before the trailing car could spot him—he hoped.

As Warrick got the wheel set to make that turn, another heavy car shot from the side street Warrick jerked the wheel to the left very fast and narrowly avoided a collision. He had a momentary glimpse of guns in the other car. There were two of them after him now.

Warrick straightened out and stepped on the gas pedal very hard. He managed to put some distance between himself and the two cars that were roaring after him.

"Narrow squeak," he muttered. "They intended to drive that second car right in our path, but it so happened I was going to turn the same corner they came out of and I confused them. Webb—from here on, it's up to you."

"They know I've told you everything," Webb cried. "They're after both of us now. They'll kill us, Mr. Warrick. What can we do?"

"I'm taking the next corner," Warrick said. "I happen to know this section perfectly. I used to be a patrolman on this beat. Are you game to risk your neck?"

Webb smiled wryly.

"Why not—they'll break it for me anyhow. I'll take any chance."

"Good," Warrick said. "When I turn this corner, you have the door open. Before the two cars catch up, you jump out. It will be dangerous, but as you say, hardly more so than waiting until they open fire. Webb—what's the matter? You're perspiring terribly, and this is such a cold night...."

"I—don't feel very well." Webb wetted his lips. "In fact, I feel miserable. Go on, Mr. Warrick. After I jump out, then what?"

"You'll find an alley right in front of you. Run down it, climb a fence and you'll come out on another street. Keep well to the building line and in the shadows. I'll draw off these crooks if I can. Now listen carefully. Go to the center of Varick and White Streets. You'll see a drug store there. Old-fashioned sort of place. If it is closed, bang on the door until someone comes."

"Varick and White Streets," Webb repeated. "I've got that. What else?"

"Ask for Robert Clarke. He owns the store. Tell him I sent you and that you want to see the Crimson Mask. Clarke can reach him also. Ready now? Travel fast when you hit the street."

"I'm ready," Webb said, "but what about you? They'll catch you sure and… they'll kill you, Mr. Warrick. They'll know darn well I've told you everything."

Warrick grimaced.

"I'll have to take my chances. A couple of lives—yours and mine, are small penalty to pay for putting the Crimson Mask on the trail of these beasts. Here we go, Webb. Best of luck to you."

Warrick glanced up to the rear-view mirror. The cars were closing in, but still a good half-block behind. He yanked the wheel hard over. The car skidded around the corner and straightened out. Webb jumped. He slipped on the icy street, fell, but got to his feet in a hurry and was well inside the alley before the two cars hurtled after Warrick.

Webb didn't see it happen, but as Warrick turned out of the narrow street, a man in the front car fired two quick shots. The rear tire of Warrick's car blew out. Warrick tried to handle the wheel, couldn't and ended up with the front wheels halfway across the sidewalk. He attempted to get out and run, but two guns covered him. He gave a sigh of resignation and raised his hands.

Meanwhile, Tony Webb scaled a wooden fence, reached the next street and walked briskly along it. He was about eight blocks from the designated drug store.

The snow was coming down harder than ever, accompanied now by a roaring wind. Icy particles cut into Webb's sweat-covered face. It had grown frosty because the sweat froze almost as fast as it was formed.

Webb breathed heavily. He finally removed his muffler and dropped it in the gutter. Next, he took off his overcoat, then his hat. A block further, he discarded his suitcoat and vest. Even this didn't seem to abate the furnace within him. His eyes bulged now, his mouth was open as he gasped for air.

He ripped off his shirt, not stopping to open the buttons. He was clad now in only his underwear, socks and shoes. At the next corner he removed his shoes and socks, wadded above his ankles in the snow.

He began to stagger. His lips moved, muttering words that hardly made sense. No one saw him. The blizzard drove everyone indoors. He seized a traffic pole and pressed his forehead against its ice-cold steel surface.

"Got to… go on," he muttered. "Got to reach… Varick and White. Clarke… he knows Crimson Mask. Robert Clarke…."

Once he fell and lay in the snow, seizing handfuls of it and rubbing it against his flesh. At last, he regained his feet and staggered on. Tony Webb was a very game man. With every step, he knew he was doomed. Knew that no power on earth could save him, yet dogged determination kept his legs moving.

CHAPTER II

RED HOT CORPSE

A TALL, SLENDER man was darkening the windows of the drug store at Varick and White Streets. His name— Robert Clarke, Ph.G.—was neatly printed in small gold letters on the front door.

Bob Clarke had been running this drug store since shortly after the murder of his police sergeant father. That had occurred when he was still in college. The drug store wasn't exactly in the modern trend. There were no counters laden with perfumes, coffee percolators or smoking essentials. There was no soda fountain or candy counter.

Instead, the showcases were neatly arranged with rows of physicians' equipment and the prescription room behind the store was quite large and provided with almost every available drug for the easing of pain and the curing of sickness.

Bob Clarke, however, was as modern as his drug store was old-fashioned. He maintained an assistant, stocky, apple-cheeked Dave Small. Business wasn't exactly booming and Bob Clarke could have handled the store alone, but there were times when his presence was required elsewhere.

Bob Clarke was the Crimson Mask. A scientific, anonymous crime fighter who worked beneath the protection of a red velvet mask. There was a reason why he had adopted this mask. His father had been shot in the back by crooks. Bob Clarke was in the hospital as his father died and shortly before the end, his father's face became suffused with a peculiar blood-red glow that took the shape of a mask across his features.

From that phenomenon, Bob Clarke had adopted his trademark. He decided at that moment to keep on with his studies, open a drug store as his father had long planned and wished. Yet Bob Clarke also made up his mind that he would develop an avocation, that of fighting the type of men who had murdered his father.

With this purpose in mind, he had made a study of crime, its causes, its cures and how to work against men to whom human lives and property meant nothing. He maintained a large, excellently-equipped, crime laboratory behind his prescription room. It was provided with microscopes, spectroscopes, apparatus, chemicals and many volumes on the subject of crime. He also kept an up-to-date rogue's gallery, garnered from newspaper clippings and other sources.

There were exactly three people who knew of his dual identity. Dave Small, of course, not only knew Bob Clarke was the Crimson Mask, but actively aided him in the work. Ted Warrick, who had been one of the best police commissioners the city ever had known, was the Crimson Mask's only direct contact with the outer world. Ted Warrick had been the elder Clarke's best friend and Warrick helped Bob in every way.

The third member of his little team was Sandra Grey, better known as Sandy. Blond, beautiful, she had as much spirit as beauty. She had been aided by the Crimson Mask once and had stumbled upon his secret.

BOB CLARKE promptly made her his aide. Not only because she knew his double identity, but because he liked her. This warmth had ripened into love, but there was little planning ahead. So long as he worked as the Crimson Mask, he didn't dare expose her directly to the danger which would envelop him if the crooks and leeches ever discovered his identity.

With this small but highly-efficient organization, the Crimson Mask carried on, always alert for developing crimes, always ready to step in and battle for the underdog.

As Clarke put out the lights, he sighed deeply.

"Well," he said over his shoulder, "if you have the Mallotti boy's medicine ready, I'll take it over. Thank heavens, it isn't so far away. This, Dave, is one beastly night."

Dave Small wrapped a bottle of medicine carefully.

"I wouldn't go out in it," he said. "Heck of a thing—you deliver this medicine to help that kid fight off pneumonia and you'll probably get a case of it yourself."

Bob Clarke grinned.

"Perhaps, but the boy needs that medicine badly. His mother is sick, too. How much does it come to, Dave?"

"Two bucks thirty." Dave said. "I'll put it on the bill as usual. By the way, did you know Mrs. Mallotti's account is now thirty-seven bucks?"

"I know," Bob nodded. "Much too high. When you add this amount to it, don't tally the three. Just add it to seven dollars. A slight mistake. We don't need money that badly, Dave."

Dave shrugged.

"Boy, if these accounts were ever audited and you weren't around, I'd land in prison for grand larceny. I—ah—stopped at the delicatessen on my way back from dinner. I—ah—bought a couple of roasted chickens. You know—spur of the moment stuff. Now I can't use them so I figured you might take them along…"

Bob made a derisive sound with his lips.

"Listen to the tough guy who talks hard and has a heart as soft as butter. Okay, let's have 'em."

Bob dressed carefully and warmly. He tucked the bundle of roasted chickens under his arm, thrust the bottle of medicine into his pocket and opened the door. An icy-blast made him wince.

He put his head down and walked out into the storm.

There was a thermometer outside the hardware store half a block up the street and he felt colder, as he looked at the narrow red line that read four above zero. Bending against the storm, he started his eight-block trek to the home of a sick boy.

This was a squalid section of the city. Nobody who lived here had much money, but Bob liked the people. They were honest. They held their heads high and fought life doggedly. That was why he stood willing to give them a lift now and then. His accounts were in chaos. Purposely so, because often some of his customers were forced to ask for credit. Then they saved for weeks to pay up only to find that the bill was about one-third of what they believed it to be.

Bob Clarke was a strange individual. As Bob Clarke, he was tender-hearted to a point that almost became embarrassing at times. As the Crimson Mask, he became an opposite character. He was strong, tough and deadly. Perhaps that was one reason why not a soul suspected that Bob Clarke could possibly be the Crimson Mask.

HE FIRST saw the approaching figure as the man passed under a street light a block away. With this initial glance Bob Clarke thought he was seeing things through the swirling snow. The man wore nothing but his underwear. He was bare-headed, bare-footed and... he was staggering like a drunk.

Bob began running toward him. Even if the man was so under the influence of liquor that he ventured out practically naked on a night like this, he needed help.

But as Clarke neared him, he saw that it was far more serious than too many highballs. This man was as pale as the snow he waded through. His face was covered with frost as if he'd been gently showered and thrust out into the frigid temperature.

Clarke grasped the man's arm.

"You're sick," he said. "What's wrong, Mister?"

The man made a weak attempt to pull free and he kept muttering words. Bob stepped closer to hear him.

"Got to... Varick and White... Clarke. Bob Clarke... knows Crimson Mask. Warrick says so. Warrick says... go to Clarke... drug store. Must get there...."

Bob's eyes opened wide. He forgot the cold, forgot everything, but the fact that Ted Warrick must have sent this man to see him and he would have-done so only under the most desperate conditions.

"I'm Bob Clarke," he said. "Listen to me—I'm Bob Clarke, What did Warrick want you to tell me? Speak up, man!"

It was no use. Tony Webb did his utmost but he had kept going only under the greatest physical strain. His eyes were fiery red as he looked vaguely at Bob Clarke. His lips moved again, but no words issued.

Tony Webb suddenly leaned against Bob heavily.

Bob Clarke eased him to the sidewalk, hastily removed a glove to feel for a pulse and almost cried out in horror and surprise. There was no pulse. The man was dead, but... in this, near-zero temperature, in the face of this driving snow and the fact that the dead man had divested himself of almost all his clothing, the flesh was hot. Not warm but actually hot as if inner fires burned fiercely.

Bob Clarke looked up and around. There was no one in sight. He glanced down the street and saw a shoe sticking out of the snow. Bob felt of the dead man's naked feet. They were as hot as his wrist, The area over his heart was similarly red hot.

Bob knew this internal heat was what made the stranger discard most of his clothing. He wanted to identify the man. Certainly, this was Bob's business now. Warrick had apparently sent the man to see him and he'd been killed on the way. Murdered, without the slightest doubt, for there was no known disease which would cause a temperature like the one this man had endured.

Bob laid him gently against a snow bank and then hurried off to search for his clothing. He picked up the first shoe, shortly after the second and a pair of socks. Further on, he found his coat and vest, but the pockets were empty.

SHORTLY, HE discovered the overcoat, hat and muffler. The hat bore the initials A.F.W. The overcoat was quite average. Jammed into one pocket was a wadded bit of paper. Opening this, Bob Clarke found an address written on it. He stowed it into his own pocket.

A police whistle sounded, shrilly and Clarke groaned. It meant the corpse had been discovered. He returned to the corner and saw a patrolman bending over the body. He didn't go back. Once the police took possession of the corpse, he could no longer examine it as he wished. That would have to come later—somehow.

Bob remembered the bottle of medicine and the two roast chickens under his arm. He hurried to the house, made the delivery and stopped long enough, to cheer up a very sick boy. His next stop was at a tobacco store where there was a telephone booth. He entered this and dialed Warrick's house.

A servant answered Bob's questions.

"Yes, Mr. Clarke, Mr. Warrick left the house very suddenly about half an hour ago. He took the sedan. Yes, he had a visitor. A man about five-feet-nine or ten. Wearing a dark overcoat and a gray fedora. Not the best, no. Average quality. I saw him from the upper landing."

"Did you overhear anything this man said?"

"Of course not, sir. I don't make a habit of eavesdropping, but even if I did, it would have been no use. The man talked in a very low voice, sir."

"If Mr. Warrick returns, have him phone me at once, will you? I'll call again in the morning if I don't hear from him."

Clarke walked out at the store, and into the blizzard, hardly aware of the driving snow and the stiff wind that whipped against his face.

Warrick was undoubtedly in trouble of some kind. He and this stranger had been on their way to see him. Something had happened and Warrick must have told the stranger to go on alone. That meant Warrick tried to divert the murderer or murderers away so that the stranger would have an opportunity to tell his story. He couldn't have known the man was dying, or was helpless to prevent it.

Bob walked past the spot where the man had fallen. A morgue wagon had pulled up and they were loading the corpse into it. He kept on going. At least he knew the morgue to which the body was being taken. That might help. He had to solve the eerie mystery of what made a man's flesh literally burn in zero temperature.

CHAPTER III

THE YELLOW FACE

THROUGH THE rest of the night Clarke only dozed. In the security of his crime lab behind the drug store he waited for word from Warrick. None came and he realized that Warrick was either dead or he'd been taken prisoner. Clarke inclined toward the latter idea, for a small radio was kept going beside him and if Warrick's body was discovered, it would constitute a news item big enough to interrupt the programs.

If he were a prisoner, it was for two quite obvious reasons. The murderers must know he represented the Crimson Mask and were holding him as a hostage to dull any blow the Crimson Mask might wish to strike or... to force Warrick to reveal the identity of the Crimson Mask.

In the gray dawn, Dave Small joined him and not long after Sandy arrived in answer to his call. He told them both exactly what had happened.

"The dead man's name may be Anthony F. Webb. I'm inclined to think so because I found those initials in his hat and an envelope in his overcoat pocket bearing that name and an address."

"But what about Ted Warrick?" Sandy asked in a worried voice. "Bob—if you make a move, he may be killed."

"I know," Clarke answered grimly. "Yet, we just can't sit here and do nothing because they'll eventually kill him anyhow. We must work very quietly. First, to discover who Anthony F. Webb was and what reasons there may have been for his strange murder."

"Imagine," Sandy mused, "almost naked in that terrible storm and his flesh so hot it seemed to be on fire. It's the strangest death I've ever heard of, Bob."

"That goes for me, too," Clarke grunted, "and the very method of murder is such that it may furnish a clue. Now, first of all, I want a chance to examine the corpse in the morgue. I'll need your help for that, Sandy. Put on some sedate clothes, a gray wig, low-heeled black shoes and an old-fashioned hat. Meanwhile, I'll acquire a disguise. We'll go to the morgue, looking for someone who answers the description of the victim. What happens then depends upon circumstances."

Sandy was ready half an hour later and she looked like a gray-haired lady of about sixty. There was an appearance of intense worry on her face. Sandy was a capable actress.

Meanwhile Bob Clarke had seated himself in front of a triple-mirrored table and gone to work on his own features. Adept fingers, with the aid of chemicals, created an entirely new face. His hair became jet black, his skin swarthy, his lips narrow and colder. He looked about fifteen years older. He then dressed in sleek, tailored clothes.

Leaving Dave to take care of the store, Sandy and the Crimson Mask left the premises by a rear door which took them across back alleys to another street. There they hailed a taxi and were driven to the morgue.

IT WAS deserted in these very early morning hours. A sympathetic attendant listened to the Crimson Mask.

"I'm an attorney," he explained. "This woman's son didn't return home night before last nor since that time. She is afraid he has been killed. He is five-feet-nine, weighs a hundred and sixty, has medium dark hair, blue eyes and a fair complexion. Have you anyone of that description here?"

"Well," the attendant rubbed his chin, "that's a pretty general description, Mister. We did receive a cadaver about five or six hours ago. Was he wearing a dark blue suit and a black overcoat and light hat?"

"Yes," Sandy cried in horror. "Yes, that was how Paul was dressed. It must be him. I must be sure…"

The attendant hesitated.

"Well, the police were pretty fussy about that cadaver, but they didn't say I should not show it. Maybe it would help if you did recognize him. Say, Mister, do you think she can stand it?"

"I'm not afraid," Sandy said. "Hurry, please."

The attendant led them into the morgue proper and Sandy shivered openly. The attendant checked numbers on the big filing cabinets and hauled the proper one out. There was a covered corpse on it. He raised the sheet.

Sandy felt her knees buckle. Even the Crimson Mask gave a gasp of astonishment. This was the man he'd watched die only a few hours before, but he had changed. His face was a distinct yellow. A livid yellow, as loudly colored as a Christmas necktie. Even the whites of the eyes had acquired this highly-jaundiced appearance.

The Crimson Mask gave Sandy a gentle nudge. She promptly collapsed onto the floor.

"Better get some water and some spirits of ammonia," the Crimson Mask told the attendant. "I'll take care of her until you get back. Why didn't you tell me it was as bad as this?"

"Good goah. Mister," the attendant gasped. "He didn't look like that when I checked him in. Honest—he was just paper white, not yellow as he is now."

The attendant hurried away and the Crimson Mask went to work. He injected a thick hypodermic needle and got a small sample of blood. He opened the dead man's mouth and smelled. There was no identifying odor of any poison. He would have given a lot to attend the autopsy, but that was impossible. He had to content himself with the blood.

But the dead man's hands interested him also. They were the same yellow color, like his face and the rest of his body, but there were deep purplish stains on the fingertips.

The attendant came running back and the Crimson Mask hastily knelt beside Sandy. He took the glass and held it to her lips.

Sandy put on an excellent act. The Crimson Mask helped her to stand and then slowly led her out of the room.

In the office she explained, in a voice that was still horror-stricken, that the body he had seen was not that of her son and she wanted to get out of here as quickly as possible. The Crimson Mask escorted her to the door.

OUTSIDE, THE walked through the still silent city streets. Sandy shivered.

"I didn't have to do much acting for that fainting spell," she said. "Bob—it was horrible. What on earth caused the corpse to take on such a color?"

"Jaundice," the Crimson Mask frowned. "But what caused so deep a jaundice is beyond me right now. Certainly it was not a disease, but some sort of a poison. I think the man was poisoned even before he visited Warrick and he didn't know it. Not until he was trying to find my store."

They awakened a dosing taxi driver who was parked at a feed line and were driven to another section of the city. The address the Crimson Mask had found on that bit of paper turned out to be a respectable boarding house.

They dismissed the taxi and stood in front of the boarding house for a few moments.

"We were very lucky, Sandy," the Crimson Mask said. "All we can hope for is that the envelope was addressed to the victim and not something he just picked up."

Sandy started up the stone stairs to the porch.

"Well, if we find Anthony F. Webb in his room, we'll know there's been a mistake somewhere. Let's go in."

The landlady who answered the door was helpful.

"Mr. Webb! Oh, yes, he boards here. We call him Stinky."

"Stinky?" the Crimson Mask chuckled. "Why such a name?"

The landlady laughed.

"He always fussed with chemicals and some of them smelled to high heaven. We had an agreement—when he used these chemicals, he had to provide cut flowers for the house the next day. He always kept his promise. I hope he isn't in any trouble."

Their bodies muffled the sound of the report

"What makes you think he might be?" the Crimson Mask asked.

"Well, he came home very late last night, unusual for him. We heard him moving around and it sounded as if he was breaking all those bottles and things up in his room. Shall I call him for you?"

THE CRIMSON MASK checked her.

"I'd rather you didn't," he said. "This lady is his aunt. I'm showing her the town and she decided to call on him although I mentioned that visits aren't usually made so early in the city."

"Nonsense," Sandy put in stridently. "Tony will be very glad to see me. I'd like to go right upstairs to his room. Do you mind?"

"No," the landlady assented. "You look like good people. He's on the third floor, Room B."

They both sighed in relief when she decided not to accompany them. At the door, the Crimson Mask paused to look around and listen. Then he tried the door, found it locked and drew certain keys from his pocket. There were few locks which one of these master keys wouldn't fit.

There was no one in the room, but it had the appearance of having been in the wake of a cyclone. The enameled sink, for instance, had assumed the hues of a rainbow. In one corner bottles had been smashed and there were also the remains of test tube retorts and florence flasks. Clothing had been carefully gone over and all pockets emptied.

"Look at this," Sandy said.

The Crimson Mask went over to the bureau on which lay a sealed envelope addressed to the landlady. The Crimson Mask put the envelope into his pocket.

"We'll watch her open it," he explained. "There isn't much doubt but that the dead man was Tony F. Webb. Someone came here last night, primarily to search the rooms and make certain Webb left no evidence to incriminate his murderers. Whoever handled the job did it well and also destroyed a lot of chemicals. Mostly dyes, which probably accounts for the dead man's stained fingers. He was experimenting with dyes in his room."

"He must have swallowed a gallon of yellow dye," Sandy grimaced. "I'll never forget how he looked."

The Crimson Mask sat down on the edge of the bed.

"Undoubtedly Webb was a chemist. We must work on the premise that either he discovered something valuable and was killed for the secret, or he knew too much about some other chemical business. Look in his drawer and see if there is any stationery to match the kind he used in his letter."

Sandy found some. The Crimson Mask laid Webb's envelope in front of him and copied the handwriting style expertly. He wrote a note to Webb's mythical aunt, sealed it in an envelope and addressed this. He waited until the glue dried and then ruthlessly ripped the envelope open.

"Let's go," he said.

CHAPTER IV

WARNING!

DOWNSTAIRS THE Crimson Mask handed the sealed envelope to the landlady.

"We found the door unlocked and went in. It was terrible. Everything smashed. We found two letters, one for you and one for his aunt here. The letter to his aunt says he expected her soon and asked her to go over to the place where he worked and pick up some back pay for him. It seems he is entering the armed services in some secret way to do chemical work."

"Yes," the landlady nodded over her own letter. "It says here he has to go away unexpectedly and he is sorry for the damage done and look here... twenty dollars to pay me for my trouble in cleaning up the room. He was a nice man."

The Crimson Mask frowned.

"He must have been in a big hurry because he asked his aunt to pick up the pay, but neglected to say where he worked. She doesn't know. Do you?"

"Of course," the landlady answered. "He was over at the Crawford Pharmaceutical plant. He worked there for two years, steady as could be."

The Crimson Mask thanked her and he and Sandy left. They went directly back to the drug store where Dave Small was waiting impatiently to hear the developments. In the security of the Crimson Mask's lab, he went to work.

"Go over the annual report of the Executive Committee of the Drug Merchants Association," he directed Dave. "Check on Crawford Pharmaceutical. I want all the facts. Sandy—you are to help me study the few clues we have. First though, I must call Warrick's house and see if he has returned."

Warrick hadn't and the servant expressed considerable worry. The Crimson Mask thought fast. If Warrick was being held a prisoner, his life might be in danger if the police started an investigation. Whatever was done about Warrick, had to be handled carefully.

"I'm sure he's all right," the Crimson Mask said over the phone. "In fact, he told me just the other day that he planned to make a trip soon and was only waiting for word to start. Perhaps his visitors that night carried urgent news and Mr. Warrick forgot to tell you he'd be away a few days. I wouldn't do anything about it, yet."

He hung up and groaned.

"Warrick is being held all right. Whoever has him knows darned well that Webb told his story and that Warrick was taking him to see me. They assume that so long as Warrick is held, I won't dare act. But I most certainly will."

The Crimson Mask took the hypodermic case from his pocket and ejected the clotted blood he'd removed from the yellow-faced corpse. He smeared some of this on a microscope slide and studied it without comment for ten minutes. Then he sighed.

"No evidence of blood cell destruction at all. Common poisons would have plenty of evidence. If I could only examine the internal organs—but that's impossible. We've got to track down some drug which kills slowly, renders the victim subject to extremely high temperatures and causes the skin to turn yellow."

"Picric Acid?" Sandy asked. "I got some of that stuff on my hands one day when I was in school. It certainly stained my hands yellow and, Bob—picric acid is used in munitions making. Maybe this is a spy plot."

THE CRIMSON MASK closed his eyes and sank back into the chair. "Munitions. I recall an interesting case some years ago wherein munitions workers became sick, lost weight and suffered from high temperatures. If I could only remember... thermadite! That's it!"

"Thermadite," Sandy repeated vaguely.

"Their skins also turned yellow." The Crimson Mask jumped up and selected several thick volumes on drugs and chemistry. He settled down with these and Sandy could see that what he found in them gave him considerable satisfaction."

"No doubt about it," he said a moment later. "It was thermadite. That drug, in fatal doses, actually causes the victim to burn up from inside. The body cells become individual furnaces at a white heat. Thermadite increases metabolism to a remarkable extent. In fact, it has been used as a reducing drug. And it works. It works like a charm except that it also kills or cripples the user."

Sandy drummed the edge of the lab bench with well manicured fingertips.

"You're driving at something, Bob. A disreputable pharmaceutical company might use such a drug, market it as a reducing medicine and get away with it if they could escape the Pure Food and Drug Act investigators."

"Which could be done at least temporarily," the Crimson Mask nodded. "You catch on fast, Sandy. We've connected the Crawford Pharmaceutical Company with a most peculiar brand of murder—if they use thermadite in any of their preparations. Get Dave, will you?"

Dave had a report on the firm.

"It's an old concern," he said. "Founded in 1902, but the original owners died long ago and the firm passed into various hands. At present it is owned by John H. Straben. Two years ago the firm was very rocky, but made a strong comeback in the past six months or so."

"Interesting," the Crimson Mask said. "Have you a list of their products and does that list include any preparations for reducing weight?"

"It sure does," Dave nodded. "There's one called *Sveltform*. It's been on the market for a few months."

"Good heavens," Sandy cried, "do you think that company is putting poison on the market? That Webb, who worked there, found it out and they killed him because he knew?"

"I doubt it," the Crimson Mask commented slowly. "Mostly because there wouldn't be enough money involved in the limited sale of such medicines to induce murder. We can assume that the company used thermadite and must have a supply on hand. It should not be used in any reducing medicines, but apparently it is. Perhaps Webb was given the drug by someone who also works at the plant and for a reason wholly unconnected with the firm."

Dave Small whistled softly.

"It's easy now, to realize why Webb acted so strangely. I mean in that he removed most of his clothes on an icy night. He was burning up from inside and I'll bet excitement and the exercise of running helped the drug to work faster."

"That's undoubtedly correct," the Crimson Mask nodded. "Now we've got to get busy. Sandy, go to the Crawford plant and see if you can get yourself a job. It should be very easy with manpower shortages today. Study the layout, the officials. Find out all you can without causing any suspicion. Remember that perhaps Warrick's life is at stake."

SANDY GOT up. "I'm on my way. You'll hear from me every night at six on the dot. If you don't... I need help. This is the kind of work I like."

"Don't let them feed you any *Sveltform*," Dave grinned.

Sandy looked in one of the full length mirrors in the lab.

"Dave, you're insulting," she laughed and then she was gone.

The Crimson Mask removed his makeup and became Bob Clarke once more. He donned a white coat and went to the front of the store. Dave Small was busy making up prescriptions.

While handling the usual run of business, Bob Clarke had time to give the case considerable thought. He hated to stall going into action because of Warrick's predicament, but Warrick was able to take care of himself and so long as the Crimson Mask did not strike, his life was not in danger. Obviously, they were planning to use him as a hostage.

During one quiet period, the Crimson Mask glanced at the morning papers. He rubbed his chin and figured that the crooks would want the Crimson Mask warned not to interfere. They must have guessed that Webb may have talked before he died and that the Crimson Mask may have been his sole audience. The only possible method to communicate with the Crimson Mask was by blind advertisements.

Bob Clarke hastily turned the pages of the newspaper to the advertising section. There it was, heading the personal column. An apparently innocent message.

> C.M. Best you do nothing because W. is in poor health. Activity bound to make him worse. Stay put. These ads will appear in all editions to keep you advised. When it stops, W. will be on the critical list. Please accept advice not to do anything to make him worse.

Bob Clarke slowly folded the newspaper and his face became very grim. There it was, in black and white. A full confirmation of his direst suspicions. If he stumbled on this case, Warrick would die. The man or men behind whatever kind of a scheme this was, had murdered once and would hardly hesitate to do it again.

Yet the case had to be investigated and by the Crimson Mask. It was absolutely vital that he reveal himself to some people he could trust, show that he was working on the case and get their help.

So far the only criminal aspect to the case, outside of Webb's strange murder, was the sale of a highly dangerous drug under the guise of a helpful medicine. Men who included that drug among others to compound a medicine were murderers.

BOB CLARKE passed a hand over his face. He was tired. He hadn't slept and there was no time for rest. *Sveltform* had to be driven off the market at once. That required the help of the Drug Merchants Association and it meant the Crimson Mask had to appear before them at once. If it leaked out that he was on the job, Warrick's life would be sacrificed.

Bob Clarke didn't hesitate very long. His war against crime was similar to the global campaign against Hitler and his satellites. Men were sacrificed to gain certain objectives. They were all soldiers and knew circumstances might mean their death. Yet they went into battle willingly.

Warrick was part of the Crimson Mask's little army. He knew what the consequences would be, but if he died to save the lives of scores of innocent people, it would be a small price. Warrick thought like that. In fact, he'd often mentioned it openly to the Crimson Mask.

Bob Clarke called Dave to his side.

"I'm going to work," he said. "Sandy may get some results if she is very lucky, but I can't wait for that. The first move is to get *Sveltform* off the market and quick. I'm going to call Tim Barlow, Chairman of the Executive Board of the Drug Merchants Association and have him arrange a meeting of the board at once. I'll attend the meeting as the Crimson Mask."

"But Warrick…?" Dave warned.

"I doubt any member of the board will break a promise not to talk," Bob said. "Anyway, I must take the chance. Close up the store around noontime. Get a quick lunch and then tour a few drug stores. Buy up some of the Crawford Pharmaceutical products. Label each preparation as to where you obtained it. They may be putting other injurious preparations on the market."

CHAPTER V

NEAR TRAGEDY

THREE HOURS later, the Crimson Mask, wearing an effective disguise which made him look like anyone but Bob Clarke, entered one of the large business buildings in midtown. He took an elevator to the twenty-second floor, walked directly to the offices of the Drug Merchants Association and stopped long enough to don his red domino.

The Association maintained a suite of offices here, but it did no general business. The rooms were used mostly for holding meetings so there were no inquisitive clerks or stenographers about.

In the outer office sat a man with iron gray hair, a ragged face and broad shoulders. He was Tim Barlow; recently elected head of the Association.

Barlow arose and extended his hand.

"So you are the Crimson Mask. Of course, when I received your phone call, I immediately arranged for the members of this Association to be on hand. We all recognize the fact that the Crimson Mask makes such a request only because it is of vital importance."

"Thank you," the Crimson Mask replied and wondered what Tim Barlow would think if he discovered that he was talking to one of the most minor members of the Association.

"This way, please." Barlow indicated a closed door. "The Executive Board is waiting for you.

The Crimson Mask stepped into a spacious board room. There were eleven men seated around a long table and he knew every one of them. They were eminent druggists, some were high officials of chain store systems and all worked in perfect harmony to protect themselves and the public from being victimized by faked preparations sold as cure-alls.

The Crimson Mask stepped to the head of the table.

"Gentlemen," he said, "before we go into the matter which brings me here, I must beg a promise from you. A vow not to tell anyone—not even your immediate families—that I have been here. Someone who works with me is a prisoner in the hands of a band of crooks whom we must all fight. That person's life will be forfeit if the crooks discover that. I am working on the case. If there is anyone who does not wish to abide by such a promise, I ask that he leave now.

Nobody moved. The Crimson Mask smiled.

"Thank you, gentlemen. My business before you concerns the Crawford Pharmaceutical Company. A manufacturing plant engaged in making patent medicines. Among their products is a highly dangerous reducing drug called…"

"*Sveltform,*" Tim Barlow shouted with obvious glee. "Mr. Crimson Mask, we discovered that *Sveltform* contains thermadite and twenty-four hours ago we banned the sale of it in any of our membership stores. You're a little late, even though we appreciate your motives."

"Thank heavens, then," the Crimson Mask sighed in relief, "that you did issue such an order. But there are drug stores which do not belong to nor adhere to your organization. How can they be stopped from selling *Sveltform?*"

"We took the matter up with the Pure Food and Drug department of the Federal Government," Barlow said. "A stop-sale order has already been issued and the Crawford Company ordered to desist from marketing any more of its product."

"Good. You gentlemen anticipated me, but I'm very glad you did. The quicker that drug was off the market, the better. Now, perhaps, you will give me some information about the firm which manufactured it. Who heads it? What is the company's financial status? Who seems to be the dominating influence behind it?"

BARLOW TOOK the floor at once.

"John H. Straben owns the firm. He was financially shaky, but seems to have gotten back on his feet. Straben has been manufacturing drugs for years. Nothing of national importance, but on the whole his products have been fairly good."

"What of Dr. Culver?" One of the other members asked. "If the Crimson Mask has something on that firm, he should know about Culver."

"Oh yes," Barlow nodded. "I was about to tell him. You see, Dr. Edward Culver has recently been placed in charge of production. I err in calling him Doctor Culver, because his right to practice was revoked six months ago by a court before which he was tried for complicity in the distribution of narcotics. They didn't have enough on him for a conviction, but he was removed as a physician. It wasn't the first time he'd been in trouble."

"I shall see about Dr. Culver," the Crimson Mask said. "Thanks to Mr. Barlow, my visit here seems to have been unnecessary and I apologize for taking up your time. The promise you made to keep my visit a secret, still holds, however. I should hate to have those crooks learn that I am working on the case because it would mean that one of you is in league with them."

Barlow laughed.

"That's rich. We're fighting the same thing you are, Crimson Mask. We have no wish to interfere with your progress in the case nor create danger for someone who works with you. Our promise certainly holds."

The Crimson Mask bowed out of the meeting, removed his mask in the corridor and took the elevator down. He felt a little flabbergasted at the speed with which the Association had worked, but would the banning of *Sveltform* put an end to the crooked influences behind the Crawford Pharmaceutical Company?

The Crimson Mask doubted it. *Sveltform* was a very minor issue, albeit a dangerous one to the general public. The profits from this product would hardly have induced the murder of Tony Webb and the kidnapping of Warrick. There was something else. Something much bigger and much more dangerous.

The Crimson Mask returned to the drug store and waited for Sandy either to phone at six o'clock or come in to make her report. She appeared personally ten minutes before the hour, but what she had to offer was mostly a repetition of what the Crimson Mask already knew.

"But Bob," she said, "the plant is big, very busy and even has war contracts. There are armed guards all over the place—thugs, if you ask me. Then this Dr. Culver is always nosing about. He's a ratty-faced man. John H. Straben seems to be all right. He's head of the plant and is supposed to own it. He comes into the various rooms and talks to the employees. Tries to be democratic and yet… I don't like him. He's too smooth."

"We'll wrinkle him up a bit before we get through," the Crimson Mask chuckled. "Suppose, Sandy, I wanted to pay the plant a visit by night. How would I get in?"

"With this." Sandy produced a key. "I swiped it. It opens the main office door. There are no night shifts, but a strong force of guards patrols the plant all night. You'd better be careful."

DAVE SMALL found time to leave the store and come back to the lab. He was excited.

"I visited a lot of small, cheap drug stores," he said, "and bought a lot of Crawford Pharmaceutical Company products. A sedative, for instance, which is supposed to contain the small legal dose of codeine. It's hardly more than sugar, water and coloring matter. There is no codeine. Products which rely on good alcohol as their base, contained about a third of the amount needed in the preparation. I'd say everything that Crawford puts out is phony."

The Crimson Mask whistled.

"That may be it, but still, what they'd save by withholding expensive chemicals from their products, wouldn't build up to any large sum of money. Not enough to induce murder. No, I feel there is something else, even bigger, and we've got to find it."

"Who is behind all this?" Sandy asked. "John H. Straben?"

"I don't know," the Crimson Mask confessed. "The ringleader is very important, of course, but finding the motive back of this is even more important because we know that the products of the firm are injurious to health and they are being sold everywhere."

"Why haven't the Pure Food and Drug investigators uncovered this?" Dave wanted to know. "Are they slipping?"

"No—the men in charge of that branch of Government are highly capable," the Crimson Mask said. "They check all products and somehow they've been given the real stuff and not this phony medicine sold over the counter. Dave, see if the evening papers are here yet."

Dave returned with two newspapers. The Crimson Mask hastily opened one and found a duplicate of the morning's advertisement. He grunted in considerable relief.

"At least they haven't discovered I'm on the job and that I visited the Association's offices this afternoon," he said. "Tonight, however, I've got to risk a great deal. I'm going into the factory. If they find me, there is going to be some battle because I'll shoot to kill. For my own protection, yes, but just as much for the safety of Ted Warrick. Once we find out what lies behind this scheme, we'll have something on which to base our investigation and find signposts which point the way to the criminal in control."

Sandy went to her apartment. Dave Small, somewhat reluctantly, continued to take over the store. At eleven o'clock, the

Crimson Mask slipped through the rear exit, made his way across the courtyards and finally took a cab on one of the side streets. He had himself driven fairly close to the drug manufacturing plant and paid off the driver.

There were two heavy guns concealed in hip holsters under his clothing. There were extra clips of ammunition stowed away too. He wore crepe soled shoes, a black suit with a black shirt. In the darkness he was almost invisible.

The premises around the plant were hemmed in by a high steel fence and there were tiny booths where guards could take refuge in bad weather. It was a large factory, four stories high and sprawling over considerable territory. In front of the main entrance was a steel gate, securely locked and—unguarded.

Apparently, the men assigned to duty outside the plant, had certain beats to cover and did not have fixed posts. The Crimson Mask found his crepe soled shoes highly effective in gaining a toe-hold on the fence and he scaled it promptly.

TAKING NO chances—because Warrick's life was in the balance, he sprinted toward the office door, but veered away and crouched behind a small platform for several minutes. It was fortunate that he took this precaution, for two armed guards strolled past and one of them paused to make certain the gate was locked.

After they had continued on their way, the Crimson Mask stepped up to the door, used the key which Sandy had furnished and promptly let himself inside. The office was large, with about thirty desks for clerks. He wasn't interested in these. Using his flashlight very sparingly, he located an office door labelled John H. Straben.

This was likewise locked, but gave way to one of his master keys quickly. The office was luxuriously furnished. A huge desk occupied a space between two big windows that overlooked the factory yard and the shipping platform. The Crimson Mask glanced out of one window and saw four guards in a group.

He covered the lens of his flash with one hand and allowed only the tiniest ray to leak between his fingers. For twenty minutes he searched Straben's desk, being very careful to replace things exactly as he found them. This search netted him no results.

There was a big safe in one corner but he knew the inadvisability of tackling it.

However, there were also steel filing cabinets and he opened several of these without appreciable result.

Then he discovered one set of filing cabinets which were very securely locked and seemed to be much more heavily constructed than the others. It required many minutes to pick the lock, but he succeeded and was glad of his persistence.

Inside the top cabinet were listings of drug stores. Many of the local ones the Crimson Mask knew and they were frowsy little places, some taking in more money by conducting betting rings than by selling drugs. Most had been very actively engaged in selling illicit liquor during prohibition and their owners possessed court records.

The Crimson Mask made mental notes of several of these drug stores and then examined the other two filing compartments. The second one contained miscellaneous papers, but the bottom drawer revealed a thick pile of stickers. They were meant for drug store windows to announce that the store sold Crawford Pharmaceutical products.

Thinking back, the Crimson Mask couldn't recall any drug store displaying any such signs. And anyway if they were so important, along with the listing of drug stores, why wasn't everything stored in the safe?

The filing cabinet was especially built and exceptionally strong. Perhaps, the Crimson Mask reasoned, a few employees had access to the safe and therefore things regarded as too confidential had to be placed in this cabinet. On a hunch he appropriated one of the stickers and put it into his pocket.

There was nothing else in the office of interest but the Crimson Mask wanted samples of their products, direct from the factory itself. The best place to acquire them was from the shipping room. From the platform outside, the Crimson Mask located this room. Reaching it was another matter for there were guards throughout the plant.

LIKE A black, grim ghost he made his way out of the offices, across a machine room where pills were manufactured in presses, and into the shipping room itself. Twice he had to merge with the shadows to avoid patrolling guards and each time he had a good look at the men in charge of protecting the place.

They weren't selected for their looks. Each was hardboiled, tough looking. Alert too, with heavy guns hip holstered. After they passed by, the Crimson Mask resumed his journey to the shipping room and reached it without being challenged.

There were cardboard boxes, filled and labelled and stacked in high rows ready for shipping. He took a sharp clasp knife from his pocket opened one box and extracted a bottle of a drug supposed to contain a mild opiate. He marked the bottle, indicating that it was from a shipment meant for a small chain store outfit.

From another carton addressed to one of the small stores listed in the files he had examined a few moments before, he took another, similar bottle. He repeated this with other cartons, sealing them up after he was finished, with the equipment in the room.

A white door attracted his attention and he moved toward it. It was impossible to use his flashlight and he tried to retain a mental picture of the shipping room to avoid crashing into anything. Despite all his precautions, however, he brushed against a carton and sent it crashing to the floor.

Instantly, a voice called out the alarm. The Crimson Mask ran lightly toward the white door, found it locked and managed to turn back the bolt. There wasn't time to enter, however. Four guards were hurrying into the shipping room.

He left the white door and dodged behind a row of packing cases. The guards swept the room with their flashlights, separated and started to cover the entire floor thoroughly. One headed straight toward the aisle between packing cases where the Crimson Mask was hidden.

Working fast, the Crimson Mask carefully pushed the boxes which formed the high tier so that one pile of them moved back a few inches each, actually forming a stairway. He climbed this promptly and lay flat on top of the cases.

The guard passed by without noticing anything wrong. As soon as he left the passage, the Crimson Mask descended to the floor and sprinted on noiseless feet toward the white door. The only other exits were guarded.

He opened the door and slipped into a darkened room. By the odors that assailed his nostrils he knew this was a large laboratory, probably used to compound and test the various products of the plant.

He took several careful steps forward, feeling with both hands for any obstructions. Suddenly the ray of a flashlight swept in his direction, passed across him and stopped to come back and fasten him in its ray.

"Stick 'em up," a voice ordered sharply, and it was followed by a hissing intake of breath. "It's… the Crimson Mask!"

CHAPTER VI

THE MOTIVE

IN THE light of the flash, the Crimson Mask saw that he was trapped between two long laboratory benches. Above them were shelves laden with bottles of chemicals. The bench itself was strewn with apparatus and the passageaway between the benches was very narrow.

"Don't let your mitts down or I'll put slug through you," the guard warned. "Boy, will Matty be glad to see you. He figured you'd work on us no matter if we did hold one of your droops a prisoner."

"Now, I suppose," the Crimson Mask said slowly, "he'll be murdered."

"That's right," the guard answered blithely, "and if Matty wants to reward me for nailing you, I'm going to get the right to rub out Warrick. He planted a shiner on my eye and I ain't forgetting it."

"Too bad he didn't break your neck," the Crimson Mask said. "Well, what's next?"

"Just keep backing up and remember, I'm not taking my eyes off you. Not for one second. They say you're a pretty smart guy, but I don't think so. I heard you unlock the door so I just stayed here, waiting. Go on—back up."

Slowly the Crimson Mask backed away with the guard advancing step by step and taking very good care that he did not get too close. For a second or two he considered going for one of his guns, but he realized the impossibility of this. The guard was prepared to shoot instantly.

The Crimson Mask's brain was in a turmoil. His death would automatically insure the murder of Warrick for then he'd hardly be of much use to the crooks.

Suddenly the Crimson Mask's feet encountered several small bottles carelessly dropped on the floor between the two closely set lab benches. He almost fell and had to reach one hand down quickly to brace himself on the bench. That act nearly cost him his life before the thug recognized the fact that it had only been an act of self-preservation.

"One more move like that," he warned, "and you get it. Commence backing again, sport. Boy, am I anxious to rip that mask off your face and see who you are."

In the brief moment during which he had almost fallen, the Crimson Mask noticed two sixteen ounce glass stoppered bottles close to the edge of the bench. One was labelled Aqua Regia, a powerful acid. As he moved back, his right hand was still down near the bench and he managed to quietly tip the bottle over. It required but a second to unloosen the glass stopper and acid flowed out over the bench. The guard saw none of this. He was too busy watching the Crimson Mask's face and gloating over the fate in store for him.

ELEVATING HIS arms again, the Crimson Mask marched backwards. He was being escorted to some side door. Once it was reached, he'd be done for. Everything depended now on the guard's preoccupation with his prisoner who he knew was very dangerous.

The guard stepped on the same small bottles lying on the floor. His hand—the one with the flashlight—darted down to the lab bench to balance himself. It encountered the acid. He promptly withdrew it and shook off the liquid. It required a few seconds for the acid to really begin its work.

Suddenly the guard gave a howl, dropped his flashlight and began to wave his burning hand madly. As the flash fell, the Crimson Mask moved forward in a lunge. He'd been ready for this and the guard didn't even have a chance to yank the trigger.

The Crimson Mask hit him low and they both went down. The guard's seared hand was forgotten as he awoke to the fact that he fought for his life. He managed to get the gun up a trifle. The Crimson Mask clamped the gun hand in a vise-like grip and twisted it.

Both men were fighting so close that it was really a wrestling match. When the gun went off, their bodies muffled the sound so there was only a faint report. The guard went limp, groaned once and then became silent. He'd pulled the trigger when the weapon was pressed against his own chest.

The Crimson Mask arose, breathing hard. He stood silently waiting, with two guns in his fists, for the arrival of help. None came. It was apparent that the noise of the brief scuffle and the muffled report of the gun hadn't gone beyond the lab.

The Crimson Mask picked up the flashlight, used it to locate a rear exit and then returned to the guard. He was dead, the bullet had passed through his heart. The Crimson Mask opened a large cupboard below the lab benches. This was commodious enough to stow away the guard's body. Another few minutes were required to clean up the bloodstains and the acid. It was quite possible that the guard wouldn't be found for hours.

Passing down the lab bench, the Crimson Mask's flashlight flicked across several very large wide-mouth bottles. He stopped, studied the white crystalline contents and grunted. The bottles were labeled Sodium Bicarbonate, but while bicarb is white, it is more of a powder than a crystal.

The Crimson Mask removed one stopper, sniffed and got no odor. He touched a speck of the contents to his tongue and grimaced. It was exceptionally bitter. These bottles contained pounds of quinine of which there was a terrific shortage since the Japs had taken over the Dutch East Indies. Quinine was desperately needed by troops assigned to the tropics. Even Bob Clarke had given up his entire supply of it to the Army. Yet here was enough to take care of many regiments of troops.

There was no time to inspect the other bottles. The guards were still prowling and they might decide to invade the lab at any moment. In fact, the only reason they had not done so already was because one guard had been permanently assigned to that post.

QUIETLY, HE approached the rear door. It led into the spacious yard behind the factory, a dangerous place to cross. The Crimson Mask saw a guard moving quickly toward the building. Then two others came from different directions. Apparently, whoever was in charge of them had called them into the factory to help finish the search.

The Crimson Mask got the door open easily, closed it behind him and streaked across the cleared space toward the fence. He gave a leap that carried him halfway up the fence. His soft shoes secured a grip. So did his hands and he clawed his way to the top and over. A jump to the ground insured his safety. He raced off into the night?

Some distance away he removed his mask, walked sedately to the next corner and found a taxi which took him back to the somewhat squalid section where he maintained his drug store. He prayed that the dead guard wouldn't be missed at once. If they found him, they'd know that the Crimson Mask had been at work. Then Warrick would die. There were many things to be done before morning, but none was more important than finding and rescuing Ted Warrick.

Dave Small hadn't closed up yet. The Crimson Mask entered the store through the rear, reached his quarters and signaled Dave that he was back. Then he went to work.

He removed the bottles from his pockets and proceeded to analyze them. It didn't require a very long time. From a bottle which had been destined for an uptown drug store, the Crimson Mask poured a measured quantity of fluid, carefully mixed a solution of sodium carbonate with it and watched a white precipitate form. He repeated this with a bottle similarly labeled and marked, but meant for one of the shady little drug stores on some dark side street.

"Look," he called to Dave. "The medicine meant for a good store shows a slight precipitate, indicating the narcotic content to be almost nil. The bottle which would have been received by one of those joints, contained so much morphine that it would kill anyone except... Dave, I've got it. This does the trick."

Dave nodded emphatically.

"Yeah—I'm beginning to see daylight, too,"

"It's simple." The Crimson Mask put his test tubes in a rack. "This particular preparation of the Crawford Pharmaceutical Company is supposed to contain a designated amount of narcotic. To make the stuff, that company is granted certain quantities of narcotics from the government. It is supposed to be evenly distributed, but somebody connected with that outfit has a way to get around it."

"Sure," Dave offered. "They send decent drug stores bottles of stuff that are not worth the labels on them. The joints get stuff so heavy with morphine a drug addict would be the best customer. Hey... it's a drug ring. Why not? Hopheads could be told where to go after the stuff."

"Exactly," the Crimson Mask said. "Narcotics are almost impossible for addicts to get these days. The supply is very low and easily controlled. Our friends at this factory know how to do a little controlling themselves. I've got an idea. See this?"

He displayed the trade-mark sticker indicating that the store which carried it sold Crawford Pharmaceutical Products.

"Stick that in our window," the Crimson Mask ordered. "It may draw results. If anybody comes in asking for stuff put out by that factory, say our stock hasn't arrived yet, but study the customers. Size them up. Get them to talk—especially what they expected to pay for the stuff."

DAVE TOOK the sticker.

"It'll spoil the reputation of this store, but that's nothing compared to what the sale of those faked drugs can do. Imagine somebody buying a bottle of medicine which lacks the main ingredient. What do you suppose those rats are doing? Faking everything they produce?"

"There are a lot of angles," the Crimson Mask frowned. "Individually—like *Sveltform*—they don't seem to add too much profit, but take them all together and you'll get some fantastic figures. I think we've only discovered part of their racket, but enough to show us they must be destroyed."

Dave heaved a great sigh.

"All of which isn't helping to find Warrick. Gosh, Bob, they've had him for about twenty-four hours now."

"He's still safe," the Crimson Mask pointed out. "The newspaper ads prove it because the man behind this scheme wouldn't dare lie about that. He knows darn well that if he did, there'd be no surrender when I caught up with him."

"You haven't removed the disguise," Dave commented. "That means you're going out again. How about me taking a little hand in this game?"

"Not quite yet," the Crimson Mask smiled. "Tonight I'm going to see John H. Straben, who owns the factory. Then I intend to visit a certain doctor who lost his right to practice some time ago and lately became associated with the factory as its scientific and medical advisor."

"Okay," Dave sighed, "I'll analyze the rest of this stuff quantitatively, to see how much drug each bottle contains. At least we know what's back of the mess."

"We do, but the man behind it is the most important. His scheme may result in the impairment of health to many innocent people. It may prevent convalescents from recovering. It's things like this, Dave, which show the real worth of our food and drug laws."

"I wonder how come they didn't catch up with that outfit before this," Dave grunted. "Seems plenty odd to me."

CHAPTER VII

WALK INTO MY PARLOR

JOHN H. STRABEN was fifty-five, pompous and over-bearing. In the security of his study he was going over his personal accounts with a great deal of satisfaction. Profits were really mounting up, he was solvent once more and in his mind were dreams of lengthy vacations, costly hotels, golf courses and swanky bars. It was a significant feature of John H. Straben's character that he included no such plebian things as War Bonds in his intended purchases.

He closed his checkbook, leaned back and started dreaming until the doorbell roused him out of his pleasant lethargy. He cursed his lack of servants and decided to hire a couple the next day. He could afford that luxury again.

He went to the door and found a well-dressed young man there, a total stranger. It was the Crimson Mask, wearing the disguise assumed at the start of the case.

"Well?" Straben demanded. "What do you want?"

"Some information," the Crimson Mask said. "About a preparation your firm puts out called *Sveltform*. May I come in?"

Straben lost his aplomb with the sudden decision that this young man undoubtedly represented the Pure Food and Drug's Division of the Federal Government. He stepped aside hastily and beckoned the Crimson Mask inside.

"I—ah—expected repercussions on that," he admitted. "Although not by an investigator who'd call at this time of night."

The Crimson Mask sat down in a comfortable chair, crossed his legs and eyed Straben for a moment. He decided this man was weak. Hardly the type to operate a combine trying to make a fortune from the miseries of others. Yet Straben headed the pharmaceutical firm and was responsible for its acts and its products. Also, appearances could often be deceiving.

"Tell me why you were so foolish as to include thermadite in your reducing medicine," the Crimson Mask said.

Straben flushed.

"It was a ghastly mistake. My plant superintendent used to be a physician and he swore that the addition of a small amount of thermadite, with other drugs of course, would not be harmful to the health. Naturally, I took his word for it."

"I see," the Crimson Mask said coldly. "Then what happened?"

Straben leaned across his desk, very eager to please.

"Well, I received a complaint. It seems someone purchased a bottle of *Sveltform* and used it a day or two until she became ill and consulted her own physician. This doctor discovered she had been taking *Sveltform* and had it analyzed. She came to me and demanded a rebate which she got with a handsome bonus."

"And then?"

"Naturally I had every bottle of *Sveltform* picked up. Fortunately, it hadn't moved fast so there were no serious results. My plant superintendent was still inclined to scoff, but I gave him orders that thermadite was not to be used in the preparation any longer."

"By doing that," the Crimson Mask said, "you probably saved your neck. Now we made a rather thorough investigation of you and your firm, Mr. Straben. It appears that a year ago you were on the verge of bankruptcy. Six months later your plant was running full blast again."

"Government contracts are responsible for my success," Straben said. "I was able to secure credit. Then, too, a distant relative of mine died and I was the only heir. I received enough from that to pay back bills and establish myself financially."

THE CRIMSON MASK nodded.

"Getting back to *Sveltform,* just whom did you call upon for help to get back all the medicine on the market?"

"The Drug Association," Straben said promptly. "They were very co-operative."

The Crimson Mask arose.

"Very well, Mr. Straben. I recommend that you discharge your plant superintendent at once. Any physician who suggests the use of dangerous drugs to be sold in any form, has no right to continue in a position where he might repeat the mistake."

"What if I... don't fire him?" Straben asked in a worried voice.

The Crimson Mask shrugged.

"I merely recommend. There is no law which compels you to fire him."

There was relief on Straben's face as he escorted his visitor to the door. The Crimson Mask stepped out, started to cross the porch and his lips grew suddenly tight. There was snow on the ground and someone, other than himself, had tracked it on the porch. There were vague signs that this person had stepped over to a large window through which he could have seen the Crimson Mask talking to Straben.

Walking briskly down the sidewalk, well bundled up against the cold, the Crimson Mask worried about this. Yet he knew that the crooks behind this scheme would not recognize the disguise he wore.

He turned down a side street and made his way across town to another address. Ex-doctor Culver probably wouldn't be quite as easy to fool as Straben, but the Crimson Mask intended to see the man anyway. Culver seemed to be the kingpin in the factory. Perhaps he ran the whole business, dominating Straben, who might be the owner in name only.

Culver lived in a fashionable apartment house. The Crimson Mask decided to take a chance and hope that Dr. Culver would accept him as a government investigator, too. He rang the bell.

The door lock clicked. The Crimson Mask went in and took a self-operated elevator to the top floor. When he stepped off, he saw a short, pudgy and dark-featured man standing in the doorway of the apartment.

"I'm Culver," the man said. "Did you ring my bell? I'd have asked your business over the house phone to the lobby, but it is out of order."

"I wanted to see you about a serious incident which I understand you were responsible for," the Crimson Mask said. "I'm talking about a drug called thermadite."

"Oh... that," Culver said enigmatically. "Come inside. I can explain everything perfectly."

As he passed through the door, the Crimson Mask had a feeling of walking into trouble and he was alert. The living room was brilliantly lighted and he and Culver seemed to be the only occupants. The Crimson Mask didn't sit down and he kept one hand lightly toying with the upper button of his opened overcoat. Just beneath that point was a gun.

CULVER DIDN'T sit down either.

"I can't understand it," he said. "There wasn't enough thermadite in that preparation to induce illness. That is, unless the employees at the plant were careless and put in too much. I have one of the first bottles put up under my direct supervision. Perhaps you'd do me the favor of testing it I don't want to take all the blame for this affair."

"I shall be glad to have it analyzed," the Crimson Mask answered.

"Good. It's in one of the back rooms. Make yourself at home. I won't be more than four or five minutes. I have it locked in a trunk."

Culver hurried out of the room and the Crimson Mask heard a door open and close again toward the rear of the apartment. He stepped behind Culver's desk and opened a couple of drawers. In a second he found something highly significant. It was a carbon copy of the advertisement placed in the newspapers warning the Crimson Mask to stay off the case.

He closed the drawers and resumed his original position before Culver got back. The squat ex-physician carried a bottle of *Sveltform*. He sat down behind his desk and looked up at the Crimson Mask.

"Of course, I would like to see your credentials first," he said.

The Crimson Mask felt the trap closing in on him. He was almost tempted to draw a gun, seize Culver and take him out of here.

"Come, come," Culver smiled, "don't tell me you have no credentials. I think it's against the law to represent yourself as an agent of the government. A man like you should know better... Mr. Crimson Mask."

The Crimson Mask's hand darted under his coat Culver didn't move.

"If you draw a gun," he warned, "you'll be shot through the back instantly. There is a mirror above my head. Look in it."

The Crimson Mask raised his eyes. Two men had been concealed behind a decorative screen. Both had guns trained on him. Two others came in from the hallway and Culver laughed heartily.

"I knew that you'd come to see me sooner or later," he gloated. "I felt that even though we held Warrick a prisoner, you'd hardly stop work on the case. When you searched my desk—as my men signaled you did, I knew who you were. How much did that fool Tony Webb tell you."

The Crimson Mask didn't answer. He was looking for a way out of this mess. There seemed to be no loophole. With four gunmen watching him narrowly, blocking every exit, he was completely trapped.

"What makes you think I'm the Crimson Mask?" he stalled for time.

Culver chuckled.

"I don't think. I know. Call it a hunch if you like, but—you are the Crimson Mask. Admit it! You aren't playing with fools this time. I'm smarter than you, cleverer than Warrick or all the police he used to head. He died bravely though."

"If you killed him..." the Crimson Mask said tensely.

"So," Culver laughed, "you admit your identity! People ought to study psychology. See how I made you talk? Warrick isn't dead—yet. But he is going to die. You were warned to lay off. As soon as we dispose of you, we shall take care of Warrick. You blundered into this, Crimson Mask, but I do not underestimate your skill. That is why I mean to finish you off immediately. Look here… a hypodermic needle which I can fill with any poison. Even thermadite. I could…"

The Crimson Mask went for his gun at that instant. He had been watching the mirror, saw all four thugs slowly and quietly move toward him. If he could press a gun against Culver's ribs, he might set least create a stalemate.

But the thugs seemed to have guessed his intentions and with the first movement of his hand, one leaped with an upraised gun. It smashed down. The Crimson Mask fell across Culver's desk and slowly slipped to the floor. The gun barrel struck again with savage brutality. The last thing he remembered was Culver's ironic laughter.

CHAPTER VIII

MANHUNT IN THE DARK

WHEN THE Crimson Mask opened his eyes again, he found himself in the white-tiled laboratory at the pharmaceutical plant. He wasn't tied up and there was a circle of crooks around him, all of them holding guns. Ex-doctor Culver smiled down at him.

The Crimson Mask sat up, rubbing two big lumps on his head. "Where am I?" he groaned.

Culver shrugged and looked at his men.

"See—I told you he hadn't been here before, even if one of the guards is missing. That fellow must have just walked out on us."

"He sure ain't here, Doc," one of the men answered. He was a burly individual with ascertain amount of authority.

"Then what are you worrying about, Matty?" Culver asked. "The Crimson Mask didn't pay you any visit. Put him in that chair over against the wall."

The Crimson Mask was hoisted to his feet and dragged over to the chair. Matty, who was obviously in charge of the crooks, tripped the Crimson Mask and shoved him into the chair. Culver walked over, stood there with his feet spread slightly apart and hands on both hips.

"Well, Mr. Crimson Mask," he said, "we're positive of your identity now. We found your mask… and your guns. You are quite helpless and you haven't very long to live. What's your real name? Who are you?"

The Crimson Mask remained tight-lipped, fighting to regain his strength and trying to plan some way of getting clear. There seemed to be none. At least ten men were in the lab, besides Matty and Culver. All had their eyes fixed on him. Every move he made was watched.

"Don't want to talk, eh?" Culver grinned. "All right. We don't really care who you are, but very shortly the police are going to name you a thief. A crook who got into this laboratory along with several others and stole some valuable property. You were shot by one of the guards."

Still the Crimson Mask maintained a stony silence and Culver didn't like it. He wanted this crime fighter to beg for his life, to display fear.

"It will be strange for the Crimson Mask to be buried with the label of a crook," Culver laughed and the other men snickered.

"I'm not dead yet," the Crimson Mask snapped.

They all howled at that one. Culver's laugh was cut off suddenly and his dark face became suffused with rage.

"Let's get it over with," he said. "Boys, start moving the barrels out. Everything is ready. Matty—you watch the Crimson Mask. Don't take your eyes off him for a single minute."

MATTY HAD a heavy revolver which he proceeded to cock with significant slowness. He parked himself on the edge of a lair bench and kept the gun trained directly on the Crimson Mask.

The other men fell to work. They started moving barrels lined up against the further wall. One of them miscalculated the weight of the barrel as he rolled it and the barrel fell over with a considerable clatter. Culver snarled an oath.

"Idiot! Do this without making any noise! Do you want cops around here? There are enough of them. Anyway, remember what each of these barrels is worth. You—carry out the big bottles, too."

The man given this order picked up one of the large bottles which the Crimson Mask had examined during his first visit. The Crimson Mask tipped his chair back against the wall.

"Culver," he said, "that's one of the rottenest pieces of business I've ever heard of. Those bottles are filled with pure quinine. So are the barrels, very likely. The government gave you that quinine for turning into pills. Our troops need quinine and there is very little of it since the Japs took the Dutch East Indies."

Culver snickered.

"At least it was very nice of the government to hand us more than a ton of quinine. It is valuable, as you say. Worth more than its weight in gold and I know just where to get rid of it at a profit that would make you blink. Let the soldiers go to blazes."

Culver turned to watch his men remove the barrels. Apparently a truck was waiting and Culver's scheme was very clear. He would claim that crooks had broken into the plant, stolen the quinine and left one of their number behind—a victim of some faithful guard's bullet. The Crimson Mask shuddered because that plan could work.

Matty was stone-faced, a thoroughly dangerous man. There wasn't much time left. The Crimson Mask had to think fast and put into action any suggestion his brain could contrive. Forcing himself to remain cool, he looked around the lab.

About twenty feet to his left he saw a glass enclosed electric switch box containing fuses and wires. It was about shoulder high. Very likely those fuses and wires controlled the lighting in this lab.

Deliberately and slowly, the Crimson Mask arose. Matty's gun steadied.

"Sit down," he snapped.

"I don't think I will," the Crimson Mask answered. "You won't dare shoot me while that quinine is being loaded. As Culver said, this area is thick with policemen. They'd hear the shot as long as the doors were open. Therefore, I'm going to take a little walk."

"I'll let you have it," Matty warned.

Culver came over.

"Don't shoot yet, Matty. I'll have a couple of the boys placed to intercept him if he makes a break. Should that happen—use a knife on him."

The Crimson Mask smiled and walked slowly along, keeping very close to the wall. The last of the barrels was being rolled out now. In three or four minutes the doors would be closed and the lab made practically sound-proof. Then Matty would shoot him down with relish.

Two men hurried over and took up posts on either side of the Crimson Mask and about twenty feet away from him. They were set to stop any break he might attempt.

THE CRIMSON MASK came opposite the fuse box. At this close range he saw that it would take very little to put out the light. Matty wasn't far away and his gun was held ready for instant action. His finger was white on the trigger.

Culver believed the Crimson Mask well trapped. He glanced toward the men and saw their work was about done.

"I'm leaving," he said. "Got to arrange an alibi for myself. I want to be home at the time this burglary and... the shooting of a burglar is announced. You know what to do, Matty?"

"I know," Matty said. "What's more, I feel like letting him have it right now. I don't trust that guy, Doc."

"What can he do?" Culver shrugged. "If he makes a move, you can shoot him. If you miss, the boys will nail him to the floor with a knife. Should that happen, have your guards claim the burglar had the knife and in the fight he was stabbed. Put his own finger-prints on the haft."

I'll take good care of him," Matty promised. "You can get going. When do we go for Warrick and fix his wagon?"

"Before morning," Culver said. "I'll get the car gassed up and ready. Crimson Mask—this is good-by. Keep thinking how people will curse you as a traitor who helped to steal thousands of dollars worth of quinine which our poor soldiers need so badly."

"Hey, Doc," Matty dropped his voice. "Maybe from now on, I'll work closer with you. Maybe I'll even meet the boss. It's tough working for a guy you don't know."

"We'll see—later," Culver answered and walked out.

The Crimson Mask gave him two additional minutes, saw that the men were getting ready to close the big doors and knew he had to swing into action immediately.

He stood with his back against the projecting glass case containing the fuse boxes. Suddenly the Crimson Mask reached under his coat and a split second later he leaped to one side. During that split second, Matty pulled the trigger.

He aimed for the Crimson Mask's chest and when the target moved, the fuse box took the bullet. It smashed through the glass and into the maze of fuses and switches. Cutting almost any of the tangled wires would result in prompt darkness and that was what happened.

The Crimson Mask made a neat nose-dive under one of the lab benches and stayed there, very quietly. The big doors swung shut in a hurry. The men began to mill around.

Matty called out:

"Listen, boys, the Crimson Mask is my meat. If we all look for him, we're liable to shoot one another in this darkness. I want you to leave by the factory door. Watch it now, that the Crimson Mask doesn't try to leave with you. Then wait for me. I'll find him. He hasn't got a gun and he can't get out. Two of you guard the platform doors and make sure the truck rolls away right now."

Matty's strategy was put into motion at once. The Crimson Mask took advantage of the clattering of feet to wriggle across a cleared space and very soon he reached the aisle between the lab benches where he had fought a death battle with one of the phony guards.

HE LOCATED the cupboard into which he had stowed the dead guard and hauled out the corpse. As he finished these preparations, the crooks cleared out. The door closed and the Crimson Mask was alone in the darkened room with a killer.

He heard Matty prowling around, muttering curses as if he dared the Crimson Mask to locate and attack him first. Matty had a gun and felt very secure. The Crimson Mask left the corpse beneath a bench, crawled away from it and deliberately scraped his feet on the floor.

Matty's gun blazed in the direction of the sound and the Crimson Mask learned all he wanted. Matte would shoot very promptly. At any noise. Crouched, the Crimson Mask moved noiselessly to the end of the lab bench, reached up and found a bottle of some chemical. He waited until Matty called a challenge to him, hurled the bottle and grinned because he knew it had come pretty close.

"So help me," Matty warned, "I'll put the first bullet where it hurts the most so you'll die by inches. Come on—stand up and face it. You haven't got a chance. Every door is guarded and you're unarmed."

Slowly now, the Crimson Mask returned to where he'd left the body of the guard. The corpse still gripped a revolver and the Crimson Mask took time enough to pry it loose.

Matty was coming closer and adopting a new technique of what be thought was a silent approach. He forgot that coat buttons make noise when they drag along a lab bench or that shoes might squeak very slightly.

The Crimson Mask grasped the corpse and raised it erect. The corpse was directly in line with a window and there were weak lights in the yard. The corpse was silhouetted.

Matty gave a yelp of delight and fired twice. Both bullets smacked into the dead man. The Crimson Mask let go and the body fell forward with a crash. Matty began laughing in high glee. He reached into his pocket, took out a pack of matches and lit one.

Holding it high, he spotted the prone form and hurried toward it. Evidently he suspected nothing.

He knelt beside the body and started to turn it over. Someone tapped him on the shoulder. He looked around and a fist smashed into his face. Matty dropped backwards, across the dead man. He did his best to get the gun out again, but he was much too slow.

The next time that fist hit him, it was a haymaker. After that, Matty displayed no more movement than the dead man beside him.

The Crimson Mask hurried to the big doors through which the stolen quinine had been taken. He had Matty's keys and soon the door was unlocked. Outside, two men with drawn guns were waiting to see if those shots meant the end of the Crimson Mask.

The Crimson Mask opened one of the double doors and in a good imitation of Matty's voice he called out to the pair of crooks.

"Come in, boys, and see what the Crimson Mask looks like, now."

Then he quickly stepped behind the door until both thugs had passed through and were floundering around in the darkness trying to locate Matty.

The Crimson Mask slipped through the door and raced toward the fence. He was up and over it in seconds.

CHAPTER IX

THU PRISONER TALKS

THE CRIMSON MASK used a telephone in an all-night drug store, hurried out and crossed town rapidly until he was only a block from where Culver lived. Two minutes after he arrived, a coupé pulled up with Dave Small at the wheel.

The Crimson Mask got in quickly.

"Your part of the job begins now," he told Dave. "Stay here. In a few minutes, I'll point out Culver to you. When he returns, in about an hour or so, conk him and don't hold back your punch. He's low enough not to care what happens to our troops fighting for their lives in all kinds of swamps and jungles. Remember that when you measure him for a sock on the jaw."

"He'll be good," Dave promised.

A few moments later, Matty, one of his men and Culver stepped out of the apartment-house door and were briefly revealed under the lights.

"The dumpy, dark-featured guy is your man," the Crimson Mask told Dave. "Wait for him inside. After you have taken care of him, drag the remains to his apartment. It's 'C' on the top floor. Let yourself in and wait for a phone call from me."

The Crimson Mask trailed the three crooks to a garage from which they soon emerged in a sedan. Staying well back, the Crimson Mask followed them, being very careful about it. Everything depended upon the success of his present mission.

The car rolled steadily uptown. It was almost dawn, but still dark enough so that the Crimson Mask wasn't noticed. Finally, Culver's sedan stopped with its radiator almost touching a heavy iron gate leading into what seemed to be a private estate.

There was a brass plate affixed to the gate. It indicated that this was a private hospital, no admittance. As the gates opened, the Crimson Mask was going over the iron fence. He ran across the estate, saw that a few windows in the big brick building were lit up and spotted a man in a white coat sitting on the back steps smoking a pipe.

The Crimson Mask took his borrowed gun from his pocket, held it firmly and approached the man. He was quite old and seemed harmless enough. The Crimson Mask stepped in front of him, gestured with the gun and forced the man behind the garage.

"What kind of a place is this?" he demanded.

The old man shrugged. "Okay, who do you want to get out of here? I won't stop you, Mister, so you can put the gun away. I'd quit myself if I didn't think they'd kill me."

"I asked you a question," the Crimson Mask reminded him.

"This is a private sanitarium, only some of the patients who come here ain't no more crazy than I am. The doc takes any kind of a case if there's money in it. He hides crooks and I suspect he even kills people for a price and says they died a natural death in his hospital."

"There is one man who arrived recently and of whom they probably take especial care." The Crimson Mask went on to describe

Warrick. "I want to know in which room they have him imprisoned."

With the stem of his pipe, the old man pointed at one of the darkened windows on the second floor.

"That's it," he explained. "Saw him only once. They said he was crazy. Mister, if you're the law, go easy on me. I didn't want to get mixed up with this outfit. When I came to work here, I figured it was a good job and before I knew the truth, they had me in a mess so deep I couldn't crawl out."

"You'll walk out tomorrow," the Crimson Mask promised. "And well-protected, too. Thanks for the information. I want to see that man and quickly."

The old man clutched at the Crimson Mask's arm.

"If you try to get in, they'll grab you. Doors are all locked and every window is barred just like a prison. But you could talk to your friend through the window. I know where there is a ladder. Right in the garage here. Nobody will disturb you. I'm the only man on guard back here."

With the old man's help, the Crimson Mask carried the ladder, set it up and climbed the rungs. He reached the window, found it open a crack and raised it further.

"Warrick," he said.

There was a startled gasp and then Warrick's voice came out of the darkness.

"Go away. You can't get me out. I hear Culver downstairs. He just came in. They told me if you went to work on the case, I'd be killed, but that doesn't matter so long as you get away and stop these madmen."

"They won't kill you if you do as I say," the Crimson Mask whispered hoarsely. "I'm sure they'd rather know who I am than take your life right now. When they threaten you—talk. Tell them you're willing to reveal my identity and where they can find me. Don't act too convincing. Give them some doubt and they'll let you live just to be sure you haven't lied."

"But I can't do that," Warrick said. "I won't either. You're more important than I."

"You'll be helping me get rid of them," the Crimson Mask said. "You talked to Webb, of course?"

THE EX-COMMISSIONER nodded.

"He worked in that plant and stumbled on the truth. These men are out to make a fortune before their plan is discovered. Narcotics sold almost openly in shady drug stores all over the country. Morphine which the government supplied them. Phony medicines that are not only worthless, but might be dangerous. Webb was trapped. They treated him well at first gave him drinks and tried to bring him on their side. He pretended to agree until he found a chance to escape."

"Webb is dead," the Crimson Mask whispered. "They fed him thermadite in those drinks. Did he tell you who was the actual head of this ring?"

"No."

"What do you know about Culver?"

"I helped send the rat to prison some years ago. He keeps in the background, but I had a glimpse of him although he didn't realize it."

"Then he must be afraid to show his face," the Crimson Mask said. "That's a lucky break because he'll leave everything in the hands of his lieutenant—a lug named Matty. Stall, Warrick. Hedge and bargain. Do anything until you hear a pebble hit the window. That means Culver has gone home. Then—tell Matty just this...."

Warrick listened carefully, agreed and then hissed a warning.

The Crimson Mask slid down the ladder and got it away from under the window just before the lights were turned on. He took refuge with the old man, behind the garage.

Not more than twenty yards away, Culver's sedan was parked.

Half an hour went by. Twice the Crimson Mask heard a muffled cry come from that lighted room and knew that Warrick was taking punishment But Warrick knew how to take care of situations like this. He could stall, absorb torture and when the time came, talk convincingly.

Someone emerged from the hospital. It was Culver and he walked swiftly toward his car, climbed in and drove away. The

Crimson Mask waited a moment or two, picked up a tiny pebble and threw it against Warrick's window. It attracted attention because Matty showed his ugly face for a second.

"Stay here and keep quiet," the Crimson Mask told the old man. "If you are sincere, no harm will come to you. That is a promise. Sometime this morning, the police will arrive and they'll have special instructions about you."

The old man nodded eagerly and accompanied the Crimson Mask to a shadowy spot where he could climb the fence unde-tected. There was a gray light in the sky when the Crimson Mask drove away.

CHAPTER X

ADMISSION OF GUILT

AT **TEN** o'clock that same morning, the Crimson Mask was ready to leave his drug store. Dave Small, on duty behind the counter, was grinning broadly.

"Boy," he said, "did I belt that crooked doctor! I met him in the hall, stepped up and let him have it. He's tied, gagged and locked in one of the closets of his apartment. He won't give you any trouble."

"Good," the Crimson Mask approved. "That's exactly how I wanted it. I'll have the police pick him up later. Right now I'm on my way to a meeting I arranged for this morning. The Drug Asso-ciation is going to listen to one of its lowly members—me. Only they won't know I'm Bob Clarke. Wish me luck, Dave, because if this works, I'm going to make a pretty important man break down and admit he heads a murder ring."

The Crimson Mask picked up a taxi on the street behind his drug store. Fifteen minutes later he walked into the Drug Associ-ation's offices. There were only eight men present. Included among these was Tim Barlow, who took active charge of things as usual. Straben, head of the Pharmaceutical Company, was slumped in a chair convinced he was not going to enjoy this meeting.

"Some of the members were unable to attend on such short notice," Barlow explained. "Those who are here are very eager to know what this is all about."

The Crimson Mask stepped to the head of the table. He surveyed the men for a moment.

"Gentlemen, hardly more than a day ago, Mr. Straben's firm was found to be marketing a preparation which included thermadite, which we all know is not conducive to good health, even in minute quantities. Fortunately this was discovered. However, I can tell you now that this drug was very deliberately placed on the market for the few dollars it would bring to the firm."

"That's a lie," Straben jumped to his feet. "I never knew anything about it!"

"Quite true," the Crimson Mask admitted. "You didn't know its deadly effect. Yet one of your employees did and when he complained about it to your plant superintendent, he was murdered. Killed with the very drug he was trying to prevent the firm from using. Murdered because he knew too much. Probably more than even you, Straben."

"I don't seem to understand...." Tim Barlow frowned.

"Straben's firm also engaged in the distribution of narcotics. Drugs they received from the government for use in making legal medicines. The medicines they manufactured contained either no narcotic or extremely little. What wasn't used, they placed in other bottles, mixed with harmless solvents, and arranged to sell these to drug addicts through a scheme that was extremely clever because of its simplicity.

"The illicit stuff was turned over to shady drug stores which displayed a certain trademark sign in their window. This sign was known by drug addicts. When they saw it, they knew a supply of narcotics was available there and they asked for these certain preparations containing large amounts of morphine and codeine. They paid handsomely, of course. The whole thing is an illegal traffic in drugs on a huge scale."

BARLOW'S FACE was pale.

"I say Straben should be arrested at once," he demanded.

"He will be taken care of in due time," the Crimson Mask advised. He looked at his watch and frowned. Then he spoke again. "You may think this scheme was pretty low, but there is one angle even lower. Straben's firm managed to get a government contract to make quinine pills for the armed forces. Quinine, as you all know, is an extremely precious commodity with all stocks frozen by Federal order. That makes any supply of the drug very valuable.

"Straben's firm got more than a ton of it. Last night the drug was removed from the plant. This morning the police were to have been notified that the laboratory had been robbed. Whether they were or not, I don't know yet. Certain circumstances may have prevented the crooks from revealing that the drug was gone. They may even have replaced it last night."

"Every ounce of quinine I obtained is in my factory!" Straben shouted. "I'm being crucified! This man—and we haven't the vaguest idea who he is—has stated I'm a thief and a murderer. I resent this and I say call in the police right now. Have them examine the Crimson Mask as well as myself!"

Tim Barlow chewed on his upper lip, glanced at the Crimson Mask and saw him studying his watch again.

"Talk it over," the Crimson Mask advised. "I won't try to influence you one way or another. In fact, I'll willingly withdraw temporarily. The next room is vacant?"

"Yes," Barlow said, "but it isn't necessary to..."

"I would rather." The Crimson Mask walked to the door. "Straben is entitled to make demands. You gentlemen have a right to study them. I'll return when you want me."

Before there were any more objections, the Crimson Mask disappeared into the next office. There he went to work swiftly. From an inner pocket he removed a flat kit. Opened, this kit held a fairly-large mirror and a number of materials necessary for disguise.

A quick application of cream removed the disguise he wore and for two or three dangerous moments, Bob Clarke's face was revealed. He hastily covered this with a substance that made him look almost florid. A quick-acting dye changed his hair to a straw color. He altered the arch of his eyebrows considerably with invisible tape.

There were no phony whiskers or metallic devices clamped in his mouth or nostrils. They were unnecessary, for the Crimson Mask was a master at this business.

FINISHED, HIS appearance had changed completely. He glanced at his watch again and stepped to the door, but he didn't open it. He could hear Straben arguing for the Crimson Mask's immediate arrest. Then Straben's voice petered out suddenly and a much harsher one gave a curt command.

"Okay—all of you. Get your hands in the air and keep 'em there. Which one is Tim Barlow?"

"That—that's him." Straben indicated Barlow by inclining his head.

The Crimson Mask opened the door a crack. Matty and one of his men were near the exit, both with guns. The others were lined up with their backs toward the Crimson Mask, Matty and his pal were too engrossed watching their prisoners to see the Crimson Mask silently slip out, close the door behind him and step up to join the others with his hands high.

"So you're Tim Barlow." Matty walked up to the man. "Move forward a few steps. Barlow, eh? The devil you are. You're the Crimson Mask!"

"What?" Bartow shouted. "No—no, you're making a mistake. I'm not the Crimson Mask! He's in the next room!"

"Go see," Matty ordered his companion, and the man hurried to the next room.

"Ain't nobody there," he reported, "and no doors out of the room either. Only way a guy could leave is through the window and we're pretty high up."

"You're lying," Matty said grimly. "It won't do you any good, Barlow. We know you're the Crimson Mask and that means curtains."

"But I tell you there's a mistake," Bartow pleaded. "The Crimson Mask was here. Ask any of the others…"

"Shut up," Matty snarled. "You're a funny guy, Crimson Mask. Last night you looked different, but we know all about how you disguise yourself. But you didn't act so scared. It won't make any difference. Okay, Crimson Mask, this is where time stops for you."

The gunmen leveled both weapons. Then Barlow gulped and became ghastly pale. He bit his lower lip and then seemed to make a very sudden decision.

"Matty," he snapped. "And you, Jordan. Yes, I know your names. I know all about you. I'm not the Crimson Mask. This is a trick to make me reveal myself and it worked. You leave me no choice. I'm Doc Culver's boss. I back him and that makes me your leader, too. I can name every member of the gang!"

Barlow rattled off names and then told how much money Matty had received a few days before. He went on to convince these two killers that he was on their side. They listened with mouths agape.

To one side, the Crimson Mask towered his hands and reached for his guns. Bartow looked around and recognized him as a stranger. Facts clicked in Barlow's brain and he yelled to Matty for action.

"That's the Crimson Mask! He changed his appearance! Get him…."

MATTY SWUNG to bring his gun to bear and died with it half-raised. The other thug gave a bleat of terror and tried to run for it. He reached the door about the same time as Tim Barlow.

Two slugs smashed through the panels, very close. The men turned and raised their hands. The Crimson Mask walked slowly toward them. Ten minutes later the room was filled with police. Among them was Ted Warrick, his face puffed, his lips swollen, but he grinned just the same.

"I did as you suggested," he told the Crimson Mask. "Matty started torturing me. Doc Culver stayed for a while and then got jittery. I heard him say he had to be home."

"He was always alibiing himself," the Crimson Mask explained. "Go on, Warrick."

"After he left, Matty got quite rough about it. Finally, I pretended to give in. I told him Tim Barlow was the Crimson

Mask, and that he would be here at eleven this morning. They let me live with a promise that if I lied, I'd be killed very slowly. How did you guess Barlow was the leader whom only Culver knew?"

"By purely circumstantial evidence," the Crimson Mask said. "First of all, when investigators for the Food and Drug Department wanted to get samples of the products put out by Straben's firm, Bartow was in a position to see that they'd get medicines really up to standard. Only someone connected as Bartow was, could arrange this.

"Also, in my former disguise, Barlow knew me as the Crimson Mask. The night I visited you, Straben, Barlow came up on the porch. He was going to pay a visit, too—possibly to give you the devil for putting out such stuff as *Sveltform*.

"Anyway, he saw me, guessed I was on the march and warned Doc Culver to expect me. When I went there, I walked into a trap. Barlow likewise claimed to have discovered the dangerous qualities of *Sveltform*, but Straben told me he had conferred with Barlow about this preparation. Barlow was simply trying to build himself up and avert any suspicion."

"This is all beyond me," Straben groaned. "I admit I suspected something queer was going on, but Doc Culver came to me with plenty of money, got me out of the red and took over. I got my share of the profits, but I didn't know anything like this went on...."

"That's how I knew there was a financial backer," the Crimson Mask interrupted. "You and Culver were broke."

An hour later, Bob Clarke was in his drug store. The phone rang and he heard Sandy's voice on the wire.

"I've had an adventure," Sandy said excitedly. "It happened last night at the plant. I brought an overnight bag with me and changed into evening dress. I pretended I was staying late because I had a date. I was in the laboratory all alone trying out some of the drug mixtures when a man with a gun appeared."

"What happened then?" asked Clarke over the wire.

"I threw the mixture in the man's masked face and then I ran and got out of the place in a hurry. I think we're on the track—"

"Darling," said Bob Clarke softly. "Straben is arrested. So is Doc Culver and the real head of the ring. You can quit your job now."

He blinked several times at the answer he received, grinned and hung up. It might have been Straben or Barlow who had been sneaking around the plant. That didn't matter now. Dave Small was standing at Clarke's elbow, but Dave wasn't smiling.

"Bob," he said, "we forgot something. Remember that sticker you had me put in the window? The one meant to bring drug addicts here for some of Barlow's special medicine loaded with morphine?"

"We never did find out if it worked," Bob said.

"No?" Dave grunted. "Step out front. There are four guys clamoring for the stuff. They're waving twenty-dollar bills and they twist and jerk as if they hadn't had a shot in days."

Bob Clarke sat down and leaned wearily back in his chair.

"They're your problem, Dave," he said. "You asked for more work in this case. Go finish it up."

MOTTO FOR MURDER

CHAPTER I

SLAUGHTER OF THE INNOCENT

IN THE big somber courtroom of the Criminal Courts Building the judge's voice echoed with befitting solemnity:

"Gentlemen of the jury, have you reached a verdict?"

"We have, Your Honor." The foreman smiled a little. Bill Willis wondered what that smile meant. Hope for him? Or satisfaction at duty well done?

He stood with clasped hands before the judge's bench, his angular face expressionless. Devore, his lawyer, a handsome, forceful man of forty, with John L. Lewis eyebrows which could bristle at a recalcitrant witness, stood beside him.

"The defendant will face the jury," the judge said.

Willis turned. The foreman smiled again.

"We, the jury, find the prisoner not guilty."

Sound broke in the court-room, and there was lightning display of flash bulbs. The judge's gavel cut the tumult short.

"William Willis, this Court has seldom concurred in a jury's verdict with more pleasure. You are a free man, and it is to be hoped that you will have no bitter memories of your unfortunate experience."

The babble broke out again as the judge rose. Reporters swarmed forward and fell upon Willis.

"Mr. Willis, were you afraid of being convicted?"

Willis turned somber eyes on the questioner.

"Only a fool is never afraid," he said.

The reporter, slightly baffled, let Willis go, staring after him.

"He's scared," he muttered. "Now the guy is scared!"

Willis reached the top of the granite steps which led to the street. He looked up at the sun and at the busy traffic. Then he stepped out of the building with Devore behind him.

A light delivery truck that had been parked at the curb pulled out and rolled away. Willis never saw it. Nor did he see the slender barrel of a rifle poked through the glassless window in the back. No one saw it. And in the muffled boom of traffic, no one heard the whiplike crack a .22 special makes. It is doubtful that Willis heard or even felt anything. A high velocity bullet through the temple is faster than a man's nerve reflexes.

HIS FEET faltered on the steps like a man suddenly sick. Then, even as Devore made a startled grab for him, Willis pitched in an arm-tossing heap to the bottom.

Face gray with fright, Devore scuttled down the steps, turned Willis over. Blood oozed from a wound in his head. A woman screamed, and the inevitable New York crowd began to hurry and push about the lawyer who knelt helplessly with the dead man's head in his arms.

Detective-lieutenant Hogan pushed his way authoritatively through the crowd. He saw at a glance the man was dead and his searching eyes darted over the crowd. A traffic policeman hurried from the corner.

"Get this crowd back," Hogan ordered.

The bluecoat stepped up on the curb, then stopped, bent down and picked up something.

"What is it?" Hogan elbowed him. "Homicide Squad," he added, showing his badge.

The traffic officer handed over an oblong of yellow cloth, embroidered with thread. A sampler. Hogan remembered his mother working on the things, embroidering mottos like "God Bless Our Home" and "Friendship Makes Friends." She'd had them hanging all over the walls. In his room the sampler had read, "The Devil Finds Work For Idle Hands."

But this one was different. The embroidery was in scarlet and the words were ominous.

There was a furious mêlée, and the man was subdued

"'Blood For Blood,'" Hogan muttered.

He stuffed the sampler into his pocket and began firing orders. In two minutes the street was cleared, the body of William Willis moved and the shaken Devore sent home in a police cruiser. Hogan went back into the court-room and talked to the judge.

When he came out he flagged a taxi and gave Willis' home address. Ostensibly his purpose was to break the sad news to Willis' wife. His real purpose was to find out why she hadn't been present on the last day of the trial. Surely she should have been, for an event as important as that in her life.

But Hogan discovered that her reason for staying at home was unimpeachable. William Willis had been on trial for killing her father. The double blow—her father's death, her husband's arrest—had crushed her. She was in bed. Hogan had the unpleasant task of adding the third blow. He drove away from the house feeling a little like a murderer himself.

Scare headlines on the front pages and pictures of the sampler crowded the war news for a few days. Then, when nothing happened, the murder sensation died out and a week later few remembered it.

One man did. Arthur Medford, waiting for the jury's verdict on a similar charge of murdering the father of his own wife. Lieutenant Hogan found the coincidence fascinating. Medford and Willis, charged with the same crime. And Medford had the same lawyer, Devore. Furthermore, there was as much doubt about Medford's guilt as there had been about Willis'....

Devore carefully placed his immaculately-clad self on a wooden chair in the barred room off the court-room to which Medford had been taken under guard when the jury had retired. Medford paced up and down with nervous, jerky steps.

"Sit down," Devore said, lighting a cigarette. "Be calm like me. The jury's convinced. I saw it in their eyes after my summation."

Medford sighed. "You were good. But—how can you be sure? You never know what's in a juror's mind."

"You're innocent, aren't you? Stop worrying."

"Sure, stop worrying," Medford said nervously. "Even if I'm acquitted—remember what happened to Willis?"

"Are you worrying about that now?" Devore shook his head. "There's no connection between Willis and you. You told me you didn't even know him."

"I don't. But that sampler—"

"Crackpot stuff," Devore said, as though his own voice were reassurance.

"Sure, crackpot stuff," Medford said, shivering.

A bailiff opened the door.

"Okay, Medford—jury's coming in."

Medford turned, his face blanching.

The bailiff was moved to unaccustomed kindness.

"It's okay," he said. "They're smiling. They don't do that when they're sending a man to the chair."

Dazedly Medford heard the jury free him and listened to the judge's final words. He scarcely felt Devore's hand on his shoulder, or heard the attorney's congratulations. He was free. And yet remembering what had happened to Willis, he almost wished he were not walking out of there.

WHEN HE reached the court-house steps he looked at the free sky and the sun as Willis had done. Devore, on his left, was trying to be nonchalant, but Lieutenant Hogan, on his right, was making no pretense. His hand was plunged deep in his side pocket, and Medford did not need to be told it gripped a gun.

Nothing happened. Medford walked down the steps and into a taxicab. An hour later the cab drew up before his suburban home and his wife ran down the walk with the tears streaming from her eyes. Medford hung onto her like a drowning man. Lonely as he had been, he had insisted she stay home, fearing that the trial would be too much for her. And today, especially, he had not wanted her to near if an attempt should be made on his life in case of acquittal, as it had been in Willis' case—successfully.

Hogan discreetly looked up into the trees while husband and wife embraced.

"Congratulations, Mrs. Medford," he said. "I didn't think your husband killed your father, even though I had to tag him with it. He had to go through it to clear himself and now he has."

"The police have been splendid," Attorney Devore said. "You're all right now, Medford, so we will go."

"Thanks for everything," Medford said as Devore and Hogan climbed back into the cab. "All the money in the world can never repay you for what you've done for me."

Devore spread his hands eloquently and smiled as the cab moved off....

Arthur Medford was a popular man. That night his friends threw a gala party for him. In a small banquet room at a midtown hotel they shot the works from oysters to champagne.

Devore sat at Medford's right. On his left was Charlie Irwin, Medford's partner in a real estate and insurance firm.

Irwin was an affable, ruddy-cheeked man about ten years older than Medford. He was demonstrative and highly affected by his partner's release. When affected he tended toward speech-making, delivered in a booming baritone and crammed with platitudes.

"Drop it, mug, or we'll cut you in half!" a voice rasped

"All of us here are Art's friends," he began eagerly when speech-making time arrived. "We stood by him through this mess because we knew darned well he couldn't hurt a fly." Everybody there knew that, but Irwin said it as though making an important discovery. "We're dog-goned proud of Art for the courage he's showed. So—a toast to Art Medford!"

All dutifully raised their glasses and drank. Irwin beamed.

"Now a toast to Olivia, his wife. She stood by him, even though—er—ah—it was hard to bear the gossip and scandal." He had almost mentioned her father's murder, but caught himself in time. That wouldn't have been tactful! "Here's to Olivia Medford, a real-life heroine!"

They drank to her too. Then a waiter presented a silver tray with a bell cover to the speaker which Irwin in turn set before Arthur Medford, talking all the time.

"A little token," Irwin explained. "We all chipped in. Go on, Art—uncover it! It ain't much, but... Art! What's the matter?"

Arthur Medford staggered to his feet, his chair falling over backward. In his hands was a sampler, embroidered in blazing scarlet with the words all had read before.

BLOOD FOR BLOOD

"If this is a joke," Medford said through white lips, "it's a mighty poor one."

"Who put that there?" Irwin demanded incredulously. "We bought you a wrist-watch! It cost a hundred and fifty bucks!"

The wrist-watch was there. But Arthur Medford didn't see it. His lips were working, though no words would come. His eyes seemed like frozen jelly in his gray face. Then he fell across the table and his champagne glass, knocked over, sent out a little straw-colored wave which quickly was soaked into the tablecloth.

CHAPTER II

HOGAN HAS A VISITOR

DETECTIVE-LIEUTENANT HOGAN was a tired man as he fitted a key into the door of his bachelor apartment. In the Homicide Bureau a man becomes accustomed to death, but even Hogan's nerves were a little frayed by the manner in which Willis and Medford had been struck down.

He opened the door and sent one hand toward the light switch. Before it got there he changed its direction abruptly, whipping it toward his hip holster. Deep in the room he saw a little glowing red eye and smelled tobacco smoke. One hand shot up with the gun in his fist while with his other he flipped the switch. Light flooded the room.

"Rufe!" Hogan said explosively. "Some day you're going to get hurt with these kid stunts of yours!" He slammed his gun down angrily.

Rufus Reed, private investigator, sitting in Hogan's big easy chair, stretched out his legs and yawned.

"What did you want me to do, Ben?" he asked. "Stand out in the hall waiting for you?"

"Who gave you a key?" Hogan demanded, wheeling with his coat half off.

Reed shrugged. "That's not such a good lock, I guess."

Hogan grunted, on his way to the bathroom to wash up. From his attitude it might not have been guessed that he and Reed were the best of friends; college mates, in fact. Hogan, serious, studious, a disciplinarian of himself as well as others, had naturally gravitated to the regular police force; Reed, no less interested in crime but more brilliant, headstrong and erratic, and chafing at discipline, had preferred being a private detective. They remained friends and frequently helped one another.

Hogan came back and dropped heavily into a chair opposite Reed.

"I'm bushed," he said. "Had a heck of a day. After losing Willis that way—now Medford. The Commissioner will be squawking for action in his quaint way."

"Precisely why I am here," Reed declared. "You need help, don't you? Tell me what the papers didn't print"

"They had most of it, I guess. William Willis was arrested for killing his father-in-law with a rifle. They'd had arguments, pretty hot ones too, but who's to say whether they were bad enough to do murder over? The gun belonged to Willis, but that was not conclusive. Anyone can pick up a gun known to be in a man's house. His alibi was weaker than Nazi acorn coffee."

"But he was acquitted," Reed murmured.

"Yes, circumstantial evidence was not good enough. His wife stuck by him loyally, even though it was her father who'd been killed. His friends all gave him an excellent character. So the jury thought he'd been framed although there wasn't a scrap of evidence to show who might have done it. They freed him and on his way out of court he was knocked off by a rifle bullet, like his supposed victim. And that sampler with 'BLOOD FOR BLOOD' was apparently dropped almost on his body."

"Suggesting revenge," Reed said musingly.

"Yes. Now who would be taking revenge on Willis if—as the assumption seems to be—he was really guilty? His wife?"

"You mean his wife's backing him up in public was just a front, that secretly she arranged to have him killed, believing him guilty of killing her father?"

"Why not?" Hogan demanded.

"Why not indeed?" Reed smiled. "I daresay it's been done. But what a tangled, intricate web of emotions that spins! Why not denounce the man and testify against him? Why defend him, get him released, and then—"

"How do I know?" Hogan growled.

"What about the other man—Medford?" asked Reed.

"He was poisoned, as the papers reported, at a congratulatory dinner given him by his friends. And another sampler turned up, smack in the silver dish on which they'd placed a watch as a gift."

"You think his wife had anything to do with that?"

"Well, it's always a possibility. But my hunch is that Olivia Medford is straighter goods than Lorna Willis. She grieved for her father as though it would break her heart, but she fought for her husband like a tigress."

"Olivia Medford's father was poisoned, wasn't he?" asked Reed.

"Yes."

"So each accused man, upon being acquitted, was killed by the same means he was supposed to have used to commit the crime. Willis' father-in-law was killed with a rifle—Willis was killed with a rifle. Olivia Medford's father was poisoned, and Arthur Medford was poisoned. And the samplers were left as direct warning that this was retribution."

"That's what it seems like."

"Ben, do you think either Willis or Medford was guilty?"

HOGAN SHOOK his head.

"No."

"Then someone else killed their fathers-in-law. The question now arises—were these earlier killings just a method of striking at Willis and Medford? Or did Willis and Medford just get the frame hung on them to avoid suspicion pointing at the real murderer? In other words, who were the primal victims—Willis and Medford, or their fathers-in-law?"

"I don't know," Hogan said. "The fathers-in-law were both rich—"

"Look," Reed interrupted. "We've lumped these two crimes together because of their similarity. But was there any connection between Willis and Medford?"

"No. They didn't even know each other."

"Then the only common bond is the samplers. They were alike?"

"Exactly. We went over them with a fine-tooth comb, but they're common stuff. The backgrounds and thread can be bought in any dry-goods store. Can't be traced."

"Yet there's a suggestion of a link," Reed said. "You sure those men didn't know each other?"

"I have only their own words for it."

"Better check."

"It's being done. Here's another angle. Though the older men were rich, it seems that Willis and Medford were not leeches. Both preferred to make their own way and not try to get anything out of their in-laws. That's what some of the quarrels were about in Willis' case. The old man wanted him to come into his business— owns a chain of hardware stores."

"Did you find out how the sampler came to be on Medford's silver serving dish?" Reed asked.

"Not a hint. The waiter swears he put the watch there, put the cover on, and carried it right in to the toast-master who at once set it down in front of Medford. The watch was there all right, but it was on the sampler and the waiter says the sampler wasn't there when he put the watch on the dish. Medford never saw the watch. The poison in his glass had begun to work by that time."

"It's a lulu." Reed grinned. "Bet you're glad you called me in."

"I called you! Why you—you couldn't catch a cold in a blizzard. I'll have to tell you the answer when I get it, same as always."

Reed shook hands with him gravely.

"Thanks, pal," he said. "I'll now go out and do a little of that extra-legal gumshoeing which the police don't dare to do. But which gets results, cookie. And to show you I'm a generous guy, I'll pool everything I find out—if you'll do the same."

"Okay."

"There, ahem—remains the little matter of compensation for my time and services. All right with you if I manage to get a fee from somebody in this case?"

"I don't care if you get a fee from all of them," Hogan growled. "Now get out of here and let me get some sleep!"

Outside, Rufe Reed caught a taxi and went back to his office in the midtown Forties off Broadway. He liked the noise and turmoil of this, the greatest entertainment district in the world, the crowds of people out for fun, the soldiers and sailors and girls. In fact his wife, Patricia, often remarked pointedly that he liked the girls much too well. But Reed dismissed this as enemy propaganda, not worth answering.

There was a light in his office and the door yielded readily to his touch. Pat Reed, a blonde with the kind of face and figure men look after on the street, sat in his swivel chair reading a detective magazine, with her shapely legs propped up on his desk.

"Either pull your skirt down or take your feet off my desk," Reed grunted, sailing his hat at the clothes tree. "Suppose a client came in? Where've you been?"

"Working," his wife said, yawning. "Didn't you send me out to interview Mrs. William Willis?"

Reed started a cigarette and sank into another chair.

"Give," he ordered.

"Well, I went out and rang Mrs. Willis' doorbell and when she answered it, I told her I was a reporter. She slammed the door in my face." Pat touched the tip of her nose reminiscently. "And through the closed door she told me what she thought of reporters in general and me in particular. What a fishwife! I'll bet Willis committed suicide. I'll bet—"

"Never mind your theories," Reed interrupted. "What happened then?"

"Nothing," said his wife, looking surprised. "She wouldn't let me in. What did you expect me to do?"

"Oh, fine," Reed groaned.

HIS WIFE was unaffected by his disgust.

"So then I went to see Mrs. Arthur Medford," she went on. "She was awfully nice. You know Rufe, it takes character to be that nice to a snoopy stranger when your husband's been dead only a few hours. I wonder if I'll have that much character when you—"

"Cut it," Reed ordered. "I refuse to die just to let you play the leading role in a tragic melodrama. What did she tell you?"

"Nothing we don't already know," Pat said brightly.

"You can build up to the most complete let-downs!" Reed muttered. "Well, what's your impression of the two women?"

"I told you," Pat said, opening her blue eyes wide. "Mrs. Willis is a fishwife and Mrs. Medford is swell."

"Anything else?"

"Let's see. Lorna Willis is the small type that some men go for, but she looks like a worrier. You know, forehead ridged like a washboard, lips curved down. Bet she's got nervous indigestion."

"And the other one?"

"Mrs. Medford looks like a thoroughbred. But I believe she is worried about something too."

"What did you expect? Her husband—"

"I mean aside from the shock and grief," Pat explained seriously. "She seems scared. She was almost on the defensive, answering questions. She's afraid of something that hasn't happened yet."

"So would you be," said John Reed, pushing open the door. He grinned at his brother and sister-in-law. "Who's got a cigarette?"

"You smoke too much," Rufus said, handing over his pack. "And what's the idea of snooping out in the hall?"

"Only way I ever learn anything," the younger brother said. "Do either of you ever tell me anything?"

"I'll tell you something now," Rufus said. "I'm going prowling tonight in Mrs. Willis' back yard and I'll have work for you both tomorrow, so get some sleep."

CHAPTER III

THE FINGER POINTS

I **T WAS** a long cab ride to the section in the Bronx where Mrs. Willis lived. Rufe Reed, however, never road in subways. He would have taken a cab to Nome, Alaska, if he'd had to go there.

The Willis house was fairly large, with a good-sized landscaped plot around it. The sky was overcast and trees and shrubs surrounded with inky pools of shadow just suited Reed's snoopy impulse. Leaving the silent and dimly lit street, he slipped through the hedge and stepped onto the grass of the lawn.

Light glowed dimly from one window through a drawn curtain. Reed crossed the yard and crouched below the window, pressing his ear to the sill. There was a low mumble of voices inside, but he could not make out any words. Already he had noticed a big car, all lights out, parked near the walk, and Reed was most curious about what was being said by Mrs. Willis and her visitor.

He fished in a vest pocket and found a long nail file. Gently he worried it under the window sash. When he pried up the window moved. Carefully, a millimeter at a time, he raised it no more than half an inch. But with his eye glued to this aperture, he could see and hear distinctly. And even the blasé Mr. Reed was slightly surprised.

Lorna Willis was standing in the middle of the room and her arms were locked tightly around the neck of a handsome man whom Reed had no trouble in recognizing, from newspaper pictures, as Glover C. Devore, the lawyer who had successfully defended William Willis and Arthur Medford!

"—not to talk about this to anyone unless the police come," Devore was saying. "If that happens, tell them you want me before you'll say a word. It's your right, and they can't stop you from insisting upon it. You must not talk without me. Can I trust you to do that?"

"Of course, darling," she answered. "People might misunderstand."

"Who cares about people?" Devore growled. "If we wait for the blessing of public opinion we'll be too old to get married. You're not feeling guilty, are

Reed caught an ankle and threw the whole might of his body into a savage pull

you, Lorna? We don't owe anything to Will! We can't let his ghost come between us!"

"It won't," Lorna Willis promised grimly. "But I am frightened. People are prying into my affairs more and more. If they get too deep—"

"I'll kill any man who—" Devore said in an ugly voice. "Oh, forget it. We're acting like a couple of kids afraid of the dark. Good night, Lorna. Try to calm down."

Reed was not interested in their final kiss. He ducked below the window, waiting for the door slam, to tell him Devore had left.

Somewhere in the dark behind him came a faint whisper of sound. He flattened himself against the dark side of the house, but saw nothing, heard no movement, no further sound. It might have been the breeze rubbing two branches together, but for a moment it had sounded like the scrape of a shoe on rock.

"Must be imagining things," he thought.

From out front came the whir of a starter. Then the tail-lights of the big car blinked into life and it moved off.

The light above Reed went out and after a moment another light in a different part of the house came on. Finally he slid the sash up quietly.

Lorna Willis was preparing for bed when Reed stepped, without warning, into her room. He got an interesting flash of a nude back before she screamed and pulled a flimsy negligee around herself.

"Not bad," he said.

"A bu—burglar!" Mrs. Willis stammered.

"Not at all," Reed said, offended. "I'm a detective."

"Police? What do you mean by breaking in here this way?"

"Not police," he corrected. "Private detective. Rufus Reed, ma'am. And it was the only way to get in I decided, after you slammed the door on my assistant's nose this morning."

"That blonde! Now you get out of here or I'll call the real police!"

"Just a minute," Reed said. "I think you'll want to talk to me about the murder of your father and husband."

He was being brutal to a woman to whom a terrible double tragedy had just come. But after the scene he had witnessed through the window, he was feeling no great sympathy for her.

"Why should I want to talk to you?" she said angrily. "I don't even know you."

"You want to see the murderer caught, don't you?"

"Why, of course I do!"

"Tell me this. Are you convinced that your husband was innocent?"

"Completely!" she snapped. Almost too quickly, he thought.

"The police have the idea that you haven't been too cooperative," he pointed out. "They think you're holding something back. It might spur them to an investigation of your past and your relationship with your husband."

THAT STAB in the dark scored a direct hit. She went whiter than skimmed milk and staggered into a chair, forgetting her skimpy attire and her indignation.

"It's not true!" she breathed. "I've nothing to hold back. My husband was innocent, and he was cleared. I don't know who murdered my father or why anyone would want to do it. There's nothing to tell!"

Reed simply shrugged.

"Look," she said, as though struck by a sudden idea. "You're a private detective. Who is paying you to investigate this case?"

"No one. I haven't started to work on it yet. But I think I will. I often do that when I'm interested."

She got up and came close enough for him to feel the warmth of her body.

"Suppose I pay your fee?" she asked.

"To do what?"

"To find my husband's murderer."

"And your father's?" he added.

"Yes, of course," she said, and went back to the chair.

"Look," Reed said. "If I work for you, it'll be on two conditions. One that I get a free hand to turn up whatever I find—and let the chips fall where they may."

"Yes?"

"And second, that you come clean with me."

She looked suddenly crushed, frightened.

"All right," she said, almost in a whisper. "My husband and my father had many bitter quarrels. They were not ordinary quarrels, for there was much bad feeling. Once they actually came to blows, and Will never forgave my father for that."

"What were the quarrels about?"

"Money. My husband made quite a lot, but he spent it like water. Dad disapproved violently, and he was not the kind to keep his opinions to himself. He told my husband what he thought of a man who would risk his family's future."

"But what are you leading up to?" Reed asked, puzzled.

"My husband murdered my father," said Lorna Willis. "I have proof of it."

Reed was almost caught off-balance. But he made a fast recovery.

"Show me," he said.

Mrs. Willis got up and weaved across to a desk. She unlocked a drawer and took out a crumpled sheet of paper which had been smoothed out but still bore creases.

"My husband wrote that," she said. "He always wrote his letters in longhand on any bit of paper he could find and then copied them on a typewriter. I found this in the waste-basket after the police arrested him. I kept it to myself because—well, how could I testify against him?"

"You mean legally? That the law says you can't?"

"No. I mean that after all he was my husband. But—read it."

It was just a fragment, without salutation or conclusion, evidently just a first draft. What was there read:

I'm tired of kowtowing and I'm not going to take any more nonsense from you. The next time you start that I'll take action myself and I promise you the action will be definite and conclusive.

Reed fingered the note absently.

"Why are you so anxious to prove your husband killed your father?"

"Anxious? Good heavens! I'm showing you this in confidence. It can't hurt Will now. But don't you see what it means? If Will did kill my father, who killed Will? The police are assuming the same man killed them both, but it's not true! Who is the mysterious person who is avenging my father?"

Her hand made a slashing gesture and lamplight blazed from a huge stone on her finger. Reed, who had a nodding acquaintance with precious stones in his work, decided it was not a diamond but a zircon, which was brilliant enough to fool almost anyone's casual glance, but was worth possibly thirty dollars instead of the small fortune a real diamond that size would represent.

He wondered whether Lorna Willis had replaced a real diamond with a zircon and if so where that sizable hunk of cash had gone. But he made no comment, simply handing back the letter.

"This is no proof, as such," he remarked. "And the question of whether or not you should have shown it to the police has, unfortunately, been taken out of your hands. I'd say it doesn't matter now, but if you're worried, show it to Lieutenant Hogan."

"But you—you'll protect me, won't you?"

"I'll try to find the murderer of your husband. It may still be that whoever that is, he is also the murderer of your father, in spite of this note. If that protects you—the answer is yes."

SHE WENT back to the desk and hastily scribbled a check.

"Will a hundred dollars carry you for a while?"

"Yes." He took the check and folded it. Then, in spite of himself, he said, "Don't worry so, Mrs. Willis. If you're in the clear it'll turn out okay. Sorry I broke in on you like this. Good night."

He let himself out the front door, made a swift circuit of the house and was beneath Lorna Willis' window just as she finished dialing. She told Devore all that had happened. Devore kicked up a fuss, evidently, for she defended herself almost hysterically. Devore calmed her down, and apparently gave her a lot of instructions for her end of the conversation was mostly a "yes."

When she hung up and turned out the light Rufe Reed was thinking that only one thing was clear about Lorna Willis. She had showed him the letter, had seemed to take him into her confidence, but actually had told him nothing. The letter may have been an indication that Willis had killed his father-in-law. But it was far from being proof.

Certainly it shed no light on Willis' own mysterious slaying. It made it all the more incomprehensible. Because if Willis really had killed his father-in-law, who was avenging that murder? Lorna Willis?

On the other hand, the letter could be a complete blind, and it seemed more than likely to Rufus Reed that the same hand had killed both Willis and his father-in-law. No other hypothesis made sense.

Also it was plain to Reed, that Lorna Willis had told him what she had for one reason only—to forestall an investigation into her past. If that was what she feared, then that was the thing to do.

Not that Reed was being deliberately disloyal to his client. But he had warned her that he was out to turn up the murderer and if it happened to be Lorna Willis—that would be her tough luck. A hundred-buck fee would not tempt Reed to shield a murderer. Furthermore, the very thing Lorna feared, even though it might be embarrassing to her, might provide the important clue.

And one more thing. Where did Arthur Medford and his tragedy fit into this little squirrel cage?

CHAPTER IV

MURDER TRUCK

REED SLIPPED quietly out to the dark street and looked for a taxi. He had almost reached the corner when one swung into the street and he flagged it. As the cab stopped, Reed yanked open the door and started in headfirst.

He saw the dark form inside instantly, and the hand going up with the sap in it. In the space of a heartbeat, he fought and conquered the instinct to pull back, which would have thrown him off-balance. Instead, he lunged forward, ramming his head into the attacker's stomach.

The man's breath went out in a great whoosh on the back of Reed's neck. The blackjack bounced off his shoulder and sent pain shooting through him. But he knew he had to keep going. One hand shot out and released the door catch and his churning feet carried him right through the cab and out the other side.

He ran full tilt into the driver who had scrambled from his seat and cut around to join the fray. This tough monkey was poised and waiting. He straightened Reed up with a vicious uppercut that tumbled the detective back against the open cab door.

Reed saw stars, but bounced back full of fight. His left hand whipped over with such dazzling speed that the driver never saw it coming until it exploded on his eye. Then he saw more colors than were ever in the gaudiest rainbow.

His howl of anguish echoed in the quiet street. The man inside the cab came to life and scrambled out, swinging the sap and cursing.

Reed kicked the howling cab driver viciously in the shins and the fellow doubled over with a new misery as the detective whirled to face the blackjack again. He tried to keep the man off with his rapier left, but the slugger bored in, shaking off those jabs and trying for a crusher with his weapon. Reed parried a vicious swing with his left forearm but the blackjack left the arm half numb. He got in a solid right hook to the cheek-bone, though, that slammed his man back against the side of the cab with a hollow bong.

The shriek of brakes snapped Reed's head up. A light truck had appeared from nowhere and from its doors was pouring what looked like a whole army of reinforcements, though actually there were only four.

From somewhere in the dark came a rasping voice:

"Get him, Matty!"

In that disturbing moment, Rufe Reed decided that it was better to be a live coward than a dead hero. He took to his heels like a rabbit. The dark forms of men raced to cut him off—and a streak of orange flame spat from the truck's dark interior. Something hot went past close to Reed's head. The flat crack of a small rifle followed.

Then Reed was across the sidewalk and had leaped into the rubble of an empty lot. Darkness swallowed him. But there was a swift scuff of feet behind him as the men spread to hem him in.

Reed had just got out his automatic, since guns seemed to be in fashion, when he stumbled over a loose rock. He took another step forward—and the ground disappeared from under him. He plunged downward into darkness. And although he fell only a few feet he landed with a bone-jarring crash and sprawled on the rocky ground, losing his gun.

He was hurt, he could not lie there and wait for help. He felt around, rapidly, and located his weapon. Then he dragged himself upright to see what kind of a hole he had fallen into.

A straight concrete wall rose before him to the height of his head. He had stepped off this. In a moment he realized what it was. Someone had started to build an apartment house here, had done the excavating and poured the concrete for the foundation and cellar walls. Then the building had been stopped, probably because of the war. And the catacombs that had been left had made a nice booby-trap for him.

Some distance away, one of the gang searching for him fell. There was a lot of assorted cursing.

"Look out, you guys!" someone warned. "There's a lotta foundations here. Maybe he's in them."

"Spread!" another voice ordered, low but carrying. "Spread all around it!"

Reed had visions of himself playing hide-and-seek with these killers through this modern labyrinth.

"All I want is out," he muttered.

On the chance that the men hadn't yet reached the far side of the ruin, he felt his way as rapidly as he could along the walls.

WHEN HE reached the opposite wall, looking up he could see the rear of a row of squat two-story brick houses. Light glowed behind closed shades and silhouetted a man's hat and shoulders on the outside. They had cut him off.

Reed crouched close against the wall, gripping his automatic. Feet shuffled quietly along the top of the wall and passed right over him. From the direction he had come he heard whispering, the scuff of leather on stone and a little sliding rattle as someone dropped into the cellar and brought earth and stone with him. They were closing in.

The footsteps above him started back. Reed saw a dim silhouette bulk just above him. He reached up, caught an ankle and threw the whole weight of his body into a savage pull.

A yell burst from the man he clutched. His body hurtled past over Reed's head and smashed on the stony floor with sickening impact. Then the detective was scaling the wall and running straight for the lights ahead.

Feet pounded behind him again, but the men were afraid to shoot. The crack of the rifle inside the truck had gone unnoticed, but pistol shots here would be a different thing.

Reed ran into a board fence that enclosed the back yards of the houses ahead. He was up and over like a singed cat and dropped into the soft earth of someone's vegetable garden. Crushing lettuce, beans and radishes underfoot, he sprinted for the driveway, pounded down it and burst out into a better lighted street.

The first thing he saw was the gleam of trolley rails and a car bearing down upon him. He raced alongside the car and swung himself aboard.

"Hey!" shouted the conductor. "You trying to commit suicide?"

He never knew why the panting passenger with the torn and dirty suit flopped into a seat and started to laugh. Rufe Reed finally got out of the wilds of the Bronx and home safely. He found Pat sleeping the sweet sleep of the blameless.

"Fine thing," Reed thought bitterly. "Her husband gets run over by a rock crusher, shot at, dumped into old foundations, beaten up, nearly killed, and there she lies, sleeping as though she didn't have a care in the world."

A hot shower made him feel better though it brought all his bruises to sudden vociferous life. But when he crawled into bed he was asleep almost immediately....

A second later—or so it seemed—Pat was shaking him awake.

"Wake up!" said his helpmate. "What are all those bruises all over you? Have you been fighting over a woman again?"

"Cut it out!" Reed mumbled, opening one eye and closing it immediately against the morning glare. "Quit shaking me!"

"Well, wake up," Pat said unreasonably. "What happened to you?"

"What happened to me shouldn't happen to a dog," he mumbled.

"John's here," Pat said.

John's voice immediately corroborated that.

"I thought you had work for us."

"Yeah." Keeping his eyes shut, Reed gave them a terse description of his affair of the night before, including the knowledge gained from Lorna Willis. "That puts her and Devore right up at the top of the suspects, even if she is our client. If she's guilty I'll give her back her check. If not, we'll find out who is."

"What do we do?" John asked.

"Start digging into the pasts of Lorna Willis and Olivia Medford. Assuming they have pasts. Get family histories, birth place, friends, early years—everything you can."

"He gives us the dirty jobs and grabs off all the excitement for himself," John grumbled.

"Look!" Reed yelped. "You can have any part or all of the excitement I had last night. Now get out of here and let me get some sleep!"

They went out, wrangling over who was to do the dull stuff of digging through newspapers, wedding license records and so on. Reed punched a new hole in the pillow for his head and wooed Morpheus.

SOME INDEFINITE time later the phone tore aside the curtain again. He groped for it groggily.

"Huh?"

"Darling," came Pat's voice, clear and sweet, "are you still in bed? Sleepy pie, a sluggard never makes a good—"

"What do you want now?" Reed groaned. "Can't you let a guy sleep?"

"We've got something, dear," Pat cooed. "Don't you want it?"

"Spill it." He shook sleep out of his eyes.

"Olivia Medford's maiden name was Steele. Lorna Willis was Lorna Blake. They've both been married seven years. And here's the pay-off, cutie pie—they come from the same town! Didn't know each other, huh?"

"All right, quit crowing," Reed growled. "I didn't vouch for the information Hogan gave me, did I? What else?"

"Both grew up in Gainesboro, Vermont. Came from moderately wealthy families—wealthy enough so that their fathers retired around the time the girls got married. Johnny is checking finances now... Here he is."

The younger Reed got on the phone.

"Hey, did you know those two dames could spend money like a sailor on shore leave?" he said. "Both got quite a chunk of dough from their families when they got hitched, and there isn't a nickel left. And then when their fathers died they both got another big chunk—about a hundred and fifty grand."

Reed whistled.

"Don't tell me that's gone too!"

"Not yet, but soon. At the rate they're going. The cash is pretty well used up. What's left is stock in the businesses. Medford's father-in-law owned a flock of auto supply stores and Willis's father-in-law went in for the gingham trade."

"Nice work," Reed yawned. "Now, the next bet is to watch Lorna Willis and Glover C. Devore, but don't expose yourselves. And Johnny—keep your eye on Pat. If anything happens to that pest I'll have your scalp."

"Yessir."

"And call me in a hour. We'll meet some place."

CHAPTER V

JOHNNY'S DULL EVENING

WITH UNACCUSTOMED caution, Pat Reed waited until dark before approaching the Willis house near which her husband had so nearly become her late husband. Johnny did not stay too near her, remaining where he could cover her retreat should withdrawal become suddenly necessary.

Following Rufe's description of the grounds, Pat slipped across the back lawn and reached a screened-in porch at the rear of the house. She could see and hear whatever went on in the front, and was covered by the vines on the house. If she had to move along the wall she could keep in the cover of a hedge.

Two hours of waiting taxed her patience. She could not see Johnny and wondered where he was. Her muscles ached and her bones creaked. Just when she was at the point of complete disgust, a car pulled up to the front of the house and stopped.

The porch light went on in front as though the visitor was expected. Pat saw a handsome man hurry up the walk and, from pictures and descriptions, recognized Attorney Glover C. Devore.

She slipped to the living room window under which Rufe had listened and found it still open. Apparently Lorna Willis hadn't even discovered it was open.

Lorna and Devore came into the room, talking.

"—afraid of this," Devore said worriedly. "If Reed gets onto the game before we're ready, he'll spill to Hogan. They're friends. You didn't buy Reed with a hundred-dollar retainer."

"I had to do something," Lorna said desperately. "He hinted that he'd investigate us. So I showed him the letter. Maybe that will keep him busy. I don't want him to find—"

"He will," Devore said grimly. "But it will take him time. Don't blame yourself, Lorna. It was coming, so we'll have to face the music. But I swear if anyone starts tormenting you again, I'll kill him!"

"Please!" the woman begged in a muffled voice as if her face were buried in her hands. "No more of that. I—I couldn't stand any more."

Devore slammed out and Pat heard Lorna Willis sobbing like a woman without hope. Then the light went out. Pat waited a long time but Lorna Willis seemed through for the night.

"The woman could be more cooperative," Pat grumbled to herself.

She tried to locate Johnny in the dark, but had no idea where he was. She dug into her handbag, removed the little .32 automatic Rufe made her carry and got out a pencil flash. She blinked the light twice, knowing that the shaded lens would make only a dim glow.

From off to one side came an answering blink and she knew Johnny would be coming across to her.

The wind was moaning softly in the trees. Branches tossed and whispered, leaves rustled, there was the suggestion of footsteps on every hand. A branch snapped. Was that Johnny or someone else? Remembering Rufe's experience here the night before, she began to wonder if Lorna's house was not being watched.

Then she saw Johnny's light blink and a moment later he appeared, a dark shadow moving across the grass. With appalling suddenness, two more shadows detached themselves from the shrubbery and flung themselves upon him. All three shadows began to thrash fiercely and to emit muffled sounds.

Gripping the flash in one hand and the little automatic in the other, Pat ran. But before she could reach the struggling fighters, a third man leaped from behind a bush and caught her in his arms.

He was big and strong and he held her so tightly that all she could do was kick at him. And the other two had knocked Johnny cold!

"Go ahead!" panted her captor trying to keep his shins out of the way of her blunt-toed shoes. "I'll bring this wildcat along!"

Despairingly, Pat saw the other two drag Johnny's unconscious figure away over the grass. She opened her mouth to scream. The man put his hand over her mouth and she bit him. He snatched it away and that gave her a chance to get her hand loose. She promptly whacked him over the head with her gun.

He staggered back dizzily, weaving. Pat rushed in, swung with more enthusiasm than science and nearly clipped herself. But even though she missed, the staggering man sat down suddenly and heavily on the grass. Pat bounced the gun solidly off the top of his head. He sighed and toppled over quietly.

PAT WAS seething with impatience to follow Johnny, but Rufe had said bring back information. So swiftly she emptied the unconscious man's pockets, transferring all the junk to her handbag. A small note-book and fountain pen in his pocket gave her an idea. She squirted some ink on his thumb and made an impression on the paper.

Waving it madly to dry it, she dashed out to the street to try to catch up with Johnny's captors.

The street was empty. They had gone!

What would Rufe say to her? While she had fooled around with fingerprints his brother had been carried off by thugs. Dispiritedly she turned toward home.

Rufe Reed was waiting with mounting anxiety for the phone call which had not come.

"What's happened," he demanded of Pat. "Where's Johnny?"

She told him. His lips tightened, but he did not reproach her. Carefully he looked over the stuff that she spilled from her handbag. A fat bunch of keys caught his attention.

"Auto keys," he grunted. "That guy could lift any car in the country with one of these. Let's see that thumb print. H'm, good and clear. If Hogan has the original on file, maybe we'll know where to start now. I'm off for Police Headquarters right away!"

He snatched at his hat and coat.

"I want to go too!" said Pat.

"No, you stay near the phone. Johnny might get away or get to a phone. Someone's got to be on tap."

He gave her his most perfunctory, husband-like kiss and beat it for the door before she could think up any more arguments.

JOHNNY REED woke up with the world's prize headache. There was a lump on his skull bigger than a duck's egg and a taste in his mouth like a motorman's glove.

It was pitch-black, and the floor upon which he lay felt like rough cement and it was cold and wet. A carefully outstretched hand touched a cement wall behind him.

Somehow he managed to sit up, though that started the pinwheels going in his skull again. He sat still until the darkness stopped heaving and throwing off sparks.

Holding onto the wall then, he got himself upright and began a careful tour of the four sides of the cellar. Once he felt a solid wooden door, but the rest was only bare walls. The door, of course, was locked and nothing less than a General Sherman tank would have budged it.

Searching his pockets, Johnny found he had been stripped of wallet and watch and keys and gun. The only thing left was a paper book of matches. Perhaps they wanted him to see his prison. He struck a match and blinked like an owl in the brilliant flare.

There was nothing to see—except one small detail which caught his eye. There was a tiny pile of crumbled cement at one spot on the floor. The filling between the blocks had began to crack, and in the block itself was a jagged crack which split off a good third of it.

Johnny began picking out bits of cement with his fingers. Soon he found he could lift out the broken piece of block. He had a weapon of sorts, a jagged chunk of cement block twice the size of his hand.

"Just the thing to go up against machine-guns with," he grumbled.

But he took it back to the corner with him, sat on it, and waited patiently.

A long time passed, while the throbbing in his head subsided too slowly. At last a key grated in the lock and the door swung open. The dazzling beam of a flashlight hit him in the eyes.

"Turn that thing away!" he barked.

The beam shifted, but all Johnny could see for a minute was a big red circle. When it faded, he saw an ugly gorilla with a broken nose grinning at him. The gorilla carried a gun.

"Head hurt?" the uncouth individual inquired.

"Nuts to you," Johnny said.

"Get up!" the character ordered.

Johnny got up, holding the chunk of block behind his back.

"What you got?" demanded the gunman. "Something we missed when we frisked you? Gimme."

"Aw, you don't want this," Johnny said. "Give me a break, willya?"

"Fork over or you'll loose some teeth."

Johnny drew his hand out reluctantly and threw the cement chunk in the character's a face.

He was not bloodthirsty ordinarily, but he got a wonderful amount of satisfaction out of the scream that followed and the red smear of a face that looped toward the floor.

FLASH AND gun clattered down and he dived for them. His fingers grabbed—then he froze. Light from the opening doorway transfixed him and a new voice rasped:

"Drop it, mug, or we'll cut you in half!"

Johnny's fingers straightened and he blinked. Two more men edged down some stone steps, and into the cellar room. One moved around Johnny, a stocky man with a neck that bulged over his collar. He slapped Johnny across the bridge of the nose with his gun, sending him flying back against the wall and starting the hammers to pound in his head again.

The stocky man kicked the yegg on the floor into groggy consciousness.

"Get up, you fool! You've got a job to do."

Footsteps approached down the stone steps outside the door, and the door was slammed shut. The stocky man had grabbed a flashlight from his pocket instantly. He turned it on Johnny and it blazed in his eyes so that he could see nothing in the blinding glare. Behind this effective shield the steps came close and stopped before him.

"That's Reed," an unfamiliar voice said. "Okay."

The steps went away and after a while the beam was shifted from Johnny's eyes. He couldn't see a thing, but ungentle hands propelled him forward, through the doorway, up the stone steps and into another cellar room.

"The truck's gassed up," the stocky man said. "Now here's the dope, Matty. You drive up Nine-W to that place where the road becomes one way and comes out to the edge of the Palisades. It's a sheer drop of three hundred feet there. Fred will be right behind you in the sedan. Leave your boy friend in the driver's seat and see if you can get the truck through the guard rail. Got it?"

"Do I got it?" Matty mumbled. "It'll be a pleasure. Only maybe when I conk him to be sure he stays in the driver's seat I'll conk him so hard he'll be cold meat when he goes over! Killing's too good for him!"

"All right, mug," said the stocky man to Johnny. "Turn around."

Johnny was wrapped up in ropes until he looked like a mummy, then two men lifted him to their shoulders and carted him up a creaky flight of steps.

Well, it was an ironic twist that the master villain who was about to kill him thought he was his brother Rufus. That was inexcusable carelessness. Wouldn't that villain be surprised! Johnny wished he could be around to see that.

Upstairs smelled like a garage. There was a light truck standing in the gloom. He was tossed into the back and the truck lurched into motion. At the wheel was Matty, holding a blood-stained handkerchief to his face and devising a list of atrocities he promised himself to commit upon the prisoner's carcass.

It was a situation, Johnny thought gloomily, with no future.

CHAPTER VI

TAKE ONE CLUE

LIEUTENANT HOGAN was waiting for Rufus Reed when the investigator got down to Centre Street. He studied the ink print with interest.

"I'll send it through," he said. "Sit down and wait. This shouldn't take long."

He pressed a buzzer and when he had sent the print away, he said:

"I'll bring you up to date, Rufus. There's been another murder."

"Another? The same type?"

"Yes. This time the victim isn't the kind to draw any sympathetic tears, but we're interested because the pattern is the same. The deceased is a tough monkey with a bad rep—Fitzy Munson. We had him on a murder rap but there wasn't enough on him so we had to turn him loose.

"He walked out of the court-room and got as far as the sidewalk. Then he keeled over just like Willis—and as dead. There was a thirty-eight slug in him and nobody had heard the shot or had seen anybody shooting.

"But we got one break. A cop who saw him fall was just in time to pick up a lush named Anders who was trying to get rid of one of those samplers!"

"You mean he was trying to get rid of it, or trying to drop it on the spot like the others?" Reed supplied.

"I think he was trying to drop it near the body."

"Who is Anders?"

"The whole force knows him. Always three sheets in the wind and would be a quarter-wit even sober."

"And somebody gave him a buck to drop the sampler on the walk in front of the courthouse 'as a joke'," Reed said.

"You've been reading my mail. But here's something. We found the gun in an ash-can down the block. A thirty-eight with all numbers filed off so thoroughly that we can't bring out a thing. No prints, of course."

"Oh, fine. So you booked Anders?"

"What else could we do? We tried to get him to give us a description of the man who paid him to drop the sampler, but except for saying he talked like a dictionary he couldn't remember a thing."

"Unless he's playing dumb."

"Correct. Which is another reason we'll hold him a while and cool him off. There's something funny going on. That lush has been handing out religious tracts, if you can imagine that."

A policeman entered with the report on the thumb print. Hogan read it, and looked up at Reed.

"Your friend has graced our halls before," he said. "Walter Brophy, alias Fingers Brophy, alias Ed Fitzgerald, alias William Hannigan, alias Tony Colucci. Professional car thief, small-time mobster. Gun for hire. Last known hangout a garage at the end of Ormund Avenue. Want him picked up?"

"I want that garage raided!" Reed said firmly. "They've got Johnny there!" He felt a touch of panic at the thought of Johnny in such hands.

"Okay. You sign the complaint and we'll hit 'em. Let's go."

Half an hour later four riot cars converged on the garage and police with sawed-off shotguns swarmed in upon it. The doors were locked, but with such flimsy hasps that a good kick sent them flying wide open. Flashlight beams stabbed into the place from all angles.

It was deserted. They covered the whole place, then Hogan shook his head.

"They're gone, Rufe, if they ever were here," he said. "What do you want me to do now?

Reed let his shoulders fall helplessly.

"I'll keep looking," he said. "Thanks, Ben."

The neighborhood was the kind in which no crowd gathers when police pull a raid. Rather the residents disappear, and the streets are deserted. So there was no curious crowd to annoy Reed when he was left alone in the deserted garage. With his flashlight he began to go over the ground again like a questing hound.

A door in the back led to a dirty, narrow hallway. He had gone through this like a house afire and found nothing, but searching it more leisurely, he spotted some fresh scrape marks on the calcimined walls. Such scrapes could have been made by the shoes of a man carried along the hallway.

Toward the end of the hall was a narrow door, locked. Reed got out a bunch of skeleton keys and found one that clicked. The door opened on a black staircase, going down. He went down, sending his light ahead of him.

HE FOUND himself in a big vaulted empty cellar. But there were tracks and scuffings in the dust which looked fresh and some unraveling ends of rope which looked new.

On the far side was another doorway, ajar. Beyond, down some stone steps, it was a smaller room and here Reed found fresh blood on the floor, and a broken, jagged hunk of cement block.

The blood looked ominous, and Reed's heart sank. But he began to search even more carefully. He passed out into the bigger cellar, his beam darting everywhere. And near the stairway where he had almost walked on it coming down, he found the number, 9, and a W, scratched in the dust of the cellar floor, as though with the toe of a shoe.

Reed thought over all the codes and signals he and Johnny had ever used. He was haunted by a sense of familiarity about this symbol which he could not grasp. Then suddenly he had it. 9W was the highway number that went north from New York City on the west bank of the river!

"They're taking Johnny up Nine W! But why?"

The "why" was not important now. Getting after them fast was. And Hogan could not help him. For 9W ran in New Jersey up to the point where the road forked and became one way and the cliffs rose to their highest point. After that it crossed into New York State again.

But Hogan had no jurisdiction in Jersey. Reed would have to go on this himself!

It took time to get his car out of the garage, and have it serviced. Fortunately he had plenty of A coupons, for the car was used only in emergencies. It took more time to check the Holland Tunnel and the Lincoln Tunnel. Reed had a hunch about the kidnap car. He remembered a certain light truck from which rifle-fire had spat at him. Of course car thieves could have any kind of a vehicle. But cars were scarce and a light truck was fast and handy. It was some kind of a lead.

At the George Washington Bridge Reed struck the trail. Traffic was light and the bored bluecoat at the toll booth remembered a light truck, because the driver had a cold or something and held a handkerchief so that his features could hardly be seen. Maybe the guy had a bloody nose, because there had been splotches on the handkerchief that could have been blood.

Reed remembered the jagged, bloody piece of cement block in the cellar. So Johnny had scored on one of the hoodlums!

He burned up the bridge, flashed past the Jersey booths, ignoring an outraged whistle from the guardians and whipped sharp right into 9W heading north.

The road was level concrete, wide, and deserted. He roared north like a meteor. Woods crowded the road on both sides with almost no cut-offs. At Alpine he had a bad moment wondering whether the truck had turned off, but there was a State Trooper's booth there and a man on duty said he thought a truck like that had gone through heading north.

Then, above Forest Park, the road became one way, south-bound traffic disappearing to the left. The north lane ran out on the very lip of the Palisades which here dropped in massive columns of rock a sheer three hundred feet or more to the river.

A fear which had been growing steadily in Reed's mind became sickeningly persistent. In a spot like this a car might go through the guard rail and there wouldn't be enough left at the bottom of the cliff to identify it. He could fairly see Johnny slumped unconscious behind the wheel, the mug with the bloody face standing on the running board, giving the wheel a twist and leaping clear as the truck charged the rail.

The picture was so clear that he felt instant conviction he was right. He reached forward and snapped off his lights.

Moonlight washed the road in a pale glow and the concrete stood out clearly with the dark mass of the woods on his left and the open sky on his right where the cliffs lunged into the river.

He rounded a turn and red tail-lights blinked at him. A car was drawn up in the parking space of a deserted log road-house. Was that it?

Reed slid his car into the shadows and parked. Gun in hand he moved toward the other parked car, keeping out of the moonlight.

There was just one man in the car, sitting hunched over the wheel and staring intently up the road. Instinctively, Reed looked that way too and saw moonlight reflecting palely on the truck he sought.

He felt a tremendous surge of relief. He was not too late!

But this man here! Who was he? Lookout? Bodyguard? Both— also obviously he was here to pick up the man with the bloody face after the truck was sent crashing over the cliffs, leaving the murderer afoot.

REED SLID around the car to the door beside the driver's seat. The intent gangster's first intimation that he was not alone was when the door was suddenly opened.

"Come here!" Reed said.

He gripped the surprised man by the lapel of his coat, yanked him toward himself and brought the flat of his gun down on the felt snap-brim. The hat buckled, the victim relaxed and spilled down out of the seat, to mash his nose on the harsh gravel of the parking space.

Reed trussed up the unconscious man with his own tie and belt, gagged him with his own handkerchief and stuffed him back in the seat.

"That one was easy. Hope the other is as dumb."

When Reed approached the truck, silently, the mug with the battered face was busily removing the rocks he had put under the wheels. He turned to Johnny Reed's bound form which he had lugged into the driver's seat.

"This ain't gonna hurt—much," he mumbled, and grinned. "I'm gonna tap you behind the ear, take off them ropes and then you're goin' for a little ride. Like it?"

"I like it better than staying here with you," Johnny said. "Come on, get it over with."

"It'll be a pleasure," the man said.

He took one step and a gun jammed hard into his back.

"Drop it!" Reed snarled.

"Rufe!" Johnny squalled.

Matty was a fighter. One elbow slashed down, sending Reed's gun wide. In the same motion Matty whirled, his own weapon swinging round.

Rufe chopped a blow at his wrist, lunged forward to get inside the gun, and grappled. His own weapon, dashed out of his hand, thudded on the ground. Then Matty was hammering his kidneys with vicious short-arm hooks.

Reed brought his knee up hard. There was a gasp and Matty broke. Reed let go with everything he had in a vicious right-hand smash to the bruised face.

It was the sort of punch which would have been suicide to throw at a trained boxer, but Reed was counting on Matty's being dazed from the knee in the groin. He was right. The punch landed and rocked the gangster so hard he dropped his own gun. But he caromed off the truck and came in with his chin tucked down behind his shoulder and his left out.

"Hard guy, eh?" he growled.

Then the night dissolved for Rufe Reed into a stunning explosion of fireworks. He felt the back of his head strike something hard and saw fiery circles spinning like the rings of Saturn. Then the circles went away and he found he was lying on the ground, directly in front of the truck. Matty was standing beyond him with a gun in his hand pointing at him.

"Get up!" Matty said.

Reed got to his knees and hung there, pretending to be a good deal sicker than he was.

"Come on," the yegg snarled. "I got no time for foolin' around."

CHAPTER VII

SHADOWS PLAY TAG

CAR SPRINGS creaked as Johnny moved in the front seat. The next instant the car head-lights went on full, throwing the whole scene into sudden blazing brilliance.

The beams flashed full into Matty's eyes. Reed pulled his feet under him and his lunging body snapped the gangster's legs out from under him. As he came down, Reed sprawled across him and smothered his flailing arms.

They rolled in a tight-fighting, thrashing mass down under the guard rail. Matty was using knees, elbows, nails and teeth. Reed confined himself to forcing his thumbs into the man's windpipe.

Matty started to choke. His flailing blows became desperate and he rocked the detective with the frenzy of his efforts to break free.

In one wild lunge he got to his knees and, driving his fists upward through Reed's arms, broke the strangling clutch on his throat. He staggered to his feet, with Reed following.

"Now you—" Matty said hoarsely.

Reed charged him. The gangster took a step backward—and there was nothing beneath his feet.

A single terrified wail was wrenched from his lips as his body cartwheeled over in space and twisted down out of sight.

Reed checked himself, trembling, on the very lip of the precipice. He was suddenly so weak and shaken that he wanted to get down and crawl away from that cliff edge. But he managed to stagger back to the car and flopped down on the running board.

"Get me out of here!" Johnny panted.

"In a minute," Rufe said weakly. "Th-thanks for switching on the lights. He had me like a sitting duck."

"Did it with my nose," Johnny said. "Did you push him over, Rufe, or did he go over himself?"

"Fifty-fifty," Reed said, sighing. He got up, his nausea subsiding. "Let's get out of here and home, Johnny. I've had enough for tonight."

"Me, too," Johnny Reed said fervently. "This was one night I didn't have only dull work to do."

With his brother released, Reed kicked away the last chock under the front wheel. The truck crashed through the guard rail and over the edge of the cliff. There was an appalling silence, then a grinding crash far below. Immediately came the puff of igniting gasoline.

"That'll bring the cops," Reed said. "They'll find the dead guy too. Let's go."

One thing more remained to be done. He stopped at a telephone back in Manhattan and called the garage on Ormund Avenue.

A voice said, "Yeah?"

Reed cupped his hand over the mouthpiece and sank his voice to a growl.

"Matty talkin'," he said. "Lissen. The job's done but I had a little trouble with the cops and had to lam. I better hide out for a while."

"Where's Fred?" the voice demanded.

Reed grinned, getting the name of the second man he had laid out.

"They got him."

"You sure Reed's crooked?"

"If he ain't he can be dropped three hundred feet onto rock and then be burned in gasoline, and I never heard of nobody that could. Lissen, I gotta lam. I'll get in touch with you."

"Okay. Call me Monday."

Reed hung up.

"Now they believe Fred's been picked up and they don't expect Matty back, so they won't get suspicious for a few days," he told Johnny. "Otherwise they'd come looking for us with their whole gang…."

Dawn was lighting the city when Rufe and Johnny got home. Pat was sitting beside the telephone, fast asleep.

"Old Faithful, asleep at the switch," Rufe whispered.

As they tiptoed past her to go to bed, Johnny objected:

"She hasn't heard from us. She'll worry."

"In her sleep?" Rufe said callously. "Come on, it wouldn't be right to wake her."

They slept all day, and woke surprised that no explosion had come from Pat when she discovered them. A note was propped on the telephone for them.

> You know where both of you heels can go. I'm going to the movies. Maybe I'll get a divorce.
> Your ex-wife,
> Patricia.

Johnny grinned. "Always said this marriage wouldn't last."

"She'll be back." Reed yawned. "Let's go get something to eat."

AFTER THEY had eaten, Reed told his brother:

"I better go down and see Hogan. He'll want to know what happened. Want to come with me, or wait for Pat?"

"I'll wait. Nothing exciting at Centre Street."

Hogan was glad to see Rufe Reed. The private detective flopped into a chair.

"Johnny's back," he said casually. "Ben last night I didn't know myself how serious it was. I thought they were holding Johnny to get me to call off the dogs or something."

"Weren't they?"

"Heck, no! If I'd known what really went I wouldn't have been so calm. They thought Johnny was me and they were getting ready to rub him out!"

Hogan whistled.

"That means you're in danger."

"No more." Reed grinned. "I'm dead." He told the story of Johnny's rescue and the death of Matty. "Wouldn't that mug be flattered if he knew he was pinch-hitting for me?"

"Yeah, flattered," Hogan said. "Well, I'll talk to the Jersey cops and tell them to hold this Fred on any charge they can drum up. Now what's next?"

"Let me talk to the lush, Anders."

"Sure. But you won't get anything out of him."

They went back to Anders' cell. The lush was white and shaking. He was sober—and regretted it. He needed a shave—and a bath—badly.

Reed leaned against the bars.

"You want out?" he asked, rolling a cigarette between his fingers.

"They gonna let me out?" Anders whined.

"Talk," Reed suggested.

"I told them everything I know!" the man complained. "Lissen, mister, I was high. I didn't see the guy who gave me that—that—"

"Sampler?" Reed supplied.

"Yeah. I was standin' at the bar at Joe's. These two guys comes up and buys me a drink. Said they'd seen me peddling them religious papers and thought I was a good Joe, see?"

"What is this religious paper racket?"

"No racket, mister. I do it for the mission an' they give me a flop an' breakfast."

"And you haven't any idea what these two men looked like?" Anders' brow corrugated in worried thought.

"I think one called the other 'Matty'," he hazarded.

Reed glanced at Hogan.

"Remember anything else?"

"I—I think somebody said something about somebody's fingers."

"Sure he didn't call him 'Fingers'—like using a name?"

"Maybe. I—I don't know."

Reed looked at Hogan again and nodded.

"Okay, Anders," he said. "I'll see what I can do about getting you out."

"That's the mob," Reed said as he and Hogan moved away. "Now where does Brophy's mob tie in with Willis and Medford?"

The answer to that, Reed thought as he left Headquarters might be found in Gainesboro, Vermont, home town of Lorna Willis and Olivia Medford. He called the police of the Vermont town, long distance, told them what he wanted and gave his office number to be called back when the information was found.

Then he grabbed a cab and went out to visit Olivia Medford.

She was a trim, pretty brunette, without Lorna Willis' nervous worried look. She showed Reed into the living room where a middle-aged, somewhat paunchy gentleman arose from a chair.

"This is Mr. Irwin, Mr. Reed. Charlie Irwin was my husband's partner and one of our best friends."

"Reed?" Irwin repeated. "You're a detective, aren't you?"

"Mrs. Willis has retained me to find the murderer of her husband. I thought—"

"There's no connection between the Willis case and Arthur's death!" Irwin said angrily. "If that's what you're here for, I object to your submitting Mrs. Medford to any more painful questioning. She's had enough!"

"I think there's a connection," Reed said mildly. "Would you mind answering a few questions, Mrs. Medford?"

"I'll try," she said, her lips pale.

"Do you think your husband murdered your father?"

"That's exactly what I mean!" Irwin shouted. "Why don't you leave her alone?"

"Please, Charlie," Mrs. Medford said quietly. "That happens to be one question I can easily answer. Mr. Reed, I do not believe Arthur murdered my father. My father and my husband had differences, but they were never serious. Moreover, if you knew Arthur you would have understood how—how gentle he was. He wouldn't h-hurt anyone."

"I'm sorry, Mrs. Medford," Reed said. "I don't want to be inconsiderate. But I must find out certain things if I am to reach any conclusion. One thing more. Do you know Mrs. Willis?"

"No—no!" the woman cried, as if her patience had snapped. "Everyone asks me that! It's just a horrible coincidence that she and I suffered the same tragedy at almost the same time. I don't know her, and I can't stand any more questions!"

SHE STARTED to cry and Charlie Irwin, with a baleful glance at Reed, hurried over to her.

Reed apologized again and left. Outside he waited and presently Irwin appeared.

"Look, Reed," the man said as they went down the walk together. "There's no one to take care of Mrs. Medford now except me. That gives me some authority. I'm telling you to stay away from her. If you're working for this Mrs. Willis, solve her case. But leave Olivia alone!"

Reed nodded. "Where do you come in on this, Irwin?"

"What do you mean, 'come in'?" Irwin demanded belligerently.

"I mean are you only acting the good Samaritan?"

Irwin stopped dead and fixed the detective with a cold and hostile eye.

"I came here to give Mrs. Medford a check," he said stiffly. "Naturally the business goes to me, but I gave her the choice of taking Arthur's place as my partner or letting me buy her out. She chose the cash. And it's none of your business. I don't even know why I'm telling you."

"Because you know I'll find out, and it'll look better if you seem to be frank and honest!"

"Seem to be?" Irwin exploded. "I think I'll give you a punch in the nose!"

"Now, now," Reed soothed. "Act your age. Remember your blood pressure."

He wheeled away before the man could act, leaving Irwin standing there, looking after him angrily.

CHAPTER VIII

PAST IMPERFECT

PAT AND Johnny were both in the office when Rufe arrived.

"Got the case solved yet?" his wife jeered.

"Told you she'd come back," Reed said to Johnny, ignoring the sarcasm.

"I asked you if you had deduced who the murderer is," Pat repeated.

"We-e-ll, I have no proof," Reed said, sinking into a chair, "but I pretty much know who it is—I think."

"Ho-ho, he thinks!" Pat crowed. "All right, wise guy, write down the name you think and we'll seal it in an envelope and then when Hogan solves the case we'll open it up and see how wrong you are. And if I'm right—you're wrong—you take me to the most expensive night club in town."

"And if you're wrong?"

"I'll owe you a nickel cigar."

"That's why I married her," Rufe told Johnny. "Her generosity."

The phone rang.

"I'll take it," Rufe said, fending Pat off. "Hello."

"Long distance," said the operator. "Gainesboro, Vermont, calling. Is Mr. Rufus Reed there?"

"This is Reed. Put 'em on."

He listened for about four dollars' worth, then he thanked the caller and hung up. He leaned back and put his feet on the desk.

"You see," he said, "there had to be a reason why neither of those two women appeared in court at the most critical period in their husband's lives. There had to be a blamed good reason."

"That's the way he is," Pat explained to Johnny, elaborately. "Always starts his stories in the middle. All right, Mr. Bones, why didn't the two women appear in court?"

"They didn't dare. They knew that their pictures would be in papers all over the country, sent out on AP or UP photo services."

Johnny's feet hit the floor with a crash.

"You mean they're fugitives from a chain-gang or something?"

"They've got pasts," Reed said. "Pasts imperfect, you might say. Pat found out they had known each other most of their lives, though both deny it. The police in their home town just gave me the rest of the story. Those girls grew up in the Twenties—the jazz age, Prohibition, bathtub gin and all. The families had dough, the girls were spoiled. They had big allowances, fast roadsters and heavy drinking boy friends.

"One night Olivia and Lorna picked up a couple of boys at a local tavern. They got pretty loaded on needled gin and started for another joint, with the boys driving their cars. They got into a race and went tearing up the pike with the cars side by side, filling the whole road. A farm wagon was there too."

"Oh, boy!" Johnny muttered.

"Well, they killed the farmer and his son. The boys vanished. Olivia and Lorna couldn't because the cars were registered in their names. At the trial they couldn't produce the boys they said were driving and both got a nice stiff prison sentence."

"What a thing to keep under cover all these years!" Pat breathed.

"Well, apparently they served out their sentences, came to New York and got married here. The old scandal was buried and forgotten.

"But something queer happens. Both women are dead broke, though they did have lots of money. Lorna Willis is wearing a big zircon in a ring that looks as if it were designed for a real diamond. Something has happened to a powerful lot of money."

"Blackmail!" Pat snapped.

"That's the way I figured it. If one of those men involved in the crack-up years ago found them, he might be bleeding them on the threat of revealing the past to their husbands, or could have sold the information to someone else who is bleeding them.

"Now their husbands might be big and say, 'That's all in the past and whatever you did while you were young and foolish you've paid for.' Or they might get plenty sore. You can see how the women would be afraid to have their husbands know. After all, killing a couple of people is pretty much of a load to carry around on your conscience. So maybe they paid off rather than take the chance."

"So the blackmailer bled them dry," Pat murmured. Then her blue eyes flew wide open. "Rufe, do you think the blackmailer murdered the fathers so the women would inherit more money and he could get more out of them? Could anyone be so black-hearted?"

REED SHOOK his head soberly.

"That's just what it looks like and worse. I think he murdered the husbands for a similar reason. Since most of the inheritances were in the form of stocks or shares in a business, the husbands would have managed it for their wives and the blackmailer would have been unable to realize. He had to get rid of the husbands too. He tried to frame them for the murder of the fathers and when that didn't work, he eliminated them himself. The samplers, of course, were just a blind, but I believe that even with them the killer had an idea of throwing suspicion on another, in case things went wrong."

"Good gravy." Johnny gulped. "Makes you a little sick, doesn't it?"

"You shouldn't be surprised," Reed said. "After what nearly happened to you."

"Rufe," said Pat, "they play too rough. Let's go into some other business. Let's raise petunias, huh?"

"The only guy who could know that much about Willis and Medford's affairs is Devore," Johnny said thoughtfully.

"What about that letter Willis wrote his father-in-law?" Pat demanded.

"How do you know it was meant for his father-in-law?" Reed countered. "Just because Lorna said so? I don't believe it was meant for his father-in-law at all. I believe it was sent to the blackmailer."

"You mean Willis had found out about the whole thing?"

"That's just a supposition. But it looks like it."

"Rufe, you're so smart," Pat breathed. "Who is the killer?"

"Quiet," said Rufe, "while I make a phone call."

He dialed Police Headquarters and asked for Hogan.

"Ben? Rufe. Listen, the murderer knows I'm alive now, so there's no more need for secrecy. Here's a phone number I got out of the pockets of that lug Fred I knocked out. It's probably for that gang's new headquarters. Trace it and raid the joint—you'll pick up Brophy and his hoods... And look! I'll hand you your murderer tonight if you want to stage a little party for me. No kidding. Get Devore, Mrs. Medford and Charlie Irwin all over at Lorna Willis' house tonight.... Well, she's my client, isn't she? I've got to earn that hundred bucks.... Okay. Thanks."

"Go on, be mysterious," Pat sniffed as Reed hung up. "Don't forget our bet."

"All right." He got an envelope out of the drawer, scribbled on the inside of the flap and sealed it. "There. And no peeking."

"You're wrong," Pat said calmly. "Because you forgot one thing."

"What?"

"The third sampler murder. A character named Fitzy Munson."

"Oh, the Anders case. Really, Pat, that's so elemental I'm surprised at you."

"You won't laugh when you get that nightclub check."

"Well, I'd say Munson was one of the mob that fell afoul of the boss and had to be liquidated. They thought it was a swell chance to add confusion by dropping a sampler and making it look as if it was linked up to the Willis and Medford killings. It wasn't. And the best proof of that is the way they tossed in that lush Anders. That was smoke screen pure and simple. If the thing had been really linked up they wouldn't have left us any human clue like Anders."

By nine o'clock Mrs. Willis, Mrs. Medford, Glover Devore and Charlie Irwin were assembled in the Willis living room, plus the three Reeds, Hogan and a few police.

Everybody was nervous. Devore, the lawyer in him coming to the surface, paced up and down with his hands behind his back.

"Ready?" Hogan asked.

"I am," Reed said calmly. He looked around. "I'm a private investigator and I have no police authority. If I told Lieutenant Hogan how much every one of you has held out on him, you'd all wind up in the brig. However, I know who the murderer is now and I'll prove it shortly. Mrs. Willis, I've earned your retainer and you owe me some more dough. Your husband did not kill your father."

He swung toward Olivia.

"The same goes for you, Mrs. Medford. Your husband did not kill your father. The same man killed all four—for one reason."

Olivia Medford sobbed. A confused murmur arose.

"I know who it is too!" Charlie Irwin said, his eyes fixed on the lawyer. "Devore, weren't you in the Navy during the first World War?"

The lawyer looked startled.

"Yes, why?"

"You were hurt, and while recovering in the hospital you learned to embroider samplers!"

"You can't pin this on me!" Devore was on his feet, shouting. "I only did those samplers in the hospital. Twenty years ago. I haven't done one since!"

"Keep your shirt on, Devore," Reed said. "You're in the clear, even though the idea was to use samplers to throw suspicion on you, just in case. Our friend Irwin is anxious to toss red herrings. Know why? 'Cause he's our murderer."

NOBODY MOVED. Nobody spoke or breathed. Every eye fastened on Irwin. His cheeks flamed, then went pale.

"That's a serious accusation, young man!" he blustered. "Better get out your proof."

"Lieutenant Hogan has the proof, Irwin. He's already raided the new garage thug headquarters and he's got Brophy and your other boys who have been doing your dirty work. He's got their signed confessions."

Irwin glanced from Reed to Hogan. The police-lieutenant was poised as though waiting, his expression unreadable. Irwin sighed.

"And I've got a gun in my pocket pointing right at you, Reed," he said. "I'm sorry Matty bungled his job. I'll try to do better."

Something sailed through the air. It was Pat's handbag, and it caught Irwin flush in the face. His gun went off with a bang and both Reeds and three police officers dived for him.

For a second there was a furious mêlée, then Irwin was subdued, handcuffed and dragged to a chair.

"Are you shot with luck!" Hogan muttered to Reed. "I never thought he'd fall for it."

"Brophy will confess," Reed said. "I was just a little ahead of him, that's all."

The two women were huddled together, staring with fear-filled eyes at the man who had murdered their husbands and fathers.

"He—he was my friend," Olivia Medford choked. "I thought I knew him so well! I never dreamed he was one of those boys who—"

"He was more dangerous than a rattlesnake. Didn't either of you suspect it was he who was blackmailing you?"

"No," said Mrs. Willis. "We always mailed the money to a post-office box number and got our instructions over the telephone."

Hogan pulled the prisoner to his feet.

"Well, we'll see what we can save you out of the money he's taken. The other damage he's done—is done. As slickly as his sleight-of-hand put that sampler in the dish with Medford's wristwatch."

Lorna Willis came to Reed as the police took Irwin away.

"I'm sorry I tried to fool you, Mr. Reed. I see now that you were trying to help us. But you understand—"

"I know. The past is dead. Forget it."

"Mr. Devore and I are going to be married some day and try to make a new life for ourselves. Olivia, I hope and pray you can find a new life too—soon."

Reed motioned to Johnny and Pat and they tiptoed out.

"I'll send her a bill for the rest," Reed said.

"Come on, Pat, you've got a job."

"What?"

"Picking out that nickel cigar."

"You mean you had the right name under the flap?" She waved good-by to the nightclub. "Drat the man," she said to Johnny. "Why does he always have to be right?"

CPSIA information can be obtained
at www.ICGtesting.com
Printed in the USA
JSHW031932100522
25808JS00001B/9

9 781618 276544